JEREMIAH'S CODES

Paul Gilmour

ACKNOWLEDGEMENT

I would like to thank my editor Tracylee Hudson for the endless hours she devoted to my journey of writing this book. Her constant critical analysis made me strive for personal excellence.

Secondly I'd like to express gratitude to my brother Bob for his early inspiration and guidance. His support gave me the courage to continue.

CHAPTER 1

TRINITY

Alamogordo, New Mexico
July 16, 1945

The morning air was still, refreshingly peaceful yet an eerie silence clung to the group of men eagerly gazing towards the north. Most stood impatiently with hands on hips, feverish with anticipation for the event had been four years in the planning.

A scorching white flash of blinding light ricocheted out across the flat New Mexico desert as all life perished in an act of merciless incineration.

Shielded behind black shades, the onlookers squinted at the ferocity of the blast flare before the desert horizon erupted in shades of crimson red, violet blue, orange and grey that clawed upwards into the heavens above. The shock wave raced out across the desert and like a heavy door slamming in a gale-force wind it slammed unforgivingly into the group. An almighty thunderous rumble shattered the early morning stillness for a hundred miles and the ground beneath the men shook.

The scientists scrutinized and examined their lethal beast, their eyes wide from astonishment, excitement and above all, fear. The test bomb had dropped from its cradle six miles away signalling the dawning of the nuclear age. Never had so much power and destruction been witnessed in one place until now with the detonation of the world's first 20-kiloton plutonium atomic bomb.

One man of absolute importance mumbled, "Now I have become Death, destroyer of worlds."

Operation Trinity had been successful signalling a day of remembrance for many reasons, some the scientists were not afforded the privilege to know.

Further to the north in an old abandoned house, six men had sat patiently waiting with a full view towards the southern horizon. It was an ideal location to conceal their agenda from the world and the makings of the atrocity to come.

From that distance, the explosion was still breath taking, far from the faint melancholic rumble they'd been briefed to expect. The lightning enriched atomic cloud expanded swiftly bearing resemblance to some illuminated satanic Christmas tree.

One of the men turned towards the group and though clearly excited spoke softly to his colleagues. They listened intently, their eyes still fixated on the coloured atomic cloud churning furiously darkening the day. His voice resonated a strong German accent with a tone of power and expected compliance. His face presented no expression and as he cast his cold steel grey eyes over the other men, they immediately felt his dominance. The men knew his history and wrong doings though it didn't alter their views or expected destinations of their master plan.

"What you see gentlemen confirms what we suspected, the sphere is an ancient vault holding technologies of phenomenal superiority to anything we currently know. More importantly, our vision of utopia just became a real possibility but it all hinges on finding the Thirteenth Code."

He paused momentarily before adding, "Gentlemen, it will take us years perhaps decades to infiltrate and coordinate this attack on society but it starts here, today with you."

Each of the five men were handed a folder labelled '*Jeremiah*'. They all knew what was expected and the importance of their role.

They moved from the patio and manoeuvred to their vehicles parked out front before embarking on long journeys home, with the exception of one. He was ushered to his car by four Secret Service Agents. He had sworn an oath as President to preserve, protect and defend the constitution of the United States but now after the atomic bomb test, it all seemed unconscionable.

As he settled into the rear seat of the presidential car, he wrestled with his conscience, was he or the world ready for such deceit? Only time would tell he conceded as he fell deep into his thoughts of what lay ahead.

CHAPTER 2

BLUE DEATH

Otavi Mountainland, Namibia
August 1965

Matheus had finally come of age and like those before him woke with an eagerness to prove himself. Turning eighteen carried an importance for any Namibian boy, it signalled their time to explore manhood and take that all-important step towards becoming a warrior. As he gazed towards the jagged ridgelines of the Otavi Mountains west of his village, he knew this day was destined to be memorable.

The eastern mountain face was steep and rugged, perforated with hundreds of deep caves formed by the endless onslaught of seismic movement and rain over millions of years. Every day they beckoned his curiosity and every day he refused the temptation knowing they were forbidden, plagued with death as declared by the tribal elders. Countless times they told of terrifying stories about men never returning and of demons guarding a priceless mineral wealth deep inside the mountain.

He would often laze for hours gazing towards them, lost in thought at whether the rumours were true and the riches they protected. His family were poor and his parents had been suffering for months with a deadly illness no one knew how to cure and he desperately wanted to save them. Today he had that chance. Somewhere in those caves was treasure and that meant a means to buy the medical help.

He trembled with terror at the thought of challenging the age old myths, but he knew it was exactly what he had to do.

As the sun rose higher into the morning sky, he could feel its heat intensifying and penetrating his dark African skin. A few strides back behind him and stumbling on every loose stone or tree root, his younger brother Sami was already whining it was too hot and wanted to stop to rest.

Matheus had never been so close to the caves and the enormity rising above sent a shiver through his body before the coldness had even brushed his skin. Visions of carnivorous demons flashed through his mind. Many times he'd heard about a brave warrior one day appearing exhausted not making sense and rambling on how the other warriors with him exploded into flesh and blood before his very eyes. He ranted for hours about the men dying in agony, screaming for mercy while shadowy creatures with luminous blue eyes clawed and devoured their flesh. A day later the same warrior was found mutilated, his skin and flesh dissolved to a liquid bloody pulp.

He looked up at the cave entrance and into the pitch black depths where for a brief moment he thought he sensed something moving, hidden behind a blue cloudy haze. A cold sweat broke out over his body and fear took a firm stranglehold.

Sami reached his side and grabbed his shaking hand.

"Matheus are you scared? Are we not going in now?" he asked.

"No I am not afraid. You should wait outside, I will fight the demons on my own," Matheus replied concealing the terror running through his veins and hoping to throw off any doubt his brother may be having about his bravery.

"I want to come with you," Sami said in a shaken voice.

It only took them a few steps inside the cave and already it was freezing and much darker than he expected as they moved from daylight to semi darkness. Matheus had to stoop in places but then as the cave dropped steeply into a maze of tunnels, he found himself standing upright and leaning back to stop from falling. The cave floor was scattered with stone and loose dirt that in the diminishing light made walking difficult without slipping and twisting an ankle.

A small rock under his left heel broke loose and the ground trembled and cracked under his feet. He lost his footing as gravity threw him tumbling feet first and sliding on his back down a near vertical slope into a pit enshrouded in complete darkness. At the same time Sami screamed, not from fear but from the sudden intense burning, clawing and shredding of flesh from his body. His nose and mouth had started gushing blood onto the cave floor as his small body fell limp.

At the bottom of the pit, Matheus had landed mostly unharmed, the fall had been twice his height yet sliding over the loose moist soil made it forgiving. The air brushing his skin had turned colder and as his eyes adjusted, the pit wall came alight under a candescent blue light reflecting and sparkling like a swarm of fireflies on a summer's night. As he pulled himself hesitantly up onto his backside, his eyes were drawn towards the glitter of light which had an hypnotic effect on him. Like twinkling stars across the African night sky, he could see hundreds of bright luminous blue crystals embedded in the wall either side of him. Each reflected light off its neighbour and as he looked down at his hands, the dancing beauty of blue light washing across his skin stole his gaze and he knew right there, he had the proof of bravery and the treasure to save his parents.

He scrambled to his feet remembering Sami still up top in the dark somewhere and surely terrified.

"Sami, you ok?" he called out.

Only his echo made a reply.

He levered the largest blue crystal from the cave wall and pulled himself from the pit. What greeted him ripped a hole through his chest and his heart with it.

In the dim lighting cast by the crystals below, he witnessed his worst nightmare. Sami laid sprawled next to the pit entrance, his body a vision of twisted agony. Some murderous act had taken place in the short time he was in the pit, blood flooded from under his body and his face was hidden beneath a sea of frothing vomit. A putrid odour like rotting flesh smothered the air and as claustrophobia made its presence felt, Matheus fell to his knees. He lifted Sami's bloodied body up into his arms and only then did he realise the terror that his only brother was dead.

The suffocating feeling of panic and fear suddenly squeezed all breath from his lungs as he tried to motivate his legs to escape the cave. His foot clipped something solid on the floor and he looked down into the screaming skull of a twisted skeleton, jaws wide open imitating an excruciating death. Next to it were more human remains, all with shreds of flesh dangling from the bones identifying the source of the foul stench.

With Sami firmly in his arms, he sprinted from the cave into the sunlight suffering a sudden burst of blindness that forced him to stumble and ease up speed. Back behind him somewhere the demons had awoken and growled with a ravenous desire to feast on his skinny body, or so he thought.

He stumbled every step of the way until he reached the base of the mountain and the grassy plain. There he ran at speed bounding into his village, his legs fatiguing and collapsing under the strain of carrying his brother. With what little breath he had left, he called for help.

As the villagers came running to his aid, one by one they collapsed to the ground screaming in agony. Matheus froze in shock at the ghastly scene unfolding before him until a more horrifying sight appeared from behind his house. His father was staggering and crying like a small child with tears streaming down his cheeks onto the limp body of his dead wife hanging loosely across his arms. Her skin was a shade of pale blue just like Sami and blood rained to the ground beneath her as if she was riddled with a thousand holes.

His father dropped in a violent body twisting convulsion, coughing up dark red blood and howling like a wounded lion. His mother's body hit the bloodied ground with a bone crunching thud while Matheus slid to her side with Sami still in his arms. Next to him, his father took his last breath.

Matheus watched and listened as his village died around him, realising he was the only one spared. Now, he too was starting to feel a sickening ache deep in his belly and he feared the demons had found him. He looked around yet he saw nothing except death, no creatures or demonic beings.

He lowered Sami gently to the ground and with the swiftness of a cheetah, he accelerated past more slain villagers into what he hoped was the concealment of the surrounding dense jungle. There he continued to run not looking back.

What he didn't know or feel were the physical and mental changes taking place inside his body and all the while the blue crystal remained firm inside his pocket.

It would take some time for him to realise he had been chosen to carry the Fourth Code.

CHAPTER 3

BUTCHER OF VOLGOGRAD

100 miles south of Moscow
January 1992

The lightly sedated CIA operative listened as the wind growled and the roof above him rattled. It had been like this for the past week, yet how long he'd laid in his bed before that was a mystery. With his vision gone, the world around him had turned a morbid pitch black and his legs had suffered crippling injuries. Everyday a softly spoken woman with the scent of a love goddess would come to his bedside, sponge him and caress him back to health. Her voice hinted a slight accent of Georgian Russian and her touch sent sensual tingling's racing through his body. She would whisper to him and her hot breath danced in harmony with his senses. Though he was blind, he could feel her beauty and as the weeks passed, he hungered for more of his unsighted queen.

As his memory gradually returned so did his surroundings as a blind man. After an expertly planned missile attack by Georgian Rebels a few weeks earlier on a KGB building in Moscow, he was dragged unconscious from the dungeons where he had been waiting execution as a prisoner of espionage.

In a small off the map backstreet hospital somewhere south of Moscow, she gave him life and from there a bond between them fermented. She rehabilitated him back to health, walked every step of his physical frustration and picked him up every time he collapsed to the floor from exhaustion. Every day she was there in the dingy hospital room until she could do no more.

Though she wanted to be selfish and keep him close, she knew she had to rescue him from blindness. Risking capture by the Soviet authorities and certain death for her crimes, she smuggled him out of Russia and back to the United States for the eye saving surgery.

A few months later, the operative with near perfect sight shuffled with a slight limp out of a Washington DC hospital. His heart grieved for the faceless woman he had come to know as Nicholette Sponarava or the 'Butcher of Volgograd' as briefed by his CIA superiors.

He returned to the Soviet Union on his own personal mission to cast eyes upon her for the first time and feel her sensual warmth again, yet after months of searching he failed.

CHAPTER 4

BENNETT

Gracetown, Western Australia
July 16th 2001

Bennett stood gazing out over the sparkling mass of water before him. It was his favourite time of day, sunset. From the weathered deck of his secluded beach shack, the Indian Ocean looked an entrancing spectacle. At 41, Jon Bennett had experienced a life only few could imagine or even endure. Two years had passed since his retirement, publicly portrayed as his sacking from the Central Intelligence Agency. Four bullet wounds, two broken legs, unknown how many lives saved or embarrassing moments for the US Government aborted and above all, twelve years of service to the Agency had left him completely humiliated.

His life had become guarded, always peering over his shoulder for an enemy lurking in the shadows waiting to kill him. He enjoyed most of his CIA career yet it carried a high price. Constant nightmares, waking in cold sweats and knowing he had dangerous enemies across the globe made it near impossible to live a normal life. Four attempts on his life by an unknown force proved that. The last of these convinced him to flee the United States for a life of utter seclusion in Australia.

Keeping off life's grid for now was his only campaign worth accepting, and south Western Australia provided all the ingredients needed to execute that mission.

His small but comfortable fibro shack set high above the South Point surf break near Gracetown became base for his daily feast of adrenaline. Having learnt to surf throughout the Pacific during a ten year career with the US Navy, he became suitably qualified to take on the three to four metre giant left hand waves that often smacked like a full speed freight train into the western shores. Even the occasional great white shark in search of an easy meal didn't distract him from his insatiable hunger for waves.

His real passport declared his birth place as Cairns, Australia under the name Jonas Viktor Bennett who then immigrated to the United States in 1973. Living in northern Queensland until age thirteen granted him enough grounding in the Australian lifestyle to sponsor his successful return twenty six years later.

With no wife or family at his side, he soon converted to the free living lifestyle many seek, Australian life on the beach and surfing the waves.

With a square jawline, dark hair edging down to distinctive ocean blue eyes, he still retained some youthfulness. His above average height and large threatening muscular stance soon carved respect among the locals and it earned him a place in their surfing world.

Agility was his best friend, most often saving his life in the streets of Moscow or high in the mountains of Pakistan. Coordination had been his saviour many times, adapting to any kind of sport quickly and surfing had been no exception. All his school life and navy days he'd been top of his sports, champion at athletics, swimming and football until he succumbed to knee reconstruction from a snow skiing accident in Utah with his navy buddies. Adrenaline had fast become an addiction, wanting to go faster and take greater risks were what Jon Bennett was about.

He migrated to Gracetown under the alias of Phillip Augustin an ex-Accountant from New York City and kept to himself most of the time. Every now and then, he would drive the fifteen minute trip into town for supplies and each time, paranoia accompanied him.

He would spend his time looking for an enemy who was never there. The moment his cover was compromised he had escape tunnels, safe houses and emergency travel packs concealed throughout the area. It was this ritualised preparedness that saved his life on the four attempted assassinations back in the US.

This particular afternoon was no different from the previous ten or so. Bennett relaxed in his usual hammock strung between two cocas palms overlooking the South Point headland. Below he watched as a 30 knot north westerly gale fed on the remainder of the day's two metre waves. When the winds howled, it was never a pleasant time to surf, all blown out and the water stirred up like a washing machine. The air with a bitter chill was indicative of winter in the southern areas of the Australian state but didn't perturb Bennett as he swung in the breeze and enjoyed the afternoon. Even the seagulls remained firmly grounded on the grassy slopes of the south headland.

A small storm cell was racing in from the south and likely to hit within the next few hours. Around it, the sky painted a bright red and orange canvas that grew darker each minute as the sun sank deeper behind the watery horizon. He continued to laze in his hammock and fell into deep thought of his past, probably aided by the Jack Daniels he'd just finished. His eyelids grew heavier as his mind went blank under the hypnotic rocking of the hammock in the wind.

Suddenly a noise jolted him and his mind raced to find conscious stability.

An earth shattering roar unfamiliar in these parts bearing down from the north, was it the storm about to unleash its fury? he quizzed himself. But then his mind screamed, '*run Jon … run... get out now... go.*'

CHAPTER 5

ESCAPE PLANS

Gracetown, Western Australia
July 16th

From hammock to the ground, his survival instincts took control as his feet responded. The explosive clapping of thunder grew closer while flashes of lightning scurried across the darkening sky. The horizon had become a shade of deep pink reflecting off the sunken sun and with each lightning flash, the ground lit up violet white. Light rain had started to fall as Bennett accelerated across the grassy expanse of his spacious back yard.

To the north and low to the coastal horizon, he caught a glimpse of something dark and sleek, racing towards him and growing larger by the second. He knew a formidable threat was fast approaching as he pleaded more speed from his legs.

Pulling up from the hundred yard stride, he reached the house just as the whirring clatter of helicopter rotors broke through above the sounds of thunder. He slid through the back door while at the same time stretching upwards for the release switch. The helicopter blades now a thumping whack sliced the air as he yanked down on the small metal lever mounted high next to the door. As the switch engaged, electronic circuits fired up and a hatch in the floor opened while his momentum carried him to the edge of what it revealed.

At his feet, a rusted steel ladder lowered into the pitch darkness of a small bunker underneath the flooring. Back behind him the wall to wall windows had become a constant reflection of lightning with one addition as he took a last minute look outside. The inbound Sikorsky Black Hawk was a terrorising sight showcased against the evil backdrop of storm clouds illuminated in flashes of pink, purple and grey. Bulging from its underbelly, a heavy burden of air to ground missiles gave it a more intimidating presence accompanied by the increasing thud of rotor blades slicing the gusty storm winds.

Bennett jumped and skipped over the first few ladder rungs while at the same time he yanked the hatch door shut just as he felt the impact rattle the building above him. The bunker walls shook and dust fell from the ceiling.

Two Hellfire missiles had slammed into the shack at sub sonic speed transmitting a thunderous boom resonating over the countryside, most of which was camouflaged by the storm's increasing fury. The bunker with its thick reinforced steel concrete walls held tight in the impact, though the roar of exploding gas bottles up top was deafening. He had spent months excavating and constructing the bunker in the event this exact scenario occurred, and now, he was mentally slapping himself on the back.

For the next moment he crouched in the darkness not moving, collecting his thoughts for his escape plan while his house bellowed and creaked under the raging aggression of the blazing inferno.

His assassins had failed on all previous efforts because Jon Bennett was the master of self-preservation. He had come to piss plenty of influential people off, but to warrant the use of a multimillion dollar war bird meant his enemy was serious. *Who wants him dead so bad?*

He lifted himself from the floor and engaged the light. The bunker was only a small room barely deep enough to fully stand. At one end only a few steps away, a stack of shelves rose to the ceiling and on each were enough weapons to supply a small guerrilla outfit. Knowing he had to hurry, he selected his best options of guns and explosives for a safe escape. Two Beretta M9 semi auto 9mm handguns with 8 loaded magazines of 15 rounds, one in the belt and the other into his backpack. Next came six M67 grenades and four blocks of C4 explosives with detonators. Across his back he slung a Heckler & Koch MP5 submachine gun leaving him to carry a fully loaded M16 assault rifle.

At the other end of the room was a steel door slightly ajar. The unlocking mechanism had engaged when he released the hatch door. Looking like the Terminator, he stepped through into a dimly lit narrow tunnel about thirty metres in length.

Up above, the Black Hawk had landed in a nearby clearing releasing two heavily armed combatants both dressed in black from head to toe with Kalashnikov AK47 automatic rifles at the ready. They bolted towards the burning wreckage that was once Bennett's place of peace and quiet not knowing that directly beneath them, he was absconding through the tunnel.

After a few minutes of searching, the taller of the two radioed a third man waiting by the helicopter, "No sign of him... must have got out in time."

"Spread out, he must have an escape tunnel... find him but don't kill him, we have time for that later," came the reply scratching through the radio speaker.

Rasheed had longed for this day for what he thought was an eon, his revenge would have a sweet taste when it came.

"Spread out into the trees, his tunnel will surface in there," Rasheed commanded as he seated himself back in the Black Hawk in readiness for an aerial survey. He was already in deep sadistic thoughts of the torture he would inflict on Bennett's body. Years of training with the Muslim Brotherhood and later the Hamas, an Islamic fundamentalist group from the Palestinian territories, made him the grand master of torture and he knew Bennett would suffer the most inhumane death imaginable.

Rasheed's men moved forward towards the only tree line close to the house site. Both knew who they were dealing with, a professional responsible for the death of Rasheed's brother in Kuwait during the CIA insurgence of `97. They were overly anxious to succeed this time and capture Bennett after the humiliation of their previously failed attempts. Rasheed was growing more hostile by the day and needed his revengeful closure. So when Bennett's location in Australia was handed to him by another infidel he could sense the timing was right, and Allah was clearly guiding him towards his victory.

Bennett continued jogging as best he could through the low tunnel, now only about ten metres to go and the floor had become ankle deep in mud from months of seepage. He reached the limits where another heavy solid steel door sat locked yet this time a key was needed. Before he removed the key from a chain around his neck, he moved to a small opening in the wall to the right of the door. Inside, he pulled out a silver cable with the other end buried into the wall.

He had installed a fibre optic cable as a surveillance system to ensure an ambush did not await his exit from the tunnel with a camera set high in the trees looking down giving, a full 360 degree view of the exit.

All clear outside to open the door.

CHAPTER 6

ADVERSARIES

Gracetown, Western Australia
July 16th

Rasheed's men aided by night vision devices moved cautiously through the thick salt bush pausing every few feet to scan their surroundings. Both were confident that if Bennett was amongst the trees, they would spot him.

Sajid, the taller of the two called on his radio, "Rasheed, I see the infidel, he's not far away. Can I take the shot?"

Rasheed ordered the Black Hawk around and lit up the nose mounted search light, "Only shoot him in the leg, he must live. You hear me, he must survive."

Sajid raised his AK47 to take the best aim he could, hoping he could wrestle the mighty weapon enough to just wound the American. The thought of accidentally killing Bennett and the repercussions ran wild through his mind as he took a couple of deep breaths to steady his nerves.

Taking aim was the last thing he did.

A warm but numbing sensation swarmed his body as Bennett's grenade detonated a few feet from where he crouched. His life had extinguished well before he even had the chance to fire a round into the dummy decoy that Bennett had erected after exiting the tunnel. This gave him the chance to rapidly back track behind the assassins and watch their advance using his own night vision device.

At the sound of the grenade exploding, the other assailant took cover behind a clump of small bushes. He was the lesser war hardened of the two and now without a radio had lost contact with Rasheed and the pilot in the helicopter.

Rasheed had witnessed the explosion and flooded the area in search light. He knew one of his men had just come face to face with Bennett most likely Sajid, he was always too bold and confident never acknowledging his weaknesses in battle. Bennett was a formidable target and not easily put down, something Rasheed knew well. He had trained him in Afghanistan after the US Navy left him there to die.

Bennett crawled silently through the undergrowth on hands and knees approaching the unsuspecting assailant from behind. He had view of the target crouching low between two trees. He was all of probably eighteen years but in this game no matter the age, killing could never be personal. He moved in close enough to hear the young kid breathing and turning his head as he scanned the trees and shrubs in front. A tree branch snapped under Bennett's body weight and the kid spun around with his rifle out, full automatic firing in a fit of panic.

Effortlessly Bennett tapped off two rounds from his Beretta into the kid's head and all went quiet, except for the thumping roar of the Black Hawk overhead. A bright beam of light followed sliding across the ground towards him and the dead soldier.

He spun onto his back directing his rifle towards the helicopter letting loose with a dozen rounds towards the cockpit section. It started lurching steeply to the right disappearing from sight before a loud explosion rocked the air and flames spewed skyward amongst the trees east of his burning house. He had hit his mark, now two flaming beacons would definitely draw the attention of the local police.

He calmly rummaged through the dead kid's pockets, finding only some Australian cash and coins. A snappy inspection under torch light of his exposed skin revealed a number of tattoos signifying Islamic extremist involvement, at least he knew now where his enemy hailed.

The storm had firmly seated itself overhead and the lightning was nothing short of spectacular. The blaze, once his home, was hissing in its own deadly convulsion as the rain pelted down. A single shot rang out and he felt the searing hot penetration of a bullet ripping its way through his left shoulder. In the distance, a dark shape skulked towards him slowly at first and then more rapidly as Bennett remained frozen in the dark taking aim. Two loud cracks of his M16 echoed out and Rasheed dropped for cover amongst the undergrowth.

It wasn't long before the revving of an engine yanked Rasheed to his feet and commenced a wild frenzy of automatic rifle fire in the direction of a sole dark figure on a motorbike disappearing into the darkness of the trees. The tail light was a good target but it was too fast darting through a heavy tree line for him to acquire the direct shot he needed.

With the Black Hawk now a burning wreck, Bennett knew he could escape quickly into the night leaving behind whoever it was, though he felt certain they'd meet again. For now he needed medical treatment quickly before too much blood was lost.

CHAPTER 7

WORLD ENVIRONMENT SUMMIT

World Environmental Summit, Geneva
July 20th

The guest speaker stepped up to the podium at the Geneva Auditorium with the applauding rumble of three hundred guests greeting him. Professor Klieg Stronmeyer had earned a reputation throughout the environmental science world and political arena as the leader in Earth Sustainability Research. His papers reached the desks of most political leaders worldwide, though some still chose to ignore his warnings and brush the issues aside. He was here to persuade them otherwise.

Stronmeyer cleared his throat and started what he hoped would be the most influential speech of his science career. Having spent twenty years researching all aspects of Earth's sustainability from his laboratory in Stockholm, he felt the time was right.

"Ladies and Gentlemen, today I come before you with grave news. Our planet is dying."

He paused for a moment, surveying the enraptured audience before him, looking for his targets. In his eyes, they were the Earth's enemy.

"During the past ten years I have gathered data from all corners of the globe, from ground up to the ionosphere and never before have I seen such devastating evidence. The world's human population continues to expand at exponential rates, the world's forests are disappearing even quicker and our Ozone layer depletes by the day. Our natural resources are diminishing, with most not extending past the next fifty years based on our current consumption rates. Human growth becomes a greater problem with thirty per cent of the world already starving, with no foreseeable improvement. The Earth is undergoing climatic changes from overheating and there is increased natural devastation like earth quakes, tsunamis, tornadoes and hurricanes. Over fifty per cent of the world is at war based mostly on religion, greed and power. We have corruption at all levels of government with financial institutions and oil magnates manipulating and controlling them."

He paused for a brief second before adding.

"Progress, I hate to say is now killing this planet."

Many of the leaders moved uneasily in their seats on hearing these comments, for they were all true.

"My latest research shows oxygen levels dropping by ten per cent in the past decade and carbon dioxide levels rising by fifteen per cent. Our carbon footprint continues to grow larger. But this does not affect you or your people right now. No, this is most devastating for your future generations. It will be your great great great grandchildren who will need to live in domed cities, where air is generated by machines and they never get to experience wide open spaces of beautiful scenery like Australia's Great Barrier Reef, Africa's Victoria Falls or America's famous Grand Canyon. The construction costs of these brave new worlds would dwarf all previous projects in the history of the Earth. Will your governments afford that?"

The Professor continued his speech, rattling off more devastating news for the Earth, quoting statistics from his research and occasionally pausing to stare towards various leaders around the room. Many were gravely concerned, some didn't comprehend the scale of the catastrophe lying in wait and some just didn't care.

He commenced summing up.

"Today, I have preached doom and gloom, all because by the year 2250, the Earth's atmosphere will disintegrate into a mix of poisonous gases not too dissimilar to the atmosphere of Mars. As more forests are exterminated so too are Earth's oxygen generators. Our human population would have tripled by that year and our natural resources such as oil, gas and coal long depleted."

"Ladies and Gentlemen, I support that every living creature has the right to life, but we must draw the line somewhere, otherwise ALL life will become extinguished. The Earth cannot sustain this life forever. Once it is gone, it is gone and death takes us. The planet has a way of unleashing its fury on us with wild storms, earth quakes, flooding and drought already showing significant changes to our existence."

Another pause...

"As citizens sharing this great planet, we have a responsibility to ensure its existence and sustainability for thousands of years to come. Do we want to be the race that assassinated our planet after it has existed for billions of years? If we destroy our planet, we cannot simply move next door to our neighbour."

"We must act today, tomorrow and everyday to come. I applaud those countries who are making the effort to change, but it is no good with just a few changing, when the largest offenders do not. Though many of you are trying to reduce your carbon footprints by emission control policies, there are still many countries where it continues to increase at alarming rates. But it is not just about emissions, it is also about population. How many people is enough before it's too late? We must act to promote successful birth control in underprivileged countries and strive towards reducing human expansion. These are greater problems than gas emissions."

He looked directly from one target to the next, "As my research results indicate, you know who is more responsible. If you don't change NOW then I say it again, the Earth will DIE within 250 years."

He thanked the audience and walked from the stage.

Outside in the street, he was approached by two elderly men dressed in dark suits, both very distinguished. It was the second time they'd met, the first was many years previous.

One of the men opened in a quiet voice, "Professor, we thank you for your services. All has been arranged as you requested and the money transfers are in effect. The plan continues to gain momentum as predicted."

The men spoke to Stronmeyer for a while longer and he just sat listening intently to their instructions. Near the end, he had transformed into an excited man and he could not help think, how good his life had worked out for him.

CHAPTER 8

WHITTAKER

Washington DC
July 28th

Robert Scott walked defiantly through the US Customs security scanners at Washington Dulles International Airport. He knew his fake passport would survive the tightest of scrutiny by any law enforcement agency. Computer technology these days meant virtually anything could be electronically manipulated and identification fraud was well on the way to becoming the number one worldwide crime.

He hustled back through the airport negotiating the mass of anxious travellers to the departure section where he exited. An awaiting surveillance team would more likely monitor the arrivals never expecting him to leave amongst those who had just waved goodbye to their loved ones. He almost never carried luggage, only a carry on and this time was no exception. As an added bonus he made sure to stay close to single women with children or elderly couples to give the pseudo family effect. His enemies would be waiting and watching for Jon Bennett walking alone in his usual confident bold manner except not this day. Wigs, false facial hair and professional movie moulding make-up blended him into any crowd.

Bennett had been considered the best covert close range assassin in the history of the CIA. His skills in disguise far surpassed his colleagues and made it possible to successfully kill his target at close personal contact without detection.

He took a taxi to a small quiet hotel on Rhodes Island Avenue where he changed clothes and removed the false extras glued to his face. In his pocket were two disposable cell phones with sufficient prepaid credit to help remain untraceable.

Now he was ready to make contact with Dom Whittaker.

Whittaker had climbed swiftly up the ranks of the CIA, becoming Director of National Intelligence within eighteen years and now reporting directly to the President. He had not always been the bureaucratic type and never showed the motivation required to escalate the corporate ladder of Washington politics until after Bennett was dismissed in 1999. He then made the bid and success soon followed. Some said it was long overdue, others said he had dirt on people in high places. Bennett had always suspected, knowing Whittaker's arrogance, that dirt was more likely the reason.

He was a field man to the core in his early years, working tough assignments in some of the hardest terrain like the Middle East and the former Soviet Union. It was Dom Whittaker who recruited Bennett into the CIA during 1987 after spotting tremendous potential in the man. Bennett's father, Viktor, had been a highly skilled CIA operative during the Cold War era presenting a tough example to follow. Viktor Bennett had always been considered the best of the best during his thirty years with the Agency before he tragically perished in a car crash.

Bennett and Whittaker had formed a strong friendship having saved each other's lives countless times in the field. From working Russian Agents in Moscow to Indian Agents in Jaipur, they had always watched out for each other both on the front line and back in the office where their every move was tightly monitored. Though Whittaker was almost twenty years his senior, Bennett had always felt an unreplaceable mateship between them and he was the one man he could trust.

He picked up one of the cell phones and dialled the only number he knew for Whittaker.

A message service rebounded after three rings.

"Hi, you've reached Dom Whittaker, leave a message and I'll get back to you... Beeeep."

He was fully expecting the voicemail and replied without hesitation, "Yeah, Hi, this is John Spencer from the Mutual Insurance Company. We have a policy in the name of Grant McClellan who sadly passed away recently. You have been named as a beneficiary on his life insurance policy. Could you meet with us please at 9.30am tomorrow 29th at our Arlington office? It is quite urgent that we speak. Thankyou and goodbye for now."

He disconnected the call.

Whittaker would have no difficulty deciphering the coded message just left on his voicemail. In the days of the Cold War, when espionage was at its most lethal, coded speech was the norm and all good operatives had a repertoire of codes to confuse any unwanted eaves dropper.

Whittaker would know to meet him at the corner of Grant and McClennan Drive in Arlington National Cemetery at 11.30am tomorrow. It was always their rule to add two hours to the arranged time to avoid any messy ambush. Arlington signified the cemetery and the name identified the actual address within the cemetery. The name John Spencer identified it was Bennett wanting the meeting urgently.

Everything was set...

They had not spoken since '99 when he'd immigrated back to Australia. It was best that way. Keeping off the grid meant no contact with anybody connected to Jon Bennett.

At exactly 11.30am the next morning, he walked casually into Arlington National Cemetery wearing a dark baseball cap to help conceal his face. The day had broken into a beautiful cloudless sky with only the slightest hint of breeze blowing from the east. The cemetery, a mass of miniature white headstones, was busy with tourists and protracted mourners for the two sniper riflemen to be noticed sitting way up on top of a nearby building. During his earlier reconnaissance of the area, Bennett had noticed the two men setting up their weapons. Whittaker never took chances, for all he knew, it was a set up. Spies don't trust spies, it's just not the industry for such moral behaviour.

He continued walking until he could clearly see the intersection of Grant and McClennan. On a park bench sat a white male wearing a dark brown suit and it was obvious from the sun's reflection that he was now completely bald. He thought as he approached, *yep no missing this giant bald Orang-utan*. Whittaker had always been a large build, quite tall and arms that at times looked like they could scrape the ground as he walked. To make matters worse, when he had hair it was orange-red giving him the distinct impression of an orang-utan.

"Better to be bald than that bloody red hair!" he announced as he walked to within speaking distance.

Whittaker jumped up and grabbed him in a bear hug that, if he tried, could crush every living cell in his body. "Good to see you Jon, it's been too long."

They reminisced about old times for the next ten minutes, while all the time Bennett scanned the horizons for an incoming Apache helicopter or two. He was still heavily paranoid and the Australian incident had unnerved him.

"So Jon, what's so bad that you come running back to the good ol' United States of America," Whittaker finally blurted out after an uneasy pause settled over their initial greetings. Before he could get started with his pre-planned reply, Whittaker added, "I hear you ran into some trouble down under."

Bennett responded not perturbed by the Director knowing of the incident, "You been checking up on me old friend or do you still bug you're mates?"

Whittaker went on, "That little episode was all over the news in Australia, a helicopter and a house both struck by lightning in the same storm, and a Phillip Augustin killed in the house, I knew straight away it was your work Jon."

"I looked into it. The Australian Government covered it all up nicely and from the reports I'd say another attack on your life."

There Bennett had his lead in.

"That's why I'm here. Dom, I need your help to track down these clowns hunting me, I am fed up with running and looking behind. I have to end it before it's too late."

He continued his plea for help, "It's time Jon Bennett was just an ordinary man with a wife and family and no deadly risks, well, maybe a shark or two at Bells Beach or Margaret River."

Whittaker broke in, "arh... still a crazy surfer I'm hearing."

Bennett went on, "My life has been nothing but danger, killing and paranoia. I just can't play this way any longer. That whole fucking Afghanistan thing set me up for this life and I often wonder how things would be if I hadn't been shot down."

Before recruitment into the CIA, Bennett had been a Naval Aviator in the US Navy. He loved flying the supersonic war birds and the adrenalin rush swept him up into a virtual euphoric world. He was never shy of taking risks but it was that boldness with sarcasm that landed him in hot water with senior officials. He had never understood when to shut his mouth, particularly when facing likely execution at the hands of his enemy however, his demise came from the constant challenging of high ranking Government officials. He had grown to dislike the political cloud over the US and the endless cover-ups manifesting in his verbal outbursts towards prominent political stake holders. One dangerously opinionated US Senator was all it took to punt Bennett from the CIA in a shroud of humiliation and embarrassment for a war crime he didn't commit. His life as a clandestine operative had been forced on him after a brutal misfortune while serving in the Navy.

In 1986, he was shot down over war torn Afghanistan during the height of the Soviet invasion, a war the Americans were not meant to be fighting. His mission was a simple photo run, no contact and the best stealth profile he could maintain. His aircraft had been stripped of all official markings, no point in aggravating an already tedious relationship between the US and the Soviet Union his superiors had said.

Fifteen minutes into Afghan territory, his F4 Phantom was hit with a ground to air missile taking out the tail section. He ejected safely, though his navigator died during the impact. That changed his life forever. He hit the ground running, Mujahedeen rebels all over him. With very little ground combat experience, he initially found it difficult to run and hide. Despite numerous radio calls to the US battle fleet, no rescue mission was authorised. He was left stranded behind enemy lines, quite clearly alone to fight and find his own exit from that bloodied country.

One week later he was captured by Soviet forces and endured four days of torture as a suspected spy. He had no secrets to tell so his torturing worsened.

Then a miracle happened.

Soheil Mahdavi, an intelligence officer with the Iranian Government was thrown into a neighbouring cell. Next day, Mahdavi's men stormed the camp killing the Soviets and releasing the prisoners.

With nowhere to go, Bennett fled with Mahdavi. Over the next twelve months, he lived in isolation with Mahdavi running from the Soviets and learning all he could about field intelligence, mortal combat, explosives, firearms and various languages common to those parts of the world. He didn't realise it at the time, but he was becoming the ultimate CIA operative.

He later made an escape out through Pakistan and returned to the US.

Anger had pent up during the time, wanting revenge on the arsehole who refused his rescue. He hated the US Navy and immediately resigned, though the paperwork became a nightmare as his official records pronounced him killed during a training exercise in the Persian Gulf.

He had been back in the US for less than a day when a knock came at his door. There stood a man dressed in jeans and t-shirt looking like he was on a mission, all hurried and to the point. He introduced himself as Dom Whittaker, an officer with the CIA. His purpose was to recruit Bennett into the Agency and his orders denied refusal as an option.

So sitting there in the cemetery, he continued describing to Whittaker of his life in Australia and surfing, about how he still felt deep resentment over the Afghanistan debacle and how one day he would find who was responsible.

Whittaker broke in quickly, "It's all just history now mate. Look if it makes you feel better, I will help you find these people but first I need you to do something for me and before you say anything, it's a national security matter."

"Yeah yeah yeah Dom, always national security, which Congressman needs his pregnant mistress silenced or wait which uncooperative leader do you need eliminated," Bennett returned in his usual sarcastic tone.

Whittaker smirked slightly and continued, "I need you back on the ground in Afghanistan to find Uri Stananov. He has information about a terrorist attack planned for American soil sometime in the next few months. We have limited Intel but all indications point towards weapons of mass destruction, thermo nuclear we suspect and Stananov, we hope, will have acquired information for you."

Bennett said nothing just sat looking at the ground.

"Jon, you have the ground agent networks and besides no one knows the terrorist training camps like you. My friend, you are the best and the only man I would recommend for this job."

Bennett had dropped into deep thought. He hadn't been to Afghanistan since 1998 when he was stationed in Kabul and working a number of agents each week. He knew the importance of ground work and yes, he knew he had all the right networks in place.

"Alright I'll do it, but I'm out after a week."

Quickly he added; "Oh and Dom, make sure my information is ready then too. You tell me who wants me dead."

He arrived at this meeting seeking Whittaker's help, he never imagined being roped back into the clutches of the Agency.

"Yes done deal Jon, we will need you to verify what you hear and locate the weapon's position for a strategic strike, so bring back coordinates please. Use the usual finance accounts, I'll arrange you full access again. The briefing notes will be delivered to the usual place for collection tomorrow morning at nine," a satisfied Whittaker said.

Bennett suddenly asked the question, "What about Brown?"

Senator Denzil Brown was the man solely responsible for his public sacking after embarking on a witch-hunt to destroy him. With Bennett back in the game, it wouldn't take Brown long to find out and launch a fresh strike.

"Don't worry about the Senator, I have some influential backing these days Jon," was Whittaker's confident response before both men shook hands and departed in opposite directions.

Denzil Brown had been a pain in his side, relentlessly pursuing his every move after an embarrassing CIA mission that claimed the lives of innocent Kuwaiti citizens. Something he would rather forget but it happened under his alleged command and the US Government needed a scapegoat. Brown crucified his actions from the comfort of his leather chair and the security of the Senate Inquiry. Bennett loathed the man, he was smug and annoying in his summation calling him reckless and a disgrace to the American people just like his father. He would never forget listening to the short fat Senator publicly rape his father's honour and then, the next day it was across the front page of every newspaper in the US.

All through the Inquiry, pencil-pushing bureaucrats told him what should have happened, men who had never once entered hostile territory except to delude a cheated wife. He listened to them tell him how he should have acted in the heat of a bloody battle frenzy, where it was shoot or be shot. Like so many Inquiries, he felt taking a bullet was their preferred option just so the US Government wasn't embarrassed and then need to enter diplomatic negotiations. Adding to the humiliation was one important fact they covered up, he was not physically there to commit the crime. He had been framed and people who he thought were friends turned on him and gave damning evidence against him, all denying him any legal defence.

As he exited the cemetery, an uncomfortable smothering feeling descended over him, somewhere behind amongst the hundreds of headstones, he was being watched.

Dropping into a skulking manoeuvre, he ducked down behind a row of monuments and started sprinting low while using an occasional tree for cover.

The only person nearby was a woman dressed in a long black dress, kneeling down with her head bowed in prayer and clutching a single yellow flower. Maybe paranoia was finally getting the better of him he thought, as he walked closer to the woman to gauge her reaction.

He stood only a few feet away staring and for a brief moment felt an urge to hold and comfort this complete stranger. She was strikingly beautiful with long flowing dark hair while tears flooded down across her heavenly sculptured cheeks. Suddenly she turned towards him, a glint of fear in her watery eyes after sensing his swift intrusion. Like under a hypnotic spell, Bennett found himself drawn to her glistening green eyes shining like emeralds in the sun as they pulled him in closer. If she had been an assassin, he would be dead, he realised and took a step sideways while apologising using a mistaken identity excuse. She part smiled at him and said nothing, clearly disturbed by his invasion of her prayer time.

She wasn't following him, he conceded, and walked briskly away leaving the cemetery behind him. By the time he'd walked to his car he had fallen into deep heart aching thought of his urge for romance brought on by the mourner's beauty and suffering.

Back inside the cemetery, the woman watched him drive away. She had deactivated the device in her hand and placed it back inside her handbag next to the fully loaded Glock 9mm.

Her target had been acquired however, this was not the right time or place.

CHAPTER 9

SPHERE OF ANUBIS

Bavarian Alps, Southern Germany
July 28th

The observation chamber, massive and unusually sterile towered above all those inside, while more sophisticated security systems had been installed than that of the Reserve Bank of New York. Gaining access required entering two numeric codes at two different doors, swiping a fingerprint activated key card and finally a retina scan to release the three electronic locks to the internal twelve-inch solid steel door.

Overall, the room was bizarre in design and caught newcomers off-guard by its enormous stark white ceiling towering high above a weird monumental centrepiece. Known as the Sphere Chamber, the room was completely round by ten metres diameter; which was only accessible by one internal door, with the exception of a hidden escape tunnel used for emergencies.

In the center of the room, a single three-foot tall steel pedestal stood alone. On top, a dull silver sphere the size of a basketball rested snugly within a ceramic dish like some worshipped idol of a primitive world gone by. The Sphere of Anubis as it was known was actually a ball of translucent grey marble with a finely machined surface, weighing exactly ten kilograms and completely covered in three hundred hieroglyph symbols of unknown origin. Each symbol lightly carved into the surface depressed like a key on a keypad and with entry of the correct sequence of thirteen symbols the sphere would activate in a most unusual way.

Etched in ancient Latin around the sphere and translated to English, revealed a terrorising scripture.

> *... Beware the third failure ... Anubis will consume this world and bring end of days, an unstoppable plague to destroy all ways...*

Surrounding the pedestal were six benches each with a sophisticated video camera directed up towards a ceiling resembling the inside of a huge cone. Protruding outwards from each bench was a light projector aimed at the vertical white wall in front. On first glance, it gave the perspective of some weird annular IMAX theatre but it was the three black leather recliner chairs that sealed the impression. It was a viewing room of an unusual kind and was not until the sphere activated that the onlooker appreciated its purpose.

Joseph Voight, a highly regarded linguist, sat staring aimlessly at his laptop on which a mass of hieroglyphs reflected back at him. He was clearly frustrated and exhausted from yet another twenty-four hour shift without sleep. Over the years, he and his offsider, Rahj had successfully translated large sections of text and schematic diagrams that resembled a crossover of Ancient Latin, Egyptian hieroglyphics and another more advanced script not recorded before on Earth. Now they were at a loss, the symbols and text proving near impossible to interpret.

Two years ago, Voight had been working at the University of Paris lecturing in ancient hieroglyphs and chasing various research projects but never the grand scale one he wanted. His qualifications and skills in linguistic analysis surpassed any academic worldwide and after winning countless awards, he felt his skillset was wasted. Then one afternoon in March of 1999, two elderly men approached him offering him the opportunity he'd been waiting for. A week later he started at Kehlstein.

Originally excavated during World War II by the Nazi's, the Kehlstein Facility was to become Hitler's private control room where he could administer supremacy until the German surrender in 1945 annihilated his plans. Now it was owned by *The Trust*, a secret organisation with a deadly agenda.

11am...

The door buzzed open.

A tall blonde man immaculately dressed marched in, carrying a slim silver metal briefcase. Voight knew what it contained, another thirteen-symbol code and after witnessing the two previous activations of the sphere, he knew this would be another truly astonishing spectacle. The first had revealed thirteen lines of ancient script and when partly translated it resembled some kind of index. The second had revealed many more lines of text and mathematical segments similar to physics formulas that they struggled with interpreting.

The man walked over to the sphere sitting lifeless in its cradle where he opened his briefcase and removed one single colour photograph. Voight stepped closer to reward himself a glimpse of the next code sequence and looked into the eyes of a terrified African man. Two things stood out, the gun against his head and the thirteen symbols tattooed in bright blue across his bare chest.

With the photograph in his hand, the blonde man started searching for the corresponding symbol on the sphere and tapping it with his free hand. With each touch, the symbol began to glow a light tinge of blue while at the same time a low humming sound commenced resonating from within. From where Voight and Rahj stood, they could see it floating a few inches above the cradle and begin a slow rotation aided by hundreds of small air jets rising from the pedestal.

The thirteenth symbol in the sequence was entered and the blonde man took a few steps backwards keeping a tight gaze on the revolving ball of blue light.

Within a few seconds, the sphere abruptly ceased rotating and a beam of pure white light jettisoned upwards. A sudden flash filled the room and was gone just as quickly. What remained, covering the entirety of the conical ceiling was a projection of ancient text and symbols. Voight immediately saw similarities to those he was working on; yet parts appeared foreign, which meant increased frustration for him and Rahj and more sleepless nights.

Rahj moved forward and pressed the record button initiating the cameras. Each of the six captured the projection and redisplayed it as one panoramic image around the room. They had experimented in the beginning with projecting across a flat ceiling that returned a distorted mass of utter confusion. The elevated conical design gave them the perspective they needed.

A few minutes later the sphere deactivated and went silent, sinking back down inside its ceramic dish. The man placed the photograph back into his briefcase and left the room. Nothing had been said the entire time.

Voight knew his job and what had to be done.

CHAPTER 10

AFGHANISTAN

Kabul, Afghanistan
August 3rd

The Kam Air 737 touched down at Kabul International just after two in the afternoon on what was an unseasonably hot day with temperatures in the high thirties. Bennett preferred to enter Afghanistan with minimal attention and arriving from the neighbouring country of Pakistan suited this purpose. Running and hiding from security cameras was the lifestyle he desperately sought freedom from.

Afghanistan certainly was not on his top ten destinations to visit after spending an overabundance of time there running agents and working strenuously just to stay alive. Adding to his anxiety was the jet crash in '86 that started it all and now returning just reopened the gates to his fury.

Clearing customs proved uneventful. He'd chosen his cover as a freelance Australian photographer on assignment for National Geographic, one he had previously used many times. Behind the guise of Peter Munro, he strolled casually through the airport security unnoticed. Displaying 'MEDIA' across the front of his vest certainly answered any questions an official may have been contemplating. In this part of the world during heightened international tensions, there were always a plethora of media hunting a lead story whether it was war, terrorism or just plain human tragedy and so one additional lone photographer meant nothing.

He continued out the front doors leaving the cool air-conditioned confines of the airport and into the intense summer heat of Kabul. Though it had only been a couple of years, he'd forgotten how hot it could be and how dry the air was; with the irritating scent of dust already clogging his nostrils.

He slid into the rear seat of the first available taxi and gave instructions to a small hotel just north of the airport. On this particular afternoon traffic was heavy, mostly caused by a few broken down trucks and a handful of the locals attempting to push them from the road. Bennett sat relaxed conversing fluent Pashtu with the driver while policing his every move and ensuring he drove the quickest route possible. He knew the city well and he soon recognised the land marks and streets appearing either side as the driver did his best to negotiate the congestion.

It was to be a fast mission and Bennett was wasting no time, he'd already studied the CIA profile of the agent he was to rendezvous with the next day. Uri Stananov had been an operative in the Russian KGB during the Cold War, but after a short period playing double agent for the Soviets and the Americans, he decided the US was more lucrative. Like Bennett, he had spent many years looking over his shoulder waiting for an ex-colleague to either shoot or slice him but lucky neither eventuated. The Cold War ended and the Soviet Union collapsed allowing Stananov to leave Russia and start a small business manufacturing and selling rugs in Pakistan. His business grew and soon expanded into various countries throughout the Middle East and Asia.

Now Bennett was to meet this ex-KGB agent who, from all accounts was held in high regard as a reliable source of Intel. His profile certainly made him sound the ultimate agent, an absolute trustworthy human source, though strangely no photo of the man had been included. *Stananov sounds almost too good*, he thought.

After settling into his war-ravished hotel on the northern outskirts of the city, he waited until dark before venturing out onto the streets. Not only was it much cooler but fewer spying eyes. Counter surveillance proved easier at night, with so few on the streets and noise easier to detect, it allowed him to move freely undetected.

Having changed into a dark coloured long robe and baggy pants typical of the local dress, he headed out towards Stananov's house. Aside from the occasional vehicle he saw no one and by the sweet aromas wafting in the street most were at home eating their evening meal. The night sky was littered with stars and the air had cooled to a bearable high twenties.

Half an hour later, he was across the road from the agent's house sitting in the dark where he had a full view and time to prepare his next move. Like many of the houses in Kabul, it was of mud brick construction with a few small windows through which a dim light filtered. All the houses in the street were similar and densely packed together for as far as he could see in either direction.

He sat watching, assessing and listening. The night had become exceptionally dark with no streetlights to give clues of his presence and the moon remained hidden. In an eerie sort of way, it had become deathly quiet except for the distant low rumble of cars on the main road a few kilometres over towards the airport.

A sudden unnerving sound just off to his right broke the silence.

Bennett all too familiar with the click of a gun trigger hammer when it's pulled rearwards remained calm, not moving an inch. The next few seconds seemed like minutes while he waited for the trigger to engage the firing pin.

As the muzzle of a handgun pressed firmly into his right temple, a strong Georgian accented voice whispered in his ear, "You move and you die. What is your business here, watching my house in the dark?"

CHAPTER 11

STANANOV

Kabul, Afghanistan
August 3rd

Bennett straightened up expecting the single gunshot if he answered incorrectly.   He couldn't see his attacker and he never heard him approach, which right now meant the man behind him was a professional.

"Sergi, is this how you treat an old friend?" Bennett whispered sideways ensuring he made no sudden movements.

Uri Stananov didn't let up with the muzzle pressure and replied, "Jon Bennett is that really you, I thought you surely dead by now."

Bennett had realised Uri Stananov's real identity was Sergi Saranovik when he heard his distinctive Georgian accent.   Both men had worked together between 1992 and 1996 whilst Bennett was stationed in Istanbul and Saranovik played both sides.

For the next two hours they reminisced about old times and brought each other up to speed with their current life events, while slamming down vodka from the seclusion of Saranovik's small house.

Saranovik abruptly broke from the conversation to ask, "So my friend, do you want to know about the threat to your country?"

Bennett turned sufficiently sober at that question and nodded confirming he wanted to know everything.   Saranovik outlined what he knew, the vodka he'd drunk didn't affect his verbal briefing though his English was partially jaded.

"You see Jon, some Afghani Islamic fundamentalist got himself all fucked up while trying to run big weapons in Tajikistan.   Sometime in August of '99, the Soviet's Special Forces caught up with him after they had been acting on a lead.   Of course, they tortured him in their usual charming way and I believe his pain tolerance was that of a child.   He gave up information about four dirty nukes bought on the Khan Black market for 60 million Euros each.   Now… this is where it gets interesting Jon.   The buyer was Omada al-Zawah."

On mention of that name, Bennett lost any lingering effects of the booze and became more attentive to the facts.   He had spent years building profiles on al-Zawah and his terrorist outfits but never had they been close to using nuclear weapons.   They preferred the traditional terrorism tactics like suicide bombings, car bombings and occasionally blowing up an aircraft or two with their crude homemade explosives. Running around with weapons of mass destruction was entirely a new ball game for al-Zawah, though Bennett knew the man had the networks in place to smuggle nuclear material into the US.

Saranovik explained what he'd learnt from an official at the Kremlin that four nuclear warheads had been stolen from a secure facility in Obninsk sometime during 1997. All four had been partially dismantled in accordance with the Nuclear Peace Treaty; however, stolen before they were fully disarmed. The Soviet Government kept it quiet to protect themselves from condemnation by the western nations particularly the US. Bennett had already suspected the sale of weapons grade uranium and plutonium from the former Soviet Union to boost their failing economy so he was not surprised to hear it.

Saranovik continued with his briefing.

"Then two weeks ago, I received information from a young wounded Taliban fighter in the north of Afghanistan. He claimed al-Qaeda had possession of four nuclear warheads and were rebuilding the trigger mechanisms. It didn't take much convincing for him to divulge the intended purpose was to strike four major US cities."

Bennett sat listening intently committing the information to memory, he would prepare detailed notes later.

"Do you know where the warheads are?" Bennett asked.

Saranovik hesitated a minute with one finger to his lips as a way to signal silence and stood to kill the light. Bennett had already heard the rough idle of a car engine as a fiery blast engulfed the small dark room. Mud bricks exploded in all directions, flames leapt up as both men were swallowed by the walls and ceiling. The rocket propelled grenade had been effective from the closeness of the car that now sped away narrowly missing people as they ran from their homes to aid Saranovik.

Inside the carnage, Bennett was alive and crawling towards Saranovik sprawled under a sheet of shredded iron roofing. In the flickering glow of the flames, he could see Saranovik's body was a bloodied mess, his left leg ripped from his hip by the jagged iron sheet and bright red blood streamed from his mouth. He was pinned down with blood flowing like a flooded river from his femoral artery and it was obvious from his fading appearance that death was walking swiftly to the man's front door.

Bennett had been lucky in the blast, suspecting what was about to occur he had dived sideways into a nearby room that ended up being the bathroom.

Saranovik looked up at Bennett and they made eye contact, he too, knew his time had come.

"Sergi, where are the warheads?" Bennett asked anxiously knowing time was running out for his friend.

Saranovik responded in strained gasps for air, "The mountains north of Khan Abad... be careful... friend." His head fell forward and he was gone, knowing he'd just betrayed one of his closest friends and would certainly go to hell for it.

Bennett clambered from the rubble, keeping low and avoiding the eyes of the onlookers. He made quick work of returning to his hotel, needing sleep before his journey the next day into the mountains of northern Afghanistan. There was no time to mourn the loss of a friend, he wanted to be out in two days and there was still much to be done.

The next morning he awoke early to the sound of gunfire in the street behind his hotel prompting him to take an earlier taxi ride to the airport. He bought a ticket to Kunduz and lucky for him, a Pamir Airways flight was leaving later that morning. A small domestic flight packed with military personnel greeted him as his walked up the air stairs and found his seat towards the rear. A few rows back, a group of loud Americans sat together and judging by their arrogant language he was sure they were mercenaries presumably there to reap rewards from the heroin trade in the north.

Arrival into Kunduz followed an hour later without any problems. The surrounding barren landscape displayed a once war zone with Soviet gunship helicopters laying crippled on the ground, victim of ground to air missiles fired by the rebel forces during the Soviet invasion. With his Media flag showing, he paraded unapproached through the small neglected terminal onto the outside road. He had to find a way to Khan Abad where he knew an old friend who would surely help him.

As he stood on the kerbside, three black trucks pulled up outside the terminal. Each had signage on the door displaying the name, United Mining Corporation. Bennett thought nothing more of it until he saw the Americans leave in them just as one gave him a hard intense stare.

Bennett didn't see the other American inside the truck take his photo and make an immediate phone call.

CHAPTER 12

DOUGLAS

Khan Abad, Afghanistan
August 4th

Hitching a ride with the Afghani soldiers from the flight, Bennett made his way to Khan Abad stretched out at the southern base of some of the world's most inhospitable mountains. There he made swift work of finding the man he once knew as Scott Douglas, an ex-intelligence officer for the Australian Secret Intelligence Service. If anybody knew about Russian nukes in Afghan territory then he was the man.

Douglas had spent five years in Afghanistan in the 90's however, decided he loved the country too much to leave. The truth of the matter was different. He had entered into a life of crime making huge profits in the heroin trade, growing vast fields of opium poppy in the valleys of the northern mountains. Most of his trade fed to the west including Australia where an arrest warrant waited the moment he stepped foot back into the country.

Bennett walked into the small secluded dingy bar late in the afternoon, a favourite drinking hole for Douglas and his criminal cohorts that he hoped had not changed. The bar was nothing special, transformed from an old mud brick house in the outskirts of Khan Abad that only the locals frequented which, he knew, meant being shot the moment he pushed the door open.

At the rear of the bar sat a tall muscular man fit in stature, in his late 50's or early 60's, and from his overall rugged appearance clearly someone not to mess with. Around him sat four other men of various sizes but all of local ethnicity. On the table in front of them stacked up were about a dozen empty beer bottles and a number of semi auto handguns.

At the appearance of a stranger creeping through the front door, all guns vanished from the table and aimed confidently towards Bennett's head. He halted in his tracks, no sudden movements as he stared down the muzzles of at least six guns each with a set of wild angry eyes behind it. The clicking of trigger hammers snapping rearwards was almost synchronised as a loud overpowering deep belly laugh deafened the room.

Douglas on seeing Bennett, had raised his massive frame from the table and almost ran towards him while the goons just stared wondering whether to shoot or not. Douglas reached him and in one swift action almost dance like, swooped him up into a bear hug. It had been five years since the two men had seen each other after they had spent time working together in the fields of the Middle East. When Douglas chose to start trading opium on the side, Bennett knew it was time to move on. It had always annoyed him that the opium trade financed terrorism and before that, the CIA covertly handed out the financial backing to buy their weapons.

Douglas in his usual growling harsh voice bellowed out for all to hear, "Look here, a fuckin ghost I see before me... Jon Bennett is back everyone."

As the beers came in plentiful supply, Bennett wasted no time getting to the point and asking about the nukes, hoping Douglas wasn't too far gone on booze already to give up accurate information. The man had been drinking for most of the afternoon and was looking jaded behind an already aged face. Though only a few years older than Bennett, he gave off the impression of a man in his sixties, his face heavily wrinkled and sun hardened from the Afghanistan wilderness.

Douglas stared down at his half empty beer before replying, "You know Jon, there is something going on in the mountains fitting with what you are telling me about dirty nukes."

He guzzled the remainder of his beer before adding, "My men won't go up there anymore. No villagers to care for the crops mean half a dozen poppy fields unattended and dying, that's like ten million green for me mate. There are myths of entire villages dying horrific agonising deaths like some new black plague is loose in our hills. To me it sounds like extreme radiation exposure, the symptoms I hear are the same as what the people of Hiroshima and Nagasaki suffered."

He called out in fluent Pashtu to one of the goons idling near the bar, "Omar... go find Suresh, tell him I need him here now."

A short while later, a small skinny Pakistani man ran into the bar going straight over to Douglas, "Boss you wanted me."

"Yes... Tell my friend here what you saw in the mountains near field four last week and no bullshit."

Suresh turned towards Bennett still looking at Douglas out of fear mostly and said, "Yes Boss, I go to field four like I always do twice a week to check poppy. This time there were no villagers caring for crop or protecting from crop raiders."

Douglas interjected, "Fuckin Taliban come steal our crops so I pay the local villagers to stand guard 24/7, that's if the fuckers get past the land mines of course," he laughed.

Suresh continued, "No villagers anywhere but still a full crop, so I went to find them. Their village is not far from field so I walk there."

He stopped and shifted his eyes from Bennett back to Douglas as if he needed approval to continue. Douglas nodded and Suresh went about telling his story.

"Nobody there, nothing and then when I walk back to field is when I seen it."

Bennett looked towards Douglas for confirmation of the truth, receiving an affirmative nod.

"Next to the field was a big hole in ground with many dead body, all blue in colour, blood running from eyes, nose, ears but it was the look on their face that was most scary. They died in much pain. There were no wounds and much more stench than normal death. I just ran not look back, I'm sorry Boss. It was the devil's work."

Douglas broke in, "Jon, this has only happened at fields four and five, I reckon your warheads maybe up near those fields somewhere, the deaths sound like radiation exposure... so much mountainous terrain up there, would be like a needle in a haystack looking for em."

Bennett asked, "I need to find the warheads, where are the fields?"

"I'll take you, we can leave in the morning but first we drink."

A night of drinking with Scott Douglas was never anything short of toxic shock. He knew his friend's drinking habits and knew the carnage waiting for him the next day.

CHAPTER 13

THE FIELD

Khan Abad, Afghanistan
August 5th

The sun's warm rays fell hard across his face; morning had come quickly with the sun appearing low over the mountains bordering Pakistan to the east. He scavenged his memory to recall the endless volley of vodka shots coming in fast all night and how Douglas remained impervious to the attack from years of acclimatisation. His head pounded like mortars exploding all around, his eyes were narrow slits fighting the incoming beam of daylight and he knew deep down his belly was ready to start protesting.

An hour later, they rolled out heading for the northern mountains and the poppy fields in two purpose built ex-military Humvees. Fully expecting radiation, they carried along Geiger counters hoping they would give off enough warning to stay alive. Bennett and Douglas rode alone in the lead Humvee while behind them in the second, four of Douglas's men sat surrounded by a cache of weapons sufficient to start a small war.

Douglas explained as he drove, "We used to fly up there but damn Taliban have shot three of my birds down with RPGs, just became too expensive replacing them."

"Come on Scott, you've never bought a damn thing in your life, those helicopters were stolen I bet or won in poker games," Bennett laughed. He knew his Australian friend too well. Douglas laughed it off, he knew he was right but he didn't care, his life was good and the drug trade earned him fifty-fold any other job he ever had or was likely to have.

The Kunduz River clung closely to the mountain's western base feeding the adjacent agricultural valley. Their track took them north west through the farming lands before taking a steep right turn up into the barren mountainous landscape. The tracks were narrow, winding and treacherous with no scope for error. In places, previous mortar fire had gnawed massive divots in the roadway forcing the extra-engineered tracking control to grip the ground harder. Douglas explained mortar attacks in the mountains were a common event and he didn't know whether they were entertainment for the Taliban or just practise. He had already lost a dozen good men and five vehicles but the profits far outweighed the risks especially when replacing workers was easy from neighbouring Pakistan.

Already the temperature was well into the thirties and showing no signs of cooling, it would breach forty by midday. All around, Bennett could see nothing but an alien landscape, steep rock ridges reaching high above, barren ground in every direction, no life and potential ambush sites every few hundred metres.

They reached poppy field four just inside two hours after drawing no attention from the Taliban, an unexpected phenomenon, Douglas indicated as he slowed the Humvee to a halt. The huge expanse of a flat field covered in tall poppy stretched out before them onto a narrow mountain platform.

Suresh had been right, there was no sign of the villagers at the field or indication they'd been there at all in the past week. The nights often dropped to below freezing so to keep themselves warm they lit fires. The only fireplace remnants they could find near the field were over a week old and the same could be said for the dried up footprints.

Douglas looked down at his Geiger counter. He was pleased to see it showed a zero reading.

"All good mate, no radiation here."

Following Suresh's recount of his experience, they trekked towards the village searching for the mass grave along the way. The rough rocky track led back down into a steep ravine a short walk from the field where Bennett and the others all abruptly stopped in disbelief at what lay ahead.

At the base of the small ridgeline, blackened ashes still with a hint of smouldering smoke trails signified where the village once carved its place amongst the rocky valley. There was no evidence of life and the area was devoid of bodies conveying a somewhat uneasy feeling that both Bennett and Douglas noticed but didn't care to elaborate on. It was the same scenario at field five a further short drive to the north.

Bennett had fallen into deep thought as he studied the smoking blackened wasteland. *How does an entire village of one hundred or so people just vanish? Who torched the villages and why?*

Douglas piped up, "Jon, my guts not right with this, you know me mate, got an instinct for trouble."

Bennett replied, "Know what you mean, who burnt these villages and where are the bodies? Something is not adding up here mate."

Five minutes into the drive back towards Khan Abad Bennett noticed something unusual.

"Scott… stop!" Bennett called as Douglas slammed down hard on the brakes while the second Humvee skidded wildly off the track to avoid a collision.

"What the fuck, what's up mate, you suddenly remember you need to pee."

Bennett half laughed and pointed out his window towards a patch of open ground about twenty feet from their vehicle.

"Look there, does that seem right to you?" he replied to Douglas who had swung his gaze in the same direction.

They both climbed out of the vehicle and walked towards it yet neither were sure of what was laid out before them.

CHAPTER 14

BANNISTER

North of Khan Abad, Afghanistan
August 5th

Bennett led the short walk to the patch of ground that appeared dangerously different to that around it. Douglas followed an arms distance behind while his men not so sure remained back near the vehicles. They shared nervous glances and watched as their boss and Bennett stood staring at a section of ground they thought had been burnt.

"Seen anything like this before?" he asked Douglas.

They were both looking out over a perfect circular patch of charred ground that on closer inspection gave no relevance to a fire at all.

"No can't say I have, the ground looks like it's been melted at an incredibly high temperature. See how the sand has been fused into one solid piece of resin," Douglas answered.

A circular section of flat ground twenty feet in diameter had been cauterized by something of immense heat with no distinct impact crater, which they both knew, ruled out a missile strike. Off to one side where the scarred area was partly broken open, Douglas bent down and scratched around with his rifle butt and boot.

"Check this out," he called back over his shoulder.

Bennett walked over just as Douglas unearthed a bloodied and stiffened dark skinned hand.

"Well we know where the villagers disappeared to," Bennett said looking down at the partial remains of a human body.

The heavy thud of rotor blades cracking the air somewhere north caught his attention just seconds before Douglas signalled his men back into the Humvees.

"Time to get going mate, that sound is never good in these parts," Douglas announced.

A small dot appeared low on the northern mountainous horizon and through binoculars it resembled a Russian made Mi-24 attack helicopter capable of carrying eight soldiers and enough armament to destroy a small town. It turned east and descended into a distant valley. This had Douglas's complete attention and he yanked hard on the wheel spinning his Humvee into a northward slide followed quickly by the second vehicle. He hadn't seen these war machines this far north in the mountains and nothing is out there anyway, except a few dozen of his poppy fields.

"Perhaps these are the swine who pilfer my fields and not the Taliban after all," he mumbled angrily pushing the accelerator harder and forcing Bennett to grab whatever he could to prevent himself being thrown across the cabin.

The helicopter had landed inside a narrow valley about half a mile ahead and dark figures were climbing out. It didn't take the Humvees long to announce their arrival; both roared in pulling up abruptly on either side of the chopper. Bennett thought the whole manoeuvre was over aggressive considering they didn't know who was on board or its purpose. There was a chance they were friendly but more than likely they were not he convinced himself. He hated being unprepared if it did go to shit, and now Douglas had driven them right to their front door.

Bennett had witnessed these massive Russian gunships during his CIA service throughout Eastern Europe and the Middle East. They were always burdened with an overkill of slim missiles hanging underneath however, this one appeared to be equipped differently. One of the underbelly pods had an unusual looking electronic type device attached. On first inspection, it gave him the impression of a pregnant stinger missile with cat whisker aerials covering the nose. On the side of the chopper was the name United Mining Corporation, the same he'd seen on the trucks outside Kunduz Airport the day before.

The same mercenaries wearing desert fatigues appeared carrying an assortment of weapons and each offering an expressionless greeting. Instead they just stood and observed their intruders.

One of the men stepped forward of the others and introduced himself as Logan Bannister, commander of the security detail for the United Mining Corporation. He was a tall muscular man of 40 years and clearly by the lines on his face had been exposed to years of harsh weather. His stance showed leadership and most likely ex-army probably American going by his Texan accent. The men with him looked similar, but younger. All seemed cocky with fingers prepped on triggers and ready to kill anything stepping in their way.

Bennett jumped in, "Why does a mining company need a security detail?"

"And you are?" was the immediate reply from Bannister.

"Peter Munro, journalist and photographer here on assignment for National Geographic covering the opium trade in these here parts thanks to Scott over there," he responded using his cover name and pointing towards Douglas standing a few steps back behind.

Bannister glared across them both to look towards Douglas's four men with their assault rifles half poised in defence. He looked back at his own men as if he was calculating the outcome of an attack just as Douglas signalled his men to lower their weapons.

All men shook hands before Bannister finally answered the question, "United Mining has a lease to explore these mountains for oil and gas."

Bennett took a sideways glance at Douglas and repeated his question, "Yeah, but why a security detail?"

The mercenary commander started to become noticeably defensive and almost aggressive with his reply. "If the fucking Taliban would just let us get on with it then all would be happy but no, they keep resisting our efforts, hence the weapons and us... United Mining have mines in almost every country on the planet but fucking Afghanistan is the only place where the company needs hired guns."

Bennett thought that was a fair reason and let it rest. The remainder of the conversation was relatively general in nature and nothing was said about the opium fields scattered throughout the area to the satisfaction of Douglas.

Just before parting ways, Bennett returned to Bannister asking if he had seen or heard anything about the mass death of the villagers. He responded negatively and curiously didn't ask any questions. Bennett and Douglas left the same way they arrived but their suspicions had been heightened. They both thought it unusual Bannister didn't ask questions and it was obvious from his silence he knew something about the deaths.

Inside the helicopter, a computer downloaded an image of Bennett and his detailed CIA profile as two bright red warning lights flashed on the monitor. The profile was over fifty pages in length and displayed most of Bennett's life history, his combat skills, missions, weapon capabilities, and his confirmed kills, mostly assassinations. It was top secret information requiring the highest level of release only authorised by a Senior Executive of the US Government.

Less than a day later, Bennett flew out of Kabul International not realising the web he had just entered.

CHAPTER 15

THE CHAIRMAN

30,000 feet over Indian Ocean
August 6th

Somewhere over the Indian Ocean, a highly encrypted satellite phone rang. The receiver answered and repeated the required access codes.

Immediately another person came onto the line. "Sir, we are ready to start excavating, but the Taliban continue to sabotage our efforts. We can't keep this up, already we've suffered the loss of ten men and more vital machinery has been destroyed."

The receiver was displeased with the continual interference, it was time to initiate the attack and remove the threat. Trillions had been spent spearheading himself into the Chairman's seat at the helm of the six continents however, without the Afghanistan mine operational then it would all crumble around him.

The caller added, "Sir, we have another problem. Jon Bennett is snooping around, he knows about the missing villagers."

"Does he know about the mine?" the Chairman quickly asked.

"I think there is a good possibility he suspects something. He met with Saranovik in Kabul and then next day he turned up in the mountains with Scott Douglas."

The Chairman replied, "If Bennett gets as much as a sniff of the blue rock then *The Trust* has a big problem. Make sure Bennett doesn't become that problem."

"What about Douglas?" the caller asked.

"Don't worry about him, he knows not to talk," the Chairman answered before terminating the call.

He turned to the five other board members on board the Gulfstream business jet and proudly announced, "Gentlemen, we are ready to start excavating, soon we'll have enough blue crystal to commence the next phase."

CHAPTER 16

STELLA

Washington DC
August 6th

Stella Van Horne, a highly respected journalist from Washington DC, walked into the small cafe just off Pennsylvania Avenue. Her hair long and flowing in the gusty morning breeze resembled the colour of rich dark chocolate. She glanced around the room at her many admirers, her face a picture of pure indulgence with accentuating soft full lips, penetrating crystal green eyes and a smile of perpetual seduction. As she paraded across the crowded floor squeezing tightly past both men and women, she couldn't help feel the mental ecstasy of touch as the men penetrated her with their fantasies.

At 36, she was in the prime of her journalistic career, a ruthless investigative reporter with a passion for the truth. She hated the cover-ups by governments and the endless lies told just to keep some bureaucrat in power. Unlike many of her colleagues, Stella Van Horne disliked bending the truth to sell newspapers and magazines, she preferred the actual un-dramatised truth. If there wasn't drama already in the facts then it wasn't worth putting pen to paper, she often declared to her colleagues particularly during heated arguments. She was a unique reporter and one that easily made enemies within the political arena of Washington, though it never perturbed her from chasing the real facts. Her controversial articles enticed endless public debate, continual denial by Government leaders and the support of conspiracy theorists around the world.

The cafe had started flooding with workers breaking for their morning ritual of coffee and the momentary escape from the office grind. This part of town so close to the White House was reserved for bureaucrats, would be bureaucrats and of course journalists chasing that career altering front page story. She had become fascinated with conspiracy theories after receiving a lead in 2000 about an international private organisation called *The Trust* controlling governments worldwide and in particular, the American government. In addition, her theories were considered too radical for most focussing on how the organisation was behind many of the planet's significant man made historical events of the Twentieth Century.

Her informant on this particular day was late.

Twenty minutes after their arranged time, a short man of ex-military appearance dressed in a black Italian made suit came hustling through the doorway. Everyone in Washington DC knew Stella Van Horne, her reports were worth waiting for and her looks captured every man's sexual desire. The man walked over to her table and sat down. He had news she was desperately seeking.

"Jon Bennett flew out to Afghanistan last week," were his first words as he sat scanning the entire place in one smooth action like he'd done so many times before.

The man now had her full attention. Her eyes fixed firmly on his as she moved in closer as if to embrace him in a deep sensual lover's kiss. The man was aroused. She wanted to know everything, but there was not much more to tell except that he had travelled to the north where the man's source had lost him. No records yet of him returning to the US.

She was curious, her journalistic hormones raging, and most definitely excited right now. For the past two years, she had chased that one exclusive interview with the world's greatest spy, a man with, no doubt endless secrets about CIA actions and cover-ups by the governments of the world. She had never felt comfortable about his sacking, suspecting something was missing and not disclosed to the public, which for her meant a huge story.

A week ago, she had her chance at Arlington, except she hadn't expected Bennett to meet with the National Director of Intelligence in a cemetery of all places. Her immediate thought was something big was going down for their meeting to appear unusually covert. Luckily for her, she avoided an awkward moment and sabotaging any future chance of an interview by playing the mourning widow.

Her informant rose from the table and opened his briefcase. He reached inside and produced a black A4 cardboard folder. "Oh, here's what I found on *The Trust*, got blocked by some seriously high security protocols so isn't much in there."

He dropped the folder onto the table and vanished out the door, hoping that one day his cooperation would land him a shot with the beautiful reporter.

Receiving less than expected on *The Trust* didn't bother her, she was deep in thought about why Bennett had been meeting Dom Whittaker so secretively and then raced off to Afghanistan. This was developing into a story, *The Trust* conspiracy would have to wait, she thought.

CHAPTER 17

WASHINGTON DC

President's Office, Washington DC
August 12th

The US President sat behind his commanding red cedar desk in the Oval Office and listened intently to the briefing taking place before him. The Secretary of Defence and the Director of National Intelligence were taking their respective turns to provide information and bow to the man's every command. No one else was present or invited.

An hour earlier in a nearby park, Dom Whittaker had met with Bennett, where details of the Afghanistan mission were handed over. In total, it took him ten minutes to rattle off, probably the quickest debriefing he'd ever delivered. At the end, Whittaker produced ten large A3 sized glossy black and white satellite images showing traces of nuclear hotspots close to the area of poppy field four. Strangely, one appeared separate from the others and Bennett knew exactly where it was, the site where they had spoken to Bannister. *So, the mercenaries may be involved,* he thought.

He did not mention Douglas or the opium fields. Likewise, he made no mention of United Mining, wanting to first verify some kind of link between the company and the villagers. He had learnt many things while in the CIA and one was to always hold a card up his sleeve.

As agreed, Whittaker handed him an unmarked brown plastic folder. Bennett exited the park knowing that inside it were details identifying his enemy and the start of his new life.

After both men ended their respective briefings to the President, Whittaker took the floor. "Mr President, I believe we have a situation, the intelligence is reliable and we need to strike while the weapons are still on the ground." He had spread out on the table a set of satellite images with the four hot zones circled for the President to inspect.

The Secretary of Defence interrupted, "Dom, you can't be serious, a military strike on Afghanistan. It would be the Soviet fiasco all over again."

"Mr President, Secretary of Defence, I strongly urge a military action using precision strike weaponry before they find their way to the US. Each one of these weapons could kill hundreds of thousands of Americans," Whittaker pleaded.

The President now interjected, "Dom, how reliable is your source?"

"Mr President I sent Jon Bennett in last week, he's completely trustworthy and was the best man for any Afghanistan job," replied Whittaker.

The Secretary of Defence jumped to his feet and clearly outraged declared, "Whittaker, now I know you're not serious and a fucking idiot. Mr President, Jon Bennett was sacked from the CIA in 1999 for the Muslim Brotherhood incident. If you remember, it brought this government under political fire from NATO and almost cut off our oil supply from the Saudis."

Whittaker in defence of Bennett returned fire, "Sir, there was not a shred of proof that Bennett was responsible for that incident and he should not have been blamed for those deaths. Jon Bennett was the best CIA agent this country has ever had and his intelligence has saved this government and the previous two countless times. Bennett's Intel is good and we need to act on it immediately."

The President dismissed Whittaker from the room to talk privately with the Secretary of Defence. He walked out knowing there would be no strike on Afghanistan.

He hurried back to his office where he made one short encrypted phone call. He was confident no record could ever be produced of the conversation. He was also aware that treason was punishable by death.

CHAPTER 18

THE REPORTER

Washington DC
August 12th

The afternoon rainstorm had sweetened the air over Washington City. The streets now washed clean were glistening in the breaking sun while Bennett walked swiftly through the steam rising from the suddenly cooled road tar. He had to make a fast track back to his hotel and feed his rising curiosity about what the envelope in his hand would reveal.

On his return from Afghanistan, he had spent a few days travelling to various destinations throughout the United States collecting personal items hidden during his final year of CIA life. Amongst those items were weapons, money and a relatively unused range rover. Maintaining a covert lifestyle meant keeping an abundance of personal affects hidden throughout the globe, in bank deposit boxes and underground vaults from any one of his pseudo lives. The range rover, he'd left in an old abandoned warehouse off the main highway just north of Petersburg, Virginia that he never thought for a minute would remain without being stolen or forfeited to the state. The battery had long died but he knew it would and with a small battery cell he quickly gave life back to his beast. In a concealed compartment in the rear were five sets of false number plates for five different states. All had been expertly crafted to avoid any unnecessary tangles with the law.

Walking through the streets while making his way towards the rover parked two streets over on Constitution Avenue, he suddenly felt a threatening presence not far behind him. The sidewalks were cluttered with people going about their everyday lives both business and personal but something was not right, he thought.

Feeling his hairs stand up on his skin and his heart rate explode, he knew someone was following him. He slipped swiftly into CIA mode and the machine he knew well.

Shop windows, vehicle side mirrors, occasional quick glances all came together into his scanning ritual. Then he caught sight of the target. A dark haired woman only one block back was slinking between parked vehicles and trying to conceal herself every step of the way.

Stella Van Horne had been tailing him since he'd left the meeting with Whittaker after her journalistic instincts had paid off. For days, she had followed and watched Dom Whittaker throughout the streets of Washington and eventually it led to her master prize. She had never thought covert surveillance could be so easy and she was quickly becoming cocky with self-achievement. As she stepped in and out from behind parked cars thinking she was well hidden, she had absolutely no idea of her failings.

Bennett moved like a ghost into a side alleyway making sure to use the surrounding hustle and bustle of the crowd as cover. His Glock 9mm handgun was out but concealed to keep publication to a minimum.

While he stood waiting in the shadows, Van Horne continued to walk her path but now more urgently after losing sight of him. A narrow side street loomed into view. Hastening into a slow run, she turned the corner into the alleyway. Her lack of training in covert surveillance at that very moment became her enemy.

With one swift hand action, Bennett pulled her from the street into an empty shop, gun pressed firmly against her back and his hand over her mouth. His hold briefly paralysed her every move and the door slammed shut behind them. It took less than three seconds and not one passer-by noticed.

Pressing his weapon harder into her back to inflict more pain, he spoke softly but forcibly, "Who are you and what do you want with me?"

She grimaced from the sharpness of the muzzle and she could feel his hot breath brush her ear. Her heart rate quickened and she started shaking from the terror of her possible encroaching death.

Stella van Horne was not a new comer to deadly encounters. She had reported in some of the world's most dangerous locations, Algeria, Bosnia, Afghanistan and she knew what it took to get the prize winning stories. This she conceded to herself was worth the fear and threat of death.

Bennett realised he was holding an athletic woman with tightly carved arms, biceps well defined and long deep brown hair pulled back in a ponytail now resting softly against his face. Her seductive womanly aroma and sweet perfume danced through his nostrils almost hypnotising him. He had not experienced the smell and aura of a beautiful woman for a very long time and now it was catching him off guard. He had always been shy around women and he struggled to accept the feeling of attraction it sometimes presented, a subliminal weakness inherited from his training and psychological torture. His mental issue aside, it was his lack of trust that generated most problems for him.

Perhaps not an assassin, he thought, but threat or no threat this woman had been following him. With his body hard pressed against hers, he pulled her back slightly and released his hand so she could speak. Now with her off balance, he felt in absolute control of his prisoner.

"My name is Stella Van Horne, I'm a reporter for the Washington Post, you're Jon Bennett, right? I have been following you, hoping for an interview."

"Look lady, my name's not Jon Bennett, you've got the wrong fella."

"I know exactly who you are. You are Jonas Viktor Bennett born 15th of May 1960 in a little town just north of Cairns in Australia. Your father was Viktor Nicholai Bennett who like you, was in the CIA. You were disgraced from the agency a few years back and no one has ever seen you since, until now."

Bennett broke in, "Miss Van Horne, or whoever you are, I'm not this Jon Bennett person you talk of, so if you value your life, you will just run when I let you go."

He started to loosen his grip gauging her reaction before fully letting go. She instantly took three steps away from his clutch and spun around to face him. She stopped abruptly when she caught sight of the gun muzzle aimed directly at her head and his ocean blue eyes locked on hers.

"Are you going to kill me now?" she asked not knowing if he would pull the trigger or not.

"No... Now get going out that door and don't look back."

She started to walk reaching for the door handle. She stopped and in one final bid to make contact she said, "You know Jon, an organisation called *The Trust* killed your father and my mother. They both died in the same car crash in 1975. I dug up some unofficial police reports to say the break lines had been cut. Oh and if it makes any difference I don't believe you were responsible for the Kuwait incident."

She opened the door and stepped through into the crowded street outside, not a single person even noticed her messed up hair and scuffed face. She hoped her quick talking had been enough.

He just stood there in the dim light of the empty shop. Now, he was unsure about her, what was her purpose, what did she know? He must find her, he decided. He threw himself out onto the street into the bright afternoon sunlight, looking left, looking right, however, she was nowhere to be seen.

Deep down, a foreign emotion was surfacing, one that had not floated for many years.

The street had become chaotic with office workers emerging and commencing their homeward rituals. In every direction, men and women moved swiftly that made his search more difficult.

He ran the length of the street, looking along every side street he crossed. She had vanished. Then as he turned to retreat, he caught a glimpse of her. Half a block away, he spotted a tall athletic woman, her long ponytail swinging in the breeze as she maintained a brisk walk. Her shape was breath taking with a knee length skirt accentuating her long muscular legs and though distinctly a woman built for speed, she displayed the grace for the catwalk. He moved quickly to catch her.

Sensing his swift approach from behind, she turned to once again, engage her contact. In the full light, he caught real sight of her physical beauty. Her pouty full lips screamed a soft long touch, her face radiated a softening glow with little makeup and her crystal clear green eyes were tantalisingly hypnotising. He couldn't help feeling as if he was under her spell and breaking eye contact was impossible until an unexpected but familiar noise broke above the sounds of pedestrians and cars.

CHAPTER 19

AMBUSH

Washington DC
August 12th

A volley of gunfire rained down from somewhere above them onto the surrounding pavement. People screamed and ran for their lives, including Stella. Bennett threw himself behind a nearby trashcan and raised his gun high, ready. Four bullets spiralled into his flimsy cover and exploded their way out the other side with a crack of metal snapping. He narrowly missed being struck as he scurried on hands and knees across the pavement out of sight of the shooter.

As the shooting eased, he eyed Stella hiding behind a parked car across the street looking timid. They briefly made eye contact with her eyes screaming, *save me*, as a black van skidded to a halt behind a screen of blue tyre smoke and breaking his view of her.

The back door swung open and two balaclava-clad men jumped out firing their automatic rifles towards him forcing him back further off the pavement. Three slower moving bystanders around him fell victim and bled out onto the concrete while the bombardment continued. As they reloaded, Bennett jumped to his feet letting off a full magazine of fifteen rounds at them and the van.

They had completed their part of the mission and had already fallen in behind the cover of the van while two other masked men dragged Van Horne into the rear while she screamed franticly for help. As quick as it came, the van and its men were gone bulldozing through the busy traffic shunting vehicles in all directions.

Up above, the shooter started his attack again now that Bennett had emerged back out into the open. Diving back behind a parked vehicle, he spotted his shooter perched high up on the fifth story of the apartment block across the street. The shooter had made an error. He had stood up to take a more unrestricted aim, and in doing so, gave away his position.

Bennett entered the apartment block at full stride bounding three steps at a time for greater speed. He was heading to the fifth level with a rough mental picture of which room to smash his way into. Room 514 was locked as he expected. He pressed his ear to the door to listen. Silence, then the buzz of a cell phone rang somewhere inside and a man's muffled voice echoed out.

With one powerful kick, he shattered the flimsy lock and the door burst inward. Gun at the ready he charged into the room just as his assailant startled by the noise turned to face him. Both made eye contact and each knew only one would survive this encounter. Bennett with the quicker of the weapons had twice squeezed his trigger a split second after crashing through the door. The first round smashed into the man's chest while the second pierced through his skull.

Already the sirens could be heard hurtling towards his location as he knelt down next to the dead man and quickly searched his pockets. Inside one pocket was a piece of paper with an address scribbled, inside another were two photographs. He looked down and saw his own reflection on one, the other was Stella Van Horne.

He had never laid eyes on the man before and he needed to identify him. He had no means to take a fingerprint impression so he did the next best thing. With his knife, he sliced the right index finger from the corpse.

A cell phone on the floor next to him buzzed to life. As the detonator activated, the tightly packed C4 exploded and obliterated the room.

CHAPTER 20

COUNCIL

Kanchenjunga, Nepal
August 12th

The old Buddhist Monk sat sipping his tea while outside the freezing Himalayan winds swirled and blasted down off the snow covered mountaintops. His temple presided high on an eastern cliff face of Kanchenjunga Mountain in Nepal bordering India and from there, he looked out across the roof of the world. Rugged frozen mountains were his everyday spectacle and he had found sanctuary in the peace of knowing he resided inside one of the most remote locations on Earth. Getting there was near impossible without a helicopter, otherwise mountain climbing for seven days was the only option.

The Monk was a peculiar looking man with bulbous dark eyes set deep into an elongated face and skin that in the daylight appeared translucent. He gave the appearance of one who had never touched the sun's rays yet he had travelled to all ends of the Earth to build his sacred army. His back was bent so that he walked with a stoop and it was no wonder people around him claimed him an old man of 150 years. Others closer to him shared a more radical view when removed from his hearing, one claiming the true origin of humans on Earth and extra-terrestrial in nature though it could not be proven they often argued.

He gazed across at the other council members sitting around the large stone table and he struggled to remember the last time they met like this. All the religious denominations had a rightful place at this table and though there were many conflicts in the world, these men and women knew their true fate rested with the decisions made inside the Temple. The World Supreme Council accommodated all religious faiths no matter their disagreements because their respective leaders shared a dark secret with the Monk. It was a secret of enormous importance and one, that if exposed could collapse the pillars of society particularly in those nations driven by religion.

The Monk began to speak in a fragile voice at first, one that sounded scared and unsure.

"My friends… Gaia is screaming helplessly in terror of what our future has in store. Everywhere we look, we can feel her pain and sorrow. The wars, the poisoned air, the continual rape of her land, the irresponsible governments, the religious unrest and conflict, and above all, humankind becomes overburdened with greed each day. Our existence is no longer based on the foundations of love, it is the dissatisfied greed for wealth and power that drives our populations into oblivion. What I have seen is devastating."

The Monk was greatly acknowledged around the religious sectors as a Prophet possessing a window into the future however, his prophecies never extended past the Temple's occupants. He carried with him a message of Earth's future and another more controversial Biblical Scripture that remained tightly held within the walls around them. One day, Earth's leader would return and restore peaceful order to the World and reunify all religions back into the one true Faith. On that day, peace on Earth would be resurrected.

He continued talking to the Council Members.

"*The Trust* grows more powerful each day and now the Thirteenth Code is within their reach. The ultimate destructive force they have no respect for is now almost theirs and they have no understanding of what it will do, yet their greed for world supremacy remains too strong to comprehend our warnings. We all know what that Code creates and we all know the destruction that comes with it. My friends, I am sorry to say but the widely prophesised *End of Days* is fast becoming a reality for our planet."

Fear enveloped the members. Never before had they contemplated this could happen. Everything was always so controlled and their directions gave faith to all no matter the sin committed. The Monk had always given them guidance and provided a safe haven but now it all seemed to be vanishing. The *End of Days* was only a myth, it was nothing to be taken seriously, or so they all thought.

"Our Nobel Guardians hold our fate in their hands. They stand in unison against *The Trust* and it is they who have the vision and faith to prevent this tragedy happening. My friends of the Supreme World Council I ask you to pray for their success," the Monk added.

He bowed his head and commenced praying. He hadn't revealed one important secret. Their hope really rested on the shoulders of one man, Jon Bennett.

The Council Members all prayed.

On the opposite side of the world, Bennett slept while his head filled with subliminal messages. He would wake not knowing how important his trip to Australia would be.

CHAPTER 21

TREASON

Terrorist Training Camp, Sudan
August 12th

The covert meeting had been arranged by the American who now appeared out of place in the desert landscapes of north-western Sudan. He'd been planning this contingency for months, an event so despicable yet the end result would be far greater than anyone could imagine.

He and three Middle Eastern men dressed in their usual long white robes sat around a fire warming their hands. No introductions took place as he produced detailed architectural drawings of four buildings in the US. Ayman, clearly the leader of the three, looked at the drawings and nodded to his brothers. They contained precise target points for the most effective impact and complete destruction of the buildings while the rest would be up to Ayman and his followers on-board the aircraft.

The meeting continued for another hour before the American left feeling confident the attack would be a success for *The Trust*.

CHAPTER 22

CIA

Washington DC
August 12th

Wide spread pandemonium spread throughout the fleeing pedestrians like a rampant virus as more gas lines exploded inside room 514. The detonation showered the street below with shattered glass slicing those unfortunate to be under it.

The cell phone had appeared old and unusually heavy when Bennett picked it up. The black tape binding around an oversize battery signalled suspicion but it wasn't until it started beeping and the screen flashed that his gut instinct screamed at him to run. His last few steps through the door confirmed what he thought.

The force of the blast blew the door off its hinges knocking him face first onto the hallway floor. Over his head and scraping his back he felt and heard the rush of sizzling fire as it searched for victims. One second longer inside the room and he would have been incinerated like the sniper's body now an investigators nightmare to identify.

The wall had been demolished behind him while smoke and flames swarmed the building. The door had shielded most of the blast wave and as he lifted himself to his feet his ears thumped to the beat of a deadened siren as his eardrums suffered the percussion of the explosion.

He dashed back to his rover keeping watch over his shoulder the entire time for further trouble or the police. In his hand he still clutched the two photographs taken from the dead man. He needed answers why the journalist was a target alongside him.

A short drive across town and he barged his way into the Director's office to the surprise of Dom Whittaker slouched behind his desk. A long legged blonde secretary scuttled along behind him in hot pursuit and making excuses all the way for her deficiencies in security. He was in no mood for protocol, politeness or general conversation and it was these mannerisms that earned him the trademark as the rule breaking agent. The secretary knew her boundaries and challenging Jon Bennett was well outside them.

Somewhat surprised, Whittaker looked up from his mound of paperwork, "Jon what the fuck, you can't just come barging into my office like this. You better have a damn good reason."

Bennett ignored him and replied, "Turn your television on, gun battle and explosions in downtown DC should be enough for you. A group of shit bags just tried to kill me but I managed to bag one before he went up in that black smoke. Some tall blonde fella with a bad aim had a photo of me in his pocket and before you say anything, it wasn't the same arseholes hunting me."

"Who do you think it was then?"

"That's why I'm here. I need system access to find some answers. Does the name Stella Van Horne mean anything to you?"

Whittaker clearly annoyed surged to his feet and quivering on the edge of yelling he said, "Jon, giving you access to a restricted database is not fucking possible, you should know that. You were only reinstated for the Afghan trip two weeks ago and it simply cannot be allowed. As for Stella Van Horne, I am assuming you mean that stupid bitch of a reporter?"

"Yes, the fella trying to shoot me had her picture as well," Bennett responded.

"No I have no idea about Van Horne except that she's a pain in the arse for us here in Washington. She's always sticking her nose where it doesn't belong, I'm surprised she hasn't been bumped off already. Shit I'd fucking do it if I could get away with it."

"Well Dom, you might just have your wish. Van Horne was dragged into a van by four men less than an hour ago while they pinned me down with gun fire."

"Let the DC cops deal with it Jon. You're out of the game now remember! I suggest you just focus on staying alive and that's my advice to you as a friend," Whittaker responded as he stepped around his desk to front Bennett. He extended his hand towards him inviting Bennett's hand in return as a farewell gesture.

Bennett responded as Whittaker hoped and they grasped hands as if to say goodbye. Like a magician, Whittaker covertly slipped him a small plastic access card and whispered, "There's an empty office, two doors down the hall with computer access and no cameras, you've got thirty minutes before I'm reporting it stolen, ok."

Whittaker pulled his hand back and said his goodbyes in his usual loud voice while Bennett turned glancing up at the surveillance camera mounted high in the far corner of the office. The Agency had become inwardly paranoid and now they were spying on themselves, Bennett laughed as he moved quickly past the secretary perched at her desk.

Bennett and Whittaker had forged a strong friendship over many years in the field and could never let each other down in time of need.

Whittaker was a man of honour and had been through his own share of personal traumas in his time. Ten years earlier his only son, Josh, then eighteen became involved in the social drug scene of Washington. First he started using amphetamines, cocaine and fantasy before sliding over into the dark abyss of heroin. His life plummeted quickly and no matter how hard Whittaker tried to clean him up and protect him, it grew worse. Then one day he got that call no father wants to hear. His son had been admitted to hospital suffering a massive heroin overdose and his internal organs were shutting down. By the time he arrived at the hospital his son had slipped into a coma, brain function severely reduced and life support was the only option to maintain his breathing.

Four painful weeks dragged by with no progress. Josh had lost all ability to sustain his own life and that raised the big uneasy question. For the next week Whittaker battled a long hard war with himself, drinking to excess, abusing everyone around him, not sleeping and all because he didn't know how to terminate his only son's life.

Then the time unavoidably arrived. Whittaker walked into the intensive care unit and announced the death of his son. It was the hardest thing he ever had to do and all the while Bennett had been by his side supporting him through it.

Bennett hurried down the hall out of sight of the secretary where he found the room Whittaker suggested. The access card logged him onto the single computer and to his surprise gave him the highest level clearance. He had taken the time to use the ink pad on the desk to roll a print off the shooter's severed finger he carried in his pocket and fax it through to a buddy at the FBI. A hit came back sooner than he expected and identified his dead man as a low life street criminal with no apparent special skills except snatching handbags off defenceless old ladies.

A search through the CIA database returned nothing.

His research confirmed Whittaker's take on Stella Van Horne. She had a history of confrontations with lead personnel at the CIA and all because of some obsession for the truth. He could see why the Director didn't like her. She had been the cause of countless briefing notes to the President placing Whittaker in the hot seat. Someone at the CIA was leaking embarrassing information and Van Horne was probably using her seductive looks to gather it. Bennett hated the media most of the time, they never told the exact truth only a manipulated dramatised version to sell a story. They had no respect for people's lives or the damage their stories caused and he held them responsible for most of the world's conflicts, all because of their irresponsible reporting regime.

He continued researching what he could on her. She was born to

Nora and Nicholas Van Horne in Belgium and immigrated to America when she was five. They mostly lived in the northern parts of the US moving frequently with her mother's work, a journalist covering international political events. Her father died from a heart attack when she was seven and Nora took it hardest resulting in two major mental breakdowns between 1972 and 1976. Then in 1978 she met Viktor Bennett before becoming romantically involved. Bennett thought back to his teenage years and could remember his father spending many nights away from home at some woman's place. Then the car accident in 1980 claimed his father's life however, he didn't know it had claimed Nora's life too.

Stella Van Horne was only moderately recorded on CIA files mostly for her antagonistic approach to the US Administration and her pursuit to open the lid on government cover-ups. She had made outrageous claims of a clandestine organisation called *The Trust* harvesting control of the world's governments and how it murdered her mother. With this accusation, she had been classified as a security risk traumatised from psychological issues arising from the death of her mother.

In the search field, he typed the words *The Trust* and pressed enter.

The screen started flashing a bright red warning.

… ACCESS DENIED…

Unusual! Bennett thought, *Whittaker should have full unrestricted clearance.*

He found himself wondering if there was truth to *The Trust* killing his father and Nora Van Horne, particularly as he also hated government cover ups if this was one. The *Access Denied* message opened the door to his own suspicions and when high ranking officials like the Director of National Intelligence were denied access then there was always something serious to hide. Plausible deniability was what government officials would often rant on about and now he was thinking, *Stella Van Horne may not be a nut job after all.*

In the rush to see Whittaker, he'd forgotten the piece of paper taken from the dead street criminal. An address of '190 Station Avenue' was printed on it and nothing else. Quickly he entered the address into the CIA search field and it immediately returned an old warehouse once used to store chemicals in the north east side of Washington. Nothing of interest he noted and still owned by the same chemical company only it was scheduled for demolition in two days time.

He left the Director's office heading for the old warehouse with a hunch that Stella was held captive there. He still had no idea why or what organisation the men worked for but whoever they were, he and Stella were their targets. He was confused or for a better word, curious why they both made the target list and that was enough in his mind to go pick a fight.

Further south at the headquarters of the CIA, a warning alert was blinking on a computer screen. The security officer peered down from behind his metal rimmed glasses and became annoyed at the Access Violation when he was due to terminate his shift in less than five minutes. He had never seen this type of warning before and what was *The Trust* he wondered.

He lifted the telephone and dialled the required number as per protocol.

CHAPTER 23

CAPTIVE

Abandoned warehouse
190 Station Avenue, North East Washington
August 12th

The old weathered warehouse appeared nothing like its newly constructed neighbours and on closer inspection it became clear why it was destined for demolition. Set at the end of a narrow alleyway within the industrial part of north east Washington, it showed signs of decay with parts of the roof and timber walls already collapsed. Once used as a chemical storage facility, it had been gutted leaving behind a huge open floor space under a four story high flat steel roof.

Darkness of night had fallen as Bennett sat watching the building from a safe distance further along the alley. The street lighting was sparse, though an almost full moon sitting high in the sky shed enough lighting for him to make good use of his surveillance. He had been there concealed among the shadows of another building for an hour deciding on his best approach and entry. The warehouse was larger than those around it and offered only a few windows and doors at ground level. Up above the roof housed massive vents that were once used in emergencies to release the toxic gases in the event of an accidental chemical spill.

He could make out the muffled illumination of an interior light somewhere deep inside the building while high up on an adjacent roofline he had spotted two snipers lying low and ready behind their rifles. He would have to take them out first, he thought, as he delicately screwed the silencer onto his rifle. At a range of 100 feet, both men were easy targets using the night vision scope attached to his M40 sniper rifle.

This assassination was different to others he'd completed. Usually he would have detailed knowledge of his target and who or what they represented however, he was only assuming these were the enemy. A slight steady rearward squeeze of the trigger and the bullet exploded through the skull of his first target. The second target unaware that his colleague was bleeding out on the next rooftop continued to scan his sector of the street and buildings. The high speed bullet entered through his left eye taking most of his brain with it just before his corpse fell flat onto the roof surface.

Using a propelled grappling hook, he climbed his way up the side of the building to reach the roof about fifty feet above the ground. He scanned the warehouse floor with a small fibre optic camera pushed through a vent which presented a complete view of the interior.

Off to one side was a group of four men sitting around a table playing cards and drinking beer. Directly below him was Stella tied to one of the building support posts. Her bare feet were submersed in a bucket of water and electrical wires hung from her arms and shoulders. A fifth man stood at her side holding a small black device and then as Bennett watched, she arched back and screamed in intense pain. The electric current pulsated though her water soaked body, she was being tortured. Her clothes were ripped exposing her breasts while blood trickled from her mouth and with each zap, cheering and laughter erupted from the other men.

The remainder of the building floor was empty.

With various weapons strapped across his body he leapt headfirst into the vent.

CHAPTER 24

EXTRACTION

Abandoned warehouse
190 Station Avenue, North East Washington
August 12th

Just above the floor the bungee cord went taut. No sounds were made until Bennett flipped over and released his weight towards the floor while at the same time unfolding the M16 rifle from its harness and depressing the trigger.

The closely packed table of men proved easy prey. They had drunk too much and their reactions were slow to escape the bombardment of bullets. A dozen rounds carved their way through the group killing all four men in a matter of a few seconds.

The fifth man he knew would be the problem just as a sweeping volley of gunfire confirmed his thoughts. He released from the drop cord and dived for cover behind an adjacent thin timber wall. The fifth man though taken by surprise had turned and engaged fire, shooting at every inch of the wall trailing at Bennett's feet as he accelerated to full stride out of sight.

Without warning, the wall to his left exploded in a blizzard of timber and shrapnel knocking Bennett off balance to his knees. Through the black smoke raced the fifth man with his grenade launcher rifle up and ready to shred Bennett until sudden movement out the corner of his eye spun him around.

Bennett had dropped his weapon in the explosion and instead had launched himself at the attacker with his hands out stretched to deflect the rifle skyward. The attacker had squeezed the trigger letting off half the magazine into the ceiling until Bennett struck him with three debilitating strikes to his throat and one solid upper cut to the solar plexus. The man dropped without a fight and Bennett ripped the rifle from his hands spinning it back towards him now in a coughing lump on the floor.

"Who are you and what do you want with us?" Bennett asked in a demanding voice staring down into the wild eyes of a red haired man in his thirties.

"Fuck you Bennett," was all the reply he gave as he pulled a handgun from his ankle.

The time needed to pull it from the holster, aim and then fire was nowhere quick enough. Bennett emptied the magazine into him ripping his chest cavity open.

Back behind him, Van Horne made a muffled noise.

He hurried over, removed the wires and cut her down. Her body flopped to the floor before he had time to break her fall just as a bullet slammed into the post beside them scattering splinters in all directions. He turned to see one of the four staggering to his feet, gun in hand firing it towards them. The man was covered in blood and grimacing with pain as the gun shook in his hand from the repeated firing.

Resembling some high scoring acrobatic move, Bennett threw himself over the top of Stella and at the same time twisted upside down to face his attacker. His handgun outstretched as an involuntary reflex had already released six shots by the time he hit the floor, most of which struck the chest and head of their attacker. This time the man was without question, dead.

Bennett walked over to the other men sprawled on the floor almost floating in their own blood. There he verified all were dead before any more little lethal surprises popped up spewing bullets at them. Stella was in shock, her body shaking and her eyes had glazed over without recognition. Suddenly a radio somewhere in the room blurted to life with a crackle and a man's deep voice.

"Mack, we got trouble out here. Both roof guards are dead, shot in the head."

A moment of silence followed.

"Mack, answer me. Are you there?"

Bennett mumbled to himself, '*hey fool, Mack is dead*'

He turned to look at the half naked and bloodied woman on the floor next to him.

"Ok reporter lady things are about to get bad, it's time we weren't here. Can you hear me, we gotta go."

No response...

In one strong action he swooped her up onto his shoulders and ran for the closest door. She was heavier than he expected making his progress that bit slower. By the time they reached the door he could see the headlights of two vehicles heading down the alley at speed towards the warehouse. He turned and headed for another door towards the rear, fortunately it was unlocked. It opened out onto another dark narrow lane way, crowded by more warehouses and a vast selection of hiding places. Back inside the warehouse a barrage of shouting signalled the discovery of the dead men.

Stella was semi-conscious but not yet ready to support herself and her weight was starting to weaken his stride. He stopped to rest in the dark of a nearby building where he found his bearings and calculated his rover shouldn't be too far. The still night air carried the sounds of his pursuers as they burst out into the alleyway from the same warehouse door.

It was right then as they rested that he felt the unnerving presence of a dark shadow moving towards them from across the street.

CHAPTER 25

SHADOW

North East Washington
August 12th

Bennett released Stella from his clutch and she slipped with a thud to the hard asphalt while he turned to engage the dark figure moving slowly in the shadows of the opposite building. The figure ceased its advance the moment Bennett stepped forward behind the sights of his handgun.

"Show yourself… your hands first."

"Bennett don't shoot, I have orders to help you," came the reply.

Bennett wasn't about to trust anyone and maintained his sights on the dark unknown figure, Stella was totally oblivious to their new problem clumped on the ground next to his feet.

Out of the semi darkness stepped a heavily built man with a young but rugged face in his early thirties and carrying a handgun in each hand now surrendering towards the night sky. Bennett kept slight pressure on his trigger, ready to shoot as he scrutinised him from head to toe searching for a sign to squeeze harder. In the dim lighting of the alleyway he could sense the man had an aura of military, most likely Special Forces. His stance and confidence gave that away.

"My name is Pierre Rousseau. We don't have much time. I work for a covert group of men that has an interest in what you seek. Your activity this afternoon on the CIA system set off some serious alerts around the world. *The Trust* seeks what you want and will stop at nothing to get it. That means killing you and everyone around you. That back there in the warehouse was a trap to catch you using the woman as bait."

Around the corner they could hear the scuffle of boots crunching down on loose gravel as the men pursuing came within line of sight, gunfire already ricocheting past them.

As Rousseau returned fire, Bennett pulled Stella to her feet and they retreated further along the alley.

"Get going, I'll hold them off," Rousseau yelled above the clatter of more gunfire.

"Hey, who do you work for?" Bennett called back struggling to be heard over the sounds of retaliation.

"You will find out in time. Now you both need to get out of here. Capture is not an option, OK… so fucking move."

Another small group of men appeared from around the corner each adding to the hailstorm of bullets, Bennett knew Rousseau was outnumbered with poor odds for survival. He felt the urge to stay and fight though he knew somehow his and Stella's survival was more important right now. So he lifted her to his shoulders and ran the final block to his rover. Back behind him, the sounds of battle grew louder and echoed through the alleyway as Rousseau fired off his last few rounds.

After gently lowering Stella onto the back seat, Bennett catapulted himself into the driver's seat just as the first string of bullets smashed their way across the rear window shattering the glass. He turned the key and slammed his foot down against the accelerator. The V8 engine roared to life and spun the rover's rear tyres into a fishtailing frenzy as more rounds sliced the tail end.

Bennett knew the best way to avoid capture was to lay low for a few hours and avoid satellite surveillance. A heavy band of clouds was building in the south with an approaching cold front and it meant they'd be better concealed however, right now they needed somewhere to hide. Not far ahead, he spotted the lights of a large shopping mall and a multi-level car park. *Perfect*, he mumbled to himself as he took the exit ramp and assimilated into the long line of vehicles hunting vacant lots.

He slipped into an empty park off to one side of the fourth level where he quickly emptied a can of black spray paint over the roof. It was only to disguise the vehicle and elude the eyes watching the satellite's monitor as their attention would be focussed on white roofed range rovers and not black. A few years back he got himself into a dangerous situation in Moscow running from the Russian mafia. If it wasn't for the quick paint job to his Volga coupe he'd be dead from a rocket grenade. Nowadays, he always carried a few spray cans in case someone just pops up wanting to kill him.

Stella had fallen into a heavy sleep on the back seat and remained unaware of Picasso outside at work. Half an hour waiting for the paint to dry, he drove out slipping in behind a mass convoy of cars leaving after a movie session had finished. His passenger still slept deeply behind him as he disembarked from the security of the traffic congestion and turned onto Connecticut Avenue heading south.

Back at the warehouse, the commander assessed the carnage. He had been told to expect it if the mission was to be a success. His cheap labour was expendable and certainly not highly trained and definitely not formidable opponents for Jon Bennett. He hadn't counted on interference by the Guardians but the end result was the same.

Bennett and Van Horne were on the run.

CHAPTER 26

MEREDITH'S VENOM

Woomera, South Australia
August 12th

Young Billy looked up from his backyard into another cloudless cobalt blue sky typical of the Australian outback landscape and waited for the aircraft flyovers. The local air force base always provided him hours of entertainment, he loved watching the fighter jets soar and dogfight high above the horizon and hear the sonic boom as they smashed through the sound barrier.

For the past hour, he'd played quietly not disturbing his mother who still slept inside their house recovering from another late night of binge drinking. Every few minutes he raised his eyes skyward hoping to catch his first glimpse of the aerial combat display but it was something else that caught his attention.

To the north, a small speck of glistening light was streaking upwards from the desert floor. He stood watching as it transformed into a long silver and orange blaze shooting towards the sun.

Without warning, a bright blue flash rushed down at it from above as if appearing from nowhere and it sent a weird shiver of fear through his tiny body. The silver object had vanished into a downward spiral of black smoke with a loud distant snapping crackle like a massive fireworks finale many miles away.

Billy ran inside to wake his mother though he doubted she would believe him.

In the distance, a clean-up team was already approaching the crash site. Their mission was to keep it top secret. Meredith had never died, she had returned more powerful and the time was fast approaching for her unveiling.

CHAPTER 27

RETREAT

Virginia, USA
August 12th

Bennett continued driving in the same manner as his neighbours, focussing on not drawing attention while around the heavy night time traffic was slow going which helped conceal their getaway. Up above the buzz of helicopter activity increased while he pulled onto Highway 66 and headed west for Strasburg where he knew of a safe house.

He drove for another couple of hours and only after he was certain there were no followers did he turn off the highway into the protection of a deep forest. It wasn't the helicopters he was hiding from, it was the satellites he knew would be systematically searching for them.

Under the darkness of night, the forest floor was alive with nocturnal creatures running for their lives at the roaring sound of the rover's engine. Occasionally a deer would dart through the headlights or collide into the rover's side chassis before franticly fleeing in fear. The engine revving to find traction and the persistent sounds of tree branches whipping the cabin exterior were all he could hear and it surprised him to look back to see Stella unconscious through it all. The torture had taken its measure on her.

After a few more miles of wild driving, he left the forestry track diverting out onto a wide open grassy field bordering a small deep lake the size of a football field. On the opposite side, a tiny log cabin appeared in the moonlight behind the shimmering reflections off the water. His father Viktor had built the cabin in the sixties as a safe house and more importantly a family fishing retreat. Only two other people knew of its existence, himself and Dom Whittaker. For many years it had become their asylum, somewhere they would drown their occupational guilt in bourbon and counsel each other back to reality. Their jobs were tainted everyday with killing and deceit, yet in the company of Jack Daniels and drunken fishing it all seemed so far away.

He slowly drove the last half a mile with the rover's lights extinguished before stopping a short distance out where he sat and scanned the cabin's surrounds. Outside the car he listened to cicadas chiming in unison while over further in the dense pine forest small animals screeched and squealed. The lake gave off a distinct impression of a black mirror reflecting the night sky until a jumping fish shattered the surface. He sat there relishing in the peace and tranquillity until a murmur from the rear seat startled him.

"Where are we?"

"A forest just outside Strasburg, you've been asleep for some time but we are safe for now," he replied.

"Thankyou, if you hadn't come I'd be dead," she murmured through her shaking lips.

"Do you know who they were and what they wanted from you?"

"They kept asking me about Jeremiah, some code book and YOU," she responded in an almost angry tone for what she endured. "Who is Jeremiah and what code book?"

"I don't know," he replied as he drove the short distance to the cabin.

The moonlight was enough to show the cabin's deteriorated condition and that it hadn't been used in years. A large creeping vine had cocooned the rear wall and grown across the entire roof giving the cabin a feeling of nature. From the sky, it would blend to its surroundings and better still, from an orbiting satellite it would be completely undetectable.

He walked to the front door and it creaked open to reveal a single dusty room with kitchenette, fireplace, two old leather recliner chairs and a couple of low beds. It was cold and had the mouldy aroma of absence. The three small windows each had faded curtains blocking the reflections of light bouncing off the water. The small but quaint timber porch overlooked the lake only a few steps away and like the rest was badly deteriorated with wood rot.

"Wow, not exactly the Hilton Hotel," Stella announced as she trailed in behind him.

He ignited the fireplace and the cabin quickly transformed under the warm orange lighting into a cosy habitat.

"It's only for tonight, takes a while to grow on you but it does. Wait til you see outside in the daylight, quite breath taking really, you'll see."

The warmth of the fire was finding its way around the room and already it had taken on a new homely feel. The fire's earthly aroma had finally smothered the musty odour and a slight breeze had started wafting through giving added revitalisation.

He looked her up and down under the fire light. Her physical injuries were minimal but as for her emotional and psychological scars, that would reveal itself in time, he thought.

They settled themselves inside the cabin and to her surprise, he had come prepared with plenty of tinned food to last weeks.

"Are you always this prepared?" she asked admiring his caring for her.

"The food you mean? Yes I carry enough in my car, in case of emergencies. Never know when you have to run and hide in my line of work."

"But you are retired?" she quickly added.

"Lady there is no such thing as a retired CIA operative, we develop many enemies and unfortunately they don't go away unless eliminated."

"You mean killed."

He shook off her comment and dished up a serving of corn beef for them both. There was much he needed to ask her and it was still early in the night.

"So you have no idea at all who they were?" he asked.

"I'm guessing *The Trust* and their attempt to shut me up. My research is getting close and no one likes the truth especially the government. My guess is that this Jeremiah has something to do with it," she slowly replied while eating.

"*The Trust*, what's that?" he asked.

"Best I've found it's a secret organisation, possibly made up of high ranking officials worldwide."

Losing focus a little and becoming sceptical Bennett suggested, "Secret organisation, next you'll be talking Holy Grail, Knights Templar, Illuminati, come on let's get back to reality."

"Yes I know exactly what you are thinking. I'm some lunatic conspiracy theorist, right?" she added sensing his sarcasm.

"Ok, let's say this *Trust* does exist. Back in DC you said something about it killed my father and your mother as well? Well... my father did die in a car crash and yes they found a woman among the incinerated ashes but it was just a tragic accident, I read nothing of foul play."

He always had a suspicious mind, something inherited from his father but the car accident wasn't an event he ever questioned. His father loved fast cars and driving like he was a Formula One Champion. The police report had declared his vehicle lost control on a tight hair pin bend coming back from the skiing slopes in Montana. The car had burst into flames and both bodies were incinerated beyond recognition.

"I was fifteen when it happened, I'll never forget receiving the news," he added falling into deep thought of his father.

"Were you close to your father?" she asked.

"Yes in a kind of way. He spent so much time in the field while I was growing up that he wasn't really in my life everyday like most fathers. But when he was, we had some great times like coming here to the cabin and fishing."

"Well if he wasn't there then who looked after you? I know your mother died when you were very young," the journalist in her came through.

"My aunt Rose, while I was young and living in Australia," he answered.

She looked into his eyes and for the first time she was witness to a look of sadness something he wasn't well known for. He had earned himself a reputation of being a hard ass, someone who always got the job done without guilt or emotions. Now she was seeing something in his eyes, a small tear forming in the corners. She found herself attracted to his masculine looks and his aura was dangerously powerful, tugging at her to move closer.

He sat opposite at the old mahogany table a relic from the 1920's and looked away quickly realising he'd shown his guest a side not many had seen. He wasn't feeling comfortable talking about his private life to a woman he hardly knew. Under his bravo exterior he suffered shyness around most women and never took chances building intimate relationships. It was always best to have minimal baggage and someone close was a potential hostage for his enemies. In his line of work a girlfriend or wife was simply a death risk.

He was anxious to find out what else she knew about his father and the circumstances surrounding his death. Stella on the other hand wanted to know everything she could about Jon Bennett, the man she suspected was sacked from the CIA because he got too close to the truth. She had always suspected he shouldered a wealth of classified knowledge and together they could expose the wrong doings of the US Government to the world.

He spoke quickly to divert her attention.

"Ok, convince me about this *Trust*."

She broke from her thoughts and started revealing what she knew.

"Your father had been seeing my mother when they both died in that car crash. I believe they met in New York and had only been together a few short months before the crash. I was only fourteen but I can remember a man coming around to our house and she called him Vik."

Nora Van Horne had been a successful journalist like her daughter, back in the sixties, mainly choosing to work the political scene. She'd met Viktor Bennett at a political function one night in New York City while he was on a stop over from LA to London. He'd convinced her to run a story on conspiracy theories he'd been unravelling and after a month they had fallen into a romantic relationship.

She continued, "A few years back I found some old diaries belonging to my mother, they were mostly about her work appointments except for one. That one gave details about her interviews with your father. From what I could tell, he had been disclosing classified information to her corroborating a number of conspiracy theories about government cover ups. There were references to Roswell, the Bermuda Triangle, Hitler, the Catholic Church and throughout the notes reference was constantly made to an organisation called *The Trust.*"

"On the day they died, her diary was marked for a meeting at 11am with Bob. Next to it was written, *The Trust finally revealed.*"

"Where are these diaries now?" he asked.

"Don't know, I had a burglary last year and the thieves took them."

"What... they just took the diaries?" he questioned suspiciously.

"No they took my laptop, cameras, SD cards and my diaries too. Don't worry I thought the whole thing seemed a bit weird but the cops said it was normal."

"Did the cops ever find who did it?"

"No, from what I found the investigation didn't go far. They said there was no physical evidence or suspects, and that I should be happy there was no damage done to my apartment," she answered.

"Didn't you think it was suspicious the thieves only took diaries and a laptop, like maybe they were looking for information you might have?"

"Yes of course, I am not naive. That's why I've been chasing you all this time. The whole thing got me looking for evidence of *The Trust,* researching Viktor, Rose and you."

"Hang on... what's my aunt Rose got to do with it?" he asked somewhat confused.

"My mother's diaries didn't just have references to *The Trust* but also Rose held some secret codes... When you mentioned your Aunt Rose just now I realised who Rose was in the diaries. Up until then I had no idea. And before you ask, I have no idea what the secret codes relate to except that *The Trust* was searching for them."

She continued, "On the day before our parents died, a note was written in bold and circled."

THE TRUST MUST NEVER FIND THE CODES

"The next diary entry showed the scheduled meeting with Bob and that comment about *The Trust* finally revealed. Then the car accident the same day, all too coincidental I think... Now can you see the connection?"

She explained how her contact in Washington found *The Trust* blocked by some heavy security protocols and failed to reveal any useful information. Bennett listened in agreement, remembering that he too had the same problem even using the Director's access codes.

"What did the police report reveal about the car crash?" Bennett asked.

Stella gave him a summarised version of the report she'd come to read a hundred times and how it claimed faulty brakes and high speed caused the crash. Their vehicle had broken through a road guard at over 100 miles per hour and plummeted down a hundred foot ravine spearing into the ground like a missile. The fire had been so intense, the bodies were both unrecognisable requiring dental records to identify them.

She added, "But the strange thing about it was in the unofficial police report. I had a contact at the local Sheriff's office who gave me a copy of the original report. It stated the brakes failed due to severing of the brake cables. However, I was told by the investigators that speed and alcohol were to blame. Toxicology reports showed excessive alcohol levels in their bodies and it was no wonder the brakes failed to respond at such high speeds. That report was taken during the break in too. Oh and my mother never drank a drop in her life."

Bennett was catching on to recognising the suspicion surrounding *The Trust* and his father's death but they didn't have the diaries or police report. They needed to verify the information somehow.

"Well we need to find out more about *The Trust* then. I think it's time to pay my aunt a visit."

"Where is she now?" asked Stella.

Bennett thought for a moment with his head down. He and Rose had been close all his young life after his mother died and then after she was struck down with an aggressive cancer everything changed.

"Last I'd heard she'd been transferred to St Marika's Hospital in Greensboro, its specific for unusual psychiatric patients. She'd been in the final stage of lymphatic cancer and wasn't expected to live. An opportunity came along to test a new drug that doctors claimed could cure her or at least improve her lifestyle. It was successful however, an unexpected side effect fucked her up. Doctors claim it somehow caused large scale brain cell mutations that have left her a zombie most of the time."

Bennett paused in thought and added, "Though don't expect anything, she has not uttered a single word in twenty years. I stopped going to visit a few years back, it was too traumatic sitting there next to her bed watching her mental decay. It's inhumane that a once lively woman can be like that, it's not a life. Dom won't give up on her though, he's paying the bills and making sure she is comfortable."

"Do you mean Dom Whittaker, National Director of Intelligence?" she asked.

"Yes, Dom and I have been friends for a very long time, you could say he's my best friend, one of the very few who I actually trust with my life. He took it on himself to provide Rose the best care available no matter the cost. The guilt I think became too much for him and he feels responsible for what happened."

"Guilt? Why?" she asked.

"Whittaker was the one who arranged for Rose to be tested with the trial drug."

They talked for another two hours about his experiences in the field and his views on the CIA. She was quickly acquainting herself with the deadly side of Jonas Bennett. Her personality profile of him was building though most was not destined for any newspaper or magazine.

The political corruption and government cover ups were however, worth throwing out there for public persecution. Just like Bennett she had an extreme distaste for bureaucrats and their power hungry attitudes. She learnt he had an extremely negative attitude towards the American government, had no respect for any political leader no matter where they reigned and he held a deep grudge for the government's failings to rescue him from Afghanistan.

She could see he was an angry man, a man wanting revenge and closure. She learnt he was a man of his word and would give his life to save a true friend.

"How you feeling anyway, electrical torture can be a bitch?" he asked realising it was late and she would be tired.

"Ok I think, arms and legs are sore but I'll live. Never been tortured before, must admit wasn't my happiest moment."

"Well now you need to rest. Tomorrow we pay Rose a visit," he ordered as he headed outside to take one last scan of the area.

Back inside, wearing an old shirt of his, she laid down on the bed wondering about her immediate future. What had she gotten herself into? Her thoughts faded as tiredness took over and she drifted off into a nightmarish sleep.

Next morning she woke early to the scent of coffee and Bennett gone. She walked outside and felt the eerie presence of someone watching her from across the lake, she looked but saw no one. Then from behind her, Bennett appeared dressed in green army fatigues and an automatic rifle resting casually across his arm.

"Morning, how you feeling?" he asked as he stepped towards her.

The morning sun was breaking over the forest onto the lake surface while the black mirror had turned to a mixture of blue and aqua. It was breath-taking she realised just as he had suggested the night before and as she stood gazing out over its beauty she wondered what life would be like if this was the view every morning.

Enjoying a strong coffee they sat together as the forest came alive.

Half an hour later, they were back on the road heading towards North Carolina and the search for clues.

Across the lake in thick underbrush, a pair of bloodshot eyes had watched them drive away.

CHAPTER 28

ROSE

St Marika's Hospital,
Greensboro, North Carolina
August 13th

The head nurse wasn't expecting Rose to have visitors today. It was late in the day and almost her knock off time after another exasperating ten hour shift dealing with the mentally insane.

She had come to know Rose as their special patient, one the doctors could not explain or adequately treat. She had been admitted in the early eighties after an experimental cancer treatment had developed a number of unexpected side effects. A treatment never trialled before but without she would have died, they'd been informed at the hospital. What the doctors found impossible to explain was her youthfulness. Rose was eighty three years old yet on appearance, she resembled a woman in her early fifties. She was just one of those very rare cases they all conceded was unexplainable.

St Marika's Hospital was set well back on 500 acres of lush maple forest and grasslands in the northern outskirts of Greensboro. To the first timer it rose up high above a long straight driveway and resembled an old historical white brick prison with its windows barred and the perimeter fenced with razor wire. Bennett and Stella felt an eerie cold presence pass over them as they drove slowly towards it while guards stood among pedicured lawns watching them suspiciously.

It was more than a hospital, it was an asylum for potentially the most dangerous people in America. As a privately funded facility controlled by the Rheineck Group, it catered for the more unusual cases of psychiatric disorders and Rose was right at home among them. It was home to patients with mental inadequacies unbecoming to society, people with genetic mutations often considered alien to human life. It was more the unknown of what they could do that doctors and officials feared. For most of these people or entities as some doctors referred, St Marika's was their last home, many too far gone for any successful treatment and return to common life was considered impossible.

Five minutes later, they were walking down a long brightly lit corridor in pace with a short rotund nurse from reception. Like the other patients, Rose had her own private room, just off to their right but that was not the nurse's destination. Further along the hallway was the Director's office, or in this case, the warden.

No visitors were permitted to visit Rose without the express permission of the Director herself. Bennett thought it a little weird but went along with their rules to avoid any confrontations and prevent their meeting.

The Director was a grey haired woman in her late fifties and clearly well educated in the field of psychiatry and the associated research. Her office wall illustrated her academic life with an overabundance of certificates and awards from about ten different universities and various medical research clinics throughout the world.

They were ushered into the room where the Director remained seated behind her cluttered desk and returned a suspicious gaze from over the top of black thick rimmed spectacles.

"Mr Bennett to be quite honest I am quite shocked to see you here with a reporter of all people."

The Director had recognised Stella Van Horne the minute she'd walked through her office doorway, and she wasn't an advocate of glamorous television personalities. But Jon Bennett she welcomed as a mysterious hero and like so many women, she admired his masculine looks.

Bennett ignored the comment and asked, "Doctor, I am very sorry for the lateness and no prior warning but Stella and I are here to see my Aunt Rose. It has been a long time since I last saw her and I hope this is not going to be a problem."

"Does Mr Whittaker know you have come here?"

"No he does not know I'm here, I didn't realise I needed Dom's permission to see my own aunt."

The Director continued, "No of course not, you don't, but there is something you should know. Rose has started talking in the past three days, not making much sense and she has mentioned your name a few times."

Bennett now curious, "What is she saying and does Dom know about this?"

"Yes I inform Mr Whittaker of every event down here involving Rose. It was his strict instructions that we record everything she says. As to what she is saying, well it's like she is learning to talk again and we are finding it doesn't make any sense."

"I'd like to see her please," he insisted. He took a sideways glance at Stella and stood in an effort to accelerate the meeting and visitation.

The Director obligingly took to her feet and quickly moved towards the door, "Follow me then."

The three walked back along the hallway and exited out into a side grassed court yard which was about fifty feet square. The late afternoon sun had settled behind the distant trees and a chill was moving in on the back of a strengthening breeze. The yard was empty except for one dark haired woman sitting alone on a wooden bench seat near the western wall.

The courtyard gave the distinct impression of a prison exercise yard with twenty-foot concrete walls towering along each side. He abruptly stopped in disbelief as he stared over at his aunt looking absent amongst the loneliness of the enclosure and it hit him hard that she'd been sentenced to life inside this institution.

He had been told his mother died from a rare blood disorder when he was four yet his memory of her was sadly restricted to a few family album pictures held closely by his father. So when this tragedy struck the family, it was Rose who appeared on their doorstep barging her way inside and without negotiation, demanding she care for Jon. She had no family except Viktor and after a string of her own failed personal relationships she fell effortlessly into the role of raising Jon. She did what most mothers tried to do, nurtured him into a teenager and prepared him for the world. With Viktor away on CIA assignments for most of Jon's teenage life, Rose was the one there for him when he had trouble at school or when he had his heart broken for the first time by a girl. It was Rose who taught him the human side of life and it was his father, who proudly showed him how to fight.

Then his father died and Rose was all Jon had left as family.

Bennett reached the seat and stood at her side while she continued to gaze forward at nothing. Strangely she appeared younger than he ever remembered and if not for her milky white skin that appeared almost translucent in places, she was an absolute picture of health. Her body no longer resembled the fragility of an old lady but that of an athletic woman.

Rose turned her head towards him and he felt her dark penetrating eyes bore into his own except there was no recognition, only emptiness. He looked closer into irises that resembled an unusual narrowing and he noticed a cloudy sheath of skin had grown over both. But it wasn't the eyes that had caused a commotion behind him.

The Director and her orderlies had never seen Rose move of her own volition since arriving at the hospital and now she had fully turned her head without prompting. The Director pushed her way forward as Bennett dropped to his knees out of emotional guilt and the love he held for Rose. He embraced her tightly like any mother and son would do after years of separation and he felt the need to not release, but something was not right. Rose had failed to respond.

He pushed back and their eyes locked. As her lips parted slightly to speak, he moved in closer to listen. Beside him, the Director responded in the same manner as she forced her way within earshot.

At first, a strange incomprehensible language was all he heard and slowly it transformed into a more recognisable English dialect.

"Jon my boy… it's you. You and Vik come to me in my dreams."

She lifted a hand towards his face and Bennett took it in his with the Director gasping in disbelief.

For a brief second Rose's eyes closed as if she'd fallen asleep but then they sprung open and she whispered something forcing Bennett to move in closer towards her. She hesitated looking towards the Director standing a few steps away and she grabbed Bennett's arm pulling his ear to her mouth. She was remarkably powerful he noticed while he offered no resistance.

"Jon you are in danger… you must protect the codes my boy. Find Viktor's Sanctuary, the answers you seek are there. But be careful, they will kill you for the codes."

"Who?" he responded quickly.

Before she could answer, her body started shaking ferociously and her face became a portrait of contortion.

"She's having another seizure," the Director yelled to the orderlies waiting in the surrounds for the meeting to finish.

Two male nurses ran in, one restraining her while the other slammed a needle into her arm. Within seconds, Rose flopped back into the seat and was glassy eyed staring out into empty space. Bennett couldn't believe how quickly it all happened and looked to the Director for answers.

"Mr Bennett, you have to leave now," she responded pointing towards the gate.

"Doctor I want answers now," he yelled back at the Director while the same orderlies stepped in to escort him out. Their mistake was made when they both at the same time placed a hand on him.

What came next landed them both on the ground gasping for air and unable to stand from the pain flowing through their bodies. Stella simply smiled while deep down she was aroused by the level of combat skill this man just showed her and she realised Jon Bennett was exactly as she profiled.

"Mr Bennett there is no need for violence, I will answer your questions but we must leave the courtyard first," a somewhat startled Director said.

As they started walking, a sudden howling satanic growl echoed out across the courtyard.

"THE TRUST"

Rose had stiffened upright in the seat and was glaring towards them while she frothed like a savage dog. Then again, she bellowed out, "Jon … Beware *The Trust*."

Then all fell silent.

Her body slumped forward and she mumbled softly towards the ground, "Jon… beware *The Trust*." The drugs reclaimed her as theirs and she fell once again into a zombie state, like the others at St Marika's Hospital.

The Director exited from the courtyard, beckoning her visitors to keep pace.

"Was that normal?" Bennett asked as he looked back over his shoulder at the nurses strapping a straitjacket onto his aunt.

"Yes, for the last three days it has been. Very strange behaviour indeed, some would say she is possessed by the devil. I personally don't support that line of thinking."

Now back in front of the Director in her office they explored the reasons behind his aunt's behaviour.

"Doctor, what is causing this?" Stella asked after seeing the distress it had caused Bennett.

The Director stood and walked to a large filing cabinet against the far wall. She opened it at the letter B, removed a thick file before returning with it to her chair. The front of the file was marked '*Rose Bennett*.' She opened it and glanced through a number of pages before answering them.

"Rose was admitted here in 1983 after an experimental cancer drug failed. Well actually, I shouldn't say failed, it did stop the cancer but the side effect was what you see here today. Rose is a very healthy and strong woman in body but mentally she deteriorated beyond understanding. Brain scans show unusual activity in areas not normally active and the usually active areas now dormant. I just don't know what will happen with her, I would like to think we find some way of activating her idle brain cells but to be honest, it's highly unlikely."

"What has she said in the past three days?" a now very curious Bennett asked.

"Mr Bennett, I have advised Mr Whittaker of everything that happens with Rose, I suggest you contact him," was a curt response from the Director as she closed the folder signalling the end of conversation.

Stella looked at him and indicated with a sideways nod of her head that it was time to go. All three stood and made their way towards the door. The Director turned towards him and almost in a demanding tone asked, "Mr Bennett, I'm sure you understand but I will need to brief Mr Whittaker on what Rose said to you?"

"Doctor, that is confidential between my aunt and myself, you have clearly shown us today how information sharing is not reciprocated. Thankyou for your time, we must be on our way."

Stella started looking around the hallway, "Doctor I need the ladies room, is there one on this floor?"

The Director gave directions back down past her office and Stella was gone. He engaged the Director in further conversation and at the same time encouraged her to walk with him towards the entrance.

Ten minutes later, Stella reappeared next to Bennett and they left the Director standing in the Institute's foyer.

The day outside had turned black with an impending storm approaching from the north. The air had become icy cold and it would be a wild night. Back inside, the Director walked back to her office where she accessed her hidden security camera which showed Stella remove Rose's file.

Stella had slipped into the Director's office under the pretence of using the ladies room. No one had seen her she thought as she rifled through the filing cabinet and removed Rose's file. It wasn't the first time she'd done something illegal to get what she needed for a top selling story and she knew it wouldn't be the last time either.

As they drove away heading for another safe house the Director made her call announcing the bait had been taken.

CHAPTER 29

ROSE'S FILE

Highway 85, North Carolina
August 13th

Stella opened her bag to reveal a number of crumpled A4 size papers loosely packed on top. Ten sheets in total, all with the name Rose Bennett at the top. She hoped these would shed light on everything that had happened and more so, now that Rose had mentioned *The Trust*. It was more than a coincidence that Rose talked about protecting codes and *The Trust* would kill for them.

"What are the codes?" Bennett asked while he drove north on Highway 85 towards Washington.

"No idea, I didn't come across anything about them in my research," Stella replied as she continued reading through the notes.

The thing sticking out in her mind more than codes was *'Viktor's Sanctuary'*, she had seen these words before in one of her mother's diaries.

"As the Director said, Rose Bennett was subject of some new experimental cancer drug developed by the Ravensbruck Institute with an address in Portland, Maine. She was diagnosed with an aggressive lymphatic cancer and only weeks to live. That was dated 17 June 1976 and the experimental drug was administered by injection on 22 June 1976 by a Doctor Sigmund Kraus, a German medical engineer working at Ravensbruck at the time," she informed Bennett as she progressed through the notes.

She discovered references to Rose as Project Eight on several pages however, nothing in print provided insight into what it meant. The final note in the report declared the treatment a success but with an additional note next to it.

"Looks like something went terribly wrong during the two days after the injection. The notes say that after twelve hours she was up walking, talking and behaving like any healthy woman. But then she became violent and super strong. Report says she attacked three nurses, critically injuring one and then escaped the hospital by jumping from a third floor window. She was located two hours later curled in the foetal position near the outer boundary of the Institute's grounds. When she was found, she wasn't making any sense, only talking unrecognisable gibberish. She descended into a coma soon after that. Two days later she was conscious again, but lacking all motor skills and diminished brain function."

Stella read on further into the notes.

"Three days ago, she started talking in combination of some unknown language and English, sometimes calling out for you or Viktor. She has previously called out the words *The Trust* and twice before something about protecting the codes."

She noticed on the back page an added comment from the previous day.

"Ok get this one, it says that last night she called out the words *Jeremiah please save us.*"

Bennett listened intently to Stella's repeating of the notes and tried hard to fit it all together into some comprehensible briefing. With his head full of questions he wondered, what was Project Eight? What were the codes and what were they used for? What had happened to Rose and what was the drug given to her? And who is Jeremiah?

Stella suddenly screeched out with excitement, "I know where it is?"

"What, where what is?" he questioned, confused at the outburst and managing not to lose control of the rover. The highway was heavy with peak hour traffic and his sudden jerk of the wheel narrowly missed his transiting neighbour.

"I mean I know where Viktor's Sanctuary is. It's in Australia."

"How do you know that?" Bennett asked.

Stella proud of her newly found detective skills started to explain, "It was written in one of my mother's diaries, Viktor had told her he once found his sanctuary in Australia and would retire there one day. I think it was a place called Cedar Bay in Queensland."

Suddenly in accord, Bennett added to the conversation, "I was born just north of there, the Sanctuary was a small rainforest about 20 miles from where I lived. Rose and I went there for holidays when I was a kid and I can always remember her saying how at peace it made her feel. The beach was so white but that's all I really remember of it." He could feel his emotions building and his childhood memories flooding back.

Stella too was excited, she felt they were onto something big and Australia could hold the answer.

Half an hour later, she had them both booked on a flight to Australia departing Washington in three days.

Bennett continued to drive north uncertain of what was in front of them.

CHAPTER 30

MEREDITH

Command Centre, Cheyanne Mountain
Colorado, USA
August 14th

A buzz of excitement saturated the control room as General George Anders soaked up the accolades and honours. He had been in charge of the Titan Project since 1995 and finally he could report back with promising news.

Meredith at last was lethal.

The Woomera test had been the second non-simulated activation of Meredith using the remnants of the abolished Star Wars Program. She was no ordinary lethal bitch, she could take out a ballistic nuclear missile in flight no matter what stage of its trajectory or speed, the Australian test had just provided the vital proof of that.

In orbit around the Earth, she floated, waiting commands from a keyboard in the hands of the General. Developed during the Star Wars Program in the 1980s to destroy inbound nuclear missiles, Meredith was a nuclear powered killer satellite, able to remain in orbit for over a century. Though the Star Wars Program had been officially terminated, part of it remained in development under the close scrutiny of Anders and a small group of undisclosed government officials. Not even the US President knew it existed yet his administration paid for most of it through various clandestine accounts.

The success of the live test meant the laser was capable of ground contact whereas her predecessor had been restricted to sub orbital distances. She was equipped with two primary lasers and three smaller laser defence systems making her immune to any attack from below, above or the side.

Anders looked towards the massive wall monitor, recognising the ground target and entered a series of key strokes into his keyboard. Meredith turned on end and her weapon armed before a bright shimmering flash of blue light ejected from her underbelly towards the red desert of North Western Australia. Seconds later, a huge explosive rumble echoed out through the rocky surroundings fifty miles south of Fitzroy Crossing. The old shipping container planted there as a target disintegrated with the one blast of the satellite's laser canon. All that remained was a circular patch of black earth fused as one solid rock from the heat of impact.

Using GPS coordinates, Meredith could strike any target anywhere on Earth and with a recharge rate of five seconds would give the US military world superiority in time of war.

In her present configuration, she only offered enough power to obliterate cruise missiles, aircraft and small ground based structures yet the General wanted more. He could see her replacing the use of strategic missiles if they could increase the destructive force of her laser but that was still a long way off.

Somewhere behind him the phone buzzed.

"General, there are two civilians here to see you and they say it's important they speak with you," the young Lieutenant on the phone stated. The General curious why he had visitors left the room to return to the surface.

Two elderly men stood before him, one German and one English. They spoke quietly but forceful and for once, the General felt inferior. A short while later, the General returned below and his plans had changed.

CHAPTER 31

PATCH

St Marika's Hospital
Greensboro, North Carolina
August 14th

Dom Whittaker strolled past the main reception of St Marika's Hospital like he'd done so often and never once was he stopped. The staff knew him well and respected the way he would sit patiently at her bedside when all the time she made no speech or acknowledged his presence. This would be different to the other visits.

Rose laid silent and motionless in her bed, eyes open gazing towards the barred window and the outside courtyard. Around her ankles and wrists were thick leather straps holding her firmly to the bed.

The Director walked in witnessing the concerned and angry look across his face.

"Mr Whittaker, we are very sorry about this but it's for her own protection. She has become extremely aggressive and her strength levels are phenomenal. To be honest, my wards men are struggling to cope with her and she may need to be transferred to a high security ward."

It had been the strictest of his conditions that she always be given freedom of the courtyard and nothing was to change. Whittaker knew her life was pitiful, he simply wanted her to coexist amongst tranquillity and the courtyard with its lush lawn, flowering shrubs and birdlife.

"Has she had more seizures since Jon's visit?" he asked.

"Every few hours and screams out in a language that makes no sense and then there's this," the Director said as she pulled back the bed sheet to reveal Rose's legs.

Whittaker looked down and gasped in shock at the scaly appearance of her lower legs. From ankles to knees her skin showed signs of some aggressive flaky skin disorder that in places resembled dark grey coloured fish scales.

"What is it? What's happening to her?" he asked.

"We don't know, I've requested a specialist to consult but it has only just become apparent in the last twenty four hours. It could be some kind of rare skin disease but it is coincidental timing that she suddenly starts talking and responding, wouldn't you say?"

"Yes I agree that's very coincidental. You told me on the phone, you couldn't hear what she said to Jon."

"Yes that's right. I asked him but he wouldn't divulge it and prior to that as I've informed you, the only recognisable dialogue were the names Jonas, Viktor and something about Jeremiah saving us," the Director said feeling a little like Whittaker didn't believe her.

"Thankyou Doctor, I appreciate you informing me immediately of this, now I would like some time alone with Rose please."

The Director headed for the door and stopped before exiting, turning back towards him she added, "Mr Whittaker there was one thing Rose called out as they left the room yesterday, she called out the words *The Trust*. Does that mean anything to you?"

He shrugged in thought, "Rose like her brother, Viktor were into conspiracy theories thinking an organisation called *The Trust* was taking over the world. It's all bull shit, just paranoia rubbish. Perhaps it's remnants of her illness."

He was left alone in the ward with Rose, her breathing shallow and her eyes still staring out the window. On first impression, he thought something had changed, her face dragging down with sorrow. He walked over and sat next to her bed, "Hello Rose it's Dom, can you hear me?"

This had been his standard opening line for the past ten years and though he had a special monetary fund set up to accommodate her, he found it difficult to sit and watch his friend die. He and Rose had once shared a romantic past carved during the `50s when he was a teenager fascinated by the sexual lure of an older experienced woman. It lasted on and off for years until he met his wife, but even then he struggled with his erotic desire for Rose.

She turned her head towards him, eyes still deeply sunken and spoke in an almost distant voice, "Is it ready?"

He replied, "Yes but are you sure this is what you want?"

A few years back, just like she did for Bennett, she started uttering a few words to him. He'd kept it secret from the hospital staff seeing no point in exciting the shrinks as he knew it would only make her life of mental testing worse. She nodded her head, looked towards him and for a glimpse, he thought he witnessed the true blue beauty of her eyes from behind the thin membrane that gave them the dark appearance.

"Rose what did you say to Jon yesterday?" he asked.

Rose went back to staring out the window and said nothing. He had come to appreciate his short conversations only lasted a few seconds at best and this encounter was obviously no different. He sat watching her transform back into the zombie the hospital staff best knew her as.

He removed the syringe from his pocket and squeezed the red fluid deep into the back of her neck.

By the time he'd walked to his car, Rose had found her peace.

CHAPTER 32

SPONARAVA

Kangchenjunga West, Nepal
August 16th

Nicholette Sponarava paraded with purpose into the Temple's main meeting room overlooking the western snow covered face of Kanchenjunga Mountain. Her blonde elegance and sleek physique demanded a lustful gaze from all those seated at the table and for a brief moment the Council members were distracted from their arguing.

She took her seat at one end and from there she couldn't help feel the men strip her naked, yet criticise her very presence inside their holy shrine. Most were intimidated by the way she killed without remorse and the mere threat she could reach out and snap their necks at any time. Once trained by the Russian Special Forces she soon broke free of the disciplined militant life and made a living off freelance assassination contracts for the KGB and various private European organisations. It wasn't until the Soviet Government decided she was a liability and contracted her death that she vanished underground to join a rebellion group fighting the Russian Regime. She never fully understood why she did what she did for the KGB when after all, she had despised her father, a long serving KGB officer, for the murderous atrocities he once sanctioned. Her hatred ran deeper with terrifying memories of the same man molesting her at a young age while growing up in Moscow.

Firelight flickered from the burning flares scattered around the walls of the room dwarfed by the single massive stone table and the twelve robe clad men seated before their leader. She sat and glanced around at each before casting her attention towards the Monk sitting at the other end.

For ten years Nicholette had pledged her allegiance to supporting the Supreme Council and the Monk, leaving behind her Soviet high society lifestyle to become an international spy and warrior in a holy army. Still she found it unnerving entering the great temple where tradition meant her place was insignificant and every action needed justification. It didn't bother her that the men were mostly arrogant and though it was sinful, only wished one thing from her body. She was there because she followed the Monk's vision of a harmonious future and he needed her to make it happen by eliminating the leaders of the enemy. The Monk had always preached the importance of her actions and that it would one day avoid a war of never imagined power and destruction. It would be a war no man could win.

Her mission involved the infiltration of wealthy conglomerates around the world where she covertly singled out members of *The Trust* before executing them in cold blood. Using various aliases, she moved from continent to continent working to orders sent down by the Monk and never once questioning his decision. He knew the prophecies of his elders meant maintaining their direction for the future of Gaia and the return of the true Higher Order. *The Trust* had to be stopped and Gaia's Guardians were the chosen ones to do just that. In all, she'd terminated over fifty high level executives yet still she had not found the group known as the Six who controlled *The Trust*.

She had been summoned to the Council to report on her progress after some of the more cynical at the table raised doubts about her actions and whether it would maintain the secrecy of the Council or worse expose the truth to the world. There were still some in need of convincing that killing was the best course of action when already so many lives had been lost.

Her verbal report was no different to the last three she'd presented. Each time she gave a new recount of the lives she'd snuffed out and what position they played within *The Trust*. Nicholette was intelligent and never revealed too much fearing she was expendable in their overall plan to save the Earth. She trusted only herself and she knew the moment her guard dropped, death would be swift. So she gave them what she decided they needed to know and not her full plan. There was one mission she failed to mention and she knew the Monk would not ask about it in front of the others.

He had assigned her the deadliest target of all and if she succeeded could mean the demise of *The Trust*. She remembered late one night in the back streets of Prague he had appeared from nowhere and gave her the new instructions but made it very clear the mission must remain a secret from the other Council members.

She convinced the members she was closing in fast on *The Trust's* primary controllers, men she believed were high up in American, British and German Governments. The controllers were the pinnacle of her mission, with them gone she hoped for a normal life, something she had lost all concept of the meaning.

The Council members all conceded her course of action was required to dispel the reign of terror in wait on the horizon. They knew what the Sphere could provide and if the Thirteenth Code was ever released, no God could save them, not even the Elders could protect them.

Sponarava was dismissed from the meeting and departed knowing there were many things she purposely neglected to say. One day, she hoped, it would all make sense.

CHAPTER 33

MEMORIES

Whittaker's Residence,
Baltimore, USA
August 16th

A few hours earlier Bennett's cell phone had rung and an encrypted message from Dom Whittaker had come through. He took no time to translate the jumbled letters and numbers while he laughed to himself thinking how Dom loved his coded invites. The message was simple, an invitation to dinner at Whittaker's house in Baltimore and time to catch up as old friends.

He and Stella weren't scheduled to leave Dulles International for a couple of days and so they took the time to take care of personal business before their trip to Australia. Stella had returned to Washington to close off a few overdue magazine articles leaving him to do whatever unemployed secret agents do, she'd jokingly suggested.

Now sitting in his rover outside Whittaker's house in the north of Baltimore, he couldn't help feel the warmth of the neighbourhood, kids on bikes, kids throwing balls, neighbours chatting across fence lines, the roar of lawn mowers and the tantalising aromas of home cooking. He longed for that kind of life, one where he'd come home each day with no tales of near death or blood on his hands. It was something he didn't dwell on, he knew too well his life couldn't permit such simplicity.

The late afternoon was darkening as he walked up the path towards Whittaker's front door. The air had become crisp and the weather forecast was for severe thunderstorms later that night. He looked to the west and already dark threatening clouds were clawing their way up drowning out the setting sun and spilling early night across the Baltimore suburbs.

The door opened, Whittaker stood with a big grin as usual and a beer in each hand. Bennett accepted one without hesitation and strolled inside. He loved his liquor, it had become his friend during his early CIA career when killing was mentally hard to digest and Dom had often been the emotional punching bag.

They exchanged their usual greetings and pleasantries before the conversation turned abruptly to his recent events at the warehouse.

"Dom, do you know anything about an organisation called *The Trust*?"

"Just that it doesn't exist. It's all a ridiculous conspiracy theory about some organisation controlling the world. Don't get yourself all twisted up with shit like that, Jon. Anyway why are you asking?"

Over the next couple of beers, he briefed him on rescuing Stella at the warehouse from men she believed were part of *The Trust*. He informed him about the man who helped them escape and he rattled off Stella's story about *The Trust* killing Viktor. He mentioned the secret codes yet he didn't say anything about Rose or Viktor's Sanctuary.

Whittaker listened intently and kept silent while Bennett had the floor. He'd been witness to Viktor's paranoia in the years before his death and knew what it sounded and looked like. Now he was seeing it all over again in Bennett.

"I went to see Rose a few days ago," Bennett announced at the conclusion of his briefing.

"Yes I know the hospital called me, how was she?" Whittaker said happy to change the subject.

"Not good, ranting and raving in some satanic verse, none of it I could make sense of."

"Yeah the Director told me, seems she started talking a few days ago and just demonic ranting is all they could gather from it. So she said nothing to you that made any sense?"

"Yeah she said *The Trust* will kill me for the codes. Do you know what she is talking about?"

"No… never heard that one. Your father got himself in deep with some hard core conspiracy theorists in the few years before the crash which destroyed his reputation at the Agency. He often babbled on about the end of the world and secret codes to unlock all hell. Maybe Rose is recalling some of that."

Bennett knew Viktor's plight into humiliation during his last two years at the CIA and the condemnation was something he always had to dispel during his career there. In the early days, he was known as Viktor Bennett's son, and wasn't till he made it on his own in Russia's killing fields that he became his own respected entity.

As a quick change of topic, Whittaker asked, "What's the latest on your assassin friends, are they all dead yet?" He knew Jon Bennett better than anyone, he knew his style, he knew his way of thinking but most of all he knew his mental drive to complete a mission. It was something Jon Bennett was admired for in the Agency, his dedication to total commitment.

"No I read the brief, it would appear they are revenge attacks by the ILF. They hold me responsible for the strike on their headquarters in Kuwait which both you and I know is complete utter bullshit."

"Yeah Jon, long dusted that one off. Please don't go opening that can of worms, you don't really want Senator Brown sinking his teeth back into you," Whittaker almost pleaded with him.

"Bit hard walking up to some revengeful Islamic Extremist group with no other wish than to slice and dice me and say hey sorry fellas you got the wrong guy, I wasn't even there. I really don't think it would cut it. I'm not real optimistic they'd say oh sorry Jon boy have a cup of tea instead!" he responded to Whittaker.

Whittaker took the point, he knew Bennett's predicament and only two viable options, one impossible with the Senate Inquiry changing its verdict and the other simply killing them all, terminating the threat.

"Jon, you know my position. Officially I cannot help, but unofficially I can arrange for a small strike team to help you out. That's the least I can do but as usual it would be off the radar and I would completely deny it."

Bennett knew this all too well, running clandestine ops in countries where the US had no standing, they were always collateral damage in order to save the US Government embarrassment. He and Whittaker had taken their fair share of assignments knowing imprisonment in a foreign country was likely until broken out by some undercover pack of lethal goons acting without the President's knowledge. That was everyday life on the edge for Bennett in the CIA.

He said his thanks to Whittaker knowing full well it would be a job he'd solely execute when the time came but first he wanted to explore more about *The Trust*, the codes and where his father fitted into it all. He had so many unanswered questions.

At that moment, Whittaker broke into an exuberant smile and stood to greet a third person entering the room. Silvia Whittaker had been his first wife and mother of their only son but then after he died from a drug overdose, the grieving process took its toll and they separated. Now ten years later and knowing their love for each other was still strong, they naturally gravitated towards each other again. Whittaker had always struggled with the decision to terminate his own son's life but the choice had been without alternatives and she had come to accept it.

Bennett and Silvia had been close, often spending countless hours talking alone into the nights while Dom slept. She was the only person who understood Bennett and the creature he had transformed into and here she was again standing in Whittaker's house like old times.

Whittaker rushed to her side wrapping his huge arms around her in a lovers embrace while Bennett watched on feeling a sense of warm familiarity flood over him.

"Jon, Silvia has come home to me and we are back together."

On seeing Bennett, Silvia broke from Whittaker and ran to him, her feelings on full display and though she was fifteen years older, it was difficult to distinguish between romance and a family reunion. He and Silvia had been tight friends but after Whittaker made the decision to terminate life support for their son, she moved away and became a recluse. Her twenty years of marriage to Whittaker had taught her many things, one was how to disappear and not even Bennett could find her, though not from a lack of trying. Now she was in his arms, this beautiful warm and caring lady, the only person to have exposed his inner depression.

They spoke like long lost lovers before she broke and asked, "And Dom tells me you have a woman now?"

"That is not true, Dom speaks bullshit as always. I can assure you nothing has changed there," he replied.

Only Silvia knew truly how he desired the intimacy of love and companionship of a woman yet she could never help him dispel the romance demons that continually plagued him. He was once married, in love and bathed each day in the ecstasy of happiness until one night his wife was brutally murdered by members of a South American drug cartel. That day his blood went bitterly cold and with it, forged Jon Bennett into the anger fuelled deadly assassin the CIA applauded as theirs. Silvia Whittaker knew everything there was to know about him and she was the only person who acknowledged his pain and suffering.

"Arh come on Jon you can't be running around with Van Horne without some kind of romance. Shit I don't like her but she is the second best looking woman I've ever seen. My Silvia here is number one of course," Whittaker said taking the physical gratitude from the warmth of her smile across the room.

Bennett shrugged off the suggestion and denied anything was or likely to happen between him and Stella.

They drank a few more beers while Silvia talked of her time away. The hours flew by and they all laughed while reminiscing the great days of the past. Whittaker spoke of a mission in their early CIA days when in the former Soviet Union, a time when communism was at its most dangerous and stealing secrets was the norm for operatives. He and Bennett had entered under the alias of private businessmen selling more efficient western farming machinery, something the Soviets needed but their pride prevented. The recruitment of Russian soldiers working at a military base in Obninsk was their real objective.

One night they sat drinking in a local bar where they were meeting an agent by the name of Sergi Saranovik, a Russian soldier who had plans for the military's new stealth tank. They had only been seated for a few minutes when confronted by two members of the KGB, the National Security Agency for the Soviet Union. An argument broke out and Bennett was arrested at gun point.

Whittaker had been detained by two more officers while the other two led Bennett out the rear of the bar. Whittaker knew this signalled Bennett's death and he swiftly removed a concealed knife from under his shirt. Within a split second he had slit both officer's throats in full view of the bar patrons while no one lifted an eyelid. In that part, and like many areas of the Soviet Union, KGB officers were most hated. Whittaker then ran outside and rammed the knife into the back of one of the officers as the fourth officer stood with his pistol aimed at Bennett's head ready to shoot.

The executioner swung his head around to see his comrade collapsing to the ground and Whittaker charging at him knife poised to strike. In the seconds it took, the KGB officer had taken his focus off Bennett allowing the victim to become the aggressor. Bennett had disarmed the officer at the same time Whittaker drove the knife deep into his stomach and upwards under the rib cage, a fatal strike. Bennett knew at that moment he owed his life to Dom Whittaker.

Silvia sat listening to the same old war stories, hearing them become more exaggerated and thought how close these two men were. They had depended on each other so much in the field and now they still depended on each other.

Another few hours of reviving the past, the conversation turned to Whittaker's health and the strain on him. Silvia complained he was doing too much between his job as Director of Intelligence and his new business ventures.

Whittaker defended his position, "Silvia dramatises everything, you know what she's like Jon. I have a couple of small business ventures underway at the moment, a little nest egg for retirement, that's all."

"For a little nest egg, you are certainly very secretive about it and is it worth all the increased stress it causes?" she protested.

Bennett entered the conversation, "What is it Dom?"

"I met a group of bankers a few years back, they presented a lucrative proposal, one I couldn't turn down and now it means I will have enough for a very healthy retirement for us. Nothing special about it, just shares in a money lending institution giving support to various third world governments. There are big risks with it but if our plans succeed then it means greater wealth than we could ever imagine."

"Third world countries…   I have to agree with Silvia, very risky mate?"

"Actually not really Jon, you see in return we get full mining rights. I never realised but Africa has some of the largest unmined reserves of gold, tin, copper and uranium than anywhere else on the planet. That's how we will make our money," he proudly explained.

Bennett conceded knowing Whittaker was a smart and shrewd businessman, he would have it all worked out and Silvia would be given everything she ever wanted.

Whittaker's cell phone rang and he excused himself. Silvia kept chatting with Bennett like old times feeling herself still in tune with the warrior's emotional side.

Whittaker spent the remainder of the night locked away in his den and by two o'clock Bennett and Silvia were falling asleep.

Bennett departed on his drive back to a small guesthouse just off Highway 95 in Columbia where he was booked in under a false name and a different set of plates attached to his rover. There he would remain until it was time to fly out to Australia, not actually comprehending the importance of what was to be discovered at Viktor's Sanctuary.

CHAPTER 34

ROBERTS

North Queensland, Australia
August 20th

The aqua blues and greens rolled out for as far as Bennett's eye could see. He had been keeping vigilance on the horizons like all good pilots do, while below the mass of coral reef skimmed past as they flew north towards Cooktown. Viktor's Sanctuary was concealed somewhere amongst the vast stretch of white beaches and lush green rainforest common in these parts of Northern Queensland. He remembered as a teenager Rose taking him there in her noisy old Land Rover a couple of hours drive south of Cooktown.

He and Stella had flown into Cairns International Airport during the early morning of this beautiful but hot humid day. She had made arrangements with her editor to take leave, explaining she wanted to spend some alone time in the Australian wilderness.

Their flight had been occupied with polite conversation yet nothing that allowed him to trust her any more than when they departed Washington Dulles International. He didn't give in easy to trusting people and spent the entire flight on guard against revealing too much about himself. She maintained her usual reporter facade asking him more questions about his CIA days than anything else and he reciprocated with various quizzes of her past but nothing too personal. He learnt she was once married to a Soviet foreign trader who immigrated to the US to be with her. They both had busy lifestyles and spent more time apart than together which also meant no children. He loved to race cars on weekends and was tragically killed in a charity race a few years back. From that day on she immersed herself in her work and committed herself to being the best reporter she could.

Once landed, they had taken a taxi to the Sheraton where they caught a few hours' sleep in the comfort of the air-conditioning after both realising it was much hotter than they anticipated. Before that, he'd made two phone calls, one to secure the hire of a small single engine aircraft and the other call was to an old loyal friend.

As they continued to make good flying time in the small Cessna, a row of savage looking thunder clouds had started rolling over the western mountains threatening their flight path. He pushed their rental aircraft to top speed and kept a close eye on the approaching storm while Stella sat beside him terrified. Flying wasn't something she enjoyed and the thought of a single engine over water added to her fear.

They approached Cooktown's only runway overflying what seemed a deserted airport. He taxied the aircraft across to where a lone man was standing and cut the engine.

The man in his forties wearing a singlet top, shorts and flip flops, typical attire of life in the hot humid north walked over clearly happy to see Bennett by the grin unfolding across his face. He had become rather unhealthy from what Bennett remembered. Life as Mayor of a coastal town and owner of the local hotel obviously meant he drank too much and ate too many free meals. At school he'd been a skinny kid yet consumed every bit of junk food he could, now Bennett could see the effects of such a life.

"Jon Bennett, I can't believe it, is it really you mate after all these years? I thought you'd be dead for sure mate."

Bennett hurried over to the man, shook his hand at first and then they grabbed each other in a bear hug acknowledging a long-time friendship. Stella soon realised these two were old friends, he'd been his second phone call back in Cairns. Bennett broke loose of the welcoming embrace remembering Stella was not far behind him.

"Jim, this is Stella Van Horne, a journalist from the states here doing a cover story on North Queensland. Stella, this is Jim Roberts, my best mate from school."

Both shook hands and immediately she witnessed his eyes roam over her that gave an unwanted first impression, he was a sleaze. She never cared about men wanting a piece of her, she knew when the time came she could handle herself ok. She also knew her body and looks were her best assets to obtain what she wanted.

Roberts and Bennett had been best mates at school in Cooktown for ten years and together had done almost everything young boys do including fighting over girlfriends from time to time. They had always vowed to look out for one another but then Bennett moved to America while Roberts remained in Cooktown becoming the Mayor and marrying one of those hard fought over girlfriends.

Five kids later, Jim Roberts was the king of his land.

"Hey Jon, I got that car you needed, one sucker that will drive anywhere no matter how hard the tracks. I hope you're not taking this gorgeous girl down to the Sanctuary?"

"Yes Jim, I am, thought I'd show her the most beautiful uninhabited place on Earth. Is it still hard to get to, or I suppose it's all commercialised now with its own fast food joints?" he asked hoping for the answer he wanted.

"I don't reckon that'll ever happen. It's been listed as native land, so no commercial progress there my friend. The tracks would be all overgrown now and entry is prohibited to vehicles after it became native crown land, so good luck getting in mate," Roberts replied.

Bennett was never one for obeying rules when on a mission and he got the impression that Stella wouldn't be too perturbed by it either. Roberts added, "Well mate no matter what you have planned, you can't go anywhere tonight, that storm down south is heading our way and gunna be a nasty one. So I have you both booked into the pub, you can leave tomorrow morning."

He knew he was in for a big night, Jim Roberts loved his booze and by the size of his belly it loved him too. All three drove into town in an old Land Rover jacked up a few extra feet above the ground that rode rough like a truck. It was their vehicle to tackle the tracks into the Sanctuary. Bennett knew the drive would be the easy part he just hoped what they discovered would be problem free, without the backing and support of the Agency he now had to clean-up after himself. In his Agency days, there was always a team of professionals behind his every move just to clean up any kills and conceal the CIA's involvement.

An hour later, with beers in hand, Bennett and Roberts had started the night's binge. It would be a big night they both knew, so much catching up and with it endless laughs. Stella dressed in a short blue and yellow sundress showing her long muscular legs entered the bar aware of the eyes that were about to strip her naked. It was six o'clock and the local watering hole was full of the town's men folk filling up after a hard day in the sun. Instantly the raucous roar of thirty men drinking stopped as they all turned to stare as she walked across the room to the small group out the back.

Bennett turned at the sudden freezing of chatter to see her parading towards him and smiling in her usual seductive way. He found it hard to drag his eyes from hers and again the hypnotic effect clawed deeply at his emotions. Her face had gained just enough colour in the brief few hours of the Australian sun and now radiated a glow of perfection. Her hair sat lightly over her bare shoulders framing her slightly squarish jaw and high cheek bones. He could now clearly see what all the fuss was about.

Roberts found himself staring as he slammed another beer into Bennett's hand. She preferred vodka in hers.

They all drank into the late hours reciting old school day stories. Stella hung close to Bennett like some rock band groupie listening and taking in some of his past adventures as a kid. She had her own war stories to tell but it wasn't the time or place. Every now and then they caught each other's eyes lingering a moment before they awkwardly looked away.

Later into the night, a drunken local wrapped his sweaty arm around Stella's waist hoping his bravado was enough to conquer her sexual attention. Before Roberts could step in to persuade the man otherwise, he fell unconscious to the floor. Bennett had been quicker than his drunken school buddy and released one well aimed punch to the man's neck striking the right pressure point all while Stella stood there unaffected by it all. No one else in the room witnessed it, his speed was phenomenal and Roberts stepped in to explain the man was a clumsy drunk. Bennett thought to himself how for a split second he felt the rage of jealousy and acted impromptu at striking the man, something he'd never encountered before.

Drunkenness set in fast with Bennett and Roberts reliving ten years of friendship in a couple of hours. They had been inseparable in their younger years and after a dozen or more beers the long forgotten memories started flowing and like dominoes falling, led to more stories. Stella kept up for a while though feeling left out of the reminiscing she retired to her room.

As she walked out the hotel's front doors and towards her room, she was scrutinised by a local Aboriginal man waiting in the darkness of the building across the street. He wasn't interested in her though, it was Roberts and Bennett he came to watch. Stanley Wilson had seen their plane land and Roberts collect Bennett and the pretty girl from it. He was curious about a few things, but mostly a conversation he'd overheard in town earlier that afternoon.

CHAPTER 35

VIKTOR'S SANCTUARY

North Queensland, Australia
August 21st

At seven the next morning, Bennett woke with the worst headache he could remember. Stella had been up for hours enjoying the morning tranquillity of Cooktown and running off her vodka. She tried to keep an exercise regime of walking or running each morning and though already humid she loved the tropical coastal landscapes. She didn't think any amount of exercise would remove what Bennett had drunk with his mate until the early hours, but he would pay the price she anticipated.

On her return to the hotel she found him perched at the same bar this time downing his third coffee and resembling death. He groaned a morning greeting and she just laughed as she slapped his back on her way past.

Within an hour they were heading out of town driving south on Highway 81 towards Cedar Bay National Park. Stella sat next to him gazing out over the mountains to the east and thinking how beautiful the area was and what lay ahead at their destination. Bennett was mentally praising the hotel staff for the hearty breakfast of bacon and eggs they'd served up, it had been just what he needed to make him feel human again. A good greasy feed after a night out on the turps was a necessity, he always said.

She broke the silence, "So you going to drink again?"

"Not for a while I don't think. I wouldn't want to keep up with him too often, he's lethal."

Another awkward moment of silence passed before she attempted to start a conversation again.

"So does Jon Bennett have a little lady waiting for him back in the US?" she asked knowing she was pushing the personal boundaries. She had heard he was once married that ended in tragedy and it wasn't wise bringing up the topic. Stella Van Horne had never been one for shying from the truth and like Bennett she was bold enough to give it a go.

She added, "I'm sorry, none of my business, right?"

He nodded and replied, "No woman back home."

"Wow progress, four words, now we're getting to know each other," she said in her sarcastic tone.

He turned and half laughed with her, he always thought he was the sarcastic one.

"Ok… no woman but you were married once, about five years ago if I recall correctly… right?" she asked.

The vehicle's interior suddenly turned icy as Bennett clenched down hard on the steering wheel, his knuckles completely whitened from the strain. He slammed on the brakes and the Land Rover skidded to an abrupt halt in the roadside's loose gravel. Her first thought raced back to her work colleague telling her once to never mention his wife. Now she was about to find out why.

He turned to face her and though he was clearly angry by the clenching of his jaws, she couldn't help notice how handsome he was. His eyes sparkled like the ocean and his face bore the warm tanned glow of the sun's rays. A few years in the Australian waters had rejuvenated his looks and now she wondered why he didn't have a plethora of women begging for a place at his side.

She snapped from her own sexual arousal to realise Bennett was unleashing at her.

"Who the FUCK do you think you are? You are lucky I don't kill you and leave you here in these barren lands," he yelled pointing out the window at the endless horizon of scrub. "My private life is none of your damn business and if you ever ask again, I swear you will disappear."

He turned back and pushed his foot hard against the accelerator sending the cruiser fishtailing back onto the road and leaving Stella sitting there in a state of shock not sure whether he meant what he said about killing her.

"I'm sorry, I was out of line," she managed to blurt out after a few minutes. He made no response and continued to focus on the road ahead.

She went back into thought but this time recollected what she knew about Jon Bennett. Five years ago he had married a young doctor from Ohio during a time when he was working a CIA operation somewhere in Northern Columbia targeting a well-established drug cartel. They had been married about seven months when one night while he was away, their home in West Virginia was raided by masked men. His pregnant wife was strung up, gagged and then slowly gutted with a knife. It took an hour for her to reach an excruciating death with the entire ordeal captured on video that was later mailed to Bennett. It destroyed him, he didn't just lose the love of his life that night but also his unborn son.

Stella sat looking at the man driving them south and she couldn't help feeling for him. After the attack, he went on a warpath hunting the murderers, suspecting the Columbians. He never found the men responsible but the cocaine trade suffered a sizeable downgrading from his efforts along the way. Two lords and their lieutenants fell along with their manufacturing labs. Up until then the CIA were losing the war on drug importations into the US but Bennett's mission of vengeance changed everything.

Her contact in Washington had sourced the information from classified CIA documents that she held back in her reports knowing he'd suffered enough. To save government embarrassment, Jon Bennett would have been hung out to dry even though he was eradicating the streets of the poison that only wrecked families and lives. His reaction was expected, she thought. Her source suggested Bennett blamed himself for his wife's death and he never found closure not identifying the perpetrators. It was one of the many demons he constantly battled.

"Do you have any idea what to expect where we are going?" she asked hoping he was receptive to carry on the conversation after his anger outburst.

"Not really, assuming whether I can remember how to get there and you heard Jim say the tracks are all over grown."

They reached the turn off to the National Park and from there it was a narrow sandy track heading east towards the mountains and coastline on the other side. It had been twenty five years since he and Rose had driven this track and most of it now looked unfamiliar. Soon the landscape transformed from open fields of wild grass and eucalypt scrub to dense rain forest where the terrain became more difficult to engage.

Roberts had been right, the tracks were hard to find and they had already past several "Access Prohibited" signs staked out in red and white. He kept pushing forward deeper into the forest along narrow openings that he knew were once tracks. The ground was cluttered with loose rocks and fallen decaying trees which made it slow going. Every now and then their vehicle slipped sideways as the rocks broke away under the vehicle's weight and they sideswiped the trees each side.

Stella sat next to him in awe of the beauty and enormity of the rainforest scenery, how the overhead tree canopy closed in making the day become night. Though it was only ten o'clock in the morning, the vehicle's headlights guided their way.

Nothing was said the whole time inside the forest, she left him to concentrate on not getting bogged and keep the vehicle on the track. In places, erosion had gouged the ground away forcing Bennett to slow the vehicle to a crawling pace and edge their way through, precariously on the edge of becoming stuck in axle deep mud.

Another half an hour of the same tedious driving and Bennett stopped where he slouched over the steering wheel staring out into the forest on both sides. He was searching for something very important from his childhood memory, something to confirm his mental road map.

It was there somewhere just up ahead, the distinctive sound of water falling he remembered so well but as he prepared to exit the vehicle, another more deafening and threatening noise broke from the tree line above them.

The outline of a dark coloured helicopter hovered low to the tree tops and moved slowly above them appearing in and out of small openings in the canopy.

"Who is it?" she asked.

Bennett replied as he pushed the vehicle into gear, "My guess someone looking for us." As he started to drive forward, he stopped and swung the driver's door open to lean out. Under the ruffle of the rotor wash he could faintly hear the same water sound and he knew exactly where it was.

"Come on, we don't have much time," he yelled as he jumped from the vehicle.

Stella was confused but fell in behind as they made their way on foot through tangled tree vines, rainforest palms and thick tree trunks before breaking out amongst a vast rocky outcrop. Set behind, they could just make out the top of a waterfall fifty feet high and ten wide. At the base, water crashed into a deep dark lagoon no larger than a back yard swimming pool. All around tall lush rainforest grew at the water's edge while the tree canopy engulfed most of the falls making detection from the air virtually impossible.

A slither of sunlight penetrated down through a small split in the tree tops. It reflected off the water cascading and sparkled across the surface to give off a soothing flickering light show. The air was refreshingly cool and it soon became clear why Rose had claimed it as a place of peace. So close to the roar of water, Bennett could no longer hear the helicopter though he knew it wouldn't be far and if his instincts were right then armed men would be rappelling their way down into the jungle.

"What are we looking for?" Stella asked looking out into the darkness of the thick jungle expecting a bevy of marauders to come running through at any time.

"We used to camp in a shack closer to the beach from here, my father built it and I'm betting that's where we need to head. Just got to work out where," he mumbled as he headed for a small clearing in the forest wide enough for one person to squeeze through.

He knew the beach was east of their location so leaving it all to luck they proceeded in that direction pushing through dense clumps of ferns and palm bushes. The roar of the waterfall had soon become a distant rumble when the bright glare of a white sandy beach came into view up ahead, behind that the glistening Pacific Ocean lapped softly.

She walked out of the rainforest onto a pristine section of white beach with the mid-morning sun digging deep into her skin. Bennett further in front was having fleeting thoughts of him and Rose fishing from that spot prompting a clear memory of where the shack was and he quickly made his way back into the forest.

It didn't take him long to find the shack where he stood in shock at the sight of its weathered condition, the walls and roof mostly collapsed probably from the onslaught of cyclones that battered the coast each year. On a post out front a deteriorated sign was hanging by one remaining rusted nail.

It read *Vik's Retreat.*

"This is it. This is Viktor's Sanctuary?"

Stella stood staring at what she thought was a pile of old timber and rusted iron having expected something a little more architectural. "Well it could certainly do with a makeover, so what now?" she asked.

"There has to be something here. Somewhere hidden would be my guess. Start looking for anything out of place," he responded as he took a quick look around the forest for any threat.

They both commenced searching through the remains, lifting and pulling up every piece of debris until it caught his eye.

CHAPTER 36

DECEPTION

Viktor's Sanctuary, Nth Queensland
August 21st

The sun had broken through the tree tops casting a slither of bright light onto the ground at their feet and as Bennett looked down he caught a glimpse of a metallic object protruding from the sandy soil.

He fell to his knees and using his hands like a shovel he scraped and dug to unearth a chain welded tight around the base of the sign post and disappearing into the ground. Stella joined him and they worked in silence until at an arm's depth they reached the chain's end.

A rusty metal canister, the size of a shoe box became more exposed with every handful they dragged out until Bennett gave the chain one powerful yank that broke it free of its grave. He reached down and picked it up surprised at its weight. There was no visible opening or locking mechanism and inside something was loose sliding from side to side. It was void of any markings just a deep reddish bronze from the ongoing rusting decay, which now resembled some mysterious archaeological treasure.

"What do you think is in it?" Stella asked.

"No idea, we need to find a way to open it."

"How are we going to do that?"

"A good hit with a hammer might do it, the rust is cracking along the edges," he replied still turning it over in his hands searching for hidden access points while his mind drifted to Indiana Jones and one of his crusades.

"We need a rock or something hard," he suggested looking around hoping to find what he needed close by.

"Don't move, hands where we can see them," bellowed a deep voice from behind them. Bennett turned as two armed men pushed their way clear from among the thick bushes lining the rear of the shack and quickly moved to within a few feet of them.

Bennett snatched Stella's arm and pulled her back behind him as a third man walked into view carrying his own weapon pointed directly at Bennett's head.

"What the fuck!" Bennett said.

He and Stella both glared in disbelief as Jim Roberts walked towards them.

"Jon, we'll take that thanks," Roberts announced pointing towards the canister at Bennett's feet and maintaining his gun squarely on him. Stella screamed as she was pulled rearwards from Bennett's grip while at the same time a rifle butt to the back of his legs dropped him painfully to the sandy ground.

"Jim… why?" Bennett asked pulling himself up into a kneeling position.

"Jon, you can't seriously think you can win against *The Trust*. They own us all now and this canister here will convince the world of that," Roberts replied.

He turned to the man holding Stella and ordered her execution. The man looked her up and down and thought he'd have some fun before she died. Why waste such beauty without first giving her some of his manhood he laughed to himself. He dragged her away kicking and screaming into the forest whilst Bennett yelled profanities in protest with the muzzle of an assault rifle hard against his back.

"Jim don't do this, let her go, you have me and the canister," he pleaded.

Roberts ignored him and went about examining the canister and how to open it.

"Then at least tell me why you betrayed me?"

Roberts snapped his head around, "I haven't betrayed anyone, you betrayed yourself for getting involved. Your father died doing the same fucking thing and here you are following in the old man's footsteps. We needed the canister and you lead us to it. Simple enough for you Jon boy?"

Showing his boldness Bennett growled, "I will kill you, you know that don't you? I WILL kill you."

"I hardly think so Jon. I've been a loyal servant to *The Trust* for fifteen years and nothing or nobody can touch me now. Not even you Jon."

Roberts, underneath his friendly exterior hated Bennett for leaving their friendship behind and he particularly hated that he'd become the notorious spy, a mysterious hero to so many. So when he was approached by two elderly gentlemen fifteen years ago he couldn't resist his opportunity to show up his old mate.

From somewhere deeper in the rainforest, a single gunshot rang out and Bennett lowered his head in sorrow.

CHAPTER 37

STANLEY

Viktor's Sanctuary, Nth Queensland
August 21st

With a handful of powdery sand Bennett flicked it into the face of the gunman guarding him and made his move. Like a jungle cat he pounced and knocked the overweight Roberts to the ground using their weighted momentum to carry them both over the edge of a nearby bushy gully.

With a small rock in his hand, he smashed it with all his brute force into Robert's face breaking the man's nose on first strike. A burst of gunfire split open the trees above his head as he grabbed hold of the canister still clutched inside Robert's hands and fled into the shadowy cover of the rainforest. The gunman had cleared his eyes of sand and was firing fully automatic in hot pursuit narrowly missing Bennett with each arc of shots.

He continued to chase him stripping the trees all around, while Bennett kept low using the foliage as cover. Meanwhile Roberts had regained an upright position and though in excruciating pain he had to recover the canister, his family's life depended on it.

Bennett continued to run pushing through huge prickly shrubs and darting between massive palm trees as a new round of gunfire sliced through the trees to his right. One round struck his leg tearing flesh and he fell, tumbling at first until the ground below him gave way and he dropped further into the scratchy embrace of a massive fern tree. There he laid twisted among the long tentacle like fronds as his attacker appeared high above him with his gun ready to fire the final verdict.

In the fall, Bennett's body weight had pushed one of the huge fronds back like a catapult ready to launch. He rolled slightly and it released with incredible speed striking the gunman mid chest and knocking him backwards. The impact ripped the rifle from his hands and sent it flying through the air, with Bennett on his feet diving for it. He locked hands with it, spun it over in the same movement and pressured the trigger. The resulting barrage of rounds obliterated the attacker's chest and dropped his lifeless bloodied body to the ground at Bennett's feet.

The other gunman and Roberts to go, he thought as he scrutinised his own wound realising it was only a graze and soon the bleeding would cease.

He made his way back to the Land Rover, stopping every few minutes to check his surroundings. Limping slightly, he edged forward out of the concealment of the forest towards the car not aware he was being watched. Just then a shot pierced the air only inches above his head and slammed into the trees behind the rover.

He flung around, dropped to the ground and raised his gun until he was staring directly into the muzzle of a Beretta handgun.

"Drop the gun Jon and hand over the canister," Roberts announced with a bloodied smirk.

Bennett slowly lowered his rifle to the ground and lifted himself upright using the vehicle behind him as support.

"Steady Jon, no sudden movements or I will kill you."

Bennett replied, "Fucking kill me then you arsehole but you'll never find the canister, it's well hidden, and I'm betting your own life depends on returning with it. Or let me rephrase that, your family's life depends on it." He slowly pushed one foot forward until a shot stopped his advance.

Roberts had fired a round into the ground inches from Bennett's boots and quickly had raised the gun back to his head. It was obvious the man was accurate with a gun, Bennett realised as he stopped mid step recalculating his next move.

"Don't try anything stupid Jon, I won't hesitate to shoot you. Now get down on your knees," he demanded as he walked closer to amplify the threat of the gun in his hand.

He lowered himself to his knees and with one lightning quick hand action Bennett speared the concealed knife from his ankle through the air into the neck of his school buddy. Blood gurgled and Roberts grabbed his throat, eyes disbelieving and realising his own death was imminent just as his fat body slumped forward onto his knees.

"See if *The Trust* can protect you now arsehole," Bennett declared as he rose back onto his feet and brushed the dirt from his trousers. He walked over to the corpse and scooped up the handgun as somewhere behind him, a tree branch snapped.

He spun anticipating the third gunman and prepared to fire.

To his complete shock, Stella pushed her way through the forest wall. Next to her a robustly built Aboriginal man dressed in a green uniform appeared pointing his rifle at Bennett. Covering one of his arms was an ugly mangled scar depicting a once serious burn he'd received as a kid during a time when he was regarded as the town's troublesome youth. Bennett caught sight of the disfigurement and he looked hard at the man's face.

Stella ran to him throwing her arms around him, her body shaking and overly excited they were both alive. The Aboriginal broke into a massive smile, bearing only a few teeth and it was then Bennett realised who he was.

"Hey white fella, I know you, you Jon Bennett, I thought you were dead man."

Stanley Wilson had been one of the problematic indigenous youths at school during Bennett's time, one he thought was destined for a life of prison and nothing else. After burning down Rose's house in `77, he'd been sent to youth detention but released after a few weeks because he should have been punished by indigenous law and not white man law. His punishment had been a lashing and a life sentence to the care of the native lands around Cooktown. His elders had administered the punishment and Stanley wasn't about to upset them. But today white man had come to his land trying to kill his friend Jon Bennett and his girl.

The night before he had sat and watched the hotel where Bennett and Roberts drank into the early hours of the morning. He wasn't sure what to do after earlier that afternoon he'd overheard one of Robert's men talking about some code book and killing Bennett at the Sanctuary. He hadn't laid eyes on Jon Bennett since school days yet recognised him the moment he appeared with Roberts inside the hotel.

"I don't believe it, Stan Wilson, I thought you'd be in jail or dead from booze," Bennett said.

"No boss, me been good for long time now. What you white fellas doing on my land and why the killin. I thought you and Roberts were mates."

"Yeah I thought so too and I don't really know why the killing, they jumped us. I wanted to show Stella where Rose loved to come," Bennett lied.

At the mention of Rose, Stanley went pale. Aunt Rose had been the most feared person in the whole of Cooktown and the world for all Stanley knew. All his childhood he had nightmares about Rose and was always more pleased to receive punishment from the tribal elders than face the wrath of Rose Bennett. Then one day he accidentally burnt her house down and he ended up ironically with a life sentence to protect her Sanctuary. A sentence he loved and wouldn't trade for anything else.

Bennett sensing the shame in Stanley quickly added, "It's ok mate, Rose forgave you a long time ago. She wanted me to show Stella her

Sanctuary and she will be so pleased you are looking after it so well." He was eager to get out of there without raising Stanley's suspicion too much.

Stella piped in.

"Stanley saved my life back down on the beach. If it wasn't for him then I would have been shot after that arsehole tried to rape me. No sooner had the prick dropped his pants had Stanley appeared and shot him in the head," Stella said as she looked towards Stanley with gratitude.

"Always knew under that wild exterior of yours, you were a good man Stanley," Bennett added.

"Jon, I hear talk back in town, Roberts was going to kill you so I come here to stop it happening," Stanley said as he looked down at Robert's bloodied corpse sprawled on the ground at their feet. He had always hated Jim Roberts so he wasn't upset to see him lying there with blood flowing from the knife wound in his neck.

"Did you hear why?" Bennett asked.

"Nah, just something about a codebook, that's all."

Bennett and Stella traded a quick glance.

"Did you hear anything else?" Bennett asked.

Stanley shook his head and the conversation turned to catching up on old times. Lucky for Bennett and Stella, Stanley wasn't a bright individual and he didn't ask many questions about why Roberts would want to kill them.

"Hey Jon what bout the bodies, can't have dead white men on me land, don't want any coppers here asking questions, they think I kill em and I go to jail."

Bennett thought for a minute.

"Are there still crocs in the creeks around here?" he asked.

"Yeah big ones hey, you don't want to take your girl there."

"Stan you were never real smart were you? Take the bodies to the creek and leave them, the crocs will destroy the evidence and everyone will just assume they were taken by them. Make sure you leave some of their things next to the creek so it looks like a croc attack."

Stanley finally caught onto what he was saying, "Arh Jon Bennett you smart white fella, yeah that's how to do it."

Leaving Stanley to move the bodies, they salvaged the canister from where Bennett had stashed it under the fern and they high tailed it back to Cooktown. Within less than an hour they were driving into the outer surrounds of the airport to yet another surprise and a forced change of plans.

CHAPTER 38

TAKE DOWN

North Queensland, Australia
August 21st

Waiting impatiently on the small tarmac at Cooktown airport were six heavily armed soldiers giving off the distinct impression they were preparing for a battle. Bennett scanned the area from three hundred metres away using a set of binoculars he found in the Land Rover, confirming six soldiers with an unknown insignia on their dark uniforms. One thing for sure he thought, they weren't Australian forces or American for that matter. Then a familiar person came into view.

Logan Bannister, the mercenary he'd met in Afghanistan a couple of weeks earlier appeared out of the shadows of a hangar and hurried over to the group. By the way he was waving his hands around, it became clear to Bennett he was sounding off orders to the soldiers.

Knowing that getting past seven mercenaries to access their plane was definite suicide, meaning only one option a long drive south to Cairns. He quickly shared his plan with Stella who was more curious why one of the world's largest mining companies would be involved. United Mining had featured prominently all year with their corporate takeover of the second and third largest mining groups in the world, estimated at over 500 billion dollars. It had been aired as the largest on record and signalled the company now controlled eighty per cent of the world's crude mineral deposits.

Two hours into the drive, Bennett spotted the familiar sight of a helicopter low on the horizon back behind them.

"We got trouble," he announced as he pushed down on the pedal.

"What… where?" Stella replied startled by his voice. She had been slipping in and out of sleep for the entire drive only to be woken by the shudder of the car as it careered through the seemingly endless sections of road works.

"Back behind us, chopper coming in low at speed. I reckon we've got three minutes before it's close enough to start shooting."

She turned to look out the back window as it loomed larger into view.

"How do you know it's coming for us?"

"Big fucker of a gun hanging out the side might give it away," Bennett replied in his usual sarcastic tone.

"How long to Cairns you reckon?" she asked looking back out the rear window.

"An hour, maybe more," he replied watching the road ahead and at the same time keeping an eye on the chopper as the thumping sound of rotors grew closer.

Less than a minute later the vehicle's engine noise was swamped by the turbine roar as the shadow of a Bell Huey passed across their path and the chopper banked into view. Hanging from the open side door was a mounted electric minigun capable of shredding them and the car into tiny pieces at 4000 rounds per minute.

"Fuck that's one big gun," she screamed in a developing state of panic. It had been the first time he'd heard her swear.

"I have an idea, just do what I tell you and we will be ok," he impressed on her before looking back at the Bell banking wider around them and preparing an attack.

"Wanna be a good fucking idea Bennett," she mumbled to herself never once taking her eyes off the massive gun barrel hanging out the door as the helicopter made its final turn towards them.

It came in low from the right, the rotors biting the air with a loud growl and the minigun whining with a barrage of metal striking across their path. Bennett swerved the vehicle from side to side to avoid the incoming bullets as they tore through the roof into the back seat.

Up ahead a dirt road came into view and he pushed his foot flat inviting the full grunt of the engine. The helicopter had banked back around for another attack and was returning fast. Bennett knew from the way they attacked their mission was capture and not kill, demobilise the vehicle only.

He tapped the brake and yanked hard left on the wheel as the dirt and gravel road appeared in full view. The Land Rover had been nicely modified for extreme country driving and what he was asking was nothing special. He slammed his foot back down brewing up a windstorm of dust fish tailing the most he could. It was all part of his plan.

"Here you drive," he screamed at Stella while dragging her into the driver's seat.

He hurled himself over onto the back seat and armed himself with an AK47 machine gun taken from the dead men at the Sanctuary. Stella had responded quickly to his surprise and continued to build the wild dust storm in pursuit as he clambered half out the rear passenger window. He lifted the weapon towards the chopper now coming around for a strike at their engine. As he did he yelled to Stella to brake hard and he held tight as the dust engulfed the vehicle like a sand storm racing across a desert city.

An entire magazine of thirty rounds was expended in the next few seconds as he obliterated the rear rotor assembly. He knew without it, they had to land or crash if the pilot wasn't sufficiently skilful and right now he was witnessing the Bell spinning out of control. He smiled to himself, he knew the men inside were probably thinking they were dead. The pilot hadn't seen the manoeuvre coming. He had pursued the car not expecting it to brake and vanish inside the trailing dust where Bennett had his shot.

He climbed back inside to the unexpected sight of Stella in full control at the wheel racing towards Cairns on the main highway again. She had wasted no time spinning the car around and hitting a good solid speed.

Bennett eased back in the passenger seat thinking their problem hadn't gone away. The lack of thick black smoke meant the chopper hadn't crashed and so the threat was still active.

By the time they reached Cairns, night was starting to fall and they headed straight to the airport. The first available flight out was to Sydney but not for another three hours. He knew that once they reached Sydney, he was confident of vanishing into the western suburbs, his Muslim contacts in that city were immense. But first they had to hide for three hours.

Having dumped the Land Rover they caught a taxi to a nearby motel where they could wait and inspect Viktor's canister to reveal what was inside.

CHAPTER 39

THE CANISTER

Motel in Cairns,
Queensland, Australia
August 21st

Bennett raised his boot and slammed it down hard onto the edge of the canister, splitting one end open an inch, yet not enough. He raised his boot again and slammed it down for a second time.

In one loud metal snapping sound, the box split in half shooting its contents onto the floor. Bennett and Stella stood staring at the two items that had just flung out of the rusty box. A strange looking metal disk about the size of a mini compact disc but much thicker had rolled out coming to rest against the far wall. The other resting at Bennett's feet was a small brown leather bound notebook.

He bent down and picked it up. It had an old feel to it resembling the size of a policeman's notebook with no markings front or back. He turned it over in his hand and opened it to the first page. Across the old lined paper were the words.

Jeremiah's Scriptures

Stella walked across the room and picked up the metal disk. A spark of blue light shot out striking her arm and she shrieked in pain dropping it back to the floor. Bennett had witnessed what he thought was a static electricity discharge, probably built up from the contact with the carpet as it rolled across the floor. He rushed over to her and already her arm was blistering from what looked similar to a cigarette burn. Unusual for static discharges to cause burns, he thought.

Driven by curiosity, she picked it up again though a little more delicately. This time nothing happened, no strange blue flash. The disk on first sight appeared silver but up close was a grey crystal material. On one side were shallow grooves in the shape of semi circles. On the other were thirteen strange symbols etched deeply into the surface.

Bennett sat down on the bed and opened the notebook. Inside the front cover appeared the name *'Viktor Bennett'* and the words *'Property of the United States Government'*. At the bottom was stamped *'November 29, 1941'*.

It was his father's work notebook he realised, perhaps his first official notebook going by the date. Viktor had been recruited into the CIA, then known as the 'Office of Strategic Services' in late 1941 during World War II. He'd spent many years running secret missions into Germany and then the Soviet Union after the war but that's about all he knew of his father's work.

The greying pages were covered in strange symbols, weird hieroglyphs and in places, his father's hand writing, Bennett assumed. The entire book had been filled, every page back and front had writing and symbols. On first inspection it resembled the writings of a mad man.

Stella didn't know what to think of the disk, she'd never seen anything like it before. It was definitely machine made, too smooth and round for anything else. On the opposite side to the symbols, a fine screw thread was visible around the outer edge perhaps designed to be screwed into something. She was not sure what the symbols meant and looked towards Bennett who was sitting only a few feet from her with the journal open on the bed.

Across the page were hand drawn symbols similar to those on the disk.

"Jon, look the symbols are the same," she remarked pushing the disk towards him.

He took it from her and compared what they had in the book however, none exactly matched. They were similar but different in some odd way like the ones in the book were unfinished.

"Weird that they look similar but something seems wrong like they are missing a certain depth of field," Bennett suggested holding the disk and book closer together.

The first two pages of the journal outlined an interrogation of a ten year old boy found adrift off Bermuda in December 1941. It didn't share many details except the boy had a strange tattoo across his chest depicting thirteen symbols scribed in blue ink. They inspected the symbols drawn on the next page, they also made no sense just formations of intersecting lines and geometric shapes. Hieroglyph text forming no distinguishable pattern smothered every line and strangely after that page no more symbols appeared anywhere else in the book.

"Hey I don't want to sound disrespectful but you sure your father wasn't a nutter. Look at it Jon, it's like the ramblings of a mad man in a foreign scripture and his graffiti artwork," Stella said taking back the disk expecting Bennett's angered response.

"Here have a look at these," was his only reply as he flipped slowly through more pages.

On various pages were phrases written clearly in English.

Beware the Blue Death, unleash it and the Earth will surely die
The owner of the Sphere and the 13th Code becomes the true Destroyer of
Worlds
Jeremiah's Codes are no longer safe…The Trust will come searching for them
The Trust must never find Jeremiah's Codes

On the last page written in large letters:

The 13th Code will annihilate all that we know…

Stella finally broke the silence, "So I'm confused, where are the answers Rose talks of?"

"Not sure, we must be missing something or that disk holds it."

He flicked back to the first pages and explored them in more detail. Still nothing jumped out at him. He knew they were in possession of something perhaps highly classified and realised he had to bring Whittaker in on it. Ten minutes later, he had reached Whittaker fast asleep and the initial greeting wasn't exactly pleasant.

He briefed him on the events at the Sanctuary, the death of Jim Roberts and then the appearance of Logan Bannister at Cooktown Airport before finally shooting the helicopter down. He described the canister and its contents. Whittaker listened to everything Bennett said before saying, "Jon, you sound like Indiana Jones on some crusade. I really hope you're not letting Van Horne get into your head."

"Actually I'm starting to see some truth in what she says and perhaps my father was killed because he got too close to the truth."

"I don't buy it Jon, but I will help anyway I can, you know me. I know an expert in Ancient linguistics who should be able to help decipher what's in that book. Just don't be disappointed when it turns out to be bullshit. I will get back to you soon," Whittaker said before terminating the call.

Bennett sat back with a strange almost sickening feeling building stronger in his gut. Ever since leaving the Sanctuary, he was starting to develop minor stomach cramps that felt more like something vibrating deep inside his body. On opening of the canister, the cramps had abruptly stopped. Now it was more of a numb cold feeling.

He just didn't know the disk was doing one of its jobs. The entities were spreading and gaining strength by the hour.

CHAPTER 40

GAMES

Cairns Airport
August 21st

The disk and journal were safe inside Bennett's jacket pocket as he and Stella sat waiting in the departure lounge of Cairns Airport for their 8.15pm flight to Sydney. They both knew they had much work to do, answers to find and the next step of their investigation to decide. He had been on edge since killing Roberts and shooting down Bannister's chopper knowing it meant their presence in Australia had been detected and more trouble was no doubt, coming their way.

Stella sat beside him deep in thought about reporting to her editor and didn't hear him whisper, "We have a problem."

Bannister and three men strolled into the lounge area and stood trying their hardest to avoid eye contact with Bennett, which only made it more amusing for the man who once lived and breathed being invisible. He sat there watching and laughing to himself while each man would occasionally throw him a glance.

Bennett leant across to Stella and whispered, "Just follow my lead, time for some fun with the three clowns opposite." She returned a confused look as Bennett stood and encouraged her up at the same time by pulling her arm.

As a mercenary, Bannister's missions were usually always restricted to those countries where questions by law enforcement were less likely and his threats made a difference. He usually opted more for the intimidation approach with large powerful weaponry and not the close one on one confrontation he was resorting to at the airport.

His orders had been simple enough. Meet with Jim Roberts, take possession of some codebook and then deliver it to a predetermined address in southern Germany. He was to kill Roberts once he had the book but then Roberts failed to show at Cooktown Airport and their plans changed.

Bennett and Stella walked casually over to where Bannister and his men were waiting. In his usual bold confident manner, Bennett reached out and grabbed Bannister by the arm, "Hey mate, didn't I meet you in North Afghanistan a few weeks back, you were there with United Mining?"

Bannister turned quickly but then paused realising Bennett was playing with him and said, "Ah, Mr Munro, yes I remember, you were there taking photographs for some magazine."

Bennett maintaining a friendly atmosphere added, "Are you here in Cairns on business or pleasure?"

"Business, always business, and you, what is your business in Australia?" Bannister asked.

Bennett replied as he pulled Stella in close under his arm, "Pleasure with my new fiancée here." Feeling a sudden rush of blood and warmth all over she ignored Bannister and played along with the correct response by kissing him tenderly on the neck. Bennett camouflaged his own shock at the affection by maintaining his steely eye contact with Bannister, though they both knew each other were lying and made no further effort to converse.

Bannister said his goodbyes and pushed past Bennett while his men glared at him as they passed. Bennett made a quick phone call and laughed to himself, he'd just given himself and Stella a decent head start.

Ten minutes later they boarded their plane, all except Bannister and his men. Within a few minutes of his phone call, airport police had stormed the lounge area, guns raised towards Bannister and his men, yelling to get down on the floor. A bewildered Bannister complied but quickly acknowledged Bennett's triumph.

Inside his left jacket pocket was a tiny improvised explosive device, one capable of destroying half the plane. Bennett had several of them all made from ceramics and other undetectable parts perfect for any terrorist wanting to blow up a commercial airline. He'd slipped it into Bannister's pocket when he grabbed his arm, his plan from the moment Bannister arrived unannounced in the lounge. A quick call to the airport police that four men were planning to blow up Qantas Flight 68 to Sydney and it was over.

Back inside the aircraft, Bennett sat smiling to himself not because he'd out smarted Bannister but because Stella was his pretend fiancée and her closeness felt satisfying against his body. From that first encounter in Washington where he held her tightly at gunpoint, her scent had tantalised his sensual desires every time she was close. From the seat next to him, she caught a glimpse of his smile and asked, "What? What are you smiling about?"

"Huh, no nothing, just thinking about the look on Bannister's face when the coppers searched him and found the detonator I slipped in his pocket," he replied laughing with Stella joining in.

He explained to her how he met Bannister for the first time in

Afghanistan a few weeks earlier which then opened a line of questioning from the nosey reporter.

"Why were you in Afghanistan? Did it have anything to do with your meeting with the Director of National Intelligence at Arlington?"

He looked at her with a smirk and said, "I wasn't sure whether you were watching me or Dom that day but I guessed you were just snooping for a story."

She returned a puzzled look.

"What you didn't think I would know, your face is plastered all over the political reports on television. Nice job with the crying act by the way, it would have fooled most however, Dom had already told me you had followed him so I was expecting you there," Bennett said.

"Now to answer your question, I was in Afghanistan gathering information on a terrorist group, nothing newsworthy. I ran into Logan Bannister in the north where he was working security for the United Mining Corporation. My guess, he was there for the opium poppy fields up there."

"I just remembered something. United Mining is the biggest contributor to Senator Brown's political campaign and it was listed a few times in my mother's diaries," she said.

The name Senator Brown made Bennett's hair stand on end, the man had ruined his life.

"I'm not surprised about Brown, he's someone I'd like ten minutes alone with. You know, deal out my own summary justice. United Mining doesn't just deal in the mining sector, it has interests in weapons, medical research, nuclear power, space exploration, communications and a vast number of financial institutions worldwide. They are also heavily into human relocation mainly focusing on the most war ravaged areas of the world, relocating refugees to safer places," he added, proud he'd done his research after returning from Afghanistan.

The flight would only be a few hours and they had plans to prepare, where to go next. They had the codebook but what did it mean or reveal? What was the purpose of the disk? Bennett had so many unanswered questions and wished his father was alive to shed light on it all.

CHAPTER 41

ILF

Qantas Flight 68
August 21st

Bennett sat there on board the Boeing 737 with Stella beside him looking out over the darkness of the night sky and the occasional lights of a town in the distance. Bennett had lapsed into deep thought about his life and his dream of complete separation from a world of espionage. Every corner he turned a new opponent wanted him dead. So many years of running, fighting, killing, hiding and often not knowing exactly who the enemy was had cause for him to wonder how this last group tracked him down.

Reaching inside his bag, he pulled out the brief handed to him by Whittaker after returning from Afghanistan. He had inspected the contents but not thoroughly enough he knew and so as the plane flew south he started shuffling through the ten A4 pages and five colour photographs of various Middle Eastern men including the two killed in Australia. The CIA profile revealed an Islamic fundamentalist group calling themselves the Islamic Liberation Front or commonly referred to in the newspapers as the ILF. Formed from the Muslim Brotherhood in 1995, they became responsible for suicide bombings across Syria, Iran, Iraq and Egypt. They had not progressed to outside the Middle Eastern sector and the group lacked sufficient funding for any large scale attacks. They were in his opinion a low threat organisation limited to car bombs and strap on dynamite.

Not much intelligence on the members, he noticed. The leader, Rasheed Omar Allah was not well documented in the brief and no photo of him to make matters worse. At its strongest, the ILF was alleged to hold membership of over fifty believers. The latest brief showed its strength had dwindled to just over fifteen men after most were killed during a CIA led attack on their Kuwait headquarters in 1997. That attack resulted in the death of twenty two members and forty civilians including women and children. Bennett shifted uneasy in his seat, palms became sweaty and his heart rate accelerated from the sudden burst of anxiety.

Stella sensed his tenseness and broke from her scanning of the document out the corner of her eye. He knew she was looking at the brief, no journalist could resist a peek at a classified document in the hands of a CIA agent.

He turned to her and asked, "You said to me back in Washington, you don't believe I was responsible for the Kuwait incident. Why?"

"I covered the story over there and it stank of a cover-up."

She looked at him, "I think the building in Kuwait was hit with some kind of experimental weapon, launched from where I don't know and covered up by the government."

He looked at her confused and she explained what she knew.

She had been sent to Kuwait to cover the attack once it became public knowledge. The Whitehouse wanted the media to report on the matter so the American people knew the truth. Her suspicions were aroused instantly. The government only ever wanted the media there when they knew there was no chance of it going bad because they had it covered. As a journalist this was enough to rush her onto the next flight available.

What she quickly discovered soon after arriving in Kuwait was that no one was talking about the attack and very little information existed worth reporting. Most of the persons involved were either dead or had vanished. Her instincts persisting, she continued the hunt for information until a week later the big breakthrough came.

On inspecting the attack site, she was initially surprised to find the four story building completely demolished. Her briefing back in Washington and the news coverage had reported a squad of elite soldiers led by the CIA had stormed the building killing all those inside. She had expected to see the building pitted with bullet holes and perhaps the aftereffects of grenade explosions. Instead the building had been flattened like it was hit with a cruise missile except something appeared unusual. She had reported during the Gulf War and knew the carnage left behind by the Tomahawk cruise missiles yet this looked more similar to a detonation of extreme heat. Towards the centre of the rubble, the stone and debris had been fused together into a mangled solid mass while around the border the ground had been charred black.

The official statement released by the Whitehouse provided a three page insight into an unsanctioned campaign led by Jon Bennett acting on information that the building contained electronic components to build nuclear weapons. It was alleged that the information had never been verified by Bennett and he was acting on his own gut feeling. He attacked the building with a squad of ten men that developed into a bloody gun battle for over three hours. His source declared the building to be vacant except for the members of the ILF who were using it as their headquarters. It turned out to be a residential building where various members of the ILF and their families lived. The same version of events was relayed to the Senate Inquiry that crucified Bennett from the CIA.

"Something didn't sit right with me, the locals wouldn't talk about the attack and the military were all evasive in their recount of what happened. What really aroused my suspicion happened on my last day. A ten year old boy told me there was no gun battle but a big bright flash of blue light from the sky. After that he said there was a loud explosion that shook the ground like an earthquake and a searing hot wind melted the skin from the people's bodies. He said he escaped most of it but his face and arms were badly scalded with festering blisters. What was also suspicious was the lack of survivors, he was the only one I found, I couldn't find any locals with similar burn marks and when I asked the boy, he said the soldiers came and took them all away but he hid."

"So how did you report it back to the Whitehouse?" Bennett inquired.

"As I found it, exactly how I just told you. The next day as you would know, it was headlines, you were deemed a rogue agent and guilty of mass murder. Then the Senate Inquiry was demanded into all CIA activities abroad."

Bennett had gone quiet remembering the humiliation and condemnation from his colleagues over the incident.

"I wasn't even in the Middle East at the time and the Agency knew that," Bennett said after a moment of silence.

"Yes I suspected as much when my sources were unable to find anything tying you to the attack."

"Who changed the story then?"

"My editor had the final say and I confronted him over it however, he denied changing it and then an hour later I was sacked with no explanation, just told I was no longer needed after ten years of loyalty to that newspaper," she replied before asking, "So if the CIA knew you weren't there then why did you get the blame? Surely it was proven at the Senate Inquiry."

"I couldn't provide proof without revealing the mission I was on and placing countless lives at risk of prosecution by the Soviet Government. I sat there in the Senate Inquiry unable to say anything about it, I had the bigger picture to think about. As CIA operatives we know all about sacrifices for the better of the people. If I was forced to reveal the details of that mission, then I'd hate to think what political consequences it would have had for American and Russian relationships. The Agency knew this and kept quiet, happy to let me take the fall."

She listened resisting the urge to explore, it was a huge story she knew but irresponsible reporting wasn't her style.

"I am confused why it was me they chose to frame. I have enough information inside my head to bring the entire US administration to its knees and a few others. You don't spend years in the political bowels of the world's most corrupt nations not to hear a thing or two. Recording conversations and taking snap shots of political leaders making deals to suit their own agendas was one of the things we did best. I could make a killing out of blackmail if I wanted to, but that would be in violation of my ethical standpoint."

"So the CIA just sat by and watched you go down for something you didn't do. What about Whittaker? Why didn't he protect you?"

"You must hate this. Sitting there wanting to get inside my head knowing your Pulitzer Prize is waiting there. The things I have seen would bring you to a journalistic climax. It certainly would fill every newspaper around the world," he said as he started thinking about the Kuwait incident, "Perhaps Kuwait was a test to whether I would talk or not?"

"No I don't think so. I think something bigger is at play and my gut feeling screams *The Trust* is involved somewhere. I don't know why but so far it is popping up everywhere we look," she replied before adding, "Journalistic climax! Well that's a new spin on it."

"You are right, I would give anything to get inside that head of yours but right now I think *The Trust* is the Pulitzer," she added after a short moment of silence.

He nodded in confirmation.

"So, the ILF hold me responsible for killing their families. Certainly explains the persistent attacks, it's simple, they want revenge. Either I kill them all or we find who is responsible for framing me and expose it. I just want it all to end."

"I vote we find the responsible ones, you don't need to be killing anymore Jon," she responded knowing he probably wasn't ready to take her advice.

Realisation dawned on him, she was not the enemy but someone with a similar cause, someone who could help him find his solace in the sun. He returned her gaze and for a brief moment that same flicker of emotion sparked between them.

CHAPTER 42

BLIND

Qantas Flight 68
August 21st

The Sydney bound flight continued south through the night sky, an hour out from its destination.

Stella always the curious journalist asked, "Weren't you almost killed in Moscow during 1991? Word I've heard was you were rescued by the Butcher of Volgograd, the infamous ghost tormenting the Soviet Government and the CIA back then."

He looked at her more in shock that she had sources who actually knew this. It was a piece of his life's history not even the CIA knew much about. It was highly classified and it meant she had reasonably well placed contacts and he started wondering what else she may know.

Thinking back over his clandestine days inside Russia, his final assignment had been to identify the Butcher of Volgograd, recruit her at whatever cost and by that, ending his Soviet deployment. After that, he was destined for the Middle East where new political tensions were building that had been declared more volatile than the collapsing Russian super power.

Much of his early career had been spent in the underbelly of Soviet espionage late in the Cold War when political structures were disintegrating and a struggle for power engulfed the State's remaining Communist machine. He had more than once penetrated deep inside to find the State's best kept secrets, weapon designs far beyond those of the US but without the finance never reached maturity.

The most difficult assignment of all was finding the Butcher. Working in the CIA, the name 'Butcher of Volgograd' was well known and millions of dollars had been spent hunting her without success. The Agency only knew her as a professional assassin believed of Soviet origin but aligned with extremist groups fighting the communist rule. Her fame came one day in August 1991 when she casually strolled alone into the KGB stationhouse in Volgograd and killed 17 officers with two silenced handguns. Limited surveillance footage showed a blonde haired woman dressed in black, boldly walk through the building calmly executing everyone she encountered, all shots precisely accurate finding her victim's head.

No operative came close to finding her except Jon Bennett.

During late 1991 at the height of the Communist breakdown, he had secured three Agents inside the KGB all with vital information of rogue government officials with plans to seize State control and declare war on the US. Their plans included deployment of their nuclear arsenal, an absurd action no one would win but a last ditch effort to seize back control. He infiltrated a high society Russian organisation deep inside Moscow controlled mostly by departed members of the KGB, men true to the old ways and men who had the financial backing to succeed.

On December 12, 1991 his cover was blown and he was taken into custody by KGB officers charged with espionage punishable by execution. His cell time lasted three hours before a missile slammed into the KGB building in Dzerzhinsky Street followed by another one two minutes later, both with unknown points of launch. Georgian Rebels stormed the remains finding Bennett badly injured amongst fallen rubble and blinded by the blast.

He spent the next three months in what he thought was a hospital somewhere inside the Soviet Union. With two broken legs, four fractured vertebrae, scalded retinas and a dislocated shoulder meant most days he laid motionless, heavily sedated to reduce movement. Nurses would come and go never saying anything to him and occasionally he was visited by an old Chechen doctor always mumbling in a southern dialect that he found difficult to tranfistslate. Yet it wasn't these people who saved him it was the Rebels' leader, the Butcher of Volgograd.

Now he sat on the plane in shock that Stella knew of the secret. No harm in teasing her a little, he thought.

"Your source is correct. My life was saved by the Butcher," he answered with a slight smile.

"So who was she?" she asked sensing something perhaps romantic may have developed.

"She introduced herself to me as Nicholette Gelashvili but our sources later identified her real name as Nicholette Sponarava, daughter of Vladimir Sponarava, a senior official in the Second Chief Directorate, a man responsible for the deaths of hundreds of innocent lives," he replied without really caring about information security.

"And what happened between you and her, I mean what really happened? I'm sensing perhaps some romance," she pressed trying hard to get to know him.

"No nothing."

"Then why the smile tough guy?"

"There was something about her that touched me deep inside, some connection between us I can't explain and even though I was blind the whole time, her radiating warmth gave me life. My injuries had been crippling but it was her who taught me to walk again and persevere each time I collapsed under the pain and strain. It was her softly spoken words of encouragement that kept me going through the agony."

Bennett stopped abruptly, he realised he'd said too much and was slightly embarrassed he had shown his soft side.

"What happened after hospital, how'd you get out of Russia?" she asked.

"They could do nothing for my eyes and needed more advanced medicine than what they had, so I was shipped south to Georgia and eventually out through Turkey. She stayed with me the entire time guiding me around until she left me sitting on the front porch of the Station Chief's house in Kars. I think we were both surprised when he arrived home to find me waiting, news was out that I'd died in the missile attack. Within a week I was back in the US where laser surgery gave me my full sight back. My other injuries healed fine though one leg is shorter than the other and I can't run marathons anymore. Not real disappointed about that I must admit," he laughed.

She broke into a snigger feeling the same way about marathons.

"So there you have it. A blind CIA assassin mothered back to health by the very person he was hunting. Go figure, someone we all thought was a cold heartless killer ended up being warm and caring," Bennett added.

"Warm and caring you say but she has killed so many people, how is that caring?" Stella threw back at him.

"How many people do you think I've killed?" he asked looking her in the eye to gauge her reaction.

For a brief moment she thought he was about to confess but before she could utter a word he laughed out loud. Other passengers turned to look at them wondering why the sudden outburst.

"If you could have seen the look on your face, it was priceless. You really thought you had that big story then," he laughed again.

"Yeah you CIA arseholes are all the same, all bullshit and lies."

The seat belt light illuminated and the Captain announced their descent into Sydney.

Twenty minutes later, they were walking through Sydney Airport, destined for a safe house in the Western Suburbs.

The security monitors identified Bennett immediately and a phone call was made.

Paul Gilmour
The Monk would be pleased.

CHAPTER 43

BLUE MINE

North Afghanistan
August 25th

Abdul hated the Americans and he particularly disliked greedy money hungry corporations invading his loved country to steal their wealth. The mountains of North Afghanistan had never received any interest from the West until the last few months when some new precious rock discovered had the westerners in a spin.

For the past month, heavy mining machinery on trucks would arrive and one by one he and his brothers of the Taliban would destroy them with their rocket propelled grenades. He knew they were winning this war and the United Mining Corporation had no chance or so he thought.

A rich vein of blue crystal ore had been discovered one hundred feet below the surface, much deeper than the Namibia mine and in far greater concentration. During prehistoric days, the area of North Afghanistan had been bombarded by meteors with a small number deflecting off the main cluster and impacting Africa. Highly enriched in blue ore they had originated from somewhere deep in space, well beyond the scope of any telescopic survey. Small scattered deposits of radioactive material similar to Plutonium 239 and Uranium 238 drew frenzied attention from *The Trust* after initial tests showed unprecedented potential for a new weapon of mass destruction.

United Mining had failed on every attempt to extract the ore with conventional mining machinery. Specialised equipment was needed to withstand the radiation while the miners required full radiation suits as split second exposure was lethal. Transporting the machinery in, soon became the greater problem and though it was done illegally through Pakistan, it was the local Taliban tribesmen who were dealing the final blow.

The only access was via the winding roads through the mountains and the tribesmen had them all heavily guarded. Six convoys had arrived and all had been destroyed frustrating *The Trust* and leaving them no other option but to execute their contingency plan.

Somewhere in the desert of Western Sudan a Middle Eastern man answered his cell phone and the final payment was transferred. The call lasted a few seconds after which he made a number of longer phone calls to the US declaring Allah would have his victory in seventeen days.

CHAPTER 44

SIGMUND KRAUS

Wilmersdorf, Berlin, Germany
August 26th

The old grey haired German sat sipping his morning espresso outside his favourite cafe in one of Berlin's more affluent areas. He had finally reached contentment away from the murderous clutches of *The Trust*. His family had long gone and the strangling noose around his neck had subsequently been cut, there was no longer a need for him to look nervously over his shoulder. At eighty years of age, his life had been a roller coaster of excitement and secrets.

Doctor Sigmund Kraus had worked at the Ravensbruck Institute for thirty years until it was burnt down in 1987 under suspicious circumstances. After that he was shipped back to an underground facility in the south of Germany where he continued his research into human cellular engineering. It was something accelerated by the secrets locked inside the Anubis Sphere and knowledge tightly policed by *The Trust*.

During his time at Ravensbruck, he learnt many secrets and he knew disclosure would be a fatal error on his behalf. For so many of those years, *The Trust* had held his family hostage in return for his cooperation and he had loved his wife and three children too much to cause them trauma. Then one heartbreaking day in the summer of 1996, his family were killed in a train crash whilst holidaying in Spain, a catastrophe claiming the life of fifty three people. The deaths had removed the threatening noose and so he walked out of the research facility expecting to be shot. To his surprise nothing happened, he was allowed to leave unquestioned and no last minute bullet piercing his chest.

A few months later, an unmarked letter arrived under his door. It simply read *Sig, get out, they are coming to kill you.*

He didn't stop to question the message, he knew a colleague had sent it. So he outlaid a large sum of Deutsche Marks to change his name, wipe his existence from the planet and settle into his new life in the Wilmersdorf region of Berlin.

He had fallen into a regular routine of morning coffee and reading the local newspaper while casually watching people hustle and bustle their way to work each day. He glanced up at a long legged brunette parading down the street and he couldn't help admire her exquisite shape and goddess face. A new comer to these parts, he thought, and the way she was dressed in tight jeans and a loose low cut blouse she was one of the many tourists who flocked to Berlin for the party scene. As she moved closer she smiled a warm hello and took a seat a few tables over. Kraus felt a surge of excitement as her sweet perfume wafted by on the breeze and enticed his sexual desires to once again take a young woman in his bed. It had been a long time since such pleasures and he found himself drifting back in time.

Two days prior, Bennett and Stella had flown into Berlin searching for Kraus and shed light on the circumstances surrounding Rose and *The Trust* or at least give them another line of inquiry. Their time spent in Western Sydney gave them the chance to study the book for clues but nothing came to light, it remained confusing and meaningless. They went over what she remembered from her mother's diaries but still too many pieces of the puzzle were missing. It left the investigation hinging on finding the doctor who administered the drug to Rose. A number of phone calls to various contacts in Interpol and the Australian Secret Intelligence Service gave Bennett a rough location to find him.

Stella had made a point of dressing like the young tourists roaming the street and walked straight to the café where their intelligence suggested Kraus indulged each morning. Bennett still had trustworthy contacts throughout Europe and most owed him favours so it took one phone call to the German Federal Intelligence Service for the pre-arrival surveillance of Kraus and collation of his daily routine.

The café on Wegener Straße was like any other with tables scattered on the sidewalk and waiters running a constant stream of hot coffee to the patrons. After making eye contact with Kraus, Stella confirmed they had their target, it was him, she was certain of it. His spectacles sat low on his nose as he constantly looked over the top at passer-by's and then occasionally he threw an extended glance over at Stella with an accompanying smile.

Now it was just a matter of him leaving and following him back to his home for the intercept.

An hour passed and the day turned to light rain as Bennett moved silently to the front door of Kraus's small dark brick apartment. There he tapped lightly on the heavy timber door knowing that any louder and it would spook their target.

Stella had been briefed on her part and waited with the rental car in a nearby street.

Another round of taps on the door, then it slowly opened.

CHAPTER 45

PROJECT EIGHT

Wilmersdorf, Berlin
August 26th

Kraus had grown confident under his pseudo life and identity, not concerned about opening the door to a man dressed in everyday German business attire. It was ten o'clock in the morning and he was most likely another door to door salesman from the local telephone company pushing their new deals. He never thought for a minute that *The Trust* would come knocking before they executed him, he had always expected it would be someone or something moving swiftly under the darkness of night.

In his usual German dialect he answered the knock, "Morning, can I help you?"

Bennett responded in German but a different dialect, "Excuse me, but I am looking for Rose Bennett, do you know her?"

An immediate look of terror smothered Kraus's face and Bennett knew they had their man. He took two steps back and attempted to close the door, "I am sorry I don't know this person, I must go, goodbye."

Bennett had anticipated the reaction and was already pushing through the doorway, Kraus too old to move fast was an easy victim.

The old doctor was forced backwards into a chair inside his living room where he sat waiting his death or so he thought. Bennett wasted no time in commencing the interrogation and came right to the point.

"Doctor, I am not here to harm you but before you attempt to persuade me you're not Sigmund Kraus, you need to know who I am. My name is Jon Bennett, I am the nephew of Rose Bennett who you once administered a trial cancer treatment drug to when at Ravensbruck. I believe it was referred to as Project 8."

Bennett noticed recognition in the doctor's old weary eyes as he listened while no resistance was obvious. "Doctor Kraus, I have many questions for you, I just hope you can answer them. I need to know what happened to Rose at Ravensbruck and what exactly Project 8 is?" he asked.

"You are Viktor's son, I cannot believe it," Kraus slowly said looking deeply into Bennett's face searching for similarities.

"What do you know about my father?" Bennett responded thrown off guard by the mention of Viktor.

He and Stella had researched what they could about Ravensbruck and the medical research that occurred there, though most had been unpublished to the open world. He had learnt it was an institute for advanced and often radical medical treatments, only for those patients on the last line of hope. From all accounts, Rose was a perfect candidate for the cancer treatment with only a few weeks to live.

"Project 8, arh, I haven't heard that in a long time. It was my first successful case until poor Rose died from an unexpected complication."

"What! Rose is not dead, she is not mentally well but certainly alive at St Marika's Hospital in Greensboro."

"That is not possible I saw her die with my own eyes. I was the doctor who pronounced her dead, I remember that well. Rose's cancer was cured, her brain just couldn't adjust to the changes and she stopped breathing. Poor thing just couldn't cope."

"Well doctor it is possible, I have seen and spoken with her only two weeks ago. She's not in a good way but she is alive, I assure you of that."

Kraus sat back into his chair in thought before asking "I cannot believe it, they must have revived her, but why not tell me. You said she spoke to you. What did she say?"

"Something about protecting codes and *The Trust* would kill for them. Do you know what she was talking about?"

For the second time, Kraus became openly terrified, fear flooded his eyes and his arms began to shake. "I have said too much, you must leave if you know what's best for you," he uttered softly but forcefully as he pushed himself up from the chair.

Bennett pushed him backwards into the chair but this time he rammed the muzzle of his handgun into the old man's left knee. Explanation was not needed. The old man sat defiantly in his chair, "Go ahead shoot me as many times as you like, *The Trust* will kill me anyhow. They are probably outside right now waiting to kill us both."

A few seconds later, Bennett squeezed the trigger and the silenced weapon responded.

CHAPTER 46

INTRUDER

Berlin, Germany
August 26th

The bullet drilled the polished timber floor next to Kraus's left foot shattering his shoe with splinters. Bennett sensed the doctor had been bluffing, why would he spend so much money with re-identification if he had no desire to live. Kraus looked up at him in fear knowing he had missed on purpose. He had grown accustomed to his new life in Berlin and long forgotten the dangers of escaping *The Trust.*

"Doctor are you going to help me, I won't miss next time."

"Yes yes, I will tell you what I know but not because you threaten me with your pistol but because your father was a friend of mine and he died at the hands of *The Trust.*"

"How do you know *The Trust* killed my father?"

"Mr Bennett you must understand *The Trust* is a powerful organisation. If I tell you everything I know then I am surely dead."

"Aren't you curious why Rose is alive when you say she'd died?" Bennett returned hoping the curiosity alone would persuade his captive to talk openly.

"Mr Bennett, yes I am but it is not my position to start questioning the actions of *The Trust,* they are made up of some very influential men, not you or anyone else can protect me from them."

A sudden noise caught Bennett's attention.

He looked towards the front door and through the inlayed stained glass panel he saw movement just as a loud knock echoed through the small apartment. A man's deep voice sounded next.

"Hallo Herr Müller...ist alles in Ordnung? Ich höre eine merkwürdiges Geräusch. Sind sie o.K.?"

Bennett spoke German fluently and right now he had a problem. The man outside was asking if Kraus was alright because he'd heard a strange noise.

He grabbed Kraus by the shoulders and pulled him in close holding his hand over his mouth to muffle any sound he foolishly chose to expel.

"Who is it?" Bennett asked.

"Herman Schlitz, he is my neighbour. He will know something is wrong if I don't answer."

"Tell him to leave."

"I can't, he is a good friend… always checking up on me because I am old," Kraus replied.

"Ok, open the door but don't let him in. Tell him all is good, you just knocked something over. "

They edged their way towards the door while outside Bennett could see the dark shape of a man trying to look in through the coloured glass. "Don't do anything stupid Sigmund, you don't need your neighbour's death on your hands," he whispered as he pushed the gun firm into Kraus's ribcage and reached to turn the door handle. The door creaked open enough for Kraus to say his piece.

The door burst inwards, knocking them both backwards.

Kraus's body was flung into the opposite wall like a rag doll where he fell to the floor in an unconscious heap. Bennett on the other hand regained his balance in the split second he saw the dark shape charging through the open doorway.

With a gun in his hand, the intruder turned it towards Bennett and fired off a few quick rounds all smashing into the wall behind him. Bennett had dropped to the floor before the weapon fired and hurled himself forward across the slippery polished floor. With the combined power of his momentum he swung his leg out and around sideswiping the intruder off his feet sending him toppling onto the floor. Two more shots rang out from the intruder's gun as he fell, with each narrowly missing Bennett's head. Bennett returned silent fire as the intruder regained his balance and vanished into an adjacent room with a volley of shots in close pursuit piercing the wall.

Bennett sprung to his feet and gave chase just as he was slammed backwards by the intruder running at him like a ballistic missile. He was of herculean proportion with a good twenty kilos on Bennett but considerably shorter and lightning fast on his feet. Within a few seconds both weapons fell uncontrollably clanking to the floor and punted away under the hustle of boots. Both men were evenly matched in fighting prowess throwing punch for punch and an array of kicks that knocked them both off balance momentarily, yet not enough to gain victory.

Both men bled profusely from facial wounds as more punches found their mark upon their opponent's head while below them, the two guns remained within arm's reach. Bennett took a massive swing striking the intruder's jaw followed by a kick that connected with his chest knocking him backwards into the wall behind. It was the opportunity Bennett was looking for, a chance to grab his gun. As he dropped to his knee and reached for his weapon he felt the rush of excruciating pain shoot through his body and his vision go blurry. The intruder had taken his chance too. As he fell backwards against the wall, he grabbed Kraus's hatstand and in a whipping backhand manoeuvre he hurled it across Bennett's head and shoulders. The timber stand shattered in two across his shoulders knocking him flat to the floor and giving the intruder time to scoop his gun up.

Three life sucking shots quickly followed.

Bennett slumped back onto the floor to catch his breath but still watching the intruder's body jerk and spasm as his nervous system fought to accept the three bullets deep in his chest. After the hatstand broke across his shoulders, Bennett had teetered on the edge of unconsciousness to roll and fire his handgun at the intruder who had been slow to take aim.

Across the room, Kraus laid face down in his own sea of blood.

CHAPTER 47

SNIPER

Berlin, Germany
August 26th

Bennett lifted his cell phone and dialled a prearranged number. Stella knew her part and so when her phone blipped four times, she drove their rental to Kraus's house.

Bennett appeared from behind Kraus's front door and she knew things hadn't gone as planned. He had Kraus's unconscious body slumped over his shoulder and blood streamed from his head. Judging by the state of Bennett's battered face she hoped he hadn't been beaten up by an eighty year old man, that would be embarrassing she thought as Bennett ran to the car and threw Kraus into the boot.

"What happened?" she called as he climbed into the passenger seat.

"Get going, stick to the plan," he commanded while she sat staring at him and the blood trickling down his neck.

"NOW," he yelled back taking a wide sweep of the neighbouring houses in case someone had seen them.

They wasted no time driving out of the city and heading towards Ahrensfelde in the north east of Berlin. There he knew of an underground safe house that was perfect to remain undetected while he interrogated Kraus.

Rain had started to fall heavier and the midday city traffic had crowded in around them. Stella continued to drive at the pace of her neighbouring vehicles not drawing any unnecessary attention while Bennett scanned behind for anyone following. If there was someone there, he couldn't make them out amongst the other hundred or so travellers on Landsberger Allee that day.

"So what happened? Why is he covered in blood?" she persisted in wanting a briefing from the house.

"Got ambushed by a Black Beret masquerading as his neighbour," he answered while watching a red Porsche scream by.

"You mean American Special Forces, how do you know that and why, I don't understand?"

"Yes me neither, but he was Special Forces, he had the tattoo to prove it. Perhaps Kraus can shed some light on it when he awakens. He copped a scrape from a bullet ricochet nothing serious. He'll live."

"What about the Beret?" she asked suspecting his response.

"Dead!"

A sudden thumping noise vibrated through the car. Kraus had gained consciousness and was advertising his dislike for imprisonment in the trunk. Bennett glanced rearwards as a semi-trailer to their left swerved viciously across their path.

Stella slammed on the brakes taking evasive action the best she could. The car's automatic braking system kicked in with a series of violent lurches giving back some control but it was too late. They sideswiped the truck both doing ninety kilometres per hour amongst a storm of blue smoke from the tyres ripping and tearing at the asphalt. Their small Mercedes sedan fishtailed and smashed through the timber road barrier before sliding at increasing speed down a grassy roadside bank into a wall of thick bushes.

Up topside on the road, chaos had unleashed for the daily commuters.

Six other cars had careered into the crippled truck causing a massive pileup. The driver was dead from a single gunshot to his forehead.

CHAPTER 48

HOSTAGE

East of Berlin, Germany
August 26th

Bennett and Stella worked themselves free from the wreckage, black smoke belching from the engine bay and a muffled hysterical scream resonating from inside the trunk. Bennett flipped the boot lid open to a wild eyed and aggressive old timer who started unleashing a verbal onslaught of his anger until Stella caught his attention. He stopped mid slander replaced by an expression of bewilderment.

"You were at the café this morning," he stuttered looking back at Bennett, "What's going on, what just happened?"

"This is Stella Van Horne, she's working with me. We just had a car crash but I have a feeling it wasn't an accident."

Up topside, people scrambled to safety while some dragged others from the smashed vehicles. In all the turmoil, no one saw the two armed men hurry down the embankment towards the crashed Mercedes.

A shot rang out and careered through the left door and then another pierced the trunk compartment next to Kraus. Bennett turned to see the men a hundred yards away and running towards their position both with their weapons up firing controlled bursts.

"RUN," he yelled while dragging the old man from the boot.

Kraus scampered the best he could for his age while Stella using her athletic prowess disappeared into the darkness of the thick forest. Bennett kept a strong hold of the old man's arm pushing him forward until they fell in behind the cover of a large birch tree alongside Stella crouching and looking fearful.

The assailants dressed in grey and green army fatigues advanced at a fast rate towards the tree line. Bennett slunk low keeping watch while he planned his next move in his head. Two handguns and 18 rounds was all he had to fight against the explosive power of the gunmen's automatic assault rifles.

As the first few bullets smacked into the trees either side, Kraus was already running and stumbling over fallen logs trying his hardest to escape both the gunmen and his captors. Bennett took aim at their enemy but then as he realised Stella was still at his side he turned his attention towards her.

"Stella get the fuck out of here, I need you to keep a leash on Kraus. We can't lose him now. I'll take care of these guys. Now get going."

He paused as she took a few shuffling steps backwards and he yanked his second handgun from his belt.

"Hang on, take this. Use it if you have to," he called before throwing her the gun.

She caught it and immediately chambered a round without a hint of hesitation or difficulty. It was a side of her he hadn't seen before and was almost arousing. To see her standing there, hair messed up, dirt and sweat streaked across her face and then push a loaded pistol down her jeans was a beautiful sight in his eyes.

The commotion up top on the road had grown deafening with sirens and people yelling and screaming. As the two men entered the tree line, a little further north a third gunman slipped unnoticed into the forest.

Bennett raised his gun and took aim at the head of his first target who had moved a few yards forward of his partner. He knew once he fired, the other man would release all hell on his concealed position amongst the undergrowth so accuracy was the key.

He squeezed off three rounds to be certain.

The first two rounds entered the gunman's chest while the third climbed higher to his neck as he fell forward. He was dead before he hit the ground and as expected, his companion swung around to let off a long blast of shots into the bushes. It did nothing but strip the tree of leaves and branches.

As the firing eased, Bennett tapped three bullets into the man's chest missing the heart and knocking him backwards to the ground. Within a few seconds Bennett was on his feet peering down into the desperate eyes of the bleeding man who frantically snatched at his side arm. Bennett didn't bother with an interrogation, quickly firing two rounds into his head and eliminating the threat.

A scream echoed through the forest from somewhere behind him.

He spun around and sprinted until a small clearing came into view. On the ground, Stella knelt in front of a heavily set man holding an assault rifle to her head. Kraus laid on his back a few feet over and wasn't moving.

"Bennett, I know you're out there. I want the codes or your little girlfriend bitch gets a nice bullet through her head," the gunman called out in an American accent. He reached forward, grabbed a clump of her long brown hair and yanked her head backwards. Tears were carving tracks down her dirtied face and she shook in fear.

"Please don't kill me," she pleaded.

Bennett slowly edged his way out into the clearing to the sight of the gunman's second weapon aimed at his head.

"Mate whoever you are or work for, I don't have the codes you speak of. I am trying to find them myself, maybe we can join forces," Bennett suggested while moving slowly closer.

"Stop right there, drop your gun or she dies," the gunman commanded taking his attention off both his hostages yet keeping the rifle firmly against her head.

The sound of two gunshots abruptly broke the forest tranquillity. One shot had penetrated the gunman's right ear exploding out the other side of his head while the other drilled through the side of his chest. Bennett stood with his gun raised, quickly assessing what had just happened and where the shots had come from. He'd been beaten to the target by only seconds.

Next to the dead man, Kraus leant perched up on an elbow, one leg missing and a small black handgun in his hand. Next to him, a prosthetic leg laid tossed across the ground, a subtle reminder of a boating accident ten years earlier. Inside it had been the perfect concealment for a weapon and though he thought he would never need it, today had proven him wrong.

"We can't stay here, too many police up top and too many questions we can't answer," Bennett suggested as he scanned the area to find the best exit from the forest.

"That man I just killed worked for *The Trust*. He used to be a guard on my floor at Kehlstein, I never liked him anyway always pushing us around," Kraus voluntarily announced.

"Kehlstein, what's that?" Bennett asked looking Stella up and down surprised at how quickly she'd found her feet to find a place at his side.

"I worked there after Ravensbruck burnt down, carried on my research. It's *The Trust's* primary facility in the south of Germany built during World War II for the Fuehrer, but the war ended before it was fully finished."

Kraus added, "The guard asked you for the codes. Do you know what they are and what they mean?"

"Doctor, that's the whole reason we are here. Are you going to help us or not?"

Kraus only gave a brief nod of his head in reply.

"What now? Where to with him?" Stella whispered to Bennett.

"The plan hasn't changed. We still head for the safe house in Ahrensfelde."

He turned back to Kraus.

"Kraus how well did you know your neighbour?" he asked.

"Apparently not well enough, *The Trust* had been watching me from right next door. I played cards with the man every Wednesday night and not once did I suspect *The Trust* was babysitting me. Just an average working man he was."

"You sure he was from *The Trust*?" Bennett asked.

"Well who else could it be? Who else would want me dead?" Kraus asked.

"How do you know he wanted you dead?" Bennett asked while leading them all off in the direction of traffic sounds on a side street. Kraus never thought for a minute that Bennett was the target.

It didn't take long before they found a car parked on the roadside and Bennett had it running. With the traffic mayhem blocking the road behind them they drove north on the almost deserted highway.

Meanwhile in two separate cities of the world, they were being intensely scrutinised via satellite feeds and new orders were given.

CHAPTER 49

THIRTEEN

Ahrensfelde, Germany
August 26th

Bennett peered down into the dark and musty interior of the old Ahrensfelde bunker. It was pitch black but somewhere deep inside he could hear movement. A family of large brown rats scuttled and squealed at the anticipation of intruders about to enter their domain.

Built below an old bombed church during World War II, the bunker had vanished among the rubble. To the untrained eye, the entrance appeared well camouflaged and to a few it had become a safe haven. During the communist days of East Berlin, the mass of underground tunnels stretching out for miles provided the perfect refuge for western operatives evading the East German Stasi. Right now Bennett couldn't think of anywhere better to extract the answers from the doctor and remain undetected.

He led the doctor below while Stella walked behind trying not to scream. Her fear of rats had been a long lasting childhood phobia and one she now wished she'd sought therapy for. The air was scented heavily with rodent and the ammonia taste of excrement made breathing difficult.

Tunnels spread in all directions a few metres below the surface. Age and seepage had taken its toll on the timber supports making the manoeuvring treacherous, made worse by cave-ins along the way.

Using his hands to guide himself along, Bennett recalled the path and pushed ahead while the others clung close behind.

He abruptly stopped.

"We're here!"

The room ignited in green light and he came into view with light stick in hand looking surprised at how the room looked so familiar. It was only a small room with a table, two chairs and a narrow bed. He had spent many days and weeks hiding out in this exact location during a time when he was number one on the Stasi's most wanted list. Even the light sticks were where he'd hidden them and to his complete surprise, still worked.

The car ride had revealed a few missing pieces. Kraus had explained how he'd been recruited in 1962 by the World Health Organisation to develop vaccines for lethal pathogens, mostly originating out of Central

Africa. While he was there, he travelled to Namibia to investigate the extermination of a village, every man woman and child killed by a rather unusual new strain. It was more aggressive than anything he'd seen and death occurred violently in just a few seconds which the locals called the 'Blue Death' due solely from the blue scaly appearance of the victims.

A few days after returning from Namibia, two elderly men approached him. They offered him a chance of a lifetime, an opportunity to conduct research using advanced technologies on a limitless budget. It came with one important condition, one that meant he could no longer speak of his work with anyone. His findings in Namibia were to be publicised as a new strain of a deadly virus transmitted by jungle monkeys and restricted to that remote location of Africa. In particular, he was never to mention the Blue Death.

He took the job with its conditions not knowing what it really meant for him and his family.

He was taken to Ravensbruck Institute in Portland where he was briefed by a man claiming to be from an organisation called *The Trust*, a secret organisation few knew about. It was then that he realised his mistake. The man not only briefed him on his expected work for *The Trust*, for they would also kill his family if he ever spoke about the organisation or his work at Ravensbruck. A day later, his family were shot at while driving along a busy highway in Portland. Their car was hit by a sniper with all six bullets clearly missing the occupants. He took the message as intended.

His work at Ravensbruck started with the Blue Death determining it was not a virus but a new lethal radiation type, more deadly than plutonium. Origins of the Blue Death had remained unknown until a few years later when the same man from *The Trust* came to visit him. This time it was not to make threats but to reveal a secret they'd been hiding.

The man explained how the Blue Death emanated from a blue crystal found in caves near the dead village and possessed unimaginable destructive forces. Alien in nature, it was believed to originate from space and implanted on Earth by a meteor millions of years in the past. The problem they had was harnessing the energy and avoiding death from the radiation.

Kraus sat opposite Bennett at the dusty old table and continued, "*The Trust* have in their possession a device, one that provides technologies that can harness the full power of the blue crystal. They call it the Sphere of Anubis and I was led to believe it was stolen from a secret facility inside the US Government's Area 47 in 1945. The same person who told me this also told me it revealed the technology to build the atomic bomb."

"The Sphere of Anubis, where did it come from?" Bennett asked looking at Stella who too was thinking about how the codebook made reference to a sphere.

"Its origin was largely unknown except that it was discovered amongst treasures in the Ancient Egyptian tomb of Anubis, the Egyptian God of Death. Archaeologists had no idea what it was and its construction wasn't consistent with the period of Anubis. The final verdict was extra-terrestrial I believe. Anyway it was transported from Egypt to the US in 1940 where months of testing proved it too dangerous to explore further. An inscription on the outer rim written in ancient Latin declared a warning. It said three failed attempts to open it would release a planetary plague. Most just thought it was a superstitious Egyptian curse but still, no one was prepared to test it."

In his time at Ravensbruck and Kehlstein, Kraus had never laid eyes on the Sphere but learnt from colleagues it was completely covered in unusual geometric type symbols.

"In 1941, a young boy named Jeremiah was discovered floating in the sea off Bermuda after a freighter was sunk by a German U Boat. Tattooed across his chest were thirteen symbols all similar to those on the Sphere. This renewed the Government's interest and those thirteen symbols were entered one by one into the Sphere," Kraus continued to say.

"What do you mean the symbols were entered into the Sphere?" Bennett asked.

"The Sphere is like a library of advanced technologies that can only be accessed by depressing the right sequence of thirteen symbols or I suppose you could say the right code. Once they are entered then what comes next is truly fascinating I have been told. A bright white light explodes outwards from inside the Sphere projecting a light show onto the ceiling. The technologies appear as detailed schematic plans and instructions however, it hasn't been easy interpreting the text. One of my friends at Kehlstein was Joseph Voight, the Linguist in charge of translation, he told me they were making progress and had deciphered some kind of catalogue."

"Catalogue, what is it?" Stella piped in.

"In the 1960's, Archaeologists discovered a new Mayan Temple deep in the jungles of Guatemala that at the time didn't mean much until the photos were published in National Geographic. What they showed were the moss covered walls of an inner chamber with the faint resemblance of thirteen symbols carved into the stone. Only a handful of people knew what their purpose was or had seen similar symbols before this discovery.

The Trust entered them into the Sphere and what it cast upon the wall was exactly thirteen lines of ancient text, nothing else. Voight told me it took the original Linguists six months to translate them into what they deciphered was a catalogue or index to what's inside the Sphere."

Bennett and Stella were enthralled at what they were hearing, neither had any idea it would be so like an Indiana Jones adventure.

"So Doctor what's inside the Sphere?" Bennett asked.

"Strangely enough, thirteen advanced technologies," he answered.

"Yes but what kind of technologies?" Bennett asked beginning to sound frustrated.

"The third on the list gave the world the Atomic Bomb and was the same set of symbols found on the boy's chest. That was how the Linguists worked out it was a catalogue, they used the third as a reference to decipher the others. I am not certain of the other technologies but I know the weaponry and stealth capabilities will mean our future wars will be nothing like they are now. Now all of that is dependent on one thing."

"What's that Doctor?"

Bennett sat listening waiting for the answer.

CHAPTER 50

THE EIGHTH CODE

Ahrensfelde, Germany
August 26th

Kraus took a few seconds to rest his voice and then answered Bennett.

"*The Trust* finding the Thirteenth Code is what we hope never happens."

"Why, what's so special about that code?" Stella asked beating Bennett to the question.

"It was common knowledge among my colleagues that the Thirteenth Code releases plans to build an orbit based directed pulse energy weapon sufficiently powerful to decimate a small nation, more deadly than over one thousand 500 Kiloton atomic bombs. To build it they not only need the plans but also a substantial quantity of that blue crystal I told you about. There is speculation that if the weapon is fired enough times at the Earth then it will set off a cataclysmic chain reaction within the planet's crust that can't be stopped. It is likened to a mile high land tsunami that keeps going, building momentum as it travels and nothing survives."

"It's only speculation, Right?" Stella asked while Bennett acknowledged his support of the question.

"Yes it is however, the weapon is more than conjecture I have heard of it from my source inside *The Trust*," Kraus answered.

"Doctor, ok, you have told us about an ancient Sphere and codes needed to open it, but can you tell us about Project Eight," Bennett asked starting to sound more disbelieving.

Kraus had sensed his scepticism and replied, "Mr Bennett, I know you may be thinking this is all science fiction, I assure you it is real and *The Trust* has already spent billions on pursuing the remaining codes."

"Project Eight, what is it?" Bennett reminded him.

"Yes, yes, Project Eight came from what was the eighth technology of the Sphere. I don't know how they found the sequence of symbols to release it but I was given the plans and specs for a seriously advanced human engineering program. Most of it took me years to fully understand and I believe it had taken years for the linguists to translate before reaching me."

"What was the human engineering program?" Stella asked.

"It was plans to build an advanced human race with strength beyond comprehension, immune to any disease, increased brain function and extended life tenfold. *The Trust* saw it as a chance to build their ultimate warriors and all from cellular robotics at the most advanced level."

"Cellular robots, I don't understand," she asked.

"The Eighth Code gave us designs to build micro robotic organisms, that self-replicate once activated inside the human host and from there they take complete control at the cellular level. Composed entirely of synthetic cytoplasm and a gel CPU, they develop their own neural networks throughout the body. Simply, they transmit new commands to the existing cells."

"So what you are describing is a parasite?" Bennett interrupted.

"No far from it. These organisms are your friends, designed to fight disease, heal injuries and improve the efficient functioning of your natural life support system. They self-learn at a remarkable rate and from what we observed they adapt to eradicate any illness including cancer. It was the greatest breakthrough in human life longevity we'd encountered and estimates presented the average person could live up to ten times longer."

He stopped talking for a brief moment in deep thought.

"At that time, I had only tested it on rodents but I needed a human host to prove its capabilities. That's when your Aunt Rose was presented to me. She was perfect, aggressive lymphatic cancer had riddled her body and well, we all knew she had less than two weeks to live. That was the best case scenario," he continued.

A tear spilt from Kraus's right eye and glistened in the green light as it fell to his lap. He had become a little emotional and his voice quivered slightly.

"Within a few hours of her injection she was showing dramatic improvements and then after about a day, the cancer was completely eradicated. She was up and walking like any normal healthy woman but then two days later..."

"What, what happened?" Bennett asked.

"She became aggressive with super human strength and not responding to any form of verbal negotiation. I'm not a believer in the spiritual world but if I had to guess I'd say she was possessed by some satanic entity. Anyway, she seriously injured three orderlies and fled jumping from a three story window without as much as a scratch on her. A few hours later we found her collapsed and murmuring complete gibberish. None of it made any sense and within a few more hours she had slipped into a coma. Sometime during the next day, she started convulsing like I'd never seen before.   Eventually she just stopped breathing."

"Do you know what went wrong?" Stella asked.

"I never got the chance to conduct the post mortem and now thinking back it was unusual why *The Trust* ordered her body to be cremated immediately," Kraus answered as he thought back to his last few weeks at Ravensbruck.

"So it was called Project Eight because it involved the Eighth Code," Stella confirmed.

"Yes correct," Kraus responded and continued.

"*The Trust* threw billions of dollars at this project wanting the master race, the next generation of humans. It is the Fourth Reich taking over where the Third failed during World War II and they again want complete domination of the planet."

Stella asked, "How do you know all this?"

"When I worked at Ravensbruck, I struck up a friendship with my caretaker."

"What's a caretaker?" Stella interjected.

"He was the man who originally briefed me on my first day at Ravensbruck and he kept me in line mostly by reminding me of the threats to my family if I didn't comply with their orders. Over the years he started letting his guard down and told me many things. Some I'd heard from other scientists working at Ravensbruck and Kehlstein."

Bennett asked "So who was this man?"

Kraus ignored this question and went on.

"You know the Aids virus was a result of my research. *The Trust* had me experimenting with ways of controlling the human population, a way that would defeat the enemy without a need for war and bloodshed. I failed at making it aggressive in design and not sufficiently contagious as a bio weapon. They may have suspected I designed it this way on purpose, I wasn't about to become another Adolf Hitler, a mass murderer so I left out a few steps."

Bennett and Stella were both stunned at this latest revelation. *The Trust* had to be stopped.

"The code book must have all thirteen codes written in it. That is why it is so important," Stella announced before turning to Bennett and whispering, "Who possess the book can rule the world. Remember what it said, the Thirteenth Code will annihilate all that we know."

Bennett didn't know how Viktor was part of it, how Rose knew about the codes or how *The Trust* killed his father? Still many questions unanswered.

He turned his attention back towards Kraus, "Ok but how does my father fit into this and why did *The Trust* kill him if in fact they did?"

"Mr Bennett what I am about to tell you may seem incomprehensible but please hear me out."

He looked towards Stella hoping he had her support, he was still having problems placing exactly where he'd met her before and he was sure it wasn't the lingering thoughts of the café that morning.

Kraus continued, "The man from *The Trust* told me many things about their master plan, the sphere and on top of all that, directed me to undertake many inhumane experiments. Over the years it was always he who came to see me, no one else. My colleagues at the Institute once saw another man with him but they would not divulge who he was, though I suspect it was someone high up in the American Government."

Kraus hesitated like he was attempting to recall a distant memory.

Then he finally spoke, "Then one day he came to me and told me of a dissention in *The Trust* and that the leadership had split. I remember how afraid he sounded and quite frankly scared the hell out of me."

Kraus's voice quivered a little as he added, "Sadly that was the last time I saw him, a week later his replacement arrived and it was only then that I learnt his name, it was Walter Stanley. I had always only called him Sir and he never once divulged his name to me in the ten years. The replacement took great delight in telling me of his death for betraying *The Trust* and that I should learn from his mistakes."

Bennett's patience had all but evaporated and he burst out in frustration, "Ok I get all that but where's my father fit into it."

Kraus turned at the sight of a cloudy mist filling the room and the sound of hissing gas coming from near the doorway. "It is too late, they have found us."

Bennett knew there was nowhere to run or hide as he could feel the effects of the nerve agent filling the room. His legs and arms growing heavy, his brain slow in response to act quickly. Stella was already unconscious on the floor, her body paralysed and spasms starting to quicken. The gas had acted fast on her smaller body mass.

A hand reached out at Bennett, his vision blurred he could see it was Kraus trying to get his attention. Both men fell to the floor with a thud, the men outside watching their every move through a fibre optic cable now under the door. Kraus tried to speak, his voice all muffled and Bennett tried his hardest to listen.

"Walter Stanley... not real name... it... Viktor Bennett... your father..."

A sudden white blinding flash and all went silent inside the small room.

CHAPTER 51

EMPTY

Ahrensfelde, Germany
August 26th

The blinding white flash tore its way up the fibre optic disintegrating the soldier's retina. He fell back in burning agony and screaming as his eye sizzled like bacon on a hotplate. The field commander pushed him aside and kicked the door in.

The bright light had lasted a split second but now as the Commander stood in the small room, there was only the soft green haze cast out by the single light stick resting in a puddle of water on the floor. His gun was out in readiness to shoot however, the room was empty. The table, chairs and bed remained as they were. A strange acidic odour brushed his nostrils and he thought how it smelt similar to burning flesh.

He stood thinking for a moment while his men scoured the area. He had his suspicions of what just occurred but he thought the Eleventh Code was not possible under current quantum physics theory. Bennett, Stella and the doctor were gone.

Outside in the concealment of a thick cluster of trees, three men dressed in brown robes stood watching a group of soldiers searching through the ruins of the old church. A few minutes earlier, they had watched the soldiers arrive and hastily enter the same bunker where Bennett and the others had climbed into only half hour before that.

They had stood back watching and waiting until it was time to engage their device and even though the targets were underground, the energy readings displayed a success.

They walked from the trees unnoticed to their vehicle and drove away.

As they did, one of the men dialled a number on his cell phone and made a long distance call.

"Master, it has been done. Readings show three positives."

CHAPTER 52

BOTSWANA

Ghanzi District, Botswana
September 11th

The warm morning desert winds skated across the Ghanzi District of western Botswana. The day was already hot and dusty. The ground was hard and cracked from the scarcity of rain and the trees were loosely scattered across the landscape. For the newly arrived visitors, it appeared like some alien inhospitable planet they'd just landed on.

Bennett had walked for the first two hours in a dazed state, not fully remembering what had happened. His body hurt from what he only assumed was some form of torture however, he couldn't be sure. His last memories were in the bunker with Stella and Kraus just before a nerve gas rendered them unconscious.

Now he was walking almost staggering along an old dirt track somewhere unsure of his whereabouts. His bearings were all messed up, he didn't know which way was north or south and for some unexplained reason, he felt different. He wasn't sure of the time except the sun was high in the cloudless sky. How long had he been out here he wondered and where was Stella? None of it made any sense.

Another hour passed and he was feeling like himself, fully aware and thinking clearly. He had been stripped of weapons and all other devices, which meant no cell phone. He still had the same clothes and shoes but nothing else. His stomach ached and cramped as it did after Viktor's Sanctuary in Australia and he was sure he had an ulcer developing.

In the distance, he could see a dark shape on the ground. From fifty metres, it was clearly the shape of a person sitting slouched forward on the track. He slowly approached with caution.

He stepped to within a few metres, the person did not move. He called out, no response. He edged his way around off the track through a few clumps of spindly grass to approach from the front while still keeping a watchful eye over his back.

It soon became apparent the person was dead. The skin reflected a shade of dark blue under the sunlight while blood still oozed from festering blisters on the arms and legs. Most disturbing of all, he thought, was the facial expression. The face was frozen in extreme agony with mouth wide open and the tongue had been bitten clean off.

He walked closer suddenly realising who it was.

Sigmund Kraus still wearing the same clothes he had on when in the bunker.

It had all become more confusing. How did he and Kraus get here and where was Stella? He was too busy running possible scenarios in his head to notice the sudden change in air pressure and temperature drop. A deafening roar, a white flash followed swiftly by the sudden expulsion of air from his lungs and everything went silent. He fell to the ground lapsing back into unconsciousness.

Sometime later he woke in a fully alert state and Kraus's body had vanished leaving just a patch of black congealed blood on the ground.

A voice broke the silence, "Jon are you there?"

He turned quickly to see Stella staggering towards him. Her face was smeared in blood, clothes were ripped and she dragged an injured leg.

"What happened?" he asked after lunging to break her stumbling fall.

"I don't know, can't remember, I can't see, why can't I see, where are we?" a confused Van Horne responded.

"It will pass, your eyesight will return. The same thing happened to me and to answer your last question, can't say for sure but we don't seem to be in Germany anymore."

"Something feels wrong, I feel like there's two of me," she said.

"Yes I felt the same but it passed, you will feel normal soon," he reassured her.

For the next two hours, he comforted her and discussed their versions of what happened. Both had similar recall, no memory after the bunker in Berlin.

They walked another hour along the track arriving at a road. An old fallen down sign showed they were ten kilometres west of Ghanzi in Botswana.

"Botswana… how the fuck did we get here?" she exclaimed clearly shocked.

Bennett was just as confused still wondering whether they were caught in some dream or perhaps under the effects of a mind altering drug and in reality they were still inside the bunker.

Moments later, they hailed a passing farmer on his way to town with a load of corn. At first, the man was curious of their presence in his land but became suspicious when he spotted they possessed the mark.

On the back of their necks was a single blue symbol, neither had seen before. Appearing as a triangle with a circle inside, it was the marking of an ancient civilisation that once ruled the land. The farmer had been told as a boy the marked ones would return one day to take back what was theirs.

"That on your neck, what it?" the farmer nervously asked Stella in his broken English.

He pointed towards the back of her neck and she turned to look at Bennett for the answer. He had seen the tattoo when they entered the farmer's truck but declined to make any commotion about it.

"It is a religious symbol, we carry the mark of our faith," Bennett quickly responded with his premeditated explanation. The farmer being a religious man accepted this and carried on with his driving.

They needed money and plenty of it particularly as they were walking in a land of corrupt militant tribes where only cash or sex would save them. Once they arrived in Ghanzi they found a public phone inside a bullet plagued Capital Bank. Knowing the call would be surely monitored, Bennett went about executing a typical emergency money transfer. It was something he'd done many times before and with the right sequence of telephone numbers activated an encrypted line out. Another series of numbers entered and an automatic money transfer was initiated.

They had to be alert and cautious now because word would be out. It's not every day an Australian, alias American, arrives in Ghanzi without any immigration records, and then withdraws 50,000 US dollars in Botswana Pula. The Botswana Police would be all over them just as the flies were doing right then.

On Bennett's orders, Stella had remained outside the bank, no point in her making matters worse. A white woman in town was already causing a stir and soon the people walking by would see the marks on their necks. He hoped the security camera was offline but it was not his lucky day. By the time he had reached the single teller, five photographs had been taken.

Claiming international diplomatic rights backed up by the account security protocols provided the necessary authority to withdraw. Some bean counter back at Langley would have a hard time explaining the missing $50,000.

He made the transaction and exited the bank in a state of utter confusion. The money wasn't the problem, it was the calendar.

CHAPTER 53

TRUST

Ghanzi, Botswana
September 11th

Bennett walked from the bank in deep thought of what he'd just discovered.

"What's wrong, you look like you've seen a ghost or something," greeted Stella who was trying to avoid the endless stares from the local natives as they passed by.

"Today is the 11th September," he said.

"What… no way! You telling me, we just lost two weeks."

They walked across the busy road to a small store where they purchased a newspaper and a large bread roll to satisfy their hunger and a Pepsi Cola to wash it down. The Botswana Guardian was a prominent newspaper in the country and right now it forced reality to bite. They both read the date in small print on the upper right as 'September 11th'.

"Jon, what is going on?"

"I do not know, surely there must be a logical explanation," he replied becoming suspicious and overly alert to everyone around them.

"We have to get out of here, I have a bad feeling about all this. We need to find a way out," he added as he pointed towards an old bus parked further up the road.

Passengers were already boarding and on the front it displayed the destination as Windhoek in the neighbouring country of Namibia where they could head towards the coast. Leaving by plane wasn't possible without passports or identification which left their only option as boat unless Bennett could secure a military extraction from Windhoek Eros Airport.

It was going to be difficult getting through the Namibia border security but Bennett had overcome similar problems in the past and was not too concerned. Finding an empty seat on board the bus was less of a problem until what seemed like the entire towns folk boarded. The driver urged more inside until like sardines packed in a can no one could move.

Twenty kilometres away, a phone rang.

Alerted to the rare bank activity, the Commander promptly responded by sending his finest troops, six of his most loyal and skilled soldiers. Nothing happened in the Ghanzi District without the commander knowing, this was his kingdom. White people withdrawing large sums of money meant trouble in his opinion.

The bus departed the moment there was no more physical room inside and the sense of claustrophobia was overwhelming. Bennett sat alongside Stella with at least thirty local Botswana men, women and children unable to move all pushing at each other to find space to breath. The windows had no glass and were their only saviour from the rancid smell of stale body odour.

She could feel the men's eyes lusting for her and salivating with a desire to rip her clothes from her body. They rarely had visits from white women in these parts of Botswana and one so beautiful was a prize hard to resist. Her instinct for survival pushed her in close to Bennett while one man in the aisle next to her was already arrogantly touching her breasts.

"Don't react, it'll make matters much worse for us. Let him play, trust me," Bennett whispered.

The ugly foul smelling man continued to run his hand over her breasts while she struggled to fight the urge to elbow him in the groin. He moved his hand to feel her hair and face line. He was surveying his victim for the savage rape he had planned once they departed the bus.

He did not fear Bennett. He stood at over 190 centimetres and weighed close to 130 kilograms, he was a giant amongst the other passengers and he feared no one.

He lowered himself down to kiss her. His mouth was a pit of disease and stench.

Bennett spoke softly and forcibly, "Don't move, I mean it, your life depends on it."

She could hear him grunt with sexual hunger as his foul breath sprayed across her face and he yanked her ponytail rearwards while his other hand groped more violently at her breasts. Rape was common in these parts of Africa from men this ugly who could never get sex on merit alone and right now she was his prize.

She shook with fear not knowing why Bennett was permitting this Neanderthal brutality. The man's infested lips pressed towards her face while she tried to push away at the sight and smell of the gaping wounds across his cheeks. The other passengers paid no attention to the encroaching defilement, they too feared the huge man and the repercussions if he caught them staring.

With tears streaming down her face, she embraced for the inevitable.

His face pushed hard into her groin and a hand slammed across her mouth to stop her screaming.

CHAPTER 54

SAVIOUR

Ghanzi District, Botswana
September 11th

"It's over… you're OK but you must be quiet. I'm releasing my hand now," Bennett whispered to her. He glanced around at the passengers surprised to see them looking elsewhere and hadn't noticed the big man lifeless across Stella's lap.

He had waited patiently for his moment to strike. He had only needed Stella to draw the man in close enough to execute his plan perfectly. One swift blow to the man's larynx had caused him to panic for breath and instantly his sexual desire was lost. Within a split second, Bennett snapped his neck with another swift controlled manoeuvre. It all played out smooth that no one noticed the man's body slump forward into her lap.

Bennett slowly released his grip and stared into her eyes all wet and frantic.

"Just act normal, he is dead. The others don't know," Bennett reassured her as he placed his arm around her shoulders and pulled her close for comfort.

A passenger at the rear, a big man himself had been watching his brother take his victim but something was wrong. His brother was usually quick pushing his way in but not this time.

He squeezed his way forward however, stopped a few rows back in shock but not because he thought his brother was dead. Stella's hair had been pushed to one side in the short struggle exposing the blue tattoo on her neck.

He had never seen the tattoo in real life, he had only heard the horrifying tales from the village elders. It was the mark of the Blue Death. If a man came to wear it then he had survived the disease and it meant he was pure evil. Now he was staring at the mark on the skin of not just one white person but two, they were Satan's henchmen in disguise he suspected.

He pushed his way back towards the rear of the bus, screaming the presence of death to his fellow natives, as a superstitious race they responded without question. Everyone started to panic and shriek hysterically while they clawed their way towards safety, some jumping out the windows as the bus rattled west.

Suddenly, the bus slammed to a skidding halt throwing people into each other and initiating a new wave of confusion and desperation as they clambered for the exit. The driver had been first to run soon trampled by the others.

Bennett seized the opportunity hurling himself across into the empty driver's seat and with the engine still idling, he kicked the accelerator flat to the floor. It backfired and hesitantly lurched forward while belching a trail of black smoke in its wake.

They hadn't travelled far when on the horizon a dark shape appeared. A truck had stopped dispersing a squad of soldiers onto the road.

Would this never end, Bennett thought, as he slammed on the brakes pulling the wheel right and heading for cover of the nearby trees. One soldier broke from the others and with a rocket-propelled grenade on his shoulder aimed it directly towards the bus.

Behind him, Stella clutched tightly at her seat as the bus slid and bounced across the uneven rocky ground. A noise somewhere close by forced her head to turn and she realised they were not alone.

CHAPTER 55

LION'S DEN

Ghanzi District
September 11th

The rocket careered into the rear of the bus pushing it into a sideways spin as the explosion barged its way forward. Within a few more seconds the bus was ablaze and had toppled onto its side where it slid under its momentum slamming abruptly against a clump of large Jackal Berry trees.

The soldiers scampered back on board their truck and raced towards the crippled wreck as Bennett helped Stella climb out through a side window. The moment she appeared, a shower of gunfire pinged and rattled against the metal frame some ricocheting and others piercing straight through the bus.

Bennett pushed up through the same window and hurled himself onto the frame just as another volley of shots zeroed across his position. As the rounds continued he grabbed Stella and together they leapt to the ground.

"Jon, someone is on board the bus," Stella called after landing hard and near snapping an ankle.

"Help me please. Is someone there? Please help."

"Head to the trees, I'll catch up," he called back and pointed towards the closest group of spindly bushes.

She sprinted awkwardly as more gunfire came low across her path and forced her to dive behind the closest bush. Bennett watched for a few seconds and then hurled himself back on board the bus to the accompaniment of the clink and clatter of rounds piercing the thin metal skin. He was greeted by a lone man wedged under a seat, an old man with horrendously scarred eyes and clearly blind.

He yanked his trapped leg free and raised him over his shoulder before quickly pushing back out the window, thankful the old man was light. Amongst the increasing deluge of bullets he jumped from the bus just as he felt a sudden burning rush of pain slice through his shoulder.

Clenching his teeth he accelerated across the open ground towards the trees where he last saw Stella just as a loud explosion rocked the air. Birds scattered skyward and the pressure wave knocked him off his feet dropping the old man in the process. The fuel tank had finally detonated killing half the soldiers with flying shrapnel.

He clambered to his feet and hurled the blind man across his shoulders again as gunfire smacked the trees either side of them.

"You must leave me, I slow you down," the old man stuttered.

Bennett ignored his request, he wasn't about to quit. There had to be somewhere they could hide, he thought sighting Stella a short distance ahead in the shadow of a large sycamore fig tree.

"You must put me down if you want to live, I know a place they will not find us but it has much danger," the old man protested and attempted to wrestle his way free of Bennett's grasp.

Bennett only slowed up once he had the cover of the fig tree where he lowered the old man to the ground. The shooting had ceased replaced by a precarious silence that he knew meant the soldiers were probably trying to surround them.

"Be quick, where is this place?" Bennett asked watching for movement.

The old man continued, "My friend, my eyes fail me but there is an underground cave near us, I can feel it. You must find the lion's den, it is somewhere close. Once there you will find the entrance hidden by a prickly bush. But be careful, the spikes on that bush will kill you."

Bennett turned to the old man, "I see a large rock outcrop with bushes around it. Nothing else except trees?"

"The rocks, that is the lion's den. The pride is out hunting but be careful, the old one stays behind to guard the den. If you show fear, she will tear you apart."

With the old man at his side and Stella just behind they pushed their way through the scattered bushes and tall grass towards the rocky outcrop. The blind man's agility was surprising and he quickly took the lead as they drew closer to the first few rocks towering above their heads. Bennett watched on in awe that the man appeared to know exactly where he was and needed no guidance as if he had a sixth sense leading him along.

They reached the outcrop in time to see the first soldier appear from behind a row of trees behind them. He was only fifty metres away and hadn't seen them duck behind the first of the large boulders and thick bushes surrounding the rock formation.

Somewhere behind the first couple of boulders, a deep infuriated growl echoed likely to make any drunken man instantly sober.

A full-grown lioness stood before them and the spiky bush. Disapproving of their unexpected arrival the lioness raised her head and released one loud rumbling growl, it was her warning to stay away.

The lion charged a few paces towards them before stopping and bellowing a series of reverberating growls that seemed to echo back and forth amongst the rocks.

"She is calling the pride," the old man said as he pushed further ahead.

"No stop, the lion is right in front of you," Bennett screamed and reached out to grab him just as the lioness pounced with its claws outstretched and its teeth bearing ready to rip flesh from bones.

CHAPTER 56

ATTACK

5000 feet, approaching New York City
September 11th

The distant city landscape engulfed the morning horizon, growing larger by the second. Mohamed was pleased with his mission so far, it was 8.40am and all had gone to plan. From the cockpit of his Boeing 767 he was leading the charge and about to make history. Only twenty minutes before, he and his men had taken forceful control of American Airlines Flight 11 whilst en route from Boston to Los Angeles with ninety two people on board.

It would be a big day for Allah.

His target finally came into view. The North Tower of the World Trade Centre in New York City was where he would martyr himself. It was time for the American filth to fall and die. He hated the west and he hated America more, they were killing everything and no punishment was ever dealt their way. This was the start of their trial, death was to be the only sentence.

A few thousand today and millions more later when *The Trust* decided the time was right.

At just over 400 knots he closed his eyes and steered his fully fuelled weapon deep into the North Tower above the 93rd floor where it ignited into a fireball devouring the entire floor in a disintegrating thermal blast.

***

While four thousand kilometres to the west, another aircraft flew towards its target and just like Mohamed, the pilot had a destructive plan, except, it was one that would bring death to millions.

"Sir, I have the target in sight, do I have a go," the pilot asked.

"Zeta 138 you have a go, the primary initiative has been activated."

The pilot armed his weapons and let loose with all twelve missiles.

CHAPTER 57

MARK OF DEATH

Ghanzi District, Botswana
September 11th

Known locally by reputation as a superstitious witch doctor, the old man had shared many dark secrets of his great land to those who dared to listen. Only one he kept closely guarded, one that had reoccurred in his dreams from a young age. A hazy vision of a man and woman arriving mysteriously from the sky, each carrying the sacred mark upon their skin. But it wasn't their unexplained appearance that concerned him, it was the knowledge one of them held and the crusade for the truth they had chosen.

The old man had fallen to his knees as the infuriated lioness charged him and then halted somewhat subdued.

"Walk slowly to the bush but be careful of the spikes, they are more deadly than this beautiful creature. Behind it you will find the opening to a cave," he said as he lightly stroked the cat's head. Something remarkable had happened that Bennett and Stella couldn't comprehend, the witch doctor was using hypnotic powers to tame the beast.

Bennett found a small opening in the rocks under the bush where they had to crawl on hands and knees to avoid the barbed spikes. In the distance gunfire had started as the soldiers took on their new enemy. Three scarcely trained men were no match for fifteen full-grown lions all starving from an extended drought.

The screams of death echoed across the outcrop and the lion's feast had begun.

At the sound of the first gun shot, the lioness broke from the trance to join her family in the fight leaving the old man crawling towards the cave.

Once inside the cave he outstretched his hand towards Bennett as if he could see him.

"Come I must feel the mark upon your neck," he said.

He lightly caressed the small blue tattoo. "Arh, it is true. You are a chosen one," he remarked breaking into a wide smile scarce of teeth.

"But I sense something else. There is something more frightening than the mark of death under your skin, something pure evil," he added.

Bennett responded, "Who are you? What do you know? We do not know how we came to have this mark of death."

The old man suddenly moved away, "What, you do not know, you must know. You have been chosen."

Born without iris or pupils, the old man's eyes were completely white bulbs sunken deeply into a black hollow face. On first appearance, he resembled some malevolent supernatural being from a horror movie. Three ugly scars ran the width of his face from ear to ear, a reminder of his first lion encounter at a time when he knew nothing of his abilities.

"You speak the truth, you do not know your future. There is a man from Otavi in Namibia who knows the answers you seek. He is like you, he was chosen and carries the mark."

"Who is this man and where can we find him?" Bennett asked.

"His name is Matheus. You go to the Otavi Province and he will find you like I did. But be warned, many believe he is an evil spirit trapped here from an ancient time. Some say he was the one who released the blue death plague from the caves that killed his entire village though mysteriously he survived."

"How do you know this?" Stella asked remembering what Kraus had told them back in Berlin.

"My name is Tabu, I am 106 years old and I can walk the spirit world, I know this is Jon Bennett and your name is Stella Van Horne. Both of you have been in my dreams seeking the Sphere of Anubis and Matheus knows the path you must take."

Stella asked, "You said something about sensing something pure evil in Jon."

"There is an aura around this man that screams a strange deathly power. My visions always show the same thing but I cannot understand it."

"What visions?" Bennett asked.

Tabu extended his hand out towards Bennett, "Take my hand, I want you to see my vision."

Bennett took hold of the old man's hand and he immediately collapsed unconscious to the cave floor. Stella raced to his side staring at the blind man for an explanation.

"Let him rest, the spirits talk to him now. You must sleep too, we cannot go anywhere until sunrise when the lions leave to hunt."

Outside the lions had returned to their den, their appetite satisfied. Getting out of the cave was not going to be possible for a while unless Tabu could hypnotise a whole pride at once.

Inside the cave, they slept while Bennett dreamt.

Further away, the Commander was raising a small battalion of soldiers to find his missing men and the suspicious man and woman the villagers were ranting about. He had no idea another problem had just arrived in Ghanzi, Logan Bannister accompanied by ten of his mercenaries.

CHAPTER 58

AREA 47

Chalk Mountains, Nevada
September 11th

Sergeant Major Andre Matheson was fit and mentally prepared to lead the primary assault. His small group of twenty elite soldiers sat patiently waiting his command half a mile outside the front gate after arriving silently during the night. They had dug themselves in hard to prevent detection by the contingent of armed guards watching from their posts at the outer confines of the facility. It was well concealed at the base of the Chalk Mountains in Nevada and to the public eye just resembled oversized farm sheds amongst the desolate and dusty landscape.

As the sun commenced its slow climb over the eastern horizon, they prepared for the invasion. He had been briefed in complete secrecy from a silhouetted figure on a teleconferencing screen. He had no idea who he was talking with though he assumed a key member of *The Trust*. A full military attack on the United States' most secret facility was not his first choice of missions however, he had worked three financially rewarding years for *The Trust* and this latest assignment offered the greatest monetary benefits of all.

Area 47 as it was known in chosen Government departments had been built almost entirely underground and was the key vault to countless unexplained mysteries. Hundreds of sophisticated artefacts discovered during mining operations of recent times boxed and tagged on every level. Briefings held in complete secrecy suggested the artefacts had originated from an era well before the first evidence of human life on Earth and in complete contravention to the holy Bible's claims of man's origins or the evolutionary principles.

A nearby radio crackled and a muffled voice sounded. Andre, with his communication device set firmly against his bald head, listened intently, his activation command had arrived.

"Ok men listen up, we have inbound in sixty seconds so be ready, you know the drill, stick to your orders. Good luck."

Matheson moved to his observation point while his soldiers moved to their attack vehicles, weapons at the ready and all carrying breathing apparatus.

Low on the northern horizon, a dark object appeared followed by twelve orange flashes. Zeta 138 had released its deadly load and the pilot completed his part in the mission. The missiles each had a target programmed to strike at the facility that would rip its heart wide open.

At speed, Matheson and his men raced towards the front gate now only two hundred metres away as the first four missiles slammed into the four guard towers. The security detail of thirty men guarding the facility would have seen the armoured convoy churning dust towards them but by then it would be too late, their fate sealed by fire and heat from the impact.

The next four explosive spears found their mark on the two hangers concealing a squadron of attack choppers that were instantly rendered useless after the missiles tore the buildings apart. The last four came in quicker and with greater destructive force. They were a new design of bunker busters enhanced with the potency of the blue crystal that drove hard into the underground structure ripping a gaping hole at least fifty feet wide.

The underground facility laid naked to the Nevada sky, its internals torn open and ready for scavenging. A siren deep within howled and Andre knew they had to act fast. By the time the missiles had found their targets, he and his men were racing through the front gate shooting whatever moved. With the breathing apparatus firmly fixed to their faces, they released the nerve agent into the bowels of the facility.

As planned and right on time, two Sikorsky Super Stallion helicopters arrived overhead, both black and bearing no distinguishing markings. He looked up and signalled to the pilots to move in closer over the smouldering crater as his men descended into the exposed corridors in search of their target. From the pilot's view, the entire facility resembled an ant nest kicked open by some menacing child with passageways leading in all directions. But somewhere deep down the Queen sat on her nest protecting what was hers.

The soldiers raced deeper into the complex smashing their way through three massive steel security doors using crystal tipped rocket grenades. Around them the guards and scientists were dead.

Matheson walked through into a dark cold corridor, the generator had been destroyed casting darkness across the entire complex. Under flash light, he knew exactly where to find their target. He had rehearsed this mission a thousand times in his head and memorised every step of the way.

He walked along the narrow corridor with doorways either side until a familiar name caught his attention. On one of the doors was a sign.

Roswell Project
Specimens Containment

He hesitated. All his life he had wondered about the Roswell Incident and if there was truth to it and now he had the chance to satisfy his curiosity if he diverted from his orders. He resisted the urge and pushed on towards the last door on the right. It offered no markings or clues to what it shielded except a heavy construction of three foot thick steel and no apparent handle.

He raised his grenade launcher and fired to the left of the door where he knew from the building blue prints a section of structural weakness existed. Once the dust settled a hole large enough for one man to walk through had appeared.

He and two of his men stepped through both with their guns raised.

A small square room exploded in light as three beams of flashlight crisscrossed from wall to wall before finally coming to rest against what they had come for.

In the center was a metre wide metal cylinder standing vertical towering above their heads to the ceiling.

Matheson walked around it carefully caressing the cold smooth surface searching for something specific. Like braille for the blind, a single small speck of metal raised under his fingertips followed by the sudden release of an electronic keypad showered in blue light. He immediately entered the memorised six digits and took a few steps back.

A loud hiss broke the silence as air expelled from inside the cylinder and the entire outer skin slid down into the floor revealing their target. Constrained within a metal frame was a crimson red cone shaped object approximately three feet tall and glistening under the flashlights. The base was circular in shape of half metre diameter and elongated upwards to a cone point. Expertly machined and smooth, it was referred to as *Lucifer's Funnel*, origin known to a select few.

Weighing close to ninety pounds, it required two men to carry, none of whom knew the mass destruction it could deliver.

They wasted no time exiting the crippled facility. The helicopters above were hovering in wait to fly to the extraction point. Everything had gone to plan, they had the funnel and soon it would be delivered for assembly into the weapon.

They only needed Jeremiah's Codes now but that was Logan Bannister's mission.

CHAPTER 59

TRACKER

September 12th
The Cave, Ghanzi

Bennett awoke eight hours later feeling revived with his shoulder graze miraculously healed.

"What happened?" he asked.

"In time you will know but for now you must leave for Otavi, I sense more dangers for you have arrived since yesterday," Tabu answered.

"What do you mean?" Bennett asked.

"More demons walk my land, they came by plane while you slept."

Stella stood and walked over to him, placed her hand on his forehead, "You broke out in a bad fever last night, your body shook but Tabu kept telling me it was normal when someone speaks to the spirits. Do you remember anything?"

"No nothing, it's all blank."

"Tabu says we can leave soon, the lions have all left the den, even the old one."

Half an hour later, they all walked from the cave, no lions and no waiting soldiers.

Bennett had extracted from Tabu rough directions for Otavi and he'd assumed the new threat was probably Bannister and his mercenaries. The man had a way of finding him, almost like he or Stella carried a tracking device, he wondered.

Tabu took them to a nearby village where Bennett offloaded some cash for an old motorbike with enough fuel to get them out of Botswana and into Namibia.

Once Tabu had said his goodbyes and vanished into the village, they headed for the western border of Botswana. There were many ways into Namibia without a need for a passport when after all, it wasn't exactly a fiercely secured nation. They raced along old dirt tracks while Stella near strangled him from the fear of falling off.

Ducking under tree branches and skirting around rocks they were making good time towards the border with the sun rising fast into the morning sky and the warm rays licking at their backs until Bennett's thoughts got the better of him.

Without warning he yanked the bike into a wild sideways skid through the surrounding long grass and flung Stella to the ground.

"What! Have you lost your mind? What is wrong?" Stella screamed while at the same time finding her feet.

"One of us has a tracker, we need to find it now before Bannister finds us again. Get undressed we don't have a lot of time."

Somewhat shell shocked, she looked at him in disbelief and hesitation. He noticed her reluctance and screamed back at her, "If you don't take your fucking clothes off, I'm leaving you here. I don't need to be tracked everywhere we fucking go. Now do it."

She responded out of fear of abandonment in this barbaric country and started hesitantly removing her clothes. Both had taken off their outer garments while he went about searching for a device embedded in the stitching he suspected. With her back turned, he couldn't help notice large scars across her back, she had been seriously hurt once he realised.

"What happened to you?" he asked pointing towards the scars.

She became embarrassed he was looking at her partly naked body and tried to cover herself. "I was in a car accident when I was young, some drunk lost control of his Mercedes and slammed into my mother's car. We survived but the scars remain with me for life."

He turned away quickly, "I am sorry."

He hadn't seen a beautiful woman partially naked for a long time and his sexual urges were surfacing from under his hard core brutal exterior.

Ten minutes of searching and he had failed to locate any device, their underwear also revealing nothing. It had him baffled how Bannister was tracking them or it could mean Stella was a mole but that idea didn't make any sense. The only other possibility was a tracker under the skin but he needed a scanner to check electronic signals.

They got dressed, climbed back on the bike and headed west as before. Stella clung to his body thinking sooner or later the truth would present itself.

As they turned a steep corner leading out into an open field, the crack of gun shots sounded and Stella's body was flung from the bike like a rag doll. A single bullet had found the back of her head while another had struck the bike frame before the third slashed through the rear tyre.

Bennett fought to maintain control however, he and the bike slammed into a large fig tree catapulting his body across the hardened Ghanzi ground.

CHAPTER 60

THE COMMANDER

September 12th
Ghanzi

The tall skinny shooter appeared from out of the long grass with a long barrel rifle in hand. He had done his job, though taking three shots wasn't his best marksmanship.

The impact between bike and tree had thrown Bennett across the dusty ground before sliding to a halt into the base of a fig tree, where he lay unconscious. A group of African men in green army attire raced forward of the shooter and hoisted Bennett's limp body to his feet dragging him to an awaiting truck. There they tossed him mercilessly into a rear mounted steel cage usually used to cart wild animals.

An hour later, Bennett woke, quickly assessed his situation and looked down at a blood soaked body sprawled across his feet. Stella was unconscious, her face, head and hair were covered in blood and on closer inspection he realised she'd taken a head shot. He felt frantic, his heart rate thumped loud inside his chest as a feeling of uncertainty descended over him. Was she dead, he wondered? He didn't want to lose her, there was something about her he couldn't explain, and an emotional bond had been intensifying between them.

He acted quickly to rip his shirt off and bandage her head tightly to slow the bleeding as they entered a military type compound. The truck shuddered to a stop amongst the circling of armed soldiers rushing forward with their weapons aimed at the prisoners. A white skinned man dressed in similar uniform pushed his way through the line of soldiers and paused at the sight of Bennett.

The Commander of the rebel forces was a big man with a full bushy beard and by the way the soldiers shied away they feared him. With his favourite Makarov pistol casually resting in his hand, he strolled to within a few feet of the cage feeling unthreatened in any way by the prisoners.

He walked closer while his men unlocked the cage.

"This one is injured get her to the doctor now," he hollered at his men.

Bennett lifted his head to stare at the Commander while he heard the click of the lock release and the cage door swing open. He thought it was his moment to escape as Stella was dragged rearwards from the cage just as the Commander broke into a deep belly laugh.

Bennett was first to speak, "Man, were you the only applicant for this job?"

The Commander replied, "I cannot believe it, of all people with the Mark of Death, it had to be Jon Bennett."

The Commander reached forward and grabbed Bennett's arm helping him step from the cage while yelling at his men to bring water. Bennett was battered and bruised from the bike crash but nothing broken. Now as he steadied himself he was looking into the dark eyes of the Commander, an old Soviet friend by the name, Vladamir Antonovich.

As they walked, Bennett rattled off a bunch of lies of how he and Stella were chasing a terrorist cell with dirty nukes hidden somewhere inside Namibia. The mark on their necks, he'd failed to fully explain but instead convinced the Commander they were symbolic of the same terrorist group and part of their cover. The code book, Sphere and *The Trust* were things he held tightly to his chest, Vladamir may have been an old friend but still he didn't trust him.

The doctor arrived and the conversation quickly changed to Stella's health.

"The woman, she has been lucky. The bullet deflected off a titanium plate in her head and so just ripped her scalp open. It will be sutured up and she should be fine, just a bad headache I'd expect," he informed the Commander.

The Commander showed no emotion, "That is good news doctor, let me know when she is awake."

They left the medical ward and headed to the Commander's quarters.

"Jon, it has been a long time since our Soviet days together. We had much fun in those days."

"Yes Vladamir we did, what happened to you, why here?"

"Yes why Botswana. Well not much choice really. I had to escape Russia in `96 after I finally made it as their number one most wanted espionage criminal," he said and then paused before laughingly added, "I think I recall you holding that prestigious honour for about ten years."

Bennett laughed and agreed it was true, he had caused the KGB and the Russian Government much humiliation with the West by uncovering political secrets and dismantling their clandestine nuclear program. Some people inside the CIA had suggested on good authority that Bennett had assassinated all the leading physicists on the project before revealing it to the UN Security Council though nothing had ever been documented. In any event the program was blown wide open to the world and the Soviet Government never had the chance to rebuild.

The Commander continued, "Anyway I fled to North Africa and moved south until I found the best place I could to build an army for protection and well, here I am. A couple of million in bribes to the Botswana Government gave me a nice piece of the Ghanzi District and all the local soldiers I need. It's nothing special and gets fucking hot in summer but it's mine to police."

"You're not kidding about it being nothing special," Bennett said as he looked around at the barren earthly landscape stretching away in all directions.

"Don't be fooled by what you see my friend, a month ago new diamond deposits were discovered right under where we stand, worth billions I believe."

Bennett smirked, "Well you are going to need an army once the mining magnates start coming."

"I have good soldiers and each day we recruit more, I don't think United Mining will have much option but to hand over a nice percentage to us."

"United Mining?" Bennett asked becoming suddenly suspicious.

"Yeah, United Mining have the mining rights to all of Botswana, I hear it is one ambitious and ruthless corporation but this is Africa where the kids are born ruthless. Once I throw an automatic rifle in their hands, the corps don't stand a chance."

Bennett listened and chose not to say anything, he just wondered when *The Trust* would change all that.

For the next couple of hours they drank vodka while Bennett divulged parts of his life since last seeing his friend until the subject of his sacking came up. Vladamir could see Bennett's anguish and quickly changed the conversation.

By the time they had emptied the first bottle, Stella had woken and was sitting upright in her bed still dazed from the thumping headache echoing through her head. She had some recollection of the motorcycle crash though it wasn't until Bennett and the Commander semi staggered through the front door of the medical ward that it all came flooding back.

"You are one lucky lady," the Commander declared walking closer to her bed.

She returned a quizzical expression as he continued, "The bullet hit that metal plate in your head and lucky for you deflected right off."

Bennett trying hard to contain his happiness that she was alive entered the conversation, "This is Vladamir, an old friend from Russia and the Commander of the rebel army here. The Doctor says you may not remember many things for the first few hours but it will return. How are you feeling?"

She nodded her head still in considerable pain and finding it difficult to speak. The nurses had washed her up while she slept but with her head heavily bandaged, her warm friendly character was hidden.

"I am very sorry," the Commander said as he pointed towards her head wound, "would have been no shooting had I known it was Bennett on that bike."

"You just need some rest now. Tomorrow morning we fly to the Otavi Mountains in Namibia. Vladamir has been kind enough to lend us a plane to get us there," Bennett informed her as he turned to follow the Russian back out the door.

She watched them walk away more confused than Bennett realised. The doctor had been correct, her memory was suffering and she hoped her medication induced sleep would bring back what her real assignment was.

The night as Bennett expected was full of booze and memories. He and the Soviet had run undercover operations spanning two years deep inside the Soviet Government and had long forgotten the good times they'd spent together. As more vodka appeared and the soldiers downed their share, the laughter between Bennett and the Commander raged into the night until they both collapsed into unconsciousness midway through yet another story of heroics defeating officers of the KGB.

A few hours' sleep and the penetrating heat of the sunrise rudely awoke Bennett.

Stella had risen with only a dull headache unlike Bennett and the Commander who both suffered the savage bite of a hangover. She had caught her reflection in the only window and a tear ran down her cheek. The bandages had been removed revealing the gruesome array of four jagged stitches across her right temple and half her hair had been razored away.

It would heal she knew and her hair would grow back yet her vanity had suffered a gruesome blow.

"It's not that bad you know," Bennett said pointing at her head as he and the Commander walked into the medical ward.

"Yeah I never knew how lucky a girl could be to have three inches of titanium in her head," she laughed.

"Was that from the car crash?" he asked.

She hesitated slightly before replying, "Yes, my skull was fractured in six places, the plate was the only option." There had been a few crashes in her life but it was the only one she told him about.

"It is time for you to leave, there are bad storms forecast later today in the Otavi area," the Commander announced.

Hanging over the Commander's shoulder was a bulky backpack with weapons and explosives all of which Bennett had requested. The food and bottled water packed would last them a few days though Bennett hoped they'd be flying out of Namibia within forty eight hours after finding Matheus.

They were led across the compound to an airstrip where a four seater Cessna was parked. The pilot was a young Englishman fresh out of flying school keen to clock up his hours so one day he could make it into the big commercial airlines.

Bennett turned to the Commander, "Well my friend thankyou for everything, I owe you one now!"

"Well it's bloody about time you owed me one Bennett, and don't think for a second I won't hunt you down for it," he replied.

Just then the Commander's satellite phone rang and he walked away in search of privacy. Bennett headed towards the Cessna, he wanted to make his own pre-flight inspection. It wasn't that he didn't trust some aero newbie, it was more that he knew the soaring costs of maintenance were crippling small airlines worldwide and he was sure his friend, the Commander, was affected no differently.

A few minutes later, the Commander returned with a look of disbelief and grief plastered across his face.

CHAPTER 61

OTAVI MOUNTAINS

September 13th
Rebel Camp

"By the look on your face, I take it wasn't a good phone call."

"No my friend, it's seems there's been a terrorist attack in New York, Al-Qaeda crashed two commercial airliners into the Twin Towers. They're both totally destroyed, thousands expected dead," he replied with a quiver of sadness breaking in his voice.

"What, how do you know this?" Stella interjected.

"It's all over the news worldwide, and all air travel has been shut down in the US. You can't fly anywhere, the nation is on the highest alert since the Cuban missile crisis."

"How do they know it's Al-Qaeda?" she asked.

"They've already claimed it as their victory for Islam, and from what I just heard the US is already planning a major retaliatory strike against Afghanistan. I think it's safe to say there's a big fucking war coming Jon!"

Bennett nodded, while his thoughts flashed back to his mission in Afghanistan where he suspected they had nuclear weapons and why didn't they use them on America as his intelligence suggested. Saranovik had been a highly trusted source never giving false or untested information.

"It doesn't make any sense, my intel was good. These guys had nukes, why didn't they just use them if they really wanted to make a statement," Bennett said.

The Commander made no reply and instead urged them towards the aircraft where they said their goodbyes.

The small Cessna lifted off out of Ghanzi shortly after 8am heading west towards Namibia, keeping close to the ground to avoid unnecessary attention from natives taking pot shots at them for fun. Bennett sat up front next to the pilot scrutinising his every move on the controls, wanting to take over at every minute because he had never been a very good back seat pilot. Even on commercial flights he fought the urge to bash his way into the cockpit and take control.

Looking outside he could see the barren terrain unfolding towards the rising rugged mountain range to the west and behind it a wall of black thunder clouds stampeding eastward across the ridgeline. The pilot appeared nervous and sweat was already flooding his shirt, though he tried his best to conceal it to his passengers.

At 100 knots, their passage towards the Otavi Mountains was slow as an aggressive headwind mauled at their ground speed and increasingly badgered the wings of the small aircraft. Stella with her fear of flying held on tightly behind him while both her face and knuckles were white. Only one thing she hated more than big planes was small planes.

To her relief, the pilot pushed the plane's nose over into its descent towards a small airstrip hidden amongst trees on the south eastern side of the mountains. It had been over two hours and her nerves were in tatters, which only made her injuries throb all the more. They hadn't spoken much except general chit chat about the area and flying lingo she didn't understand. Bennett had made the mistake of informing the pilot he was once a navy aviator. From that point on, the Englishman didn't shut up, asking aviation question after question.

Another twenty minutes and they had landed on a rough uneven section of grass on a mountain plateau, with a steep cliff along one side rising high into a darkening sky. The pilot pushed them out the door as he spun the plane around in preparation of a quick take off.

They stood on the edge of the deserted airstrip watching the plane disappear into the south eastern sky while all around them, the rain started pelting down hard and fast. In the near distance, the rumble of thunder sounded and the lightning kept it company while three hundred miles away, their friend the Commander was brutally executed.

CHAPTER 62

THE VILLAGERS

Soviet Testing Facility, Otavi Mountains
September 13th

As the storm moved closer and the rain fell harder, a heavily burdened truck slowly negotiated its way up the narrow winding road towards a hidden facility amongst the rocks and trees. The twenty villagers inside the rear steel cage trembled with fear, and like the few hundred before them, would never see their loved ones again. They sat waiting, the young clinging to their mothers while the truck eased to a halt. Amber warning lights flashed as a towering steel door rose up to expose a brightly lit wide corridor into the belly of the mountain. All around guards stood ready, caressing their rifles and scanning for the first sign of trouble while the increasing rain edged them closer to the comfort of inside. Bennett counted at least eight patrolling the outer perimeter and then behind the door, he spotted another five all armed with similar weapons.

He waited out of sight until the door started rolling down and he darted across a short open space to duck under the final few feet before it closed. A few minutes earlier he had left Stella hidden among trees near the airstrip while he investigated the noisy labouring truck.

No one had heard or noticed him take cover behind a solitary vehicle parked just inside the entrance where he crouched and watched. A few minutes passed before half the guards exited through a side door leaving the remainder to watch over the test subjects.

Each time a villager screamed out in terror a guard stepped forward and rammed the barrel of his rifle through the cage signalling silence. Hours earlier they had been abducted at gunpoint from their homes with no explanation and herded like cattle onto the truck.

The guards spoke Russian and from the tattoos scattered across their arms they were perhaps previous or current Soviet military, Bennett thought, crawling under the vehicle for a closer inspection. As he took up a concealed position behind the front wheel, the villagers were ordered to offload. They slowly and hesitantly climbed down from the cage and formed a tight group until one chose bravery to fight his escape.

Bennett fought the angering urge to take the guards out as he watched one raise his AK47 and fire three rounds into the native's head exploding blood and brain back over his cowering family. They rushed forward to hold their dead father but stopped abruptly as the same guard fired more rounds into the floor at their feet.

He pointed to another side door and the congregation followed disappearing one by one behind it. It shut with the whining of electronic locks falling into place and the villagers were gone.

A loud siren started blaring as two men dressed in white biohazard suits with oxygen bottles strapped to their backs moved slowly and nervously towards the door. The guards had quickly vacated the corridor the moment the siren had sounded and Bennett flung himself to his feet. He dashed silently across the floor towards the closest door just as a single guard appeared from behind it. One swift hand action was all it took to silence the man's life and drop him unnoticed to the floor. It happened too quickly for the victim to sound an alarm and back behind him, the two men in their suits waited intently oblivious to the killing.

The siren stopped followed by silence.

For a brief second, Bennett thought he heard the faint sound of people screaming and then nothing. The two men waited by the door as the unlocking sequence initiated, bolts rolled away and the door swung open giving him a quick horrifying glimpse of inside.

CHAPTER 63

GENOCIDE

Soviet Testing Facility, Otavi Mountains
September 13th

Huddled together on the floor was a mass of tangled bodies, skin a distinctive blue colouration similar to that of Sigmund Kraus in Botswana two days earlier. The villagers had become victims of a bio agent and exterminated, Bennett suspected. No, he corrected himself, the Soviets were using villagers to test the Blue Death.

The men relying on the protection of their biohazard suits disappeared inside the room and the door slammed shut behind them. A second siren sounded just before the large steel door commenced opening and another truck drove in carrying a second load of villagers. Behind it a second truck, more modern in design rolled in and a familiar face appeared from the cabin.

Bannister took two steps, looked around the facility and called out, "Bennett I know you are here. Show yourself."

Bennett remained hidden behind the partly closed door calculating his escape until suddenly the situation changed. Bannister pulled Stella from the rear seat and raised his handgun to her head.

"Bennett show yourself or you're pretty little girlfriend dies like that stupid Russian friend of yours did back in Ghanzi."

Bennett fought desperately to hold back his rising anger. Vladamir had been a good friend and didn't deserve to die particularly at the hands of this madman.

"On your knees bitch… NOW," Bannister yelled as he shoved her forward of him.

"Bennett, prepare to witness her execution."

She burst into tears, it was the second time in only a few days someone had threatened to kill her. "Please don't kill me, I haven't done anything. I am only a journalist looking for a story, whatever beef you have with Bennett doesn't involve me."

"Shut up!" Bannister struck her head with the butt of his handgun sending her crashing face first to the floor.

Bennett with no option stepped boldly and confidently from the doorway. He raised and aimed his weapon at Bannister's head as he walked slowly towards him. The other mercenaries in the room all zeroed in on him unsure whether to shoot.

"Bannister, tell your men to drop their weapons. You know I can drop you as quick as they can shoot me."

"Yes Jon, I've read your profile, impressive I must say. But I don't think you have read mine."

Bennett took one more step then felt a sharp sting in the rear of his neck and he collapsed to the floor.

CHAPTER 64

CRUCIFIXION

Soviet Testing Facility, Otavi Mountains
September 13th

The paralysis lasted a few minutes, long enough for Bannister's men to move in quickly and disarm Bennett. A small dissolvable projectile filled with a fast acting neurotoxin had been fired from somewhere behind him only taking a microsecond to strangle his central nervous system from the neck down.

Stella thinking he'd been shot, tried desperately to raise herself from the floor only to be pushed back down by Bannister's boot.

"Bennett you are lucky I'm following orders otherwise you'd be dead right now," Bannister announced while he walked closer aiming his handgun down at Bennett's limp body on the floor resisting the urge to squeeze the trigger. He knew the neurotoxin would last an hour so when Bennett launched at him from the floor it took him by complete surprise.

Likewise Bannister's men didn't expect the toxin to have a shortened effect on him and acted too slow to impede Bennett's attack on their boss. Three superbly directed blows to Bannister's head were all it took for Bennett to gain the upper hand and snatch the gun from his hand. It had been a superior and lightning quick display of skill but the rifle butt slamming into the back of his head ended all momentum to kill Bannister leaving him slip unconscious to the floor.

Bannister still dazed and his face a torrent of blood climbed to his feet making sure to land a full swing kick into Bennett's ribcage. He had been humiliated in front of his men by Bennett's ease at which he took him down and disarmed him. Right now he wanted to inflict the most pain he could, his pride had been crippled and for that the urge to administer punishment was overpowering. Another cowardly kick drove hard into Bennett's belly lifting his body off the floor inviting a sudden screaming plea from Stella for him to stop.

She had lifted herself to a sitting position but a guard standing behind her had his rifle firmly pressed into her back. Bannister hesitated before laying one more boot into Bennett's belly raising a painful grunt from his awakening victim.

"Leave him alone," Stella yelled as Bannister turned towards two of his men and gave them a nod. Both raced over and lifted Bennett to his feet as Bannister pushed his handgun into his head as motivation to obey their instructions. Back behind them, Stella was dragged to her feet and coerced in a similar manner.

"Bennett, one wrong move and you both die," Bannister demanded as he tapped Bennett's head with his gun to subtly remind him it was there.

At the end of a long walk, deep inside the facility, the mercenaries threw them into a cell secured behind thick steel bars. The cell door slammed shut and both were left standing in the semi darkness.

Meanwhile another truck arrived with twenty more villagers on-board and more were expected later that afternoon. Genocide was maintaining a fast pace at the Soviet facility.

An hour passed and Bennett had talked very little. Stella too was quiet wondering whether it was all worth dying for until a light came on above them and the silence broke as Bannister appeared at the cell door.

"Bennett, I want the code book, where is it?" he demanded while two of his men aimed their rifles towards them.

"I don't know what you are talking about," he murmured in reply.

"Come on Bennett this is your lifeline, my boss doesn't want you dead just yet, he just wants the code book."

Bannister turned to Stella, "What about you pretty one, do you want to live? Just tell me where it is and you walk free?"

Without a sideways glance she replied, "I have no idea what you are talking about."

"Bannister, tell your boss to get down here and take it from me," Bennett snarled back at him.

"That's not going to be possible. You see, my job is to get the codebook from you by any means and I'm not about to disappoint my boss. But Bennett, you do disappoint me, you're not as tough as you're reputation. Must admit though, I will enjoy killing you. Oh, but not before you get to watch my men pleasure the beautiful reporter," Bannister threatened.

She glared at the animal on the other side of the bars, her talons twitching to latch onto his face and rip his eyes out. In one gigantic leap, she launched off the floor at the bars and spat in his face. Bennett sat watching, amused, it was a side of her he had not seen before and her speed was incredible, he thought. He was witnessing a feisty woman and inwardly, he applauded the show.

"Lively aren't you pretty one, but foolish I might add," Bannister laughed.

Bennett remained calm as always, just calculating his moves, waiting for the right opportunity to present itself like he'd done countless times in the past. There was no point letting Bannister under his skin, it only invited fatal mistakes.

Bannister was shocked by her sudden explosion of attitude and under different circumstances would have shot her in the head just to maintain respect among his men.

He left shaking his head, "You are fools but I have a friend who, I think, will change your minds."

The cell went dark and Stella collapsed back against the wall, "So what now?"

"Don't know yet, still trying to work out what these Soviets are up to and how Bannister fits into it all."

"I'm guessing the Soviets are working for *The Trust* and this facility belongs to them. "Any ideas what it's used for?" she asked.

"Yeah some kind of genocide or experimentation using the Blue Death, there's a room back there full of dead villagers all blue in colour like how I found Kraus's body."

"So *The Trust* is involved with the Blue Death," she announced thinking how the other pieces of information were fitting into the big picture.

"Yes looks that way, remember Kraus said the Blue Death came from a blue crystal discovered in a cave of the Otavi Mountains. That's where we are now and I'm willing to bet this is a bio weapons plant. Kraus mentioned the Fourth Reich taking over from the failed Nazi's. They killed six million Jews through genocide during World War II and I reckon this is how they intend to carry on their extermination plans by using the blue crystal."

Stella was in partial shock, the gravity of the situation had finally sunk in. "I once did a story on Nazi supremacy and the impact on the world in those years. One historian I interviewed suggested that if the Allied Forces had not entered the war when they did, then Hitler had enough support to rule at least half the world. From there, his power would have grown exponentially and conquered the entire planet within another ten years. I actually thought he was a bit eccentric and cut it out of the final story. My Editor agreed it was too inconceivable, the American people would never accept the notion of a German dominant world."

Bennett sat there non-judgemental, listening and at the same time he was thinking of an escape plan. A man's voice sounded from outside the cell and the light illuminated above them again.

"On your feet, time to play."

Bennett looked up to see Bannister standing there with his handgun aimed at his head. Behind him stood four of his armed goons, two he recognised from Afghanistan a few weeks earlier.

"Bannister you don't need her, it's me you want," he pleaded for Stella's safety more because he knew the term *play* meant torture. He feared she would reveal all they knew including the codebook's location.

The cell door opened and they were led out into the corridor, five guns aimed squarely at their heads. Now wasn't the time for an escape, he considered.

"Now why would I have Miss Van Horne miss out on having fun, and when we're finished my men will need some womanly recreation. They work very hard you know." He pistol-whipped Bennett across the side of his head and pushed him forward.

"Now get moving."

They were pushed at gunpoint down a long narrow corridor while all the way Bennett searched for an exit plan as Stella hung close behind him. Two of Bannister's men were looking Stella up and down as they guarded her from behind. It had been a long while since they indulged in sex with a woman and never one with such a fine tight body.

The torture room was small, dimly lit and stank of faeces and vomit. It had been used recently, Bennett thought. In the center was a wooden pole with chains and razor wire dangling from the top. Above the pole a set of electrical wires hung loosely from the ceiling. At the base was a horizontal timber cross beam and near the top was another. Both showed signs of dark red stains and he knew, it was the build-up of dried blood.

A sharp searing jolt of pain between his shoulder blades took him by surprise as one of the guards struck him from behind with his rifle butt. The weight behind the attack pushed him off balance as another guard drove a kick into his legs. He toppled to the floor where they zip tied his hands and feet.

Stella realising her fate, started kicking and fighting to break free. Her strength took the goons by surprise and needed three to push her struggling body against the pole. One hand broke free unleashing a retaliatory strike into the closest man's face. His nose burst into a flow of blood while Bannister stepped forward and slammed his rifle butt into her head. It stunned her enough to finish stringing her up.

Her position on the pole resembled a crucifixion with her arms spread out above her head in the cross formation. Bannister had walked over to an assortment of tools scattered on a bench against the far wall where he selected the most appropriate instrument to complete the picture.

"NO!" Bennett screamed at him, "Don't do it Bannister, it's me you want."

He fought hard against the zip ties but with each violent movement they tore harder into his skin and blood trickled to the floor.

Bannister ignored Bennett as he blasted a six-inch steel nail through each of her hands using the nail gun he'd selected. A loud high pitched heart wrenching squeal bellowed out while Bennett watched on trying harder to free himself. He knew the tactics at play, punish the weak to make the strong talk.

"Sir, it's ready, you can start anytime," announced Bannister's second in charge after he had secured the last of the electrodes to her head.

With the wires firmly attached, the pulse would hammer her brain every time he pressed the switch on the small remote held firmly in his hand. Turning a dial would increase or decrease the strength of current depending on how evil his desire.

Since joining *The Trust*, Bannister had become their best foot soldier or in the true sense, their best hit man. He had executed countless threats along the way and most often after or in some cases during torture. He believed in *The Trust's* vision for the future and would do anything to make it a reality yet he never fully understood how keeping Bennett alive was part of it.

"Miss Van Horne, I need to know where the codebook is?" Bannister calmly asked.

She looked up and from watery hate filled eyes, glared at the animal in front of her. She made no reply but instead looked over at Bennett twisting aggressively on the floor trying hard to free himself and right then, she knew, he could not be her saviour this time. Her tears flowed fast and the burning pain grew stronger as the embedded nails tore more flesh from her hands. She sensed greater pain was soon to come, this was the second time she'd fallen victim to *The Trust's* torture methods and electric current through her body.

Bannister proud of himself looked down at the remote in his hand and flicked the switch.

A few seconds and she started screaming uncontrollably while pleading desperately for mercy, but pain was not the reason.

CHAPTER 65

FEAR

Soviet Testing Facility, Otavi Mountains
September 13th

Bannister rotated the small round dial increasing the current pulsating through her head. He knew Stella's fear level would escalate quickly and it was already showing in the way she had started convulsing, her heart rate was bordering on maximum and she battled to find an escape.

He flicked the switch off.

Stella opened her eyes, relief washing swiftly across her body. Bennett had realised it wasn't conventional torture methodology he was using, it was something feeding on her fear.

Bannister turned to him and explained, "Jon let me tell you, pain and fear are too different things. Pain is what the body endures and the brain tries hard to deal with it. Now fear on the other hand causes far greater psychological pain and the brain cannot control this."

He turned back to Stella, "I can control the level of fear you suffer Miss Van Horne and just so you know, this is the lowest level."

She returned a look of terror from eyes flowing with tears.

"I don't have to turn it on again, you just tell me where the codebook is and you are free to go," he lied.

She spoke for the first time, "Tempting as it may sound, I will have to pass on your offer."

She was thinking of the warnings from Rose, Kraus and then the witch doctor not to release the codebook. Bennett looked over catching her eye and he hoped she was strong of mind. It was about to get real bad, he knew.

"Very well, have it your way," Bannister said and flicked the switch.

He turned the dial to half way and she responded. A deathly blood curdling scream vibrated through the room and to an outsider it would sound like the vicious attack of wild animals. This lasted for the next three minutes before he stopped the current.

This time her response was delayed, her energy had drained and she was finally becoming conducive to talking. She lifted her head slowly, her hair drenched with sweat dripping over her face while blood dripped from her impaled hands. Bennett fearing she was about to break called out,

"Hey Bannister you gutless fuck stop picking on a defenceless woman, or is this the only way you can prove yourself a man."

Bannister took the bait.

He walked over to him leaving Stella to catch her breath and regain some balance of mind. She watched as Bannister took an AK47 from one of his men and with one sweeping arm action, he drove the butt of the weapon into Bennett's head knocking him speechless.

He returned his attention back to Stella on the cross who had recovered enough to relinquish any thought of betrayal. His cell phone blipped, an incoming message signifying the arrival of the latest aerial dispersal weapon for testing. This pleased him and he handed the remote to his second in charge, "Keep working on her, we are close to her talking, I will be back in 30 minutes." He left the room, taking one of his men with him.

The second in charge walked over to her thinking it wasn't how he preferred his girls to behave on a pole. Greased up, naked and dancing was his preference. He reached out and grabbed hold of her shirt pulling hard to rip it open exposing her smooth flat abdomen and bra covered breasts. He took a step back to admire the sight just to help feed his sexual hunger because he knew later it would be satisfied.

"Hey bitch you're mine now, talk or your worst nightmare comes true."

She remained silent, her humiliation of being half naked was taking over. He pressed the switch and immediately her sweaty body started trembling, her screams soon following with a sickening cry for help. He stood watching enjoying the torment while the clock ticked. At five minutes, her body twisted from side to side pulling harder on her impaled hands and she let go a wild screech, "Jon, help me pleaseee."

"Let her go, she doesn't know, she wasn't with me when I hid it," he yelled out of fear for her life.

The current stopped abruptly. He turned and moved towards Bennett, "Then tell me or I'll string you up like Jesus too."

"OK, I'll tell you but take her down first."

He nodded to the other two men in the room who ripped the nails from her hands accompanied by another scream echoing through the room. With the pain finally too much, she fell unconscious hanging from the zip ties. Her head hung loosely forward while the men cut her down and she collapsed to the floor.

"Get her out of here, but save some for me and don't mark that pretty face or I'll cut yours off," the second in charge ordered as one of his men lifted her from the floor and headed for the door.

"So tell me where is the codebook, and I might let you live?"

"Now come on, Bannister is in charge here not you. I have to think a bit, my memory is not as good anymore," Bennett replied.

The second in charge punched him square in the face, lip bursting open and blood oozing down his chin. It joined the flow still dripping from the open head wound inflicted by Bannister's rifle butt fifteen minutes earlier.

"How long have you been Bannister's bitch? I'm sure *The Trust* would see you fit for his job if I gave you the book's location and not him. It's only a matter of time and I'll give it up and you know Bannister will be back very soon."

"Shut up" he screamed before turning to the other man in the room, "String him up on the cross, he will tell us."

Bennett pleased with himself, relaxed a little.

CHAPTER 66

LAB RATS

Soviet Testing Facility, Otavi Mountains
September 13th

Across on the eastern side of the facility, a helicopter had landed under a blanket of torrential rain. On board was a small explosive device, the first of its kind anywhere in the world and though, only in the prototype stage, it represented a new era in weapons of mass murder.

Bannister stepped forward to inspect the device. He knew the test was scheduled for later that day but the delayed arrival of the test subjects meant it would more likely occur into the early night.

A man dressed in a black expensive suit with an air of importance stepped from the helicopter. They shook hands, exchanged no words outside the soundproofing of the building and then walked briskly for cover.

Once inside the building, the Suit spoke for the first time, "The Afghanistan mine should be fully operational in a few weeks. We expect the Taliban will head south to fight a much bigger problem giving us free reign."

"Has this anything to do with what happened in New York?" Bannister cautiously asked.

"Details you do not need to know Logan. You just stick to what you are paid to do and we won't have any problems," the Suit replied before quickly adding, "Now, I hear you have Bennett and the girl here."

"Yes sir, we are loosening their tongues, I expect to know the codebook's location within a few hours."

"Excellent news Logan, the board members really don't expect you to get it that easy, he is too much like his father and I think you underestimate him. I suggest you do not lose sight of your mission."

"Sir, but if I get the codebook out of Bennett now, then there will be no need to complete this mission."

"True, if that happens," the Suit conceded with some doubt sounding in his voice, "You have your orders Bannister, now execute them."

Bannister hurried off to oversee the injection of crystal dust into the device, it needed to be ready for testing when the remaining villagers arrived in a few hours. The local human supply had run dry and now they were culling from further east, which meant longer travelling times.

Back in the torture room, Bennett sat on the floor hands and feet tied, anticipating his move. The second in charge stood with his AK47 aimed at him ready to fire at the slightest wrong movement while the other armed man cut the zip ties from his feet.

With his hand ties already snapped behind his back from an unexplained strength gain, he leapt from the floor grabbing the man around his throat and turning his weapon towards the second in charge. The man's body became a human shield punctured with metal as the second in charge fired towards Bennett but only killing his own man. The second in charge fell backwards as his chest burst open from an onslaught of bullets from Bennett's gun.

He dropped the dead shield to the floor and headed for the door, one AK47 in hand and the other slung across his back. He knew the sound of rapid gunfire would attract attention from everyone on site and of course Bannister. The area outside the door was surprisingly clear, no immediate opposition and so he sprinted in search of the closest cover.

A dozen or so fast strides and he found another narrow corridor in almost complete darkness.

Further back behind him he could hear the heavy trampling of running boots and men shouting, the search had begun. Everywhere in the facility, lights were illuminating making his chance of escape now more difficult. He reached up and using his rifle smashed the overhead light casting him back into darkness but he feared his chances of escape were slim.

Keeping constant check of the rear, he moved closer to two doors at the end of the corridor illuminated by a single overhead light. One was locked but the other pushed open without effort. He threw himself into the room while holding his gun high ready to fire at the slightest movement.

Nothing moved. It was dark and a strange acidic smell filled the air.

He took a lowered position to avoid an enemy's bullet and engaged the light switch. It was a laboratory of some kind and devoid of human life.

Another door was visible across the room and he raced towards it to check security. The door also unlocked led to yet another dark room this time the sour stench of excrement stole his breath. To his left, a massive steel roller door similar to that at the front entrance stood closed. To his right, he could vaguely make out the entrance to a single open doorway wide enough for roughly two men to walk abreast. A sudden sound of men shouting from somewhere behind pushed him forward in the darkness.

He ran towards the open doorway, the smell of faeces growing stronger with every step he took and within seconds, he was standing in a large room with steel bars from floor to ceiling along one side. It was a prison cell of about twenty square feet. Inside the cell, he could just make out dozens of dark human shapes, huddled together on the floor. More lab rats, he thought. Some started to move as he approached and some reached through the bars pleading in their native tongue. About forty pairs of panic-stricken eyes screamed back at him and there was no need for a translator, he could sense their cries for help.

The overhead lights started flickering on one by one, lighting up the room.

A new sense of panic inundated the room herding the terrorised villagers into a tight huddle away from the cell door and revealing a lone white woman crouched in the corner. Her face showed no expression and her eyes glistened tears. Her clothes were torn while her hair was matted with a cocktail of bloodied sweat. Stella turned her head slowly towards him and they made eye contact while at the same time she leapt to her feet in relief.

He searched around for a door release not really knowing their next move. On the wall behind him he spotted a green and red button so he pressed the green as a volley of shots hit the wall above his head and the cell gate rolled open.

Further over from the direction of the laboratory three armed men in dark uniforms kept up a constant rattle of gunfire towards Bennett's position mostly striking the villagers as they pushed and shoved to escape. Behind them and low to the floor, Bennett took a controlled aim. Half a dozen quick shots and he had killed the enemy.

He sprinted to the roller door keeping guard for more gunmen as he did and pressed the switch. The motor whined and chains rattled as the door rose towards the ceiling to reveal an open field lined with tall trees against the backdrop of the rugged Otavi Mountains. The rain had eased to a light drizzle and the sun had disappeared behind the cliff face of the mountain.

Stella stumbled caught up in the stampede of the fleeing villagers as another door swung open towards the rear and Bennett raised his weapon readying himself to fire.

CHAPTER 67

THE TEST

Soviet Testing Facility, Otavi Mountains
September 13th

To Bennett's surprise, more villagers spilled through the doorway like rats scuttling from a sewer drain. They screamed in fear and on catching a glimpse of daylight they scurried with increased commitment towards their survival.

Stella had managed to edge her way across the room as the fresh load of test cases rushed past. Gunfire from inside the building somewhere jolted Bennett into action grabbing her by the arm and joining the villager's plight towards the open field.

Once outside they kept running towards the only tree cover in view.

The villagers now about eighty in total, had mostly scampered across the field into the shadows of the tree line. Running swiftly was something they did every day and now it came naturally leaving Bennett and Stella stumbling on the uneven rocky ground.

"No... Stop!" Bennett screamed while he watched helplessly as six villagers leapt at full stride onto a twenty foot fence. For them, it was too late. Their bodies shook and trembled as the high voltage electricity tore its way through their flesh and fused their brains into a molten mess. The sounds and smell of burning flesh was sickening even for Bennett. All around, men women and children screamed in terror at the sight of their brothers clinging lifelessly to the steel mesh looking like insects on a bug zapper.

Back behind them, the steel door rolled down.

Bennett ran the fence perimeter, about a hundred metres in total however, as he expected there was no escape. Stella leaned back against a tree resting her throbbing hands and did her own assessment of the perimeter. Her bleeding had stopped but her psychological toughness had suffered after managing to fight off the rape.

The guard had dragged her from the torture room to another room where he forced himself on her. He tore at her clothes and fondled her privacy. She waited until he'd pulled his trousers down ready for his moment and she kicked him with all her might in the face smashing his nose and breaking his jaw. His revenge was swift with a number of punches and kicks into her head and body. The ferocity of his return attack knocked her winded on the floor but to her surprise and relief, he left her unviolated inside the cell.

Inside the facility, Bannister was infuriated, yelling and cursing at his men. They had lost Bennett. A board member on site to witness him failing, not a good way in the eyes of *The Trust*, he thought. The radio buzzed, "Sir, we found Bennett and the woman, they are in the testing grounds with the villagers."

The Suit had arrived and overheard the conversation, "Leave them there, the test starts in three minutes and I'm not calling the chopper back."

"Sir, Bennett will die if you leave him out there," Bannister argued.

"Logan, are you questioning my judgement not to mention my orders."

"No Sir, not at all," he replied cowering away and talking into the radio, "Leave them there, test goes ahead in three minutes."

One minute later, a siren similar to that of an air raid horn blared across the enclosure.

Bennett looked towards Stella, "I have a bad feeling about this, I think we just joined their lab rats."

Within thirty seconds, the dark shape of a helicopter appeared overhead at about 500 feet. While on the ground, the villagers were oblivious to what he suspected was about to occur, as he looked towards the afternoon sky and watched the helicopter maintain its hovering position.

"What's it doing up there?" Stella asked.

"My guess is waiting for the test to start," he replied just as a silver object fell from the helicopter's underbelly. It fell silently, impacting the ground not far from where they stood. A cloud of dust and dirt spewed up followed by nothing.

A small group of the villagers moved slowly towards it while Bennett pulled Stella in the opposite direction trying to add distance between them and the object. He had his suspicions what it was.

They had only taken a few steps when the object detonated. A blinding flash of blue light shot out in all directions followed by the sound of rushing air. Stella fell backwards from the shockwave as Bennett broke her fall and they fell together to the ground.

All around them, villagers started squealing in agony, their bodies twisting in pain while the crystal radiation devoured their bodily fluids and organs in seconds, their brains first to dissolve. For the weak, the screams lasted a few seconds while the strong lingered a little longer before all their bodies collapsed, became rigid and turned a vibrant blue.

A total of ten seconds was all it took before all the villagers had perished.

Back inside the Facility, the Suit was impressed with the results. The dispersal system proved successful at close range. He picked up his cell phone and made a call to an office in Washington DC.

"The test was a success, seventy people killed in under ten seconds at a range of a hundred metres. The dispersal system proves effective using the crystal dust and the estimates mean we can expand the range to at least ten kilometres using larger quantities."

The Suit continued talking, "No they haven't been searched yet, but it seems no one survived like all the previous tests." He broke the connection and looked towards Bannister, "I want Bennett's body restrained and prepared for shipment to Kehlstein immediately." Bannister knew not to question the Suit but thought it strange why he had to restrain a dead man.

The Suit headed for his helicopter and a long journey back to Southern Germany.

CHAPTER 68

OTAVI

Soviet Testing Facility, Otavi Mountains
September 13th

Bennett opened his eyes to a bleak and morbid landscape. Everywhere he looked, villagers laid sprawled on the ground, their bodies twisted from an agonising death and already blood oozed from countless erupting skin lesions. It was a gruesome sight of mass proportion and he had to turn away shielding himself from the vision.

The impact had knocked Stella unconscious, her pulse was weak and her breathing had become erratic but it was her skin that he feared most. A light tinge of iridescent blue like that of asphyxiation had started to show and as he inspected closer a distinct pattern similar to fish scales grew noticeable.

Somewhere behind them a faint rumble could be heard as a truck approached the gate and he pulled himself tighter to the dusty ground to imitate death. He watched as the gate rolled back and two men heavily clad in white biohazard suits wearing breathing apparatus walked slowly towards them.

Beside him, Stella was gasping like a fish out of water, and with each gulp of air signalled her struggle for life. He could hear the men's boots crushing the small stones and gravel as they approached and it became clear he was their target.

He remained motionless and then when he felt a hand brush his shoulder he launched to his feet. Both men froze in disbelief and took two stumbling steps back. They had no weapons, there had never been a need, they thought after thousands of test subjects had died from the effects of the blue death.

Bennett leapt at them and in one clean swift arm action, he swiped a small razor blade concealed in his watch across both men's suits. The suits blew open exposing them to their deaths as the radiation clawed at their throats and they collapsed lifeless to the ground.

He scooped Stella's limp body up and ran the short distance to the truck, that on first appearance reflected a hint of military with its dark camouflage colourings and robust rear canopy. That perception changed once he opened the door. Inside a row of airtight human-sized clear canisters lined each side interspersed with sophisticated electronic monitors and other devices.

He lifted Stella onto the passenger seat and threw the truck into gear lurching it to life with a vibrating jolt. He drove hard all the way down the winding steep mountainside road towards the town of Otavi only fifteen miles to the south. Every twist and turn was wrestled with danger as he fought to stop the rear end fishtailing in the loose gravel.

Stella's unconscious body slumped against his as he tugged and pushed at the wheel to keep control while back behind them, a milky white dust trail peeled upwards into the late afternoon sky.

Inside the facility, Bannister knew something had gone wrong and had broken into an agitated state of pacing back and forth like a hungry animal in a cage. He was constrained by the time limit imposed for the radiation to penetrate the ground and lose its lethal charge though something more irritating clawed at him. It was the humiliation of failure that pushed him to bark new orders and send men running in fear of lethal reprimand.

By the time the testing grounds were safe, the truck had roared into the small town of Otavi where Bennett found the dirt streets deserted, unusual for late afternoon in an African town, he thought. To the north, the dark silhouette of a helicopter at low altitude was fast approaching and he knew what that meant. He slammed the truck hard right into the closest side street as two hellfire missiles launched from under the helicopter's left underbelly pod.

One tore through the rear canopy spinning the truck into a sideways slide while the second hammered the building beside them. The truck's rear end erupted into a ball of fire as oxygen bottles exploded and black smoke engulfed the driver's cabin.

Stella was slung across the inside like a rag doll and Bennett hung on the best he could while fighting with the wheel to keep some control. The side street was narrow with barely enough width for the truck. The noise of the engine revving and the destructive sounds of metal scraping on timber were deafening until the bullets started raining down.

Fifty feet above them, the helicopter was stalking their escape and had wound up its front mounted chain gun letting loose with five hundred rounds a minute of metal obliteration. Bullets ripped through the cabin forcing Bennett to yank hard left and push his foot flat on the pedal. Lucky for him the walls of the Otavi buildings were lightly constructed and the truck smashed through without much trouble into a deserted market place with rows of empty stalls in all directions. Two more missiles slammed overhead peeling away the roof and like a giant's hand scooped the truck up before tossing it onto its side.

The helicopter like some gargantuan starving beast rose up above the hole in the roof and lashed the crippled truck with its chain gun. As bullets carved their way through the already burning rear canopy, Bennett dragged Stella out and hoisted her over his shoulders as a bullet found the fuel line.

The truck exploded in a ball of fire and metal knocking Bennett off his feet and he dropped Stella. Above them the helicopter circled around to land while the rotor wash spewed dust up into a swirling blizzard of road grime that gave Bennett an opportunity to escape. The overbearing roar of rotor blades cannibalizing the air overshadowed Stella stirring on the ground beside him. She had gained consciousness and was already trying to climb to her feet reaching up at Bennett who had his eyes fixed on the pilot. They were like stunned rabbits in the headlights of a car, both frozen in time as the pilot grinned.

Her hand clawing at his arm caught his attention. Bennett looked down into her green sparkling eyes and relief washed over him, the blue death had failed to take her. He spun, raised his machine gun and squeezed off the remaining few rounds into the cockpit that only angered the pilot to retaliate with the ferocity of the chain gun.

As the gun's fiery breath of metal closed in on them, he lifted Stella to her feet and sprinted the best they could together to the closest building, a warehouse of sorts. The failing afternoon light made the interior almost completely dark and a scattering of large timber crates provided good cover.

As he stood to find an exit, gunfire swamped their position and the crates began to shred like paper.

CHAPTER 69

TANGENI

Otavi, Namibia
September 13th

Two heavily built Soviet soldiers dressed in dark grey fatigues charged into the small warehouse wasting little time finding their targets. Under the roar of the helicopter turbines, Bennett had not heard the screech of the jeep outside and the pounding of the two men's boots across the ground.

The soldiers approached in formation firing short bursts splintering timber in all directions while cautiously working their way around to outflank Bennett. One climbed to a higher position amongst the rafters into what he thought was a dominant position as a collection of shots echoed off the walls. Bennett had killed his partner with a clean head shot and was already moving to take him out.

He glanced down into Bennett's steely blue eyes, realising his mistake as he tried desperately to swing his aim sideways but it was futile. His head blew apart with a spattering of blood and brains from Bennett's double round penetrating through under his chin and erupting out the rear of his head. Death was without question immediate and there had been no suffering for the unfortunate soldier as his body fell to the floor.

In the chaos of battle, Bennett didn't notice the other body in the room, though small, it moved swiftly towards them.

He caught sight of the movement at the last minute and snapped his gun around just as a young dark skinned boy threw himself to the floor and pleaded for mercy in his best English, "Please don't shoot, I know why you here, you seek Matheus."

Feeling unthreatened, he lowered his weapon and the boy responded by climbing cautiously to his feet still mostly camouflaged by the darkness of the room. Stella pounced knowing more troops were sure to arrive, "Who are you and what makes you think we seek Matheus?"

The local boy had excelled in English at school and he was proud to show off his skills. "My name is Tangeni, this was my father's shop. Each night I have dreams about you and the man with the mark on your necks." He turned to Bennett and said, "You have a secret, but you don't know what it is, and you think Matheus can help you."

He added, "We must go fast, soon more soldiers come."

Though only ten years old, Tangeni was wise and fierce of heart for his age and he knew how to survive on his own. His father had taught him to hunt and fend for himself from the age of five which kept his spirits alive in the isolation of the deserted town.

"Are there any other people here?" Bennett asked.

"No they all gone, taken by the soldiers. Each time the trucks come I run and hide with my family. But last week they were taken too."

"How long has this been happening?" Stella inquired looking towards Bennett who was becoming edgy at the thought of reinforcements arriving and the helicopter still somewhere above them preparing for the final attack.

"I think about three months but most were taken in the last month and always at night."

Bennett looked back at Stella, they knew the fate of Tangeni's family but he probably didn't.

"Yes we are searching for Matheus, can you take us to him," Bennett shouted as the roof started a deafening rattle just as strips of roof sheeting started crashing around them. Through the gaps they could see the underbelly of the SuperCobra as it lowered closer to the warehouse accompanied by the violent hurricane off the rotors.

"Come on, we've got to get out of here and fast," Bennett ordered as he yanked at Stella's arm.

The warehouse interior lit up in a flash of blazing light as the far side exploded in fire and timber splinters. Wooden crates ignited in an inferno of intense heat engulfing everything within twenty feet and it dictated Bennett to push the others towards the only exit remaining. The helicopter had launched a missile followed closely by another that devoured the surviving section of the building and threw up a black smoke screen wide enough to offer them an escape.

They sprinted across the street searching for a place to hide as the dark intimidating shape of the attack helicopter materialised through the swirling smoke and dropped rapidly towards them. Immediately the ground erupted as the chain gun blasted their position in a shower of bullets lashing at their feet all the way til they bounded through the doorway of another building.

"Run and don't look back. I will take care of the chopper," Bennett yelled and pushed Stella through the doorway with Tangeni close behind.

He emerged out onto the roadway in full view of the pilot who was hovering just above the road and arming his next Hellfire missile to obliterate the building. He paused as they locked eyes until the sound of the chain gun whining back to life sent Bennett scuttling into a nearby yard of old timber logs. There he took cover while the helicopter gained height for the final kill and let loose with the missile into the logs.

He edged his beast back down for a closer look at the burning carnage while his finger rested lightly on the chain gun's trigger waiting to see Bennett's slain body in a sea of blood behind the blast ravaged logs. He pushed the helicopter forward focused on the flames and thick black smoke that now swirled along the street accelerated by the gusting afternoon breeze.

The turbine whining was deafening up close as Bennett moved in close out of sight of the pilot. He had used the concealment of the log stacks and a neighbouring building to emerge behind the helicopter as it floated a few feet above the ground towards the burning logs. He raised his gun towards the cockpit as movement in the distance caught his attention.

A few hundred metres further to the north, Stella ran into view with Tangeni close behind until they slid to a stumbling halt at the deadly sight of the helicopter. Resembling the threatening stance of a Tyrannosaurus Rex it turned to glare down its next meal.

The massive frame of the attack helicopter spun left sending a gush of rotor wash and dust smashing into Bennett's face and ripping his feet out from under him. His body slammed backwards across the roadway as the chain gun roared to life and sprayed a path of death towards the others now running for their lives.

Bennett found his feet and raised his weapon against the gale force of the rotor wind taking aim at the cockpit.

He pulled the trigger.

Click… nothing.

Damn Russian crap, he thought, as he tried hopelessly to fire the weapon knowing Stella was about to be shredded with bullets. He threw himself forward fighting hard to maintain his balance in the down winds and sprinted to the pilot's cockpit door.

The pilot caught sight of movement in his peripheral as Bennett yanked the door open and drilled the butt of his AK47 into the side of the man's head. He defended against the attack the best he could while struggling to maintain control of the machine as the skids kissed the ground and the rotors belched a violent dust storm skyward. Bennett clung to the cockpit and with his free arm continuing the attack until the pilot's body slumped forward unconscious.

He reefed him out and climbed into the control seat. Another few feet and all would have been lost. In the struggle, the helicopter had drifted precariously close to the burning log yard and was seconds from its own destructive finality.

As flames rose violently across the windshield, Bennett pulled up the control and squeezed the throttle lurching the machine airborne. As he threw his feet down hard against the pedals, he managed to grasp a fragile command and climbed enough to hover above the rooftops. A few hundred play hours in a Seahawk on board a US carrier as a young aviator was all he had at his disposal to command a timid control of the lethal helicopter now rising above the town.

The cockpit radio crackling to life broke his sweat riddled concentration.

"Ivan, have you got them cornered?"

It was Bannister's rough voice, Bennett realised and as he looked into the northern distance, a truck laden with soldiers sped into town.

Bennett dropped the nose forward accelerating to attack speed and though he was relatively inexperienced at rotor birds he knew how to inflict most harm. Searching the instrument panel, he caught sight of the needed switches, armed two Hellfire missiles, and charged ahead at fifty feet above the ground. At one hundred yards out, he flicked two switches releasing his payload at subsonic speed towards the inbound truck. Both missiles plunged into the target, while the unsuspecting soldiers were incinerated instantaneously.

Bannister watched from further up the road unable to act without a ground to air missile at his disposal. His face showed his displeasure and insurmountable anger as he looked among his few remaining men standing next to him. No one dared to speak instead watched on as their comrades burnt and the black smoke bellowed into the air above the town.

Back behind the burning wreck, Bennett had banked the helicopter around slapping it down hard against the road that near stripped the skids out from under it. Within a few seconds, it had bounced violently to a stop and Stella was already pulling the rear door open. He looked back into the terrified eyes of the Namibian boy as she hoisted him up into the back seat. The frightening look in his eyes said it all, he had never flown before.

Bennett powered the helicopter up and it shook as they rose.

The radio squawked in a broken crackle, "Bennett, don't think you can escape me. I will find you and when I do…"

Bennett silenced the transmission cutting the irate Logan Bannister off mid-sentence. He punched the nose over and they accelerated to top speed toward the mountains west of Otavi and away from the lifeless town.

CHAPTER 70

MATHEUS

Otavi Mountains
September 13th

Tangeni sat paralysed with fear as Stella did her best to comfort and reassure him while the brutal attack helicopter charged westward at a frightening speed. Just below at what seemed an arm's length, the tree tops raced past as a blur in the semi darkness of dusk and to the young Namibian boy they grew almost hypnotising.

His virgin flight on-board an aggressively loud military helicopter had developed into something much more terrifying for the boy's debut in the air. With each violent shudder of the sleek airframe from the gusting winds spiralling down off the mountains, Tangeni's trembling intensified and his fingers dug deeper into Stella's arms.

Up front, Bennett scoured the forward terrain and the approaching rugged ridgeline that grew darker and more treacherous the closer they entered the sunset shadow of the mountains. A familiar voice broke the silence inside his helmet as Stella announced what he was hoping for. He turned to look over his shoulder at Tangeni perched on her lap in the rear seat. He looked terrified yet somehow he'd found the courage to look further than just at the mesmerising tree tops. At the same time he had raised his trembling hand and was pointing towards a long steep cliff face directly in front of them.

"He's saying down there is Matheus's cave, close to where he is pointing," Stella called over the helmet comm set.

Bennett found the best flat site he could amongst the rocky outcrops and shrubs lining the base of the ridgeline from where they would trek uphill to the caves. The landing was nothing short of atrocious with Bennett firstly hitting the ground too quickly from the wind gusts and then bouncing ten feet sideways into a clump of bushes that buckled the left missile launcher. It hadn't been his finest flying but he'd grounded them safely and that he always thought was a success.

The dark of night crept up fast once they began scaling a narrow rocky track up the mountainside. The air had turned bitterly cold and an eerie feeling of isolation swamped them the higher they ventured. The climb was not demanding however, Stella was showing fatigue missing a few steps and slipping on loose stones into Bennett's outstretched arms.

He had seen her fumbling and caught her mid fall while up ahead Tangeni suddenly stopped in an agitated state.

"Mister, I am too close, it is not safe for the unmarked to walk into the cave of Matheus. You must enter without me."

"Why?" Stella asked as she regained her balance pushing herself away from Bennett and trying to ignore the embarrassment.

"Some men in my town say Matheus is a demon. There is a myth he is the one who released the Blue Death from these caves that killed his village and his own family. Some say he later died and became the spirit guardian of these mountains," Tangeni said while edging back down the track.

"Do you believe it?" Bennett asked.

"No. One day when I was eight, I came up here hunting for wild pigeon eggs. I fell off a rock ledge breaking my leg and I couldn't move. Then this man in a black robe rescued me and carried me home to my village. He left me outside the doctor's house and vanished back into the mountains. He told me his name was Matheus. He too wore the same strange blue tattoo on his neck like you and it was him who told me I must never go into the caves."

"Why not, did he say why?" Stella asked.

"There are blue crystals in the caves that kill anyone who goes near them, he called it the Blue Death."

Bennett quickly interjected, "Did he say why he didn't die?"

"Yes, he said he had been chosen."

"Chosen… chosen by who?" was Bennett's response.

"I don't know, he didn't say but I think it is the mountain spirits. My father always told me that bad spirits live in the mountains, spirits of men who lived here in ancient times. He said they were not men of this world," Tangeni replied.

"Not men of this world, what did he mean by that?" Stella asked.

"I do not know. I must leave now, Matheus waits for you," Tangeni said as he turned and fled downhill towards the landing site.

The ground had flattened out at the base of a sheer vertical cliff face that dwarfed their presence amongst the low scrub growing sporadically in the rock infested plateau. It was only ten feet at its widest point, but it was the rock face they were drawn to and though light was scarce, they could see it was pitted with small caves like holes in Swiss cheese.

Directly in front of where they stood the largest of the caves rose up to twenty feet above them and wide enough for a small car to drive through. They had no idea what to expect and cautiously entered one slow step at a time.

Bennett snapped the first of two light sticks he'd found in the helicopter and the cave burst into view under a haze of green light that glistened off the moist muddy walls. Deeper into the depths, the walls converged tightly to a narrow gap behind which a shimmer of blue light clawed its way out. They stood staring almost hypnotised by the welcoming tranquillity of each quivering light pulse yet both could feel the cold presence of death somewhere close by.

The noise of heavy breathing caught their attention as a tall dark figure emerged through the blue light towards them. A few quick steps backwards and Bennett lifted the light stick high to cast light over the approaching figure, its reflection revealing a dark skinned man dressed in a black ankle length robe, just as Tangeni had described Matheus. His face was gaunt with high pronounced cheek bones like many Africans but it was his eyes that reached out to Bennett's curiosity. The whites offered a strange pale blue tinge whereas the iridescent blue glow of his irises was not normal for any man, he thought.

Bennett watched and held his ground as the man continued to advance slowly towards them while Stella stepped further away not sure of the situation and feeling something overwhelming her since catching sight of the blue light. The man stopped just short of arm's length of Bennett and uttered his first words in surprisingly good English, "My name is Matheus. I have been waiting for you to come Jon Bennett."

Bennett was bewildered just as he was in the Ghanza province when Tabu spoke his name. This was becoming too coincidental, he thought, as he looked the man in the eye and acknowledged, "Yes I am Jon Bennett, how is it you knew I was coming?"

Matheus was tall at over 190 centimetres and this heightened presence gave a god like feel to the meeting. Stella had returned to Bennett's side now more curious of the man's unique appearance than thinking of her own safety.

Outside a storm was fast approaching, a storm of a different kind, one violent and merciless.

"Jon Bennett you are in danger. You possess the Thirteenth Code and they want it."

A confused Bennett looked across at Stella and back again at Matheus, "We don't understand any of this, what does it all mean?"

"Please sit, you must understand many things," Matheus said as he lowered himself down onto the hardened cave floor encouraging the others to follow.

With his legs crossed, Matheus fixed his attention on Bennett's eyes and face as if exploring his sole and commenced what Bennett hoped was the answers he sought.

"When I was a boy, it was customary for the older boys to display great courage to become village men but it was hardest for me as the son of the village Chief. One day in late summer, I had my chance to show my father I was the bravest of all his ten sons. I decided to enter the forbidden caves of these mountains like the one we are in now. It was legend that any man who entered the caves would never return but I had no belief in these stories. I never listened to the old men in my village, they were always trying to scare me and so I set out to prove them all wrong."

Matheus stopped and a tear rolled from his eye, "I have never told anyone of this. I have lived alone since my family and village all perished that day. I walked into the caves with my younger brother and there I found the shining blue crystals in the walls. Just like the ones you see behind me."

He pointed behind him through the gap and a hundred or more small blue crystals embedded in the cave wall became the focus of Bennett's attention. Each shone brightly and shimmered under the reflection of the others around it.

Matheus continued, "I took one, it was to be my passage to manhood and respect in my father's eyes. Instead it brought death to my young brother with no warning, his blood flowed from his body like a river and his skin turned blue."

He stopped momentarily before adding, "This was the start, the evil spirits had been released so I thought."

He continued while the others sat and listened, "I returned to my village with the crystal in my pocket, and they all died, my mother, my father and everyone I ever knew all dead. All but me. I was spared not knowing what I carried. I ran like the cheetah for days and never once did I look back."

"Then a few days later, the dreams started and it was then I knew my fate. I had become an Oracle of the Sphere, chosen by the Ancients. You my friend have been chosen like me, I can feel it in your aura."

Bennett had experienced dreams since the encounter with Tabu but mentioned nothing of it to Stella, they were more confusing than revealing. Visions of mass bloodshed with nothing clearly identifiable.

Bennett spoke "We met a blind man named Tabu in the Ghanza province who spoke of a spirit sending us to you to explain these marks." He turned his head so Matheus could see the mark on his neck. Stella did the same, pulling what was left of her hair to the side from under the bandage still wrapped firmly around her head. Her bullet wound was still excruciating but it was her hands that bothered her most except for when close to Bennett. She neglected to enlighten Bennett but each time she moved to within a few feet of him, her pain subsided and she felt a surge of strength rush throughout her body. But now as she sat in the cave under the halo of blue light she could feel something sinister clutching at her and forcing subliminal claws into her brain as if searching for complete control. She nervously twitched in response catching Bennett's attention and he pulled her closer as a gesture of support. In that very moment of his touch, all feeling of evil dissolved replaced with a weird tingling sensation bordering on numbness all over.

Matheus looked closely towards her and then back at Bennett.

"You hold a mighty power inside you, one that was given to you many years ago but only now does it come alive."

"What is your purpose?" Bennett asked.

"I am the Oracle of the Fourth Code. Let me explain something. Three thousand years ago, an old man walked this Earth giving hope to those around him and faith to many in their dreams. His only companions were thirteen followers and a silver metallic ball, a sphere that held enormous power. It was a gift handed down to him by his elders, men of a higher order believed to possess superior powers themselves."

He went on to explain the old man presented the Sphere to an Ancient Egyptian Pharaoh on the promise of undefeatable power. In return, the pharaoh granted him and his thirteen followers passage to live freely among the Egyptian lands as Noblemen. Engineers of that ancient era failed to interpret or understand the diagrams and meanings of the Sphere's light display and from there failed to harness its power.

"Soon after this, the old man and his followers were hunted and imprisoned. Two days later, they all perished at the hands of the Executioner's axe on orders from the Pharaoh himself. Then one day, the great Gods descended from the clouds and cast war down on the Pharaoh. A war of gargantuan power and destruction erupted across the lands and within days all the Pharaoh's soldiers had been annihilated. The same Gods remained thereafter in power, and the people worshipped them relentlessly."

Matheus paused for a brief moment.

"The old man and his thirteen followers still exist. Their spirits live in the thirteen Oracles that walk among us and it was in my dreams that I ascended to the fourth."

Bennett spoke, "We have been told the Sphere contains thirteen advanced technologies and needs a sequence of thirteen symbols to release each one. Is this true?"

"Yes it is, buried inside there are instructions to thirteen powerful technologies, some good, and some evil. Unleashing them does require a thirteen symbol code that only the Oracles and one other can reveal," Matheus replied.

"One other, who is that?" Stella asked.

"His name is Jeremiah, he was the Sphere's Architect but he died many thousands of years ago before revealing the codes."

"How can he reveal the codes when he is long dead?" Bennett asked.

"Just like the Oracles, his spirit lives on," Matheus replied.

He reached out and placed his hand on the bare skin of Bennett's arm. Just like Tabu's touch, Bennett felt something pass through him, a spirit of sorts, he thought.

"The blue crystals are what started all this, they are lethal to all people except the Oracles. Only in the presence of the crystal can an Oracle be triggered and with it the knowledge of their own code comes forth in their dreams. *The Trust* know this, they take villagers from everywhere, their goal to expose Oracles and the codes. Now, hundreds of my people are murdered every day."

Stella broke in after realising what was happening at the facility, "Jon, that's it, that's what's happening at the facility, *The Trust* and the Soviets are experimenting on the villagers, exposing them to the blue death just hoping they get lucky. We have to stop them before thousands more die."

"But why did we not die on exposure to the crystal at the facility?" Bennett asked Matheus.

"You are an Oracle like me and exposure to the crystals does not harm us. Your aura is strong, but it is what lies under your skin I fear the most."

"But then why am I alive, am I an Oracle too?" a confused Stella asked.

"I do not know why you live, you have not been chosen but there is something in your aura I find unexplainable. It is like you are part of him," Matheus said as he pointed towards Bennett.

"We learnt of rumours that the Thirteenth Code releases plans to build a weapon of ultimate power that would give *The Trust* complete world domination and if used enough times could signal the end of humanity. Do you know of this?" Bennett asked.

"The Earth or *Gaia* as we know her is already dying, people pollute the air and water, they destroy her food, each day less people respect her life and greed brings on quickly the end of days. The Thirteenth Code allows the construction of a pulse weapon of colossal strength and when used will inject death into *Gaia's* core. Each strike of that massive energy pulse will vibrate deeper into her heart and inject the Blue Death deep within her veins."

Matheus abruptly stopped talking while at the same time, Bennett felt the sleek projectile split the air past his face just before it slammed into the rear cave wall and shattered the silence.

In the brief second of impact, Bennett screamed, "Get down."

A bright light smothered the darkness and they slumped unconscious to the rocky floor. The stun grenade had been effective in close confines allowing Bannister and his men to take their prisoners without the need to fire a single shot.

CHAPTER 71

TRAP

Matheus's Cave, Otavi Mountains
September 13th

Illuminated under the beaming light of powerful torches and protected by a dark green biohazard suit, Bannister nervously entered the cave. His plan had been to flush Matheus out into the open using Bennett except now he was suffering the anxiety of knowing the blue death radiation was crawling all over his suit. One small tear in the toughened fabric and he knew it was over.

On the cave floor at his feet, Bennett and Stella sat with their hands restrained to the rear. The stun grenade had given his men time to awkwardly storm the cave, burdened by their heavy suits and secure all three.

"Arh Jon, you are awake. I am sorry for this intrusion but we really needed Matheus unharmed, his survival is too important to the plan," Bannister announced as he walked over close enough for Bennett to see him smirking behind the clear visor of the helmet.

"What plan and why is Matheus so important?" Bennett immediately snapped back.

"Oh Jon you know very little don't you? Must be hard for you not knowing what's going on. Matheus carries the Fourth Code that will give us cloaking technologies. Imagine our armies and machines invisible in the attack, the enemy unsuspecting will surely be defeated."

Bannister walked across to the far side of the cave where Matheus knelt while behind him two of Bannister's men raised their weapons ready to inflict compliance to the back of his head.

The mercenary leader stopped and reaching down with his non-gun hand ripped open Matheus's shirt to expose the man's bare chest.

His skin was dark as expected for a Namibian man but in the semi darkness of the cave that night, the iridescent blue symbols became strikingly apparent as a series of thirteen strange but distinct shapes appeared across his chest. Bannister stood back and looked over at Bennett, "Jon you led us to Matheus and the code you see before you, thankyou. As much as I would love to kill you right now, *The Trust* wants you alive and I'm betting it's not just about that codebook anymore. Your immunity to the blue death is intriguing, how is this possible?"

Bennett made no reply.

Bannister disappeared out the cave entrance for a brief moment before returning with Tangeni in tow under a tight grip on his arm.

"Let him go Bannister, he has nothing to do with any of this," Bennett yelled while at the same time trying to snap the ties around his hands.

"Tell me how you are immune to the effects of the blue crystal?"

"I don't know and that is the truth," Bennett replied.

"Sorry if I don't believe you," Bannister said as he gave the kid one hard shove in the back towards the rear of the cave.

Stella screamed in disbelief and horror at realising Bannister's intentions.

Bennett pulled harder at his bound hands, his anger lusting to rip Bannister's heart out right there and then.

Tangeni collapsed to the cave floor as blood surged from his eyes, nose and mouth. Paralysis snapped his leg bones and he gasped for air while his body shook in one violent spasm. Death came quickly for the Namibian boy and all the while he was shrouded in the blue light emanating through the gap in the cave wall.

"Now now John, don't struggle, surely a man of your experience knew the kid was destined to die, he served his purpose, his job finished when he showed you the right cave to find Matheus. It's amazing, there are thousands of caves here we just didn't know where to find him," Bannister declared.

Stella had broken into tears while Bennett just glared hatred towards their captor and yet he was trying hard to find an escape strategy. Nothing was coming to mind.

Matheus spoke but it was a deep growling voice that broke through, a sound rising up from deep inside his body, "You are weak and cowards, the Ancients are returning and they will destroy you all."

Bannister responded, "Matheus your spirit speaks but this Ancients talk is all bullshit so shut the fuck up." He drove the butt of his handgun hard into the side of the Namibian's head and with a loud thud Matheus collapsed to the cave floor.

"Take him away," he called to one of his men before turning back to Bennett and declaring, "Now Jon I have no more use for you or Miss Van Horne."

Bennett continued to struggle against the zip ties as one of Bannister's men stepped forward with a syringe in hand and small bottle of yellow liquid in the other. He filled the syringe with the liquid and injected Stella in the arm. Her body went limp and she slumped forward to the dirt floor.

Bennett powerless to stop it, yelled at Bannister, "I will hunt you down and inflict the slowest painful death you could ever imagine you fuck."

"Oh Jon I am very sorry, I don't think that chance will ever come."

A sharp needle prick in his neck was all he felt as his body collapsed to join Stella.

Bannister walked outside the cave removed his suit and made a phone call, "Sir, we have the package. I would expect arrival time at Kehlstein 1100 hours tomorrow." He listened to a series of instructions from the man on the other end, the plan had been carefully coordinated to reveal the codes.

Further off in the darkness of the mountainside, a pair of bloodshot eyes narrowed in anger as he watched Bannister's men drag Bennett's unconscious body down the track towards the helicopter. The two other prisoners were of no concern to him, it was Bennett he needed to protect and right now that wasn't happening.

CHAPTER 72

MEREDITH LOST

Washington DC
September 14th

The Secretary of Defence was not a man to piss off. He had been in politics his entire adult life and he knew how to pull the right chains in Washington DC. Many in the US Administration believed he controlled and manipulated the President and certainly was not a man to trust under any circumstances.

"You fucking what, what do you mean, you lost Meredith!" he screamed at the Chief Engineer of the Titan Project. "And where the fuck is Anders?" came blurting out immediately afterwards riding the spit of his rage.

The Chief Engineer was starting to feel the enormous pressure of the situation. Six hours earlier, all was operating as normal at the Command Centre deep inside Cheyanne Mountain. Meredith was floating in orbit in a deactivated state with the next series of tests not due for two weeks. The fifty plus staff at the centre went about their everyday tasks not noticing General Anders had failed to show for work or in the case of some just thinking he was running late probably caught up in the morning traffic. It was unusual because Anders never missed a day, even on his days off he would often just show up unannounced, an extreme workaholic many would say.

It wasn't until 8.15am when an amber warning light flashed on the control panel that the General was suddenly missed. Meredith had gone hot.

Her laser was preparing to fire and the staff failed to understand why. They scrambled for their respective places behind consoles and monitors, all thinking the same thing, it was impossible. Their killer satellite could only receive instructions from the Command Centre using the one encrypted keypad that the Chief Engineer frantically punished with his fingers tapping the shutdown sequence of digits and letters.

She continued unfolding her tentacles in readiness to extend the canon.

The engineer entered the code again and then when that failed he activated the emergency kill switch. Immediately it took effect and the arming sequence terminated. Within a few more seconds Meredith's electronics shut down rendering her motionless and she floated through orbit like the other hundred or so neighbouring satellites crisscrossing the sky that day. It also meant she could no longer be reactivated remotely.

All across the room, sighs of relief were heard while the Chief Engineer commenced a series of diagnostic commands to identify the problem, feeling confident a glitch in the software would be the reason.

"Sir, Meredith's gone."

The engineer looked towards his head technician and then up at the oversized wall screen where it was obvious, Meredith had vanished from their scope. Their other satellites were still visible following their usual orbital flight paths except the killer satellite had disappeared. This was impossible, he thought. Only one encrypted keyboard existed, one programmed with a unique software code impossible to duplicate without the insertion of a key card secured inside the President's personal safe. It had been designed that way in the event of theft, the software would unleash a virus rendering the keyboard a wasted piece of junk.

Now feeling every mouthful of abuse coming at him from the Secretary of Defence, the Chief Engineer had no answers to explain the disappearance of the Government's most secret weapon. Meredith had been originally designed to target and destroy inbound nuclear missiles high above American soil and was purely developed for the Nation's defence and not as an attack mechanism. Political pressure from abroad mostly the Soviet Union ended its completion and it was shelved.

Then some years later, a few extraordinary scientists developed a directed energy pulse weapon with sufficient ground destructive force for use in wartime against small to medium sized targets. It didn't take long before the 'Titan Project' took the lead and Meredith became the subject of top secret testing hidden from the world and destined for strategic lethal attacks on the enemies of the United States.

"Sir, General Anders didn't show for work today and no one has heard from him. He didn't answer his cell phone and he is not at home. His wife reports he left for work this morning as usual from their Colorado Springs home," replied the Chief Engineer.

The Secretary of Defence with his suspicions aroused lifted his desk phone and dialled a number, "Titan is on the loose, I need the team assembled within an hour." He turned back to the Chief Engineer and commanded, "Do not forget the contract you signed, you are not to mention any of this to anyone outside the Titan Project, now get back to the Mountain and find our girl."

"Sir what about Anders?" asked the Engineer as he turned to leave.

"Not your worry, you're in charge of Titan now. Just find the satellite before it's too late and leave Anders to me," replied the Secretary of Defence.

At around the same time in Southern Germany, George Anders guided Meredith to her new home inside the orbit garage, a purpose built docking unit designed by the Soviets to repair damaged satellites . The unit had room for two cosmonauts and sufficient resources to last several months at a time. This would be her home until the new weapon was fully assembled and ready for testing.

With the software source code changed, Anders had complete and sole control of his girl. A week earlier he had shut all her defensive mechanisms down without triggering any alerts in the control room so that the physical circuitry changes could be made in orbit. He had falsified documents approving maintenance to Meredith that on the outside looked like any other communication satellite in orbit. To the US astronauts making the changes, it was a sophisticated spy device needed for the security of their country and they needed no further explanation.

Once activated Meredith was no longer like her docile floating neighbours, she transformed into a lethal life sucking bitch, displaying aggression in all directions, opening up into a spider with 40 foot canons ready to destroy anything coming too close. Her soul was death and nothing could stand in her way once fully operational.

Executing the required command disabled the existing software and the control shifted from Cheyenne Mountain to Anders.

CHAPTER 73

TORTURE

Kehlstein Facility, Southern Germany
September 14th

The prisoner sat chained, his life lingering on the edge of total demise. A small cramped cell was all he had as his home for longer than he could remember and still they tortured him for what they needed. Each time he gave them nothing, the Eighth Code providing him the strength to conceal it from their invasive mind techniques and each time he prayed the Monk would save him before his next torture.

He could not recite the codes, it had been too long in solitude. His mind was once that of a normal man but since imprisonment his mind and soul were transforming into something he was yet to determine though he was sure it wasn't human.

Unlike all the previous torture sessions, this one lacked sadism, something had happened, *The Trust's* henchmen were behaving smugly as though they had gained the high position of their enemy. Matheus had been captured and *The Trust* now had leverage over the prisoner they thought.

He felt the thick steel chains tighten around his arms and legs just before his body was yanked rearwards into the once electric chair as it had been done many times before. He felt the probes insert into the base of his neck and the signal start its initiating bone vibrating drone through his head.

He only had to wait a few minutes before the questioning commenced usually focussed on codes, scriptures and deciphering the great Sphere but not this time. It was about a man by the name of Jon Bennett.

The electric pulse ripped through his old body and the agonising pain rose up from deep inside his weakened muscles.

A short balding man wearing spectacles making his eyes appear bug like walked over to the prisoner, "We have the Fourth Code old man, and Matheus is dead."

The prisoner made no comment just stared at the excuse of a man standing only a few feet from him.

"Oh and we have another prisoner now too, Jon Bennett."

The prisoner still made no response.

"Now old man we would like to know why Bennett does not die from the Blue Death when he shows no sign of the markings on his chest?"

The prisoner failed to answer and another crippling electric pulse was released through his body.

"A woman with him also does not die and neither of them bears the thirteen symbols. Why old man?" the interrogator asked.

The prisoner maintained his composure and defiantly refused to answer, that only frustrated the balding man further. Though he remained silent, the prisoner knew why Bennett survived because it had been his doing in the first place.

CHAPTER 74

KEHLSTEIN

Southern Germany
September 14th

"Miss Van Horne what is your involvement with Jon Bennett?" came a stern voice over the intercom.

Stella had been held captive strapped on her back to a flat steel bench for days she felt. Her view revealed a stark white ceiling in a sterile room somewhere she did not recognise. Every now and then, a man in a white biohazard suit entered the room, gave her an injection and then withdrew three vials of blood from her arm. Then he'd leave and the room would go quiet again, no sounds of any kind until now.

She tried to open her mouth to answer but no speech came out, something uncontrollable clawed its way through her body and she started panicking. "Wh... where am I? What do you want?" she managed to splutter while her throat burnt from the strangling dryness.

"Miss Van Horne, I assure you are safe for now but if you don't answer my questions then I cannot guarantee your safety. Now tell me, what is your business with Jon Bennett?"

"Who are you?" she asked.

"My name is of no importance to you. What you should know is that I represent *The Trust* and right now, you will answer my questions. If you do not, then my orders are to kill you," he answered knowing the drug in her body would release the truth and her death was without negotiation.

She could sense from his heavy accent, her interrogator was German but well educated in the use of the English language.

"Now answer the question, what is your business with Jon Bennett?" he growled displaying his sudden anger at her hesitance.

"I am a freelance reporter covering a story on Bennett since his retirement from the CIA," she lied.

"Miss Van Horne do not lie to me, I know more than you think, you have been researching him for the past two years. On top of that we know you have been inquiring about *The Trust* and the Sphere of Anubis so it's time to start telling me the truth."

"I am telling you the truth, I researched Jon Bennett because of the story I'm doing on him, I don't know what or who *The Trust* is or the Sphere of Anubis. That is the truth. Where is Bennett?"

"Miss Van Horne, it is not your concern where Mr Bennett is, your story on him is finished. Where is the code book?"

"I do not know what you are talking about," she responded as the clouded confused feeling in her head intensified.

In the previous few minutes she felt the onslaught of a strange warm sensation pass through her body and her mind loosen as the drug took hold. She tried hard to fight the feeling of violation as if someone or something had just rammed down the front door to her conscious mind. It was then she realised what it meant to have voices inside her head, she found herself having no control over the second entity interrogating her thoughts.

"The code book is in Australia, in Sydney in a house somewhere in western Sydney, Jon hid it but didn't tell me much," she said not even realising she had confessed it.

"Excellent Miss Van Horne you are doing well, can you describe whereabouts in Sydney the code book is hidden?"

"A house in Blacktown, the home of an Arabic family with the name Faheem. I cannot remember anything else," she added.

The electrodes attached to her head led to a computer behind her on a bench. A technician sitting next to the interrogator looked at his monitor, "Sir, she is telling the truth and it is true she has no more information on that subject." They had spent millions of Euro designing and redesigning a mind manipulation device capable of extracting the truth from any subject. Only one failed to respond and he was their old prisoner in the bowels of the facility.

Suddenly the thunderous boom of the door imploding deafened the room followed by a barrage of automatic gunfire extinguishing the lights. Stella felt the straps snap like cotton and her body savagely dragged from the bench. She fought but it was futile, whoever had her was vastly too strong and in a hurry.

Back inside the control room, the Six member was furious yelling at all those around him. On the surveillance monitor playback they watched the happenings until the room was cast into darkness.

One of the technicians watching the video mumbled, "She is as good as dead now."

CHAPTER 75

PRISONER

Kehlstein facility, Level 16
September 14th

Bennett laid motionless in a tiny cell somewhere near the depths of the facility. He had a vague recollection of his arrival accompanied by the echoing pain of a throbbing headache. He recalled Matheus's cave and the ambush by Bannister, the violent death inflicted on the defenceless Namibian boy and the injections he and Stella received. The injection had knocked him into a heavy dreamtime, a chance to meet something or someone he wasn't quite sure about but it was powerful and with it he had his direction confirmed. He now clearly understood his purpose and what was coming. His vision was of peace but first the evil had to be terminated otherwise billions would die.

A hard bed held his weary body and as his eyes adjusted, he could see nothing but pitch black in every direction. An occasional dry cough was the only indication he was not alone. He tried to move, his legs still paralysed from the chemical injection that had swarmed his nervous system blocking every impulse from the brain to the large muscles.

Not far away in the dark, the cough transformed into an old man's scratchy voice, "Who are you?"

Bennett answered cautiously, "A prisoner perhaps like you, how long have you been here and where is here?"

"You are at Kehlstein in the south of Germany, it's a research facility for *The Trust* and I really have no idea how long I've been here, last count was ten years but that was many years ago."

Bennett had managed to sit up interested in why *The Trust* had a man imprisoned for so long and wondering what made him so important.

"What do they want with you?" he asked the old man.

"I know many things, I know what they want but their torture is futile."

"Who are you?"

"My name is Heimdall, I think! It has been a long time since I had clear memories or thoughts. The drugs they inject have messed with my brain and now I cannot remember much before I came here."

"What is it you know old man?" Bennett asked.

The old man became suspicious thinking Bennett was a spy planted in the cell to extract what *The Trust* wanted and went silent as the cell lights activated. Bennett's eyes found it difficult to adjust and he looked at the ground to speed up the process. To his right a large steel door opened. To his left he saw three cells with steel bars, one where an old grey haired man sat staring at him, the darkened voice had a face and a wild look in his eyes that bordered on insane.

The man's skin was almost translucent from the endless darkness of the cell and he appeared strangely alien at a quick glance. The steel door to his right had fully opened and three armed men were fast approaching his cell.

"On your feet Bennett, time to go, you've got some questions to answer," the lead man announced as he opened the cell door. At the same time, one of the others fired a small dart into his chest and his body went loose.

The old man knew the drill, it was everyday life in the first few weeks at Kehlstein. In his years, many prisoners had come and gone, but this one was different in some odd way that he couldn't understand. Deep in his subconscious, a long lost memory was racing to the surface like air bubbles from the depths of the ocean.

CHAPTER 76

REUNION

Kehlstein, Interrogation Room
September 14th

The guards dragged Bennett's limp body across the polished white tiles to the only chair in the room, a sturdy grey metal seat resembling something more commonly found in a fighter jet. As they let go, his legs buckled and he fell backwards into the chair where they strapped his arms tightly to the side rests.

The sudden jolt of his back slamming against the chair's rigid frame woke his senses enough to take in his surroundings. The room was large and mostly empty. Along one side a mirror covered the wall from floor to ceiling and Bennett knew his captors scrutinised him from behind its two way design.

Within the next minute, he felt a searing pain penetrate the rear of his neck, a hot prick as the probe found its mark and a tingling sensation rushed down his arms.

The room faded to pitch black like the cellblock, before a small bright light ignited across his field of vision and the silhouetted shape of a largely built man appeared, walking slowly towards him. He focussed the best he could from behind an increasing pain in the back of his eyes that intensified with the onset of the chemical injection.

The dark figure stopped, he was close enough for Bennett to rip his throat out but the restraints held his arms tight. The man stood gazing at him for a few seconds, his dark expensive suit giving the impression he was a man of significant power.

The CEO of the Deutsche United Bank, Herman Schwartz spoke in a demanding deep voice weighted by an aggressive German accent. His forceful mannerisms were indicative of his self-convinced notion to carry on with the Fuhrer's vision. The continuance of the Third Reich now the Fourth represented everything to him and he would do whatever it took to see it reach world domination. He stepped closer to Bennett, he was accustomed to fearing no man, always able to hide behind a conglomerate of private armies and around him Kehlstein had become his castle.

"Mr Bennett we finally have you imprisoned at Kehlstein, this is truly astonishing after what I've heard about you."

Bennett forced his vocals, "Who the fuck are you?"

"Argh the ever defiant Jon Bennett, well it's time for that to change. That hot spike you felt in your neck is already transforming your mind. Oh, I do apologise for my rudeness. My name is Herman Schwartz, I represent *The Trust*. My colleagues and I have some questions we need answered so you best comply."

"What have you done with Van Horne?"

"Yes, Miss Van Horne, well we had no use for her anymore, she is dead."

Rage commenced an upward spiral through his body, an extreme haemorrhage of emotion from deep inside that he struggled to control. He bent and twisted to break loose of the straps and besiege the suited Nazi standing before him.

"I will kill you…," he screamed as the invading probe fired up its initialisation process and released the first round of brain triggering impulses. He struggled veraciously to control the incursion while something unbeknown to him and buried deep inside his left kidney activated to take up the fight.

"Now Jon, tell us exactly where you hid the Codebook in Sydney? Miss Van Horne was most forthcoming before her agonising death."

Bennett howled like a wounded animal, "I will tell you nothing, now free me and I will make your death painless." The electrode in his neck went searing hot as a series of pulsating currents shot up through his spinal cord sending signals deep into his brain and he started to lose grip of his mind. He wanted to release the sacred information, the Codebook's exact location but it was a tug-o-war between reality and what he surmised was illusion.

"Tell us where the codes are?" Schwartz yelled into his face.

Bennett refused to answer and instead focused all his strength on taking back his mind control. Somewhere behind him, a door opened and he heard the chink of chains growing louder towards him.

Schwartz stood boldly in front where they both stared at each other for a brief moment. He was approaching eighty years of age yet his appearance gave the impression he wasn't a day over fifty. His skin was womanly smooth, unwrinkled, and well-tanned for a German while his size was indicative of an ex-athlete, superbly toned and tall. Something was not right about his appearance, something was out of place, Bennett thought, as Schwartz lent in closer.

He stopped a few inches from Bennett's face, where his presence and foul cologne only tormented the restrained prisoner.

"Jon I have some encouragement for you, I think you'll see things our way."

Two guards dressed in black came into Bennett's field of view and between them they dragged the same old man he'd seen in the cells. The man looked old carrying the many scars of torture across his semi naked body while the leg chains added to the mosaic of a slave entombed to a life of misery.

"Jon tell me where the codes are and the old man lives."

Bennett laughed, "Why would it matter if this old man dies?"

"You do not recognise him? I am shocked you don't. Then allow me to reintroduce you to your father."

Bennett had suffered at the hands of various mind control tricks during his field campaigns in the Soviet Union but this was different. He wrestled hard to search for stability but the image was there in front of him, an old damaged man in chains, a man he did not recognise but yet he could feel some unusual connection.

"This is not my father, you stupid fucking Nazi. My father died thirty years ago. Is this really the best you can do?" Bennett said more confidently to throw off his tormentor.

The old prisoner hanging low and weak in the guard's arms looked up at Bennett now in full light of the overhead lamps, his memories stronger by the minute since sensing the device's activation. Bennett returned the quizzical gaze and still he failed to see anything in the man that reflected his father. The guards threw the old man to the floor and one kicked him savagely in the chest, a roar of pain bellowed out as he curled up tight into the foetal position of self-preservation. Another heavy boot slammed into the old man and he pleaded for it to stop.

Schwartz grabbed at the old man's head and twisted it around for Bennett to get a clear view. Dried blood was still caked across his face from the last torture session and fresh blood dribbled from the corner of his mouth.

"Do you want your father to die all for some old book?"

Bennett looked at the man and under the full light, partial recognition started to set in, yet he still wondered if it was a drug induced illusion.

"JoJo, if you want Sanctuary you must not reveal the location. Please forgive me my son," the old man mumbled and stared directly into Bennett's eyes.

No one had ever called him JoJo except his father and no one else knew of the nickname he'd been given as a young boy living in Australia. Then he peered deep into his eyes and behind all the blood and dirt, recognition engulfed him.

Rage boiled over, his core temperature swiftly rose and hundreds of microscopic artificial intelligent organisms extinguished the effects of the probe. The operator sitting at the monitor in the next room witnessed the dramatic spike in brain activity and nervously reached for the intercom button, "Sir we got a situation, his brain activity just went off the chart, you need to get out now so we can activate the gas."

Schwartz was a man of pride and ran from no one, his family was fourth generation Gestapo and he was proud of it. In the room, the guards had heard the intercom announcement and looked to each other for their next move, fight or flight.

The straps on Bennett's arms snapped as he flexed and wrenched himself free from the chair. Reaching behind he ripped the metal spike from his neck and he hurled his body towards the closest guard. With full brutal force, he drove the full length of the spike into the man's left eye skewering his brain. Death was immediate.

The other guard reacted too slow and lost his footing as Bennett's boot fractured three ribs. In pain and on his back, he scrambled for his holstered handgun trying desperately to remove it as Bennett leapt at him. Three shots echoed across the room and the guard rolled lifeless out of Bennett's clutch. In the swiftness of the attack, he had turned the guard's gun back on himself and squeezed the trigger.

Schwartz had hurried towards the exit leaving the old man crouched on the floor in the foetal position at the base of the chair. Unbeknown to Schwartz, Bennett had caught sight of him escaping and leapt over the second guard's dead body to intercept him.

"JoJo, he is one of the Six, he must be stopped," the old man called.

He reached the door in time to reap Schwartz by the arm and fling him back across the floor towards the chair. He was heavy set yet Bennett threw him like he was a small child. As he attempted to gain his balance he slipped on the blood covered tiles and cracked his head against the chair. Semi-dazed, he rolled himself over to face Bennett's approach.

Outside the room, an alarm screeched to an irritating drone and it signalled the impending arrival of more guards from other levels of the facility. Back inside, Bennett threw himself at Schwartz and with three driving punches to the man's face and head, ended any further likelihood of resistance.

"Who are the other five?" Bennett demanded while he slammed another bone crunching blow into the man's exposed face. His nose crushed and the cartilage shattered from which a new torrent of blood flooded his finely tailored Armani. All the while, he held firm and defiant, not saying a word except to scream, "Release the gas."

"You will not get anything from me, *The Trust* is too powerful," Schwartz managed to expel through his bloodied mouth and pushed himself up to half lean against the chair.

Bennett grabbed a handgun from one of the dead guards and pointed it at Schwartz's face, "Tell me the names of the other five?"

The Nazi remained silent boldly looking into Bennett's eyes and he knew Schwartz was a man who would never talk no matter how crippling the threat or torture would be. He wasted no more time and pulled the trigger twice as the hollow point bullets rescinded the Sixth's life. Six became Five.

He took a brief moment to search the dead men's pockets before helping the old man towards the same door where Schwartz previously attempted his escape. He raised his gun and fired four rounds through the locking mechanism and kicked it open. He could feel his body had tripled in strength and his mind was more powerful, but he had no time to query the reason why or the unusual feeling of some supernatural possession. His father's survival was unexplainable and yet there was no time to digest that either.

He pushed his way through the door into a brightly lit room now mostly evacuated. Monitors and computers lined each wall, some security surveillance, and others analysing data. In the corner, a small man dressed in a white lab coat stood shaking at the sight of Bennett now empowered on the Eighth Code and brandishing a Beretta. This was not in their contingency plan and he froze watching Bennett walk towards him aiming the weapon's muzzle directly at his forehead. He was a computer technician and lacked any tactical skills against Bennett.

"You are going to show us how to get out," Bennett demanded and the technician responded without question upon seeing the ice cold scowl in his eyes.

The alarm was more deafening outside the control room as he shoved the technician along a narrow corridor with the gun pressed firmly into his back. To Bennett's astonishment, Viktor was gaining strength fast and keeping good stride as two guards bounded into sight from a side doorway. Both raised their rifles towards Bennett but hesitated when they sighted one of their technicians held hostage in their line of sight. Then like it was everyday business, Bennett drilled two rounds dead centre into their foreheads and they collapsed with a thud to the floor leaving the technician screaming from the muzzle blast so close to his ear.

A quick jab to the back of his head with the butt of his gun was all it took to regather the man's attention and continue directing the exit path along a maze of well-lit corridors. They had only walked a few more feet when another gunman appeared, this time quicker and more precise in his movements. Dressed in black from head to toe, he had Bennett covered from behind two handguns.

"I am not your enemy, but you are in danger if you go any further with this man. He leads you into a trap where ten of *The Trust's* men are waiting around the next corner," the man said revealing a deep French accent.

The technician seized the opportunity to break free of Bennett's grasp and run for his life. Five feet was all he gained when a single projectile pierced through his back obliterating his heart.

Bennett and Viktor stood watching as the Frenchman lowered his handgun from the target now collapsed dead against the wall and returned the stare. His eyes showed a hint of excitement when he looked Viktor up and down until Bennett spoke.

"Who are you?"

Something was familiar about the accent, Bennett thought.

"My name is Pierre Rousseau, I sound like someone you know, correct? I was the one who helped you in Washington. I am here to get you and your father out alive but we must hurry, *The Trust* has many armed men on these levels and the ones above."

A sudden flashback erupted from his subconscious, Stella was dead, was that true, he wondered. "Yes I remember you now. The girl I was with then was brought here with me, have you seen her?"

"No I have not, we cannot stay here, we must get going," responded Rousseau as he started to run back the way they had come and away from the sounds of men shouting above the rumble of boots.

Bennett knew they were outnumbered so any help was better than none. He and Viktor ran in pursuit while Rousseau shot out the surveillance cameras unaware of the dark and deadly figure waiting further down the corridor.

CHAPTER 77

SPARTAK

Kehlstein
September 14th

Bennett wishing he had night vision, advanced slowly along a wider corridor that led to one of about five elevators throughout the facility. They had entered a section of the structure that screamed abandonment by the dilapidated condition and clearly a recent gun fight from the bullet holes pit marked along the walls. The overhead lights hung lifeless from the ceiling yet all the way he was cloaked under an eerie orange ambience similar to emergency lighting. He scrutinised his every step, cautious and uncertain of what lay ahead.

Rousseau and Viktor had fallen back allowing Bennett with his added strength and agility from the Eighth Code to work reconnaissance. He knew someone or something lay in wait around the next corner he could sense its presence and he needed to neutralise the threat. Since escaping the control room he had felt changes take hold, all unexplainable but strangely comforting and charging. Above all the changes, it was his eye sight and hearing that were most heightened.

He moved slowly and silent.

The others continued along behind, not aware Bennett was about to encounter Spartak, a 145 kilogram Soviet soldier who had been destined to be *The Trust's* first ultimate warrior. His condition had deteriorated badly after the injection of a newly engineered Eighth Code microorganism specifically designed for advanced military behaviour that offered no fear or pain just superior combat skills, agility and strength. His highly decorated military record selected him as the prime candidate for the trial until his body reacted adversely to the tiny invaders and chaos prevailed.

Two weeks prior, he had broken his restraints, overpowered the guards and escaped into the lower extremities of the facility. There he savagely and mercilessly attacked any person taking the risk to venture into his lair. His agility and almost stealth capabilities made it impossible for the facility guards to capture him. They had spent days at war with the beast hunting its every move but not once did they show progress. His armoured skin was impenetrable and his swiftness had seen the death of ten men so far.

Now, Bennett was about to take this ultimate angry soldier head on.

He walked out into full view, weapon raised towards the dark shape ready to shoot at the slightest movement towards him. A heavy grunting noise was all he heard and the dark figure did not move, just motionless ten feet further along the corridor.

He kept his eyes focussed on the unknown, aware that back behind him Rousseau was moving slowly towards him leaving Viktor waiting. Once he was within ear shot he called softly to Bennett. "No sudden movements, this is Spartak, he will rip you apart. He is their first attempt at creating the ultimate warrior, didn't turn out the way they'd expected, poor bastard."

Bennett whispered back, "What do we do?"

"The elevator is just on the other side but we need to get past Spartak first, a little hint, bullets not real effective against his hardened skin. Human engineering at its most lethal I should add," Rousseau informed him and pulled back slowly towards Viktor.

Bennett raised his handgun towards Spartak hoping it would be some protection for when the creature decided to attack. That was the trigger, a threat perceived by the beast.

Spartak leapt with his arms outstretched and the swiftness caught Bennett off guard. He hadn't expected a man of such size to be so quick on his feet as his handgun was knocked to the floor. An arm like a baseball bat struck his shoulder sending him spiralling across the corridor and slamming against the opposite wall in a dazed state. Rousseau let loose with a full magazine of bullets, each smashing into the super soldier and only bouncing off the reengineered skin covering. It had taken *The Trust* a decade to develop, finally they had perfected the cellular alteration of the epidermis into an impervious exoskeleton capable of retarding fast moving projectiles and medium strength blast forces.

Rousseau knew this when he fired his weapon but he hoped it gave Bennett a fighting chance.

Spartak as expected threw his attention towards Rousseau giving Bennett the opportunity he needed and lifted himself from the floor. Another step and Bennett leapt onto the soldier's massive frame, gripping him hard around the throat, the animal had to breathe, he thought. With all his arm strength, he wrestled a choke hold around the huge neck until with one hand, the giant reached behind and threw Bennett from his back as if a rag doll. Rousseau had just enough time to weave and duck the human projectile of Bennett's body as it launched off Spartak's back and slammed again into the wall, this time knocking the wind from him.

Spartak pounced, grabbed Bennett and raised him above his head ready to spear drive his body head first into the hard tiled floor.

Rousseau anticipated this manoeuvre and crash tackled Spartak's lower legs buckling the big man backwards off his feet. Bennett slipped from his hands while at the same time using his falling body weight to drive his shoulder into the soldier's head impacting the floor, knocking him unconscious.

"He won't stay down for long, come on," Rousseau called as he pushed Viktor past and headed towards the elevator. Bennett somewhat stunned struggled to his feet as the big man showed signs of life with a slight shake of his head.

With all three inside the elevator it started ascending until an explosion somewhere above yanked it to a shaking halt just below level one. As the lighting extinguished and the soft emergency ambience kicked in, they found some stability sprawled against the walls. Small gunfire echoed in the distance while more explosions rocked the facility and shook the elevator. Thick smoke quickly filled the cubicle as a blast from a rocket grenade hit the elevator's motor housing obliterating it into pieces.

The elevator broke free and careered downwards three levels until a loose section of steel beam wedged it to a slow grinding halt. There the frame squealed under the load of those inside and the continual bombardment of metal debris falling from above.

Rousseau pointed to the ceiling and yelled, "We need to climb out through the hatch and climb up the shaft well."

Bennett agreed while Viktor only nodded his head, hoping he was strong enough to stay with them. With Rousseau leading the way, it took a few minutes to clear the hatch and edge across onto the emergency ladder. Somewhere above they could hear sporadic gunfire interspersed with the occasional flash of more detonations close to the shaft head. Jagged steel and concrete fell at their backs as they clambered up taking cautious steps on the steel rungs that in places had rusted completely through.

Bennett yelled to Rousseau, "Do you know what's happening up top?"

"It's my team, they had plans to attack if I didn't return."

They reached Level Two just as the doors started opening and their position on the ladder declared them as sitting ducks. A guard peered over the edge towards them as Rousseau tapped a round into his forehead and yanked his body downwards onto the crippled elevator pod. The sudden impact on the roof shook the pod free sending it on a rapid descent to its destruction seven levels below.

Another guard appeared with an AK47 spewing bullets in their direction, he was just aimlessly pointing over the edge and firing without looking. Bennett let loose with cross fire while at the same time Rousseau swung himself over the edge open firing at anything that slightly resembled a threat. Bennett was quick on his heels bagging two guards, one precise round through an eye with a second tap into his comrade four feet to his right. Rousseau in the same time had taken the remaining three men.

With the guards eliminated, Bennett helped his father up off the shaft ladder just as the motor house lost its battle with gravity and plummeted downwards smashing and scraping against the shaft walls. They held each other for the first time since the reunion and both felt the rush of emotion.

Rousseau interrupted the embrace, "We have to get going, two levels to the surface and we're clear."

They grabbed as many weapons and ammunition as they could carry and ran to the fire escape stairwell keeping watch for more guards or worse, Spartak.

Gunfire and the sporadic thump of grenades exploding filtered down from the direction they headed, clearly a war zone was soon to greet them. Another explosion blasted the level above causing the ceiling to shake and shatter in places with chunks of plaster falling into the stairwell. They reached the hot zone hidden behind a closed steel door marked Ground Level, the noise now deafening and the heat intensifying from a fire outside.

Bennett edged forward to open the door while Rousseau prepared to provide cover fire. The door was jammed and wouldn't budge. He tried to kick it open, nothing, he fired two rounds into the lock and still nothing released. It had been fused shut by the sheer heat of an earlier explosion.

"What now?" Bennett asked the Frenchman.

"We have to go back down and come up another stairwell," Rousseau replied moving quickly back down the way they'd come not looking back. Bennett pushed Viktor in the direction and they followed.

With Schwartz dead and Bannister still out in the field, leadership and control at the facility was severely missing. In the dark, Spartak had gained consciousness and his primary instinct was to acquire better weapons. A few minutes later inside the armoury, four guards died from broken necks as the super soldier found his choice of armament. His directive was simple, kill the enemy by any means possible.

240

CHAPTER 78

VOIGHT

Kehlstein
September 14th

Rousseau knew the facility's layout well, his preparation to rescue Viktor had been months in the preparation and when the Monk received word Bennett and Stella had been captured, it was an opportunity to rescue all three. After infiltrating the facility several weeks earlier, he had explored most of the underground fortress though he never located the Anubis Sphere.

He guided the other two towards the western exit under the emergency lighting of Level Three until movement caught Bennett's eye.

"Stop, we got company," Bennett whispered.

Rousseau had missed spotting the small man skulking behind a water cooler just ahead of them.

"Show me your hands, what are you doing here?" Bennett called as he confronted the man using the intimidation of his gun muzzle.

Dressed in a white lab coat and wearing dark rimmed round spectacles, the man was the advertisement of geek, all wimp looking with a milky white appearance and cowering from Bennett's presence.

"Please don't shoot, my name is Joseph Voight, I am a Linguist here, I only translate text nothing else," the man pleaded as he started slowly lifting himself from behind the cooler.

Bennett pushed the muzzle into his head and demanded, "Who else is on this level?"

Out of fear he responded with a shaken voice, "Most of the other scientists have evacuated to the lower levels, it's only me and my colleague Rahj, no guards, they are either up top fighting or down below. Who are you? Why is this happening?"

Rousseau now intervened into the conversation, "You are the linguist working on the Sphere of Anubis. Is this correct and do not lie?"

"Yes… yes I am. Myself and Rahj."

Viktor had been listening to the conversation not saying anything, he was more concerned with escaping the facility.

"We need to move Jon," Viktor said.

Rousseau broke in cutting Viktor off, "Bennett, the Sphere is here somewhere and this linguist can take us to it. We need to find it now."

Bennett looked back at his father, they both knew what the answer had to be. Viktor nodded and conceded, "Yes the Sphere must be destroyed."

Bennett applied the muzzle again to Voight's head, this time asking, "Where is the Sphere?"

"It's one level below us, but if I take you to it then they will kill me," Voight hesitantly answered not truly realising his predicament.

"Well if you don't, then I will kill you right now where you stand. Your choice, but make it quick I suggest."

He turned away and indicated down a long semi lit corridor that gave no clue to where in the facility they were. Somewhere not far above them, an explosion rocked the ceiling which started cracking in places. The clatter of automatic gunfire was close and they realised Rousseau's men were making progress deeper into Kehlstein.

Half way along the corridor a large heavy steel door caught Bennett's attention. Though lighting was scarce in that section of the building, an object on the door glistened and begged to be noticed.

In the centre of the dull gunmetal grey door hung a solid brass plaque in the shape of a circle surrounding a red Swastika. It was large and clearly displayed a vision of supremacy to those who dared to enter. The door was locked tight requiring a six digit code manually entered into a keypad after a thumbprint scanned and a key card inserted. He stood staring at it with the urge to enter like it was calling to him.

"What's in there?" he called to Voight now further along the corridor with Rousseau.

"I'm not sure but I think it's the main control room for this facility," Voight replied as he hurried back towards Bennett.

"Open it, I want a look," he demanded lifting his weapon slightly towards Voight as inducement.

Voight inserted his security card, entered the code and pushed his hand against a flat screen on the wall. The electronic grinding of bolts retracting sounded deep inside the wall and the door released enough for Voight to pull it fully open.

"Wait," Bennett said as he pushed his gun into Voight's back and pushed past him. He wasn't taking any chances and he didn't know whether the geek was capable of lethal retaliation or not.

Both Bennett and Rousseau had their guns ready, aimed at anything moving as they entered while covering off each other. The same orange twilight of emergency lighting saturated the room and from behind their gun sights it was devoid of any human life. It was a control room of incredible size with massive flat panel screens lining three walls that overlooked an imposing oblong timber conference table capable of sitting thirty people. At the opposite end were ten computers some blinking data on the screens while most remained inactive. Overall it gave them the impression of a miniature NASA control room in between rocket launches.

Bennett looked down at the table. At one end, a gold plaque sat inscribed with the name *Herman Schwartz* and under it the words *Director, Europe Division*.

Bennett looked at Rousseau who nodded his head in confirmation while at the same time stating, "Kehlstein is *The Trust's* European headquarters and for the past decade was Schwartz's home."

Bennett searched over the various control panels in front of him looking for a way to light up the wall screens. The third of the switches initiated what he needed, the screens illuminated to display a massive deep red Swastika symbol.

"If Mr Schwartz finds us here, at least our deaths will be quick. You know it is rumoured his father masterminded the extermination of the Jews and not Hitler," Voight informed them.

"Schwartz is dead, I shot him twice in the head earlier tonight, I don't think he'll be masterminding anything," Bennett added.

The linguist stood stunned, his facial expression one of disbelief, Schwartz dead, how would *The Trust* react to this, he thought.

Bennett ignored him returning his attention back to the console, there had to be something worthwhile. He pressed a few more keys on a remote keyboard next to Schwartz's plaque. The screen transformed into lines of text and engineering drawings.

On closer inspection, it focussed into a set of instructions and schematics. Much of it no one in the room could understand, a highly sophisticated document but several printed words became clear. Blue Crystal, Lucifer's Funnel and Meredith appeared at different positions and sometimes repeated.

"They are trying to work out the Thirteenth Code for themselves," Rousseau suggested.

"I don't believe they can work it out themselves but it concerns me they know about Lucifer's Funnel," Viktor said.

Bennett turned towards him, "Lucifer's Funnel, what's that?"

"It was discovered a long time ago, a funnel shaped piece of extra-terrestrial diamond with enormous magnification powers. The thirteenth technology shows how to use it to magnify the strength of the blue crystal into an energy pulse weapon of colossal power."

The screen flickered as another grenade detonated somewhere directly overhead and a section of ceiling broke free collapsing and crushing a bank of computers against the far wall.

"We have to get going now, Bennett come on," Rousseau called already making his way towards the door.

Bennett knew he was cutting it fine, his mission he believed was to assassinate the Six and here in this room he could identify who they were. He pressed another key, this time only two screens changed their image. Across them, a map of the world now exposed with a series of red shaded circles displayed on most continents.

They stood in disbelief staring at the screens.

CHAPTER 79

TARGETS

Kehlstein
September 14th

Bennett was first to speak, "Are these what I think? Are these targets?"

The wall screens showcased multiple targets with heavy concentrations in the Middle East, United States, China, India, Australia, North Korea, Europe, United Kingdom and Canada. Most other nations had red circles but with lesser concentrations.

Viktor announced what he knew, "These are targets for the pulse weapon."

"What… it's the whole fucking world. This is madness, surely it cannot be real," Bennett responded in disbelief.

"Most of these targets are chosen on their threat level but primarily on reducing at least eighty per cent of the world's population. It is not just to enforce their New World Order but it is also to ensure the Earth can continue to sustain life under their regime."

Rousseau added trying to hurry them up, "Bennett, it's like this, your father was one of them once, the enemy, one of those ignorant fools who have no respect for Gaia. The pulse weapon if used will start a chain reaction deep inside the Earth's core that nothing can stop, total devastation, goodbye Earth."

"The Earth's enemy is us… humans. We started the murderous chain reaction back with the industrial revolution. Too many humans living here now and multiplying at a rate our planet cannot sustain. *The Trust's* solution is extermination just like they did with the Jews," Viktor added as another grenade exploded somewhere on the level above.

New cracks appeared in the already failing ceiling and more concrete fell this time smashing onto the table and shattering Schwartz's name plaque into pieces. Up above and outside the room, a fierce battle was underway that grew closer by the minute. Rousseau and Voight had already fled the room heading towards the stairs as the corridor exploded into a flash of red. Timber and metal like miniature missiles sliced through the air as Bennett and his father threw themselves to the floor.

"We have to get the sphere," Rousseau screamed above the crackle of fire and increasing sounds of gunfire. *The Trust's* men were holding off the infiltration of Rousseau's men unaware the four of them were just to their rear.

Viktor though weak managed to scream back, "You must find a way to destroy it, if I had the disk then it would self-detonate, I don't, so you must use explosives, it's your only chance."

The corridor had become increasingly noisy with gunfire, Bennett thinking he heard something about a disk piped into the yelling match, "Is that the same metal disk you left in Australia at the Sanctuary?"

"Yes yes that's it, but I don't understand, how could you possibly know about that?" Viktor asked knowing it wasn't the time for questions.

Bennett reached down and removed his left boot. Inside the rubber sole was a hidden compartment big enough to firmly house the disk. He always had a feeling it was something important and one day would be needed, so he kept it on him at all times. He removed it and raised it in full view of the others and in the dim light, the metal came to life. Under the reflection of the fires, it glistened deep crimson and the thirteen symbols illuminated under their own silhouettes. Small enough to fit inside his hand, it was purely a detonator, he realised as he handed it to Viktor.

Voight was quick to remark, "That's the same weird metal as the sphere."

Viktor almost laughing replied, "Of course it is, this disk screws into the underside of the Sphere. Once in place, it arms for detonation. Thirty minutes is all we get and it should destroy this entire facility. Think of it as a small thermo nuclear device but it must be dropped down the elevator shaft for best effect, the deeper the better for the blast."

A bullet split the air between them and then another just missing Voight. An armed man wearing the facility's black and red uniform had appeared behind them and commenced firing at his first opportunity. He never saw his own death coming at him.

Almost on hearing the trigger snap back, Bennett had swung around, dropped to the floor and raised his handgun in the direction of the shooter. Tapping off three rounds at the dark figure, he had removed the threat while the shooter's body fell limp to his knees and then flat to the floor.

"Ok time to get going people, more will be coming," Bennett called.

A minute later they reached an undamaged stairwell where they could reach the level below. Rousseau opened the stairwell door and checked for shooters, all was clear.

"Wait... Bennett, you and your father go, get him out alive. I'll take the linguist and destroy the sphere. Viktor, how do I use the disk?" Rousseau asked.

Viktor explained the sequence and handed it over. Bennett could see the logic in the plan, there was no point in them all going below.

Rousseau added, "When you get topside, head towards the western forest, about 400 metres and you'll find our base camp. My men know what you look like so you'll get the support needed." He grabbed Voight by the arm, "you're coming with me."

Rousseau and Voight disappeared down the stairwell while Bennett and his father headed up towards the surface until three gunmen appeared at the top of stairs, rifles pointing at them and nowhere to run.

Further down below, Rousseau and Voight had soon run into their own problems.

CHAPTER 80

GUARDIANS OF GAIA

Kehlstein
September 14th

Each time Bennett returned fire, a new barrage of gunfire swamped their position forcing them to retreat deeper until another blast silenced their attackers. A perfectly aimed grenade from somewhere on the surface had demolished the top two levels of the stairwell crushing their opponents in seconds.

As the dust settled he and Viktor clambered over the debris towards the surface and the remains of the building that now laid torn open by the explosives. The roof had collapsed exposing the dusk sky and across the compound fires burnt out of control.

Bennett stepped cautiously out from the rubble and hesitated as sudden movement stopped him dead in his tracks.

"You are surrounded, don't move."

They had been ambushed, Bennett realised as men appeared with assault rifles raised at their heads. A group of five soldiers dressed in a mixture of black army fatigues quickly moved forward and disarmed Bennett until one announced, "Holy shit, it's Viktor Bennett".

Immediately they all lowered their weapons and stepped back except one. He was their leader, a man in his thirties, olive complexion, Middle Eastern and by the stern look on his face a seasoned militant.

"Viktor you are alive! But where is Pierre?" he asked.

"He is down below on his way to destroy the Sphere," Viktor returned realising the men were Guardians. They gave each other a sideways glance and Bennett was unsure whether they showed fear or rejoice.

"Who are you?" Bennett asked.

"My name is Omar," he replied before turning towards his men and adding, "We represent the Guardians of Gaia. Now, we have little time, *The Trust* will send reinforcements within the hour and we must get Viktor to safety. The Monk has commanded his safe return."

Omar Mustafa claimed himself a freedom fighter from Eastern Turkey who found his fulfilment in the beliefs of the Monk and resurrection of the Earth. The Guardians of Gaia had become his only family after he lost his at the hands of a corrupt military regime from choosing not to comply with their way. Now he lived and breathed the Monk's spiritual beliefs for a peaceful planet. Their mission was simple, save the planet from total destruction and that meant preventing the release of Jeremiah's Thirteenth Code.

His passion for Gaia, like the Monk's, was intoxicating. It was the Monk's early teachings that led him to understand the Earth as a living life form and could die like any living creature. Gaia was Mother Earth and it was she, they had to protect yet under it all no one except the Monk himself knew the true reason why.

"Wait," Viktor called, "You need to know Rousseau has the Sphere's detonator disk."

"What, how is that possible?" Omar asked.

"It does not matter how it is possible, Rousseau has it and he knows how to use it," Viktor replied.

Omar went a shade of grey as he spoke, "Ok this means we have less time. When that thing goes you don't want to be anywhere near here, trust me, it has the power of a 50 kiloton nuclear device."

He added, "How long has he been gone?"

"No more than fifteen minutes at a guess," Bennett said.

They were both ushered off with the sense of urgency intensified. Viktor struggled at first but he soon showed an unexplainable speed for an old man and overtook most of the Guardians around him. It was the first time since his imprisonment that he had set foot above ground and he was enjoying the moment of clean brisk air rushing across his face.

They were guided at a fast running pace into the western forest where another group of seven men appeared covered in blood.

"Omar, our teams have penetrated level four but the enemy continues to bury deeper into the lower sections and still no sign of Rousseau?" said the one known as Fox.

"Thankyou Fox but the plans have changed, listen up," Omar announced.

Fox and the remaining few gathered around.

"Brothers, today is very special. Today not only can we destroy Kehlstein but we can destroy the maker of all this evil. The Sphere of Anubis is here in the lower levels and Rousseau has the arming device."

Fox gave him a quizzical look and he nodded confirmation in return.

Bennett was watching towards the facility but still no sign of Rousseau. It had been over thirty minutes and he was sensing something had happened. "Omar, we need to get back in there now. Rousseau needs our help."

Omar responded hesitantly, "Rousseau can handle himself, he is a master skills man and knows how to get out of tight spots. We'll give him another ten minutes."

Fox moved closer to Bennett and out of Omar's hearing he said, "Don't listen to Omar he is very stubborn. We need to rescue Rousseau, he would do the same for any of us."

Bennett stood and boldly announced, "Omar, I don't answer to you so I'm going back to rescue Rousseau and detonate the Sphere. If you want to help then come along, if not, then stay and wait, either way I'm going."

Fox was at his side before Bennett finished informing his intentions followed a few seconds later by the other men, all declaring their allegiance to rescuing Rousseau. Omar wasn't happy about the mutiny but hesitantly conceded to the plan.

"Three helicopters will be here to extract you, stay alert and alive. Bennett you're with me. Fox you have your team," he ordered and turned to collect his weapons.

Viktor hugged his son and turned to Omar, "You let my son die, I will kill you, understand."

Omar laughed it off, "Sure thing old man, your baby boy is safe in my hands."

Viktor moved in on him and without warning grabbed his arm as he said in a low almost growl-like tone, "I mean what I say, I WILL kill you if anything happens to Jon."

Omar's facial expression changed, his arrogance dissolved, and for a brief few seconds fear invaded his eyes. He had witnessed and felt something in Viktor that no one else had, something he could not explain. The old man released his hold and Omar quickly made distance between them, making sure he engaged no further eye contact with the old man.

Within a few minutes all men had kitted up with an assortment of weapons, ammunition and grenades and had moved out leaving Viktor behind to wait for the helicopters. Ten minutes later, the two teams separated as they approached closer to the damaged facility. Omar's team with Bennett arrived at the same stairwell he'd been ambushed at while Fox and his team worked their way to the main entrance, further towards the east.

The small war inside Kehlstein progressed unnoticed to the world. It sat inside a ring of five smaller mountains wedged deep in a remote part of Southern Germany. All around, the mountains were rugged and impenetrable with access solely by helicopter or plane. Next to the facility, an expertly camouflaged airstrip stretched westward through a valley carved by twenty kiloton of explosives. On the mountainous surface, the Kehlstein facility appeared as an unusual rock formation where the few building structures had been built under the disguise of limestone outcrops completely undetected from the watchful eye of satellites.

Deep down inside the facility, two groups of Guardians battled their way towards level six where the explosives would be most effective. Most were on levels three and four encountering strong resistance from the facility guards and suffering more losses than expected. They had attacked Kehlstein with a plan to detonate twenty kilograms of C4 explosives at various points to crumple the support pillars and start a collapsing domino effect of the entire facility. The unexpected high losses meant it wasn't proceeding as planned.

Omar and Bennett entered the stairwell hard and at speed, with weapons ready and the remainder of their team close behind. Both battled over the leadership, Omar wanting to go one way and Bennett the other. It was expected, Bennett thought, he understood these types of men, often it was best to play their game until the right time presented itself. For now, he complied with Omar's way.

They reached level two without encountering resistance. Fallen soldiers lined the floor of one corridor as if placed there for later burial. None were Guardians, they noticed sighting the facility uniform laid out in mass. Level three presented a similar scene and then as they opened the stairway door to level four, a barrage of gunfire hammered the steel door pushing them into retreat.

Omar tried his radio headpiece but still interference hissed and crackled. From the moment the Guardians had entered the facility their communication devices were useless, jammed from somewhere inside and contact was lost.

"Omar, the elevator shaft, I can rope down and take them out from behind," Bennett suggested as he looked around at the men with him and noticed one had rope strung across his shoulders.

Omar signalled his approval and Bennett bounded back up the stairs to the level above. It was still unguarded as he sprinted the length of corridor towards the empty elevator shaft. A few minutes and he had the shaft doors jemmied open and peered down into the deep dark pit below.

With the rope firmly anchored, he rappelled down to the level four doors, suspended himself and edged the doors partly open. A dimly lit corridor under emergency lighting was all he could see and the best he could tell, it was empty. He pushed the doors back a few more feet and slipped silently through.

For the next few minutes, he advanced slowly along the corridor listening for the enemy and scanning both front and behind. Up ahead the corridor veered left and the faint sound of men whispering emanated from the other side.

To his right, a heavy grey door beckoned his attention. Just like the control room, it displayed the same Swastika symbol on a solid brass plaque. Next to it on the wall was a key card entry pad and a retinal scanner.

He took one step closer to read the signage under the plaque.

SPHERE CHAMBER
RESTRICTED ACCESS
WARNING: LASER SECURITY

Standing and staring at the door, he wondered if Rousseau was somewhere inside arming the Sphere. His choice was without question, he had to access the chamber.

Around the corner he peered, only three gunmen sat watching the stairwell door, guns ready to engage any movement coming through. Not a particular hard task, he thought, and was perhaps unfair as he stepped out, handgun raised towards his first target. In a quick three-tap succession, he drilled a small hole into each man's head, all falling lifeless to the floor. The noise of a professional hit dragged Omar and his men from the confines of the stairs and they appeared one by one.

"Nice work Bennett, very impressive," Omar called.

"Nothing special about that, they made it easy. Come on I found the Sphere Chamber. It's back behind us," Bennett called.

He led them back along the corridor towards the chamber as a noise from behind took them off guard. The familiar rattling sound of a metal ball rolling across the hard concrete floor meant one thing in Bennett's mind.

"Grenade…. Get down," he yelled as he flattened himself hard against the floor and hoped for the best.

An explosion quickly followed.

CHAPTER 81

CONTINGENCIES

Kehlstein
September 14th

Rousseau and Voight heard the automatic rifles rattling above them in the stairwell and moved swiftly to distance themselves further from the fight. Twenty minutes earlier they'd been in the same situation under a storm of gunfire from the level four guards. Rousseau had chosen to move down to level five and work his way back up until he realised his mistake.

Half way along the level five corridor, he came face to face with Spartak carrying an experimental energy pulse weapon ready to fire. One squeeze of the trigger and their bodies would have been pulverised against the far wall like jelly.

However, while they both froze at the sight of their impending death, Rousseau couldn't help think something was not right with the big man. The massive human cyborg was behaving unusual like computer software infected with a malicious virus. He had them in his sights yet he hesitated in his actions and his weapon remained deactivated.

Rousseau tugged at Voight's arm and they rushed past him expecting him to give immediate chase. He followed but with less urgency, his internal mechanisms were in turmoil. Bennett's earlier head strike had inflicted enough damage that the micro robotic organisms flowing through his blood had difficulty mending. However, it wasn't the primary reason for Spartak's sudden behavioural change.

Voight suggested, "Wait... I know a safe place."

Rousseau stopped, dragging Voight to a halt.

They had sprinted down a long L-shaped corridor with no visible doorways and though Spartak had not come into sight they could hear his heavy breathing not too far behind. To their left was another corridor narrow and short with a solid steel door bearing no markings.

Voight removed a key card from his pocket and swiped it down through a scanner just to the left of the door.

"Hurry, our friend is almost on us," Rousseau said as he looked back out around the corner from where they had run.

The door opened within seconds with a lesser degree of security Rousseau noticed. They both entered while Voight slammed the door shut behind them, pressing a series of keys on the keypad.

"There it's locked down, no one can enter unless it's opened from this side."

"Yes but what about Spartak and that weapon he has?" Rousseau immediately returned not so sure of Voight's confidence.

"I think we are safe, he would have killed us then but instead he allowed us to escape," Voight answered.

Rousseau nodded and looked around, there was nothing special about the room, "What's this place?"

"It's an evacuation chute, in case the sphere goes hot."

Rousseau needed no explanation, he had heard what the sphere would do in the event of three incorrect codes entered. The inscription gave warning but many believed it to be ancient superstition however, the Monk claimed its truth and petitioned *The Trust* to take notice.

The emergency chute started pressurising, cold air breezing in and with the higher oxygen levels, Rousseau's mind grew more alert. "So where to now?" he asked.

Voight pointed towards another steel door at the far side of the room, about ten feet away. The room they were in was void of anything, just plain white walls and a white tiled floor. Voight quickened his pace, opened the door and stepped through while Rousseau hung close behind with his gun raised ready for the unknown.

Another corridor, this time long and slender, only enough room to walk single file with no immediate end in sight. It was dimly lit with emergency lighting like the other sections but deadly quiet, the sounds of gunfire unable to penetrate the walls.

"We are in the access tunnel to the facility's bunker. It is a long way around but part of it leads back up into the Sphere Chamber above us," Voight said.

As they moved further along, Rousseau raised his gun and Voight stopped. Directly in front was another solid steel door displaying a biohazard symbol and a security keypad.

"It leads into the sanitisation room to remove unwanted bacteria and viruses from our bodies. You'll be blinded by a white light for a split second while the scanning and sanitisation process takes place," Voight informed him.

"How do you know this?" Rousseau asked.

"Emergency protocol drummed into us at least once a week, I'm the one in the sphere chamber mostly so I'd be activating the alarm. Actually thinking about it, I'd be first to die," Voight semi chuckled at the irony of it all.

They stopped at the door.

Voight entered four digits into the keypad. Then out of Rousseau's eyesight, he pressed another key.

The door swung inwards revealing another small room surrounded by white walls and white tiles. It was different Rousseau noticed. In the center of the ceiling, a strange looking ceiling fan started to wind up.

Voight pointed towards it, "That's the scanner, remember a white flash."

Both men stood waiting, Rousseau for the scan and Voight for something else.

CHAPTER 82

THE DISK

Kehlstein
September 14th

A flash of white light engulfed the room as Rousseau felt the chilling air rush his body followed by an unexpected disorientation and light headedness. He should have trusted his instincts and slit the linguist's throat when they first met.

His mind clawed its way to find reality and he felt his weapon yanked from his hands as his legs collapse from under him. As his eyes adjusted and his mind regained balance, he stared into the black threatening muzzles of four automatic rifles. The room had settled back to normal light and the scanner had stopped. Off to his left, Voight stood with a smirk on his face.

"Fucking arsehole," Rousseau managed to yell towards him as one of the armed men whacked his rifle butt down into his head and all went pitch black.

Voight walked over to Rousseau's unconscious body and removed the small metallic disk from his trouser pocket. He turned to one of the armed men, "Well executed, a close call but we have it now."

"Sir, what do you want us to do with the body?" the armed man responded.

"We need him, the two Bennett's have gone topside, find them but keep them alive and bring them to me."

The man masquerading as Joseph Voight had learnt long ago that to be powerful and successful it meant deceit and lies. This was no exception. With Schwartz dead, that meant he was now the facility's controller and could make a forceful stand against the Five. His day had come to take the power and domination right out from under them but first he needed the codebook.

Heiden Klein had always come second, overlooked for the leadership of three different mega corporations during his thirty-year career. Some said it was his personality, always jealous of those around him and never focussing on the big picture for the company. Then he gravitated to heading up the international investment section of the Deutsche United Bank and a whiff of the master plan. It was something he didn't comprehend until he was transferred to Kehlstein as the Facility Director.

Schwartz needed a man or in Klein's case, a puppet to coordinate the daily running of the Facility. He handpicked Klein for his Nazi heritage and his sadistic nature. All through his school years he had been bullied and ridiculed for being the nerd he was. The Six had done their research, they knew a man moulded from a schoolyard holocaust carried the hatred and revenge to best lead an extermination program.

Now Klein bathed in the glory of the control he had over the Five. He knew they would do anything to regain the Sphere. He could ask any price, he thought, as he flipped the disk in his hand feeling its smooth cold metallic skin.

He walked back down the tunnel towards the Sphere Chamber. In his pocket, he held a small electronic device ready to deactivate Spartak should he appear. It was something he always held close in case his prize warrior mistook his enemy. Part of him felt some guilt for what they did. It was a shame Spartak had been a wonderful family man and so sad his wife and three children were murdered to initiate the experiment. The superior Soviet warrior had agreed to the injection of robotic controllers but never had he thought *The Trust* would go back on their word by killing his family. They thought it best to prevent the family asking questions when the experiment developed complications.

Now Klein knew the device in his pocket would render the micro robots inactive causing Spartak to cease all muscular function and eventually die from the nerve aftershock.

He hurried along another narrow corridor that led to a small elevator large enough for one person and completely blast proof. Once inside he pressed the only switch and the lift surged upwards into the large conical shaped room where the solitary metallic sphere came into full view sitting high on top of its pedestal. He stepped quickly from the elevator onto the floor of the Sphere Chamber.

The real Voight hurried over knowing protocol restricted their exit from the chamber if the facility ever came under attack.

"Sir, what's happening, do we need to commence evacuation protocols?"

"No you do not," he said as he fired two rounds into Voight's head, eyes going expressionless as his body hit the tiled floor. Rahj had been sitting at his computer at the far end of the room and now stumbled off his chair onto the floor at the sight of his colleague's assassination. Klein walked over to Rahj scrambling and slipping on the tiles, trying his hardest to get away and maintain life.

It was all too late for Rahj. Two more shots rang out in the chamber that day and one more victim bloodied the floor.

His cell phone chimed.

"Sir, we have Bennett and a few Guardians, level four ... sector five."

"Excellent, I'm on my way," replied Klein as he turned towards what he came for.

He picked up the sphere and disappeared from the chamber. The power was his now and no one could take it from him.

CHAPTER 83

THE CHAMBER

Kehlstein
September 14th

Bennett and the men had fallen victim to two stun grenades. He awoke to his hands and feet bound sitting alone while a few feet over the others were tied in much the same way. They had been dragged into the sphere chamber with its towering sterile white walls, no windows and an array of electronic equipment sitting idle around the sphere's pedestal.

Omar and his men had all regained consciousness while to their left, three guards stood watching and waiting to shoot at the first sign of escape. A short pale man wearing thick-rimmed spectacles clutching a handgun stood in front staring down at Bennett. He was runt in size and wore a finely detailed dark German suit that less than an hour before was concealed under a white lab coat. His face resembled that of a rat and his teeth were disgustingly crooked from a neglected childhood.

"I'm assuming you're not Voight," Bennett snarled towards the imposter with the handgun aimed meticulously at his forehead.

He stood for a minute or more just glaring at Bennett before he spoke in his usual strong German accent, "Yes you assume correct, I am not Voight. I am Heiden Klein now the Emperor of Kehlstein since you eliminated Schwartz."

"Yeah don't start thinking of throwing a celebration, I will be killing you soon," Bennett remarked.

Klein broke into a fit of laughter more like the squeal of a hyena.

"Mr Bennett you are so bold, take a good look around you, surely you are blind. I know you would like us all to believe you fear nothing and that you cannot be killed. That does make me laugh because right now I could easily just squeeze this trigger and well, you know the outcome of that."

Bennett said nothing.

"Mr Bennett you killed Schwartz, now that makes me in charge, and I'm not someone you should mess with. Tell me, where is the code book?" Klein demanded while waving his gun towards Bennett and trying his hardest to puff his puny chest out and intimidate his prisoner.

"I don't know where it is, it vanished a long time ago," he replied before pausing for a second and added, "Oh I believe one of your henchmen stole it, what's his name, yes that's right, Logan Bannister."

Klein stepped abruptly backwards on hearing the name Bannister, he hated the man, he reminded him too much of his abusive father. All his young life, he fell victim to his father's unforgiving disciplinary hand and his Nazi ways towards forced obedience. He always thought that once he gained power inside *The Trust* Bannister would be his first victim. He never once dreamed Jon Bennett would line up in front of him.

"Now Mr Bennett, that's not the answer I'm looking for," Klein said as he walked across the room towards the men tied up on the floor, "You will tell me."

He lifted his handgun towards one of the bound men and without hesitation fired a single round into his forehead. Blood and brain exploded rearwards to become a dripping mosaic on the pristine white wall behind them.

"No! You fucking asshole," Bennett screamed pulling ferociously at his restraints.

Omar and the remaining men did the same while Klein's guards moved in with their rifles aimed to settle the commotion.

"Jon… Jon… Jon, come on, it's senseless me killing any more of these men, just tell me where the code book is and I will consider letting you all go."

Bennett possessed the character of a hardened warrior but under that tough exterior he despised innocent people murdered for no reason.

On the far side of the room behind Klein, he glimpsed movement of someone on the floor behind one of the recliner chairs. At first he saw hands moving and then the legs started a struggling fight against the ties around his ankles and wrists. Rousseau had been tied up the same way and was just finding consciousness as he struggled to force himself free like the others had desperately tried a few minutes earlier. Rousseau caught sight of his men held prisoners and then Bennett to his left that intensified his struggle for freedom. Klein pressed his gun into the side of Omar's head and Rousseau restrained himself, he was fully aware of the life or death threatening routine.

Omar knew too much sacrifice and hard work had been bled protecting the codes for this weasel to get his hands on them. "Bennett, tell Klein nothing, our lives mean nothing, you hear me, they mean nothing," Omar yelled while keeping his eyes glued defiantly to Klein's.

Klein wasn't in the mood to dance with negotiations and pointed his gun at the man next to Omar and pulled the trigger, "Do anymore of your men need to die. Tell me where the codes are."

"Don't you fucking tell him," Rousseau yelled from across the room, inviting a guard to drive his rifle butt into his head knocking him unconscious again.

Bennett tried stalling for a moment while he thought, "So tell me, what happened to Voight?"

"Joseph Voight and his colleague Rahj sadly died a short while ago. They were incompetent at reading the ancient text and your father always refused, why Schwartz kept him alive all these years had me beat. It's a shame though, I need a new linguist now."

Bennett watched Klein proudly bounce around the room, this was his moment to shine, a long time dreaming and finally he had the controls to the world's newest war machine. He reached into his trouser pocket, pulled out the detonator disk and held it high under the light of the wall lamps where the symbols etched on one side glistened.

He turned towards Bennett and said, "You won't be needing this anymore."

"Where's the sphere?" Bennett threw straight back at him keeping him away from the murderous pursuit of the codebook. He had seen the empty cradle on top of the pedestal and assumed it had been the sphere's resting place.

"Somewhere safe," Klein replied as he turned unexpectedly towards another of Omar's men and fired a round through his head. The man's dead body collapsed to the floor at Omar's feet where it bled a river of dark blood towards him, pooling and flowing under his legs. He pushed himself back but the blood kept trickling across the floor until his trousers stopped the rising tide.

"How many men have to die, I won't ask again, tell me, where is Jeremiah's Codes?"

Bennett held silent, the killing of men loyal to a cause was painful to the heart and soul but releasing the codes would bring far greater planetary pain.

"Tell me or they all die and you included," he screamed as he paraded back and forth in front of Bennett.

"TELL ME," he howled but this time he showed the signs of a true maniac as his small spectacles slid partly down his nose from the raging tremble. His pale sickly skin had turned a sweaty pink tone and as Rousseau regained consciousness behind him he stampeded at Bennett with his gun leading the way. His trigger prepped and was ready to fire.

"Tell me, where is the code book or I WILL KILL YOU," he screamed spurting spittle into Bennett's face followed closely by the handgun butt.

The guards reacted too slowly to prevent Omar hurling himself into the air towards Klein using his weight as momentum to counteract the crippling effect of the ties. It was a move demanding absolute strength just to raise himself from the floor.

The German had not expected such a bold heroic move from a fully restrained man and his attention had been totally on Bennett, like a tiger with tunnel vision watching its prey. In the impact of the ambush, Klein's weapon released two rounds while at the same time, the rear wall shattered and erupted into a ball of fire and smoke. The gunshots had been drowned by the deafening roar of C4 exploding and desecrating the wall's structure.

Thanks to a hidden surveillance camera in the chamber, Fox had the needed intelligence to place the explosives without endangering his friend's lives. Ten minutes earlier he had discovered the damaged control room and activated the security monitors where they watched their friends die by Klein's gun.

Once the wall exploded, they charged into the chamber shooting the guards. It had been too late for Omar though, Klein had shot him twice in the stomach while Bennett was powerless to prevent it. Omar had martyred himself to save his life. In the chaos of the explosion, Klein scrambled to his feet and scurried away like a rat fleeing a cat.

Bennett was helped to his feet and the restraints removed only to then witness the devastating sacrifice lying sprawled and bleeding in front of him. The Turk had given his life to save Bennett's and he knew it was time to repay his respects.

"Klein has the Sphere and the detonator, we must find him before he can escape this facility," he called above the noise of burning and crumbling concrete.

"He must pay for what he has done here tonight and he must pay in the most agonising way possible," Rousseau yelled back as he was being cut free and climbed unsteadily to his feet.

Fox nodded in agreement looking down at his colleagues slain before him with the nightmarish staring eyes of death. "This sadistic criminal must be stopped," he declared as a tear welled in his eyes reflecting on the many friendships now brutally executed.

Fox Staunton was once a police officer with the Los Angeles PD until five years ago the Monk appeared on his doorstep and from there his life changed. Membership of a secret religious society fighting evil was something he read about in fictional novels but he never thought that one day he'd be actually doing it. Now he only thought about fighting the enemies of the Earth.

"Yes I agree, but first we must find him and take back the sphere," Bennett commanded as he grabbed Fox's handgun from under his belt and headed out the same exit where he last saw Klein scampering. The others were close behind in pursuit.

Outside in the corridor, smoke was already strangling the air and most of the emergency lighting had been destroyed in the explosions that cast their search into near darkness.

Bennett knew Klein could not have gone far and turned towards the stairwell as the ceiling above them lost its battle with gravity.

CHAPTER 84

INFECTION

Kehlstein

September 14th

The damaged wall collapsed under the strain and the concrete ceiling buckled. For Fox and his men, there was no escaping as the ceiling crashed to the floor.

Bennett had been more fortunate; he had been further ahead and turned around in time to see his new friends vanish under tonnes of plummeting concrete and steel. The C4 used to blow a hole in the wall of the sphere chamber had undermined the main central supports to the facility's armour shield protecting the Sphere's Chamber. The protective design meant nothing could penetrate it from above however, from below or the side were completely plausible. With one of the three main supports destroyed, the six metre thick steel reinforced concrete slab slipped sideways and careered downward. There had been minimal warning and as the dust settled under the flicker of spot fires, a small movement caught his eye.

Somewhere just under the edge of the rubble Rousseau had been spared and though he was spewing blood and gasping for air, he tried desperately to claw his way out flat on his belly. Blood lined his face and his blood soaked shirt was in tatters exposing heavily tattooed and muscular shoulders.

Bennett raced to his side and helped drag him free of the wreckage as more of the overhead structure collapsed amongst another torrent of dust. One end of the corridor was completely severed and somewhere on the other side, Klein was making his escape with the sphere.

At his feet, Rousseau forced his words through a splatter of blood.

"Leave me, find Klein… Sphere… get it back."

Somewhere behind him towards the empty elevator shaft, Bennett heard a noise. The corridor was in complete darkness except for a few thin beams of light filtering down through from the collapsed ceiling and the scarce pockets of emergency lighting. Random gunfire still echoed from the lower levels and the occasional shudder of a grenade exploding sent a dull shock through his body as he sprinted towards the noise.

One level below on the access ladder, Klein was slipping and clanking on the steel rungs as he clung tightly to the sphere under his arm.

His stark white shirt now an orange glow under the lighting gave away his position and it was obvious he was having difficulties by the way he fumbled with only one hand free to hold the ladder.

Rousseau had struggled to his feet and called out in a laboured breath, "Is it Klein?"

"Yeah he's climbing down, why not up?"

"Emergency exit… level five… leads to the hangar."

The same emergency exit chute used to access the sphere chamber also gave passage to the airstrip and an aircraft hangar.

"Will you be alright to get out yourself?"

"Yeah… Go."

Bennett hurled himself onto the ladder in pursuit of Klein hoping Rousseau was strong enough to climb out through three levels of rubble with his injuries.

By the second ladder rung, he heard Rousseau call out again, "Bennett… kill that Nazi bastard, show no fucking mercy, kill him." Bennett didn't respond he just kept pacing down the ladder two rungs at time.

He landed with feet firmly onto level five, the elevator doors already open and Klein nowhere in sight. The corridor like the one above stretched out in front with doorways off both sides but none offered a clue of Klein's movements.

The red blood trail on the floor was difficult to see at first. Klein had been injured in the ceiling collapse but Bennett knew he was moving too quickly for it to be life threatening. Now the trail stopped at a steel door just to his left, no markings or indication of what waited inside.

He pushed down gently on the handle and was surprised to find it unlocked. He slowly pushed it open and lowered his profile as he entered behind his gun sights.

The room like so many of the others he'd seen resembled a research laboratory, electronic equipment and computer monitors scattered throughout. In the scarce light he could sense Klein was in there, a slight movement across the room. Almost immediately, the movement was replaced with the sound of gunfire and two bullets shattering a large glass canister next to where Bennett crouched. Shards of glass and grey sticky fluid exploded as the canister smashed to the floor.

A muffled scream from somewhere further back in the dark caught his attention, it wasn't Klein's voice. Another round fired but this time clearly missing him.

"Bennett, join me and together we can make this planet a better place, with the Sphere nothing can stop us. It is the Fuhrer's vision," Klein called out hoping he could pinpoint his position.

"Why would I join a dead man?"

Klein lifted his head at the question not aware his enemy was close until he felt the cold abrupt steel of Bennett's handgun press cruelly into the back of his head. Like he'd done a thousand times before, he reached forward and disarmed his enemy. Next he reached inside his shirt pocket and removed the detonator disk while he dropped him mercilessly to his knees.

With Klein cowering on his knees anticipating an execution, the same muffled sound caught Bennett's attention but this time it had some familiarity.

Klein saw Bennett's distraction and began his torment, "Argh Jon, you are too late. The power of the blue crystal feeds on her and you weren't here to save the beautiful princess. Does this upset you?"

Klein broke into a screeching laugh, a noise like fingernails scraping across a blackboard that added to the uprising agony of what Bennett had just realised looking in the direction of the sound. He backhanded the Kraut with all his might across his head using his handgun for added brutality that split the man's ear wide open accompanied by an avalanche of blood before he blacked out and hit the floor.

He walked towards the sound, suspecting the outcome. On a metal table against the back wall was a body, a human body with electrodes and tubes hanging loosely from most orifices. Covered partly by a white sheet, he was looking at the ravaged body of Stella Van Horne, a new blue death victim of sorts. He ran to her side, removing the wires and tubes, she was alive but a light grip was all she had.

Klein started to stir behind him finding consciousness and trying to pull himself up to escape. Bennett turned in anger and ran at him grabbing him by the shirt collar and throwing his weak pathetic body into a large steel vat directly behind him.

"What have you done to her? I will kill you as you stand here."

Klein looked back into the fury of Bennett's eyes, a raging inferno demanding answers, "Jon you didn't think we would let her live did you? Poor thing suffered excruciating pain and she told us everything we needed to know."

He lost his temper and unleashed his fury directly into Klein's face. Six unforgiving punches in the space of a few seconds and Klein's bloodied face was barely recognisable. Bennett took a step back and aimed his handgun at the Nazi's head, it was time to serve up some summary justice, he thought.

He was so intensely focussed on revenge that he failed to notice the movement behind him, edging closer.

CHAPTER 85

PROMISES

Kehlstein
September 14th

Stella had lifted herself from the table, placed both feet on the tiled floor and started walking almost stumbling towards him. Her appearance and health had somehow improved inexplicably in just a few minutes, enough for her to walk.

Klein looked on in disbelief, bloodied mouth drawn open uttering the words, "What, this is not possible, no one survives the blue crystal unless they possess the Oracle gene... and she does not."

With his handgun aimed firmly at Klein's head Bennett took a few long strides to intercept Stella and hold her trembling body. He hadn't seen her since the cave in Otavi and though only twenty four hours earlier, it felt like weeks. Now he was looking at and holding a fraction of the woman she once was. Her face had taken on the appearance of someone visiting death with paleness and black rings circling dark pits for eyes. Her once seductive green crystal eyes had faded to yellow with a crisscross of red veins like an inner city street map. She clung tightly to his body and as she did, she murmured the words, "You must destroy the Sphere."

He lowered her down onto the floor and turned back to Klein, "Where is the Sphere?"

Klein remained defiant, saying nothing, just smirking back at him.

Bennett fired one single round into Klein's right shoulder at point blank ripping through and shredding his shoulder joint from front to back. The pain hit him and with the desired effect causing him to bellow in agony.

"Now tell me Kraut, where is the Sphere?"

Klein was cringing in pain, his voice shaking but still he refused to talk just glared at Bennett with his snakelike eyes.

Bennett pushed the muzzle of his gun into the wound and twisted it touching on all the torn nerve endings.

"Please no more, I will tell you but you must promise not to kill me."

Bennett not one for negotiating with the enemy responded by pressing the gun muzzle into Klein's hand, "I can play this game all day. You best tell me where it is?"

Klein hesitated a second and the gun fired.

He screamed pointing towards a small metal cabinet near where he'd been crouching. Bennett let him collapse to the floor and clutch his arm before motioning at him to open the cabinet by shaking his gun towards it. He crawled amongst his blood pooling under him, and reached up with his good hand.

The cabinet opened.

CHAPTER 86

ORACLE

Kehlstein
September 14th

Klein slouched back waiting his execution, he was silently praying for a swift bullet to his head. The pain in his shoulder and hand had intensified and the dizziness was worsening. The cabinet had opened without force and the sphere had become centre stage for Bennett while Stella experiencing an unexplained strength gain, found a place by his side.

Inside the cabinet rested a solitary dull metal object, the size and shape of a soccer ball and covered in symbols of ancient appearance or perhaps extra-terrestrial. It had an almost hypnotic calling, something that beckoned Stella's complete attention. Her strength was returning at a fast rate and already her skin showed signs of pinkish healthy tones. She bent down to pick it up.

Klein was confused with her recovery, it was unprecedented.

Stella lifted and rolled it over to view the finer detail. Each symbol was engraved in blue and recessed into its own hexagonal shaped switch pad three centimetres in diameter similar to that of a large telephone keypad.

Bennett belted his weapon and took the sphere from her. It was how it had been described to him, something sophisticated yet artistic in an unexplained way. He held it firm in his hands like a person would a priceless vase inspecting every symbol while at the same time exercising the corner of one eye on Klein.

None of them expected it to start activating.

Bennett fumbled at the first hum from inside and almost dropped it. He turned to Klein for some kind of explanation and though the German was in severe pain, it had his full curiosity. He looked at the faint blue light emitting from each symbol and looked back at Bennett searching his face and body before finally saying, "You are an Oracle of the sphere, what code do you hold? Tell me, I must know."

"I do not know", Bennett said as he handed the sphere back to Stella while it deactivated as quickly as it had energised to life. Klein turned towards Stella trying to engage a post medical interrogation of her condition, something he couldn't explain, no one survived this long from the blue death unless an Oracle and she was too sick for that. She let him take one half crawl towards her before she stepped in and with a goal scoring kick across his face, lifted his entire body off the ground and snapped his jaw in two places.

"Stella come on, we have to get going," Bennett called and motioned towards the door.

She followed with the Sphere, leaving Klein bleeding on the floor and holding his mouth while he screamed in extended choruses of agony.

CHAPTER 87

BATTLE

Kehlstein
September 14th

Bennett and Stella ran towards the elevator shaft until her screaming stopped him abruptly in his tracks. He spun to see Spartak dragging her away still clutching the sphere in her hands.

Eighteen hours earlier while Schwartz was interrogating her, Spartak had attacked and took her prisoner.

Bennett aimed his handgun towards the cyborg's head and prepared to fire when Stella screamed, "No don't shoot him."

"What, you are kidding me right?" Bennett protested as he advanced taking a precise aim at the man's head. Spartak stopped and released his hold allowing her to step free until he locked eyes with Bennett and his gun.

"Stella talk to me, what's going on?" Bennett asked starting to edge backwards away from the super human.

Knowing Spartak would not harm her, she pushed herself between them both and forced his attention from Bennett. As she did she called out, "He is my brother, I will explain but right now you can't show any aggression towards him. Lower your weapon."

She kept her eyes locked with his and raised her long slender arms to his shoulders, "Spart you cannot harm him, he is my friend, do you understand?"

For the first time, Bennett witnessed what he thought was human emotion on the face of *The Trust's* failed experiment. His face appeared as if hardened steel but his eyes softened in that precise moment and he thought he witnessed compassion. Bennett lowered his gun while running scenarios in his head. How was this Stella's brother? None of it made sense.

"Take the sphere and get going. I'll catch up," she called back over her shoulder. He edged in, took the sphere from her and headed towards the ladder while she continued to lock eyes with her brother as if in a hypnotic trance.

With one hand on the ladder rung, he looked back as four gun men appeared in the corridor and open fired. Most of the rounds ricocheted off the man's armour allowing her to drop and crawl across the floor.

"Stella, get out of there," Bennett shouted as he dropped from the ladder and sprinted towards her while at the same time firing at the incoming guards. A single handgun was no contest against four automatic assault rifles and he soon found himself pinned down with Stella within arm's reach.

Spartak lifted the energy pulse weapon towards the guards and let fire with one burst that pulverised the closest two into a mass of bloodied pulp on the floor. The next missed all together as the remaining two fled back into the depths of the corridor.

Three more guards arrived to join them and they shadowed a fourth man who stumbled every step of the way. Klein was suffering intense pain and cringed with each step.

"Stella, come on, we have to go," Bennett yelled. She had stood watching Spartak advance around the corner towards the waiting guards and Klein.

As Spartak came under a siege of gunfire, he stopped and lowered his weapon.

"No Spartak ... No," she screamed while running towards him now kneeling on the floor, weapon dropped and his head bowed as if in defeat. Bennett raced to catch up while still clutching the sphere, he wasn't leaving without her.

The first volley of shots came in high above their heads while the second smashed through the wall to their right forcing them both to take cover.

Bennett fell to the floor and slid firing his weapon towards the attackers. Two guards went down wounded while the others returned fire and Stella screamed for her brother's help. The momentum of his slide found the only cover in the corridor, the huge armour plated body of Spartak.

He grabbed the warrior's weapon and pulled him over onto his side. He was alive, his breathing shallow and soft but something had changed, his enhanced abilities gone or maybe suppressed.

He turned Spartak's gun towards the guards and released a pulse, striking one guard high and decapitating him. As he did, he caught the familiar sight of Klein crouched behind them holding his bleeding shoulder. *Should have killed that weasel when I had the chance*, he thought.

"Bennett, Spartak can't help you, I've deactivated his micro robots. His death will come quick just like you and the girl. Now give me back my sphere," Klein demanded.

A muffled voice broke Bennett's attention, a weak sounding voice spoken in Russian, "Please don't let my sister die, I beg you..."

Spartak tried to push himself up but it was useless with his enhanced robotic parasites inactive. His body had become solely dependent on the microorganisms and without it, meant he would die just as Klein had said.

"Hey Klein, I am the Thirteenth Code," Bennett called.

As he anticipated from such a comment, Klein flew into a frenzied state.

"Don't shoot, don't shoot, drop your weapons NOW," he screamed. His men looked back upon him confused and knowing their fate once Bennett raised himself. Klein was an intelligent man but greed for power had taken its toll on his mind, now he'd made a mistake.

"Show me… show me, I need to see it," Klein begged. The search for the Thirteenth Code had become an obsession for so many inside *The Trust* and now Bennett was using that greed to beat his opponent.

Bennett kicked the guard's weapons away and pulled Klein forward of them while at the same time he maintained his gun pointed at them. A few seconds spent searching Klein and he located a small black device inside one of his pockets. On the device were two buttons, one for activating and the other for deactivating the electronic micro-organisms in Spartak's bloodstream.

"So Klein let's see what happens when I press this button."

Spartak's eyes opened.

Bennett dragged Klein back towards the elevator shaft while one of the guards ran forward to sweep up his gun. Unfortunately for him, he didn't see Stella crouching behind the corridor corner.

Her kick knocked his head backwards snapping the man's neck, cracking vertebrae and severing his spinal cord. His legs buckled under the weight of his lifeless body and his gun dropped and rattled across the floor until it whacked against Spartak's feet. He reached down and picked it up while the remaining men ran for their lives until he cut down their escape with a full magazine of bullets.

With the enemy sprawled dead along the corridor, he turned and set his sights on Bennett.

CHAPTER 88

RETRIBUTION

Kehlstein
September 14th

With the energy weapon slung loosely across his back, Spartak moved swiftly to reach Bennett who continued to drag Klein kicking and screaming for mercy. He just didn't expect a tug of war from the big man.

Spartak grabbed Klein by the neck with one monstrous hand, forcing Bennett to release his own commanding grip. He aimed his gun towards the warrior's head, surely point blank would penetrate the hardened skin, he thought.

"No Jon, don't shoot him, he wants Klein," Stella screamed.

He lowered his weapon while Spartak lifted Klein higher by the throat till his feet dangled above the floor. With his hand biting in under the German's jawline, he carried him to the edge of elevator shaft where it became clear his intention. Klein's death waited for him deep in the darkness of the elevator pit.

Just then the corridor lit up in a bright flash of orange and red as a rocket propelled grenade slammed into the wall beside them. Another group of guards had found them, seen their comrades slain and switched straight to the heavy artillery.

The impact had knocked them both to the floor but Spartak and Klein were gone. The force of the explosion had thrown them over the edge crashing down onto the elevator three levels below.

Stella had already clambered to her feet sprinting to the edge to peer down into the darkness.

Screaming and kicking in denial, she resisted vigorously against Bennett as he dragged her back from the edge. Her legs buckled and she collapsed to the floor in despair clutching at her head and screaming in mental agony, "No." It had taken her years to find Kehlstein and the last of her family.

"There is nothing we can do, we have to get going," he beckoned while pulling her head around to stare into her streaming eyes.

Below them in the pit, an evil laugh bellowed out bouncing upwards off the walls. Klein felt the new crippling agony of a broken leg that had snapped back under his body in the fall and though he was bleeding profusely from his bullet wounds he laughed at the thought he had survived. Luck was truly on his side, he mused, as he caught sight of the twisted metal debris protruding out Spartak's left eye.

"Bennett you are a fool, you will never defeat *The Trust*," he called out through his evil laugh and shortness of breath. His escape was within reach.

CHAPTER 89

ESCAPE

Above Kehlstein
September 14th

The surface above the facility appeared deserted and tranquil under the failing dusk light. The wind streaming down off the mountains surrounding Kehlstein had a colder than usual bite for the September climate and with the sun fully devoured by the western ridgeline the temperature had plummeted ten degrees.

Bennett and Stella had been forced to climb out onto the ground level through the first level debris after the earlier explosions had stripped away the last dozen rungs of the emergency ladder. Once on topside, Bennett had time to prepare the sphere while hidden inside a partly demolished guard tower.

He had taken the small detonator disk from his pocket and carefully screwed it into the circular recess in the base of the sphere. Stella kept watch for the guards, feeling healthier by the minute. The whole process had only taken about twenty seconds to complete with the disk fully screwed into place but to their surprise nothing happened.

They sat there in the shadows of the building wondering their next move as the sphere remained lifeless. But then something started...

First a hum and then it vibrated like it did when Bennett handled it for the first time. He placed it down on the ground and they watched on in awe at the beauty unfolding before them. It only took ten seconds but the light show was spectacular. As if it was initialising itself, the 300 symbols lit up and commenced flashing some kind of sequence until all remained illuminated.

Inside the building, it could have been mistaken for a disco dance floor with lighting reflecting off the glitter ball. From outside was a different story, their location had become a dead giveaway to the enemy.

Slowly one by one the symbols started extinguishing, the radiating blue glow diminishing and they knew the countdown had commenced. It also meant thirty minutes to evacuate the area.

In the space of a minute, Bennett ran the fifty yards across the compound to the exposed elevator shaft where he launched the sphere.

Somewhere to the north, he could hear the rumble of incoming helicopters the rescue party, he assumed. As they flew closer, he was forced to change his mind.

"It's *The Trust's* reinforcements," Stella called as three Soviet Mi-24 Gunships flew at speed overhead accompanied by the turbines growling and the rotors thumping. "They're doing a reconnaissance run, getting ready to land," she yelled, "and that means more soldiers."

"We've got less than thirty minutes to get the fuck out of here," Bennett called back.

"Jon, someone's among the shaft debris, I just heard them call for help... sounded like someone calling your name."

He too had heard the cry. "It's Rousseau, my god I forgot him. We need a vehicle and something fast, meet me back here and make it quick. I'm going back down to get him out," Bennett commanded as he leapt down onto the twisted steel once the elevator motor house.

Not far into the shaft he found Rousseau, his legs crushed under the latest collapse of steel and concrete. Blood covered the man's face and his expression proclaimed the agony of it all.

"Rousseau, can you hear me?" Bennett called above the growing sound of attack helicopters banking around onto their return flight.

The injured Frenchman nodded his head but grimaced in pain. "Yes… but I can't move, legs broken and busted ribs I think."

His body was pinned under a steel beam, one of the four once used to hold the elevator wheel in place and wedged firmly across his legs, one knee had been completely crushed while the other bled profusely from the intrusion of jagged steel.

Bennett tried with his added strength to budge the two tonne of steel but his efforts proved nothing and as Rousseau screamed out in more pain another sound silenced his pleas. Overhead a missile screeched across the sky in low over the elevator shaft before impacting a nearby building in a blaze of fire and death. A small group of Rousseau's men had been defending the main entrance and gunning down facility guards one by one as they exited until one of the helicopter pilots spotted them. He launched a missile that obliterated their position and their lives before he depressed the switch for another that slammed into the outer edge of the mutilated shaft.

The second strike threw Bennett off his feet among toppling concrete and steel while moving the beam enough to pull Rousseau free. A strip of jagged steel had slashed his left leg to the bone causing him to pass out from the pain.

He reached the top, exhausted from the burden of the man's heavy weight. To his right in the distance was a large building similar to an aircraft hangar and a line of smaller buildings closer to his left. Directly in front were the smouldering remains of the first missile's destruction yet Stella was nowhere to be seen.

In the sky to the west, he could just make out the dark shapes of the rescue helicopters lifting up from the tree line that had grabbed the attention of the Mi-24's. Bennett seized the opportunity and ran with Rousseau across his shoulders towards the hangar hoping it was worth the effort.

Up ahead a solitary shape came running into view as a surge of relief flooded through his body. Stella stopped the moment she cast eyes on him with Rousseau slung across his shoulders and raised one arm towards an open doorway back behind her.

"Jon, there's a plane in there," she called already turning back towards the hangar only a short distance behind her.

Dangling from her other hand was the dark silhouette of a Heckler & Koch assault rifle and in the dim light Bennett couldn't help feel compelled to gaze upon her new militant look as he laboured under the weight of Rousseau. Two minutes earlier she had stumbled across a lone guard hiding in the hangar presumably waiting for them but never expecting her stealth or ability to effortlessly snap his neck.

Bennett's legs had started to cramp and buckle as a new barrage of bullets zeroed in around them. Two guards had appeared from behind the main compound building next to the elevator shaft and were running towards them, guns firing as they did, quickly closing the gap. Stella fell to the ground and returned cover fire.

Bennett reached the hangar doorway and fell inside under the momentum while Stella fired off more rounds. The hangar wasn't overly large but what had Bennett's complete attention was the Gulfstream business jet, presumably belonging to the late Herman Schwartz. It sat motionless pointing towards a length of tarmac and a runway that disappeared off towards the western mountains.

With the help of Stella, he lowered Rousseau onto the aircraft lounge and strapped him in. They didn't have much time, the man would die without immediate medical treatment and he knew more guards would burst through the hangar door at any second.

"Hold them off, I'm getting this baby moving," he called and threw himself into the pilot's seat.

Less than sixty seconds later, the dual jet turbines started whining up drowning out the gun fire now coming from the rear of the plane. Stella fired short bursts across the doorway holding them off until two appeared at the front of the hangar.

"Jon come on, we gotta get out of here," she yelled.

Bennett released the brake and pushed the throttle forward. The jet jumped to life accelerating out the hangar enclosure throwing her off balance as a string of bullets punctured across the fuselage narrowly missing her. She pulled herself up and closed the door as the jet was gaining speed towards the runway and gunfire still clattered from behind them. The diminishing chink of bullets hitting the fuselage was a good sign and Bennett pushed the throttle full with the runway filling the windshield.

In the near distance, rising up into his path was a ridge of snow-capped mountains with the lightened haze of the sun lying low behind them and he knew he needed all the speed he could find to clear them. At 140 miles per hour the business jet launched from the far end of the runway into a steep climb towards the mountains. The sinking sun blinded him the higher they climbed but still he held full power for a maximum climb rate and their only chance to escape Kehlstein before the sphere detonated.

Two minutes into the climb and one of the gunships disengaged from the Chinook pursuit and headed their way at speed. Bennett banked hard right into a narrow canyon while still pulling altitude at near maximum rate and hoping to outrun the gunship, though he anticipated what came next.

"Hold on, missile on our tail," he called as he wrestled the controls to out manoeuvre the inbound missile that had already locked onto the heat of their engines.

Impact in three ... two ... one...

CHAPTER 90

KHARMA

Kehlstein
September 14th

On top of the stranded elevator, Klein had forgotten the agony of his injuries, he was watching waiting for his demise.

Above him the sporadic rattle of gunfire echoed while a single slither of pale light from the surface enshrouded him like under a spotlight. He took a brief moment to gaze up into the light as it fell through the ruptured elevator wheelhouse exposing a reddish grey backdrop of the dusk sky.

He had watched Bennett and Stella climb out through the same opening just moments before the remaining two of his security detail were slaughtered on the ladder by the accuracy of Bennett's gun. One by one, gravity tossed their lifeless bodies clipping and bouncing off the rungs before terminating in an abrupt bone crushing thud either side of him. One landed across the hatchway blocking his only exit and as he was pushing and shoving at it, something caught his attention.

Above him a small dark object was dropping and deflecting off the shaft walls as it fell. It built up speed until it punched deeply into Spartak's chest with the sickening sound of the ribcage imploding into bone fragments. There it slipped sideways and rolled a short distance coming to rest at Klein's side.

He reached for it and for a brief moment his excitement exploded only to be demolished by fear at the same time.

Resting against his hand, the object shimmered in a beautiful iridescent blue glow, hundreds of small glowing symbols extinguishing one by one. Klein knew what was happening and finally his fate.

The Sphere of Anubis was on its way to ending his short lived reign.

CHAPTER 91

UNSEEN ENEMY

Airspace above Kehlstein
September 14th

The missile slammed into the left engine, shearing it cleanly from the rear fuselage, a precise hit and lucky for them left the tail section intact. A fire ignited and Bennett raced to shut the flow of fuel and control the crippled jet to avoid the next inbound missile, something more difficult with only one engine, he cursed.

In the failing light, the black gunship laden with missiles looked a formidable sight that Bennett failed to feel confident in defeating. He had no room to manoeuvre inside the sheer cliffs either side with the helicopter closing fast and already lining up its final kill strike. He did all he could under the circumstances, drawing the gunship in close teasing the pilot to use guns and not missiles.

The helicopter pilot as if Bennett's puppet, pulled back on his controls and squeezed the trigger breathing life into the front mounted Gatling gun spraying bullets across the Gulfstream. Bennett continued to slow his speed as the ravaging sound of shredding metal filled the cabin. Stella had buckled herself in beside him and her knuckles had faded to white with fear as they clenched tightly into fists at the thought of dying.

"Hang on," Bennett called, though Stella was already feeling the G forces ripping at her body as the jet plummeted towards the mountainous terrain below. The gunship followed like a dog chasing a cat and attacked with another blast of rounds this time slicing through the tail. Bennett pulled back hard on the controls and gave the last remaining engine full power as the gunship's pilot seized his moment to destroy the business jet.

The trigger engaged under his finger and the gun responded. As he did, a flash of blue light engulfed his tightly enclosed cockpit and cauterized his body in a split second. His machine veered sharply right out of control heading for its own destruction against the cliff face.

Another flash tore across the sky this time intercepting the Gulfstream's flight path and lighting up the cockpit as Bennett shielded his eyes and pushed the nose high to clear the highest of the mountain peaks.

"What the fuck was that?" Bennett mumbled above the sounds of the airframe creaking and groaning. Stella said nothing only stared out the windshield at the ground racing away below.

As he banked the jet to the right and witnessed the facility for the first time he spotted the burning wreckage of the gunship belching a leaning column of black smoke in the gusty mountain wind.

"Well that explains why the attack suddenly stopped," Bennett said pointing towards the smouldering wreck scattered across the snow and rock. He searched the skyline for other aircraft and the reason for the helicopter's fate but nothing emerged into view.

Towards the north and low to the ground he could just make out two groups of helicopters, one the escaping Chinooks and just behind them two pursuing gunships. He watched as one of the gunships peeled away and banked high to intercept his course while the other launched a barrage of missiles towards the Chinooks.

Another flash of blue reflected off the windshield and the jet shook violently. Bennett had kept his eyes on the inbound gunship now about two kilometres away and missed seeing the outer tip of his left wing explode from what he thought was a missile. Stella too had seen the reflection and felt the jet shudder except she knew it hadn't been a missile.

"Jon we need to get on the ground, it's only a matter of time before it hits us," Stella said reaching out to grab his arm to draw his attention.

"Before what hits us?" he asked as he turned back towards her.

She opened her mouth to reply as a flash of intense white light silenced her.

CHAPTER 92

FINAL SAY

Kehlstein
September 14th

Deep down the elevator shaft, Klein laid in his broken state just staring at the sphere, watching the blue symbols extinguish one by one.

His dreams of taking over the realms of *The Trust's* final solution were over.

Klein waited and prayed for the forgiveness from his God, he wasn't a believer in the Monk's revelations though he knew that if the truth of humanity was ever revealed it would unleash a monsoon of uncertainty across all the religious domains on Earth.

The Sphere of Anubis continued its countdown, now only 3 symbols remained.

Then two symbols and finally one extinguished.

Klein watched as a bright white tunnel of light burst out from each symbol and then nothing...

The enormous power erupted up into the Earth and heavens above.

CHAPTER 93

PULSE

5km north of Kehlstein
September 14th

The Sphere of Anubis had detonated in a display of nuclear strength fusing the facility into solid rock and entombing all those left inside for eternity.

The sky lit up brighter than the sun and as Bennett shielded his eyes, the jet slipped sideways into a powerless fall driven by gravity alone. The remaining engine had quit and the cockpit display had extinguished leaving him wrestling the controls as the shock wave tore through the jet. The explosion had devoured the ground and expanded skywards as one massive black, red and orange mushroom cloud.

Back behind them the gunship was suffering the same fate and falling towards its own explosive death while the scattered fires to the north symbolised the tragedy of the Chinooks. He had no time to reflect on the likelihood of his father's death amongst the burning wreckage while outside the nuclear thunderhead defiled his jet ripping at the wings and tossing it like a feather.

"We're going down, too many trees for a safe landing," he shouted at Stella while keeping his focus on the ground five hundred feet below. The explosion had illuminated the forest sufficiently to discover they had nowhere to land and the loosely scattered pine trees meant it would require some skilful crashing to avoid death.

Less than a minute later, the first line of trees ripped the wings clean off causing the fuel tanks to erupt and ignite the forest into a trailing blaze. Inside the cockpit, they held tight for their lives feeling the jet slip and skid as the trees smashed and clawed their way along the fuselage. Bennett could do nothing but hang on and hope for the best as more trees impeded their path forcing the jet to veer sideways.

Stella screamed as a large old pine careered through the side slicing the jet's body in two and catapulting the rear section into a densely packed clump of Silver Fir trees before slamming to a crumpled halt. The remaining half led by the battered cockpit kept its momentum straight ahead and ploughed down into a steep ravine with a trail of fire in pursuit.

What seemed like minutes to them was only seconds for the amputated luxury jet to reach its resting place wedged firmly against the rocky edges of a swirling stream forty feet down at the base of the forest.

Badly shaken and battered, they removed themselves from the cockpit, Rousseau's body still strapped to the lounge had deteriorated since leaving Kehlstein. Blood was freely oozing from his mouth and exposure to the scraping tree branches had razored his skin. They left him unconscious and headed further up the ravine to seek a way out.

Stella had taken a few steps before the display of flashing crimson light in the southern sky caught her attention. She stood mesmerised by the sight of a nuclear mushroom cloud rising like some Greek mythology beast standing up preparing to rain hell down on the ground below it.

Bennett turned to take in the same view, he figured they were about ten kilometres from the facility, which meant the downed helicopters would be somewhere close by. However, as he contemplated how they would carry Rousseau up the rocky hillside, a flash of blue light streaked across the sky stripping all limelight from the atomic display. They both watched as it impaled the jet's fuselage in one massive strike that disintegrated the wreckage and cremated Rousseau's body. The blast wave rushed out and reefed their feet out from under them throwing their bodies head first into the bushy undergrowth of the forest.

"It's a D.E.W., we have to get going and fast," Stella called as she rolled over to her feet.

He knew what D.E.W. stood for, a Directed Energy Weapon, a pulse of intense energy fired from somewhere he assumed was an orbital platform or aircraft. He didn't know how Stella knew or who had developed it, though he was guessing *The Trust*.

"How do you know this?" he asked still comprehending their situation.

Both had started climbing up through the trees as Stella found her breath to reply, "*The Trust* have been developing a pulse weapon using the blue crystal and then last month they stole the US Government's killer satellite."

"Wait," he yelled at her, grabbing her arm and pulling the woman to the forest floor, "You better start telling me what's going on, who are you?"

There in the semi darkness of the forest floor, she gave Bennett a brief run down of her mission, only a condensed version as time was scarce and soon the area would be swarming with reinforcements from *The Trust's* sweeper teams cleansing any incriminating connection to them.

"My real name is Nicholette Stella Sponarava, I am a devoted Guardian of Gaia, a servant to the great Monk, once a Soviet spy with the Russian Foreign Military Intelligence Unit," she replied before adding, "and I believe I saved your life once."

For the first time, Bennett had been taken by a formidable equal in disguise and pseudonym, a spy on a mission like him. He sat listening but not angry from the deceit, he was well accustomed to this behaviour after all, it was how he lived his life most days, not many people knew the real Jonas Bennett.

"My mission was to infiltrate, identify and terminate influential members of *The Trust*, but then we learnt of Jeremiah's Codes concealed by your father many years ago and that changed things."

She continued her short confession, "I'd spent a year in Washington DC under the guise of Stella Van Horne journalist, all to flush out and kill the enemy. Then one day my orders changed, my mission was to become something I wasn't used to, I was to become your accomplice and convince you to find the code book and all the while keep you alive."

She started laughing, "Can you imagine me protecting the great Jon Bennett and I might add the most wanted man in the Soviet espionage world. It was something I found difficult to play at and maintain my cover as the reporter but I realised your help would lead me to the Six, the ultimate targets for any Guardian. More importantly, I knew it would lead me to my brother, Spartak. It became something I couldn't refuse, I had no idea the importance of the Codes but I had to convince you to look for them. And yes before you ask, most of those things I said back in Washington were made up, all to motivate you. The abduction was not, that was *The trust* trying to draw you out."

"Nicholette, Stella or whatever your name is, you have no Russian accent and I've seen no picture of you in CIA profiles, how do I know you are telling the truth?" he asked more cautious than ever.

"If you have a profile on me then you would know what I have endured and the details of my childhood. You would know I was born in Moscow, my father was Vladimir and my mother was Olesya. And you should know this!"

She stood, lowered her pants, pulled her underwear aside to expose a cruel looking scar inflicted by her father when she was five. He had marked her for life, something to always remember the sexual assaults every night as she lay scared in their Moscow apartment while downstairs, her mother cried in denial and fear of the man's killing streak. He was influential in the KGB and would order their execution if ever the truth was revealed, the usual way for Russia's secret police. Then one night a few days after her father carved his mark into her flesh, they fled the country, defected to the US and far away from his tyranny.

Unknown to her at the time, their escape had left behind her older brother Spartak who had been stolen from the family when she was one. It was something the KGB had arranged to keep a tight leash on Vladimir. They never spoke of Spartak in front of Stella but it was something her mother always hated him for and she knew they would die if they crossed the KGB's cause.

Bennett remembered reading her story a few years back, severe molestation by her father at a young age and then she and her mother vanished, presumed dead. The fact that ten years later, her father was discovered executed in his home with a single pistol shot wound to the back of his head never occurred to the CIA it may have been the revengeful work of Nicholette.

After defecting to America, she and her mother lived in Seattle for 9 years, before her mother was killed in a car crash with Nicholette suffering life threatening injuries and third degree burns, she was only 17 at the time. After six months of hospitalisation, Stella returned to the Soviet Union coincidentally a week before her father's murder.

She didn't resurface again until a few years later when a Soviet Agent provided information on her involvement in a right wing radical group plotting to overthrow the then Gorbachev Government. Believed responsible for the assassination of over thirty corrupt Government officials, Nicholette Sponarava fast became a target for both the serving Soviet Administration and the CIA. Both sides hunted her, one to end her killing spree and the other to recruit her services. Both sides failed in their bid, none having the skills or underground contacts to reach her or better still corner her. She quickly became a legend among her people and the spy world until disappearing again in 1992.

"Who do you answer to?" he asked.

"The Grand Council but usually the Monk himself, many religions with a mission to protect Gaia, sustainability is their primary goal. Without it we are doomed," she mumbled thinking of the endless times the Monk had repeated it.

"Gaia?" inquired Bennett.

"Gaia is Mother Earth, she is what we stand on, she feels our existence but now she suffers the pain of society's greed... the Monk says it's time we stood up and fought for our physical future. *The Trust* want total domination and suppression like the communist days, I know what the Soviet Union was like back then and this will be far worse, but that's not the worst of it."

"How do you mean?"

"The Thirteenth Code releases the plans for a weapon of mass destruction, more powerful than anything this planet has faced, it is that directed energy weapon you just witnessed but with blue crystal power. *The Trust* is already trying to imitate it but they need massive quantities of blue rock and the Namibian mine is near depleted. We don't think there are other deposits but *The Trust* continues to search and they continue to search for the Thirteenth Code."

She paused, "Hear me now, if that weapon ever becomes active, it can flatten 30,000 square kilometres of land, that's the size of Belgium. It drives a concentrated energy pulse deep into the ground like a large meteor would do and the resultant land tsunami would annihilate everything within a 200 kilometre radius."

"How do you know this?" Bennett asked.

"The Monk knows many things, but I do not know how. Some say he has a spiritual connection to the sphere's maker. I just know that I've never had reason to doubt the words of the great Monk."

They had been whispering in the now dark undergrowth of the pine forest for fifteen minutes, Bennett deeply entrenched in his new discovery but he still wasn't sure whether she was telling the truth. His visions were growing stronger and with them the number thirteen had more meaning, as too did assassinating the Six.

The mountain wind was howling up above the tree canopy and the sky had finally gone black from smoke and night. He knew their chances weren't good for venturing outside the forest, their heat signatures the most obvious target for Meredith prowling in orbit.

"So is it true, are you the Butcher of Volgograd?" he asked after a brief moment of silence.

"Yes that was me and that was also me who cared for you after our missile attacks on KGB Headquarters," she replied.

He stopped in brief reflection of the search for her so many years ago and gazed closer at her. She had saved his life and nurtured him back to health, her sweet fragrance and warm touch was what he remembered most.

"Then I owe you my gratitude and it certainly explains how you knew so much about it when it was Top Secret. I was dubious when you talked about it on the plane to Sydney and it concerned me what else you may know."

Both had been deeply focussed on conversation to notice the movement in the darkness behind them. The first they knew of others nearby was the hard steel capped soldier's boot in their back as both were pushed to the ground and a rifle muzzle driven into their heads. An American accented male ordered in a commanding voice.

"Bennett, don't move if you want to live."

The night remained silent except for the howling wind and their plans had changed yet again.

290

CHAPTER 94

NEW WORLD ORDER

Marseille, France
September 14th

The privately owned cruise ship concealed itself amongst other luxury liners of similar size, all indicative of the extremely wealthy and a lifestyle expected throughout the marine precinct of Marseilles. Here, boats of enormous value slid out onto the Mediterranean each day and this particular cruise ship was a regular sight in the area. Owned by the Interglobal Banking Corporation, one of the largest financial organisations on the planet, it played host to a banquet of seduction and luring clients into more outrageously insane bank deposits or business ventures.

The sun was setting and darkness would soon fall over the ship as it prepared to set voyage, a trip to only last a few hours. A short while earlier, men and women from all backgrounds and nationalities had boarded making themselves comfortable in the main conference room in anticipation of the night's presentation.

At the front of the congregation standing on a small podium were two elderly men looking out over their expanding audience. Never before had so much wealth come together in the one location, so many people of enormous financial power from all parts of the globe.

The ship started moving out, leaving the port in its wake.

Heavily armed men took up their respective places at the doors both inside and out. This was no normal pleasure cruise, it was strictly clandestine and the guards were under orders to shoot on sight anyone trying to get in or out.

The location had been chosen for its security and camouflage. *The Trust* controlled the Interglobal Banking Corporation and a large congregation of wealthy business people onboard their cruise ship would fail to raise any suspicions.

Most sitting on board that night had previously met in private with the two gentlemen and were offered an invitation, those who declined met with fatal accidents. *The Trust* never took chances, not all agreed with their vision and so billions of dollars had been spent ensuring their new world order remained a conspiracy theory.

Now they sat growing impatiently hungry to learn the contractual details with their cheque books at the ready. Their preliminary briefing had taken place sometime in the preceding year and gave sufficient foreplay to bring them to the edge of wanting more. They all knew this meeting held the answer to what they wanted, the one thing people thought money couldn't buy, eternal life and utopia. But like all good things, it came with a hefty price.

The elderly man known to them as the German stepped forward and raised one hand above his head. Silence immediately followed.

He spoke with a deep strong German accent, sometimes difficult to understand but when he did, it resonated the authoritative sound of a leader.

"Ladies and Gentlemen, tonight is an historic moment for us all. Tonight marks the dawn of a new era for humanity and the chance to live five times longer without illness or weakness. As in our preliminary contact, we informed you of our experiments. We are excited to say, the trials have proven the aging process slows to extend an average person's life to in excess of five hundred years. It has proven to defeat any bacteria, virus or cancer in the body and it has also proven to increase brain function by two hundred per cent. This is what you all seek, am I correct?"

He paused to let the audience take it in and salivate for the next part of his speech. Around the room, most were nodding their heads in agreement to his last question.

"With longevity of life comes a price. But it is not just your wealth that secures you and your family seats in this new world we promise. There is a far greater cost."

He slowly scanned around the room into the eagerly awaiting eyes. From the beginnings in the old abandoned house in New Mexico, the Six set out and scoured the high society world for the best clientele. Researching and infiltrating the wealthiest families, conglomerates and governments all to isolate those most willing to covertly commit millions of dollars for a better life.

Today was the twelfth and last instalment of customers about to sign over their wealth to the new world and the ultimate protection when D Day came.

"The greater cost comes with war and for the unfortunate term, genocide," the German announced without a trace of emotion.

He watched and heard the audience move uneasy in their seats, some looking around at the other clients beside them. The looks on their faces was what he expected.

"You have all received preliminary briefings on the future of Earth. So this should come as no shock to you. In the next three hundred years the Earth's human population will grow past 40 billion and our planet will struggle to sustain life. Leading sustainability scientists claim by the year 2300, the Earth's natural resources will be near depleted and our oxygen levels severely diminished to the point you will need breathing apparatus during everyday life. So how does this affect you? Well quite simple really. With the Serum Eight, your lifespan is extended by at least five hundred years so you don't need to be mathematicians to understand what I am saying. The question is whether you want to live in a world of plenty or fight for your survival each day."

He stopped, took a sip of water and looked towards his associate who just simply nodded his head in affirmation. The German continued his speech.

"The future does sound uninviting but we can change it. For some if not all of you, what I am to say at first sounds criminal and insane but it is needed. We at *The Trust* believe in a sustainable future but the only way it can be achieved is through human culling. We must take drastic steps if we are to survive. It is those drastic steps, *The Trust* is prepared to initiate in order to arrive at a better world, a New World Order. How we arrive there is an ethical dilemma but your fee guarantees you full protection and a utopian life thereafter. A choice of where you wish to live with a plentiful supply of anything you want. My men are handing out your contracts as I speak, please read them carefully and be prepared to sign them before leaving the ship tonight. The fee is fifty million dollars for a family of four and seventy-five million dollars for every other family member thereafter. We require a 30% deposit transferred into the account outlined in the documents with the contract. Once this is transferred and confirmed then you will be administered the serum. On receipt of the balance, you will receive the serum for your families."

One of the men at the front of the audience stood and said, "So what happens to the people when you say culling." Others around him nodded in support of his question.

"I cannot give you specifics but the method is least painful and the end result benefits you and your loved ones, that is all you should be concerned with. You do not have to sign the contract or pay us anything but without the Serum Eight, most of you will be dead within the next 30 to 50 years. It is your choice."

He turned and walked from the podium followed closely by the other man while contracts were handed out across the room.

Only a few of those seated had reservations about the impending human atrocity and hesitated. From an observation point back behind them it was noted and orders were given to neutralise a potential threat to the master plan.

294

Jeremiah's Codes
them it was noted and orders were given to neutralise a potential threat to the master plan.

CHAPTER 95

MAYAN SPHERE

Kangchenjunga West, Nepal
September 15th

The morning mountain air cold and clean separated easily for the sleek long-range cruise missile to penetrate as it sped towards its target at over 800 kilometres per hour. The victims would not see or hear it arrive, a programmed ground hugger that monitored the forward mountainous terrain to give best covert approach and the most effective destruction. Back in the command room, the five remaining members watched the wall screen as their plan unfolded to wipe out the mistakes of Kehlstein and resurrect their final solution.

Bannister sat kitted up and ready for their assault on the Temple. He and his team were embarking on a mission of historical proportion, once forbidden but no longer after the fall of Kehlstein. The Mayan Sphere was locked away deep inside the bowels of the Temple somewhere close to the heart of the snow-capped mountain. There it sat untouched inside a tomb built thousands of years earlier.

"Sir, impact in sixty seconds," the helicopter pilot announced to Bannister as he raced the massive black gunship towards the Monk and his disciples.

As it banked right with thunderous thumping vibrations across the valley, the Temple came into view perched high on the mountain crest. It had Bannister's complete attention as the missile slammed into the hard rock surface with fire, snow and ancient timber exploding in all directions. The Temple like a domino, crumbled downwards, no longer the highest humanly structure on Earth, its history decaying in seconds. The one thousand pounds of death had done its job while the helicopter shuddered violently from the blast wave.

As if drifting slowly into the mouth of a firing volcano, the gunship floated down landing inside the calamity of burning thousand-year-old timber beams while scattered either side were the smouldering remains of incinerated worshippers.

Bannister stepped first from the helicopter clutching his rifle and barking orders while firing one loosely aimed round into the head of a lingering victim crawling at his feet. Their mission was simple, get in, steal the Mayan Sphere, execute anyone in their way and leave in the shortest time possible. The planning had been limited during the short time frame since the Anubis Sphere detonated and shock waves of disbelief raced through *The Trust's* helm.

His team of ten advanced quickly through the carnage and into the catacombs below. Like kicking open an ant nest, the missile had blown the main structure apart exposing the underlying tunnels leading to the prize chamber.

Resistance was non-existent and he didn't expect such ease as they reached the deepest point. The chamber was exactly where their map depicted, their human source had risked his life to seek its location, and infiltration undetected into the World Council was nothing short of heroic. *The Trust's* plan had been unleashed ten years prior to bring the enemy down for the final time, life within the Temple was almost impossible to achieve without the right religious sponsor or the Monk himself. Now they were using that precious Intel, the location of a second sphere. Just like the Anubis Sphere, it had been discovered during an archaeological dig deep in the jungles of Guatemala among the ruins of an ancient Mayan civilisation.

The chamber was small, dark and stank of stale seepage. In the center under the reflection of their flashlights, the lifeless dull grey sphere rested upon a stone pillar. Bannister felt the rush of adrenaline grip his body the moment he laid eyes on it and raced over to swoop up his prize. At last, he had what he always wanted, the power to control.

"Men, with this device, *The Trust* will pay any price we name. Today we have just become wealthier than any of you could ever imagine."

The men clapped and cheered, it was the promise of fortune that lured them this far.

What they didn't know was the Temple's destruction came with tragic consequences. The moment the missile struck, an emergency signal went out and soon reinforcements of unequal power would commence their journey.

CHAPTER 96

VIKTOR

US Army Base, East of Salzburg
September 15th

Bennett embraced his father for the first time since Kehlstein, now within a US military facility, five kilometres east of Salzburg. The remaining Guardians sat huddled not far away planning their return voyage to the Temple.

The team of American soldiers who, two hours earlier had extracted them out of the forest, sat waiting their next command from Washington. Their current orders had been simple, rescue Jon Bennett from Kehlstein and wait directives from Washington. Their thirty-minute pre-mission briefing had screamed national security to the highest level of secrecy however, they never expected the nuclear explosion or the swarm of helicopters crashing throughout the countryside on their arrival.

Now they just watched over their catch.

Viktor broke the silence hoping he could explain the answer his son desperately sought. Next to him on the hard concrete floor, Nicholette sat deep within her own thoughts, her only brother had died at Kehlstein and she couldn't prevent it. She had failed to save his life and though she felt angered and sad there was another more calming feeling emanating from the man next to her. An emotional attraction was building between them and she could feel the forces growing stronger. Around him an aura of complete warmth and protection had taken her by surprise that seemed to give her great strength, yet something she couldn't understand was changing quickly.

Viktor spoke quietly, "Jonas, I have much to tell you, some you may not understand and son, I do not know how I can best apologise for the pain I may have caused you. Many things have happened to me since Australia."

Bennett sat like a small child mesmerized by the teacher, his father alive, still in disbelief and craving for answers. His childhood was full of exciting stories narrated by his father every time he returned from an assignment. He would sit for hours listening and worshipping the man while Aunt Rose doted on them both with lemonade and cookies. She loved her brother more than anything in the world and felt it was her duty to care for Jon when he was gone. Their family bond was strong in those years but then the car crash ended it all and Bennett was scarred the most.

As a young 15-year-old boy, he needed a father figure in his life like all his friends at school. He liked bragging about his father to his mates, a famous CIA agent and a deadly assassin, he would claim to make it more impressive. In return, his mates treated him like a God but then Viktor died in the crash and he no longer had the messiah status. Part of him mourned his death and part of him resented it for stealing his schoolyard stature.

But all this time his father wasn't dead and the mixed emotions hit him like a head on collision with a train. He just sat there and listened and even though he was shell shocked, he couldn't help feel the beat of his heart pounding in his chest from the excitement of their latest discoveries.

"The Bermuda mission in `41 changed things for me with the Agency, I became sought after, special assignments answering directly to the President and the Director but it took me many years to realise what was really happening. By then it was all too late. Jonas, I have seen, and heard things, that scare the living bejesus out of me, things that if ever became public knowledge, would cause worldwide anarchy."

He continued to explain his absence from Bennett's life, while small tears built up in the corners of his eyes. He was a hardened man of eighty years with minimal aging lines to show for it. His skin pulled tight across his face like a Hollywood model and his grey hair flowed long past his shoulders like a man of the wilderness. Similar to his son, he had striking blue eyes, except his were set against a backdrop of translucent skin. His years in confinement and not touching the sun's rays had drained his colour but it wasn't just that, his body was undergoing a transformation, something unannounced about the Eighth Code.

"Look at me Jonas, I am 80 years old but still I feel I am 40, I am strong, fit and my mind is able even after imprisonment at Kehlstein. Why do you think this?"

Bennett as a young boy was always a smart child, quick to answer his father's pop quizzes after school but now he didn't feel so special, though he suspected the answer.

"Twenty years ago, I was injected with a trial robotic microorganism, one that had been designed to give eternal youth, a breakthrough if successful would mean enormous wealth for a select few. I was tested and then later, so too was your Aunt Rose, hers failed but mine didn't. My aging process has slowed to the equivalent of one year every five. Imagine the social impact if we all lived another 500 years, can you imagine what would happen to this planet. We all know greed would conquer any ethical dilemma and the Mega Corporations would rise up further above it all, it would mean death for millions perhaps billions of lives around the world."

Bennett stepped in, "You are talking about the Eighth Code, aren't you?"

"Yes the Eighth Code, in its raw format very dangerous but engineering refined it to give us extended life and enhanced abilities, super humans you might say. Mine was instant, unlike Rose the poor dear suffered a severe brain haemorrhage and lost all cognitive control, I believe she died sometime ago from it."

Bennett looked at Nicholette perched beside him, her face a little grey and sickly, something was happening to her, he thought. She returned his gaze knowing their next conversation.

"Aunt Rose is still alive, mentally restricted yes, but alive in a hospital in North Carolina, we both saw her a month ago. It was Rose who told us about finding answers at the Sanctuary where we discovered the disk and your diary," Bennett said while Nicholette nodded in confirmation.

Viktor looked into his son's eyes, "When you first found the canister, did you get stomach cramps?"

"Yes for a while but they went away not long after opening it."

"I put that there in hope one day you would find it," Viktor said and then added, "It wasn't just the detonator for the Sphere but also a trigger."

"What do you mean, a trigger?" Bennett asked.

"We surgically implanted a small device inside your left kidney when you were young. Opening the canister activated it and released your own robotic microorganisms just like mine. It means you have the Eighth Code running through your blood. It was a safety measure we devised to protect you from the Blue Death. *The Trust* had a plan to expose the blue crystal to the population, part of their Final Solution a continuance of the racial exterminations of World War II. This way, we knew you'd be safe from harm."

Bennett remembered going to hospital when he was young but Rose told him it was to repair a ruptured kidney, he was none the wiser and had no reason to dispute it.

"Did Rose know about it?"

"Yes ... it was her idea, she had influence inside *The Trust*," Viktor replied.

"What! Rose was also involved?"

"Yes, I am sorry to say, she was close to one of the Six at the time. That explains why they never killed her. Now where is the book? It must be destroyed. It holds all thirteen codes and if *The Trust* find it, this planet will not survive," Viktor said.

"It is safe, but first tell me, how this all started? What happened in Bermuda? Where did the sphere come from and how did you get the codes?" Bennett asked however, hesitated before adding, "And why fake your death?"

"How much has Nicholette told you?" Viktor asked.

"You know her?" somewhat confused he asked his father.

"Yes I know her, but only from my dreams. She is a loyal servant to the Council and a true follower of the Monk and his beliefs for this world. She was a young woman with demons inside her head when she first went to him. He taught her to fight them and in return she became one of his best warriors."

"She only just revealed her true identity to me in the last few hours, before that a journalist seeking answers like me with all the usual deceit of a spy securing an agent. She has told me mostly about some new weapon of apocalyptic destruction and the future of Earth rests in the hands of the Monk and his council of followers," Bennett informed his father still thinking it fantasy.

Viktor sensed the ridicule in his son's voice.

"Jonas, you must treat this serious, if *The Trust* develop this weapon it brings far greater destruction for Earth than you can imagine. Each pulse of concentrated energy derived from the blue crystal creates a chain reaction of seismic activity deep within the Earth's core. Once started, it cannot be stopped, a cataclysmic event signalling the end of our time. The Earth's core expands at a phenomenal rate releasing the crust's stability and the ground starts shifting worldwide, the human race no more. The Six see no strength in our warnings, they see an opportunity for their New World Order using the weapon."

"I don't understand, why fake your death?"

"It was something beyond my control. *The Trust* demand complete anonymity and will do anything to maintain it. I had become deeply involved within the organisation and had drawn attention from a nosey reporter. She had pieced so much of it together and it was only a matter of time before she exposed the Six. *The Trust's* solution, like so many of their solutions was to kill her. My orders were to make it appear an accident and remove myself from society."

Bennett thinking back to what Nicholette had said in Washington, looked towards her, soon realising from her return gaze she had used some truth to get to him. He added, "How did you get involved with *The Trust* in the first place?"

Viktor knew this question needed an explanation, "My first assignment working at the Agency was a simple transport job, go to Egypt collect some weird artefact and return it to a high security facility in the Nevada Desert. I did this, nothing challenging about it except it was that sphere we just detonated."

"Did you know what it was at the time?" Bennett asked.

"No, I didn't find out till many years later and well after Bermuda. I was only new to the Agency and knew my place not to ask too many questions."

"Bermuda ... What happened there?"

Viktor needed to explain further his life, close in more gaps and reveal the truths behind the sphere and the codes, he owed that much to his son now part of the plan to make a difference. Nicholette coughed deeply as blood spilled from her mouth into her open hands. She looked down in shock, the blood dark red was dripping through her fingers onto the floor at her feet.

Viktor had seen the sign in her eyes, the hidden pain, the radiation spreading and her skin changing colour. Her contamination had just reached the next phase, the suppressive field provided by Bennett's device was failing her. Her body was rapidly surrendering and soon her organs would too, a slower killing strain of the Blue Death, Viktor realised was at work.

Nicholette collapsed to the hard cold floor and began convulsing in a violent terrifying seizure.

CHAPTER 97

SICKNESS

US Army Base, East of Salzburg
September 15th

The engineered strain of the blue death was taking a veracious hold of Nicholette's body blockading the messages between her brain and vital organs.

Bennett threw himself forward, lifting her limp body from the bloodied concrete, his emotions creeping out from under his rock exterior.

"She has the blue death," Viktor called, "Jonas, she is dying, your device is failing her."

Bennett lacked the knowledge and his father could sense it by his confused look.

"The device not only spread the Eighth Code into your bloodstream, it also provided protection from the blue death to those in close proximity to you. While she has been near you, she escaped it but I fear this is a new engineered strain and your device has lost its effect," Viktor explained.

"We have to get her to the Temple, the Monk will know what to do," echoed Marcus from across the room. He was a Canadian nationalist once a soldier in their Special Ops Command, a fine marksman and tactical operative now devoting his life to the protection of the Council's beliefs. He reached down and checked her vital signs, while her body continued to tremor and shake in Bennett's arms.

She started convulsing more violently, legs shaking like some demon entity fighting to take control of her skinny body.

"What are her chances?" Bennett asked more concerned than he expected of himself.

"She has a slim chance if we can get her to the Temple within the next 24 hours. It's *The Trust's* new fuck up. They experimented with this new strain hoping it would reverse the effects of the radiation but it only prolonged the death by days instead of seconds."

"Ok, where's this temple?" Bennett interjected.

"Himalayas, Nepal."

"Who is this Monk and why so special?" Bennett asked.

Marcus answered, "Some say he is a descendant of the once Higher Order, one who can talk to Gaia. No one really knows but once you meet him you will understand. We all feel him inside us, inside our souls but it's something none of us can explain but it feels strangely safe."

Bennett turned towards the Operations Sergeant, the soldier who led their rescue, "Sergeant, we need to get to Nepal tonight."

"Sir, I cannot do that, my orders are to hold you here, a team is flying in to debrief you, arriving 0830 hours tomorrow."

"Alright can you get the Director of National Intelligence on the line then, tell him it's Jon Bennett and urgent."

"Sir my orders are for you to remain, contact no one just wait the arrival of the debrief team," the Sergeant replied in a more authoritarian tone.

Not one for obeying orders, Bennett returned his own fire at the young Sergeant, "You obviously haven't been briefed adequately Sergeant or you don't have high enough clearance but one phone call is all I need to the Director's Office."

The Sergeant knew his order but he also knew of Jon Bennett, he read the briefs and witnessed the media coverage of his sacking. The young soldier knew this man had the backing of the Director, this had been made public during the Inquiry. Now he wasn't sure if denying him access would be a good career move or not and handed him the encrypted phone.

"Jon, are my men looking after you?" Whittaker responded when he knew it was Bennett coming in on the secure line.

"Your men! Did you arrange this?" a bewildered Bennett asked thinking back to what the Sergeant had said on their first encounter only a few hours earlier.

The blast at Kehlstein had been detected by US monitoring systems high in orbit activating an immediate reconnaissance out of an unmapped US Army base east of Salzburg. A number of unmarked Black Hawk helicopters came in low over the trees arriving before Bennett had even realised, the sounds reverberating off the steep mountain walls, Nicholette too had missed the incoming roar above the wind noise.

Unprecedented in nature, both had been taken off guard, ambushed in the dark and quickly secured. Thirty minutes flying time and they reached their destination where they were joined by Viktor and four surviving Guardians from the crashed Chinooks.

Now on the phone, Bennett was trying hard to arrange air transport into Nepal. Whittaker had the access and administrative capabilities to make it happen however, convincing him became the problem. Arguing back and forth resulted in a US Air Force 737 out of Salzburg Airport and a prompt departure.

Bennett was the least surprised to discover the CIA with knowledge of Kehlstein and had been monitoring the facility for two years, mostly from orbit and some ground reconnaissance. The thermo nuclear explosion had triggered alarms across all CIA Stations in the Europe sector before sling shotting a wave of chaos across the Whitehouse.

Bennett handed the phone back to the sergeant who listened to his new instructions. He knew Whittaker had withheld information in Washington when they last spoke about *The Trust*, though it was understandable under the circumstances with his security classifications removed.

Within a few more minutes they were heading towards Salzburg unaware their destination had just been changed.

CHAPTER 98

JEREMIAH

Austria
September 15th

"You didn't tell me, what happened in Bermuda?" Bennett asked his father while they rolled down the runway for the take-off. Their departure had been delayed thirty minutes waiting a storm to pass over the airfield and all the while Nicholette's health deteriorated slowly, her vital signs weakening by the minute.

"There are many things I haven't told you. I was assigned a mission in December of 1941 to interrogate a young boy in Bermuda. Unusual assignment I must admit, but it had the highest security classification, the young boy was believed to be the sole survivor of a German U-boat attack on an ore carrier somewhere in the waters off Bermuda. The USS Nereus had been carrying bauxite destined for a US aircraft manufacturing plant when believed sunk. We knew their U-boats were using these waters to spy on American shores but this attack was unprecedented. The debris was like nothing seen before, all fused together from some kind of intense heat. We suspected the Germans had developed a new weapon and the boy may have had knowledge of it."

The plane had lifted into the air, climbing to 30,000 feet and heading east.

Viktor continued his account of the past, "The boy, a ten year old, unknown to anyone at the hospital, or around town, was found at sea clinging to the wreckage. His skin badly burnt in places and strangely, an almost blue appearance but different to the effects of hypothermia. The ship's manifest had no record of him, so we assumed he was a stowaway, they were common back then.

"He spoke good English but at times it was difficult understanding what he meant, it was as if he would start talking backwards halfway through a sentence. Then at other times, he spoke an unrecognisable language that made no sense and often was just repeated ramblings. In the beginning, I remember none of it had meaning until after about three weeks of listening to him day and night. Then it all became clear what he was saying and the message he was trying to deliver."

Viktor stopped for a brief moment in silence thinking back to the boy and added, "His name was Jeremiah and I never found out where he came from or how he ended up amongst the debris. He could not recall any of his past yet he was so detailed in his persistent ramblings."

"Ramblings?" Bennett asked.

"Talk of doomsday, end of world prophecies and the sphere becoming the destroyer of worlds. Then there were scriptures he would write on his bed sheets, lines of text and symbols written repeatedly that I copied exactly into my notebook." He paused before saying, "and then there was the tattoo."

Bennett returned a quizzical gaze, "What tattoo?"

"Inscribed in dark blue ink across his chest were thirteen unusual geometric symbols, strikingly similar to those covering the spherical artefact I returned with from Egypt. Some appeared throughout his writings but at that time I didn't understand what they meant. What I found unusual was the level of disinterest by the Agency when I reported the similarities to the markings on the sphere. My gut instinct had me suspicious and I knew there was something big to it yet I couldn't confirm it without sighting the sphere again."

Their plane had been flying for fifteen minutes at its optimal cruising speed and at just over 35,000 feet. Nicholette had slipped into a coma and was secured firmly on an inflight medical stretcher while further towards the rear, the soldiers sat relaxed talking and laughing among themselves.

Viktor continued talking seeing that Bennett was hanging off every word he said.

"I walked out of the boss's office that day, curious, angry and suspicious so I snuck back to Bermuda to continue building the profile on the boy. It wasn't like the Agency to just drop something sounding so mysterious so I kept that notebook secret. I thought someday it would be important, just a gut feeling I had at the time . Anyway, I returned to the hospital and Jeremiah was gone. The nursing staff claimed it was as if he just vanished."

He added, "Then four years later, I stumbled across a highly classified document confirming the atomic bomb had been developed using the Egyptian sphere. Though it was a brief report, it summarised the sphere releasing schematics after a thirteen-symbol code was entered to activate it. That code astonishingly was the same thirteen symbols tattooed across Jeremiah's chest. I could not believe the coincidence and that was when I made the connection. I looked back through my notebook and the sequences of codes jumped out at me, thirteen of them in total ingeniously concealed as part of his writings."

He grabbed Bennett's arm and pulled him closer.

"That book you have hidden, holds Jeremiah's thirteen codes. Do you now understand why it must be destroyed?" he whispered.

Bennett was finally discovering the mystery behind the sphere and the codes. He now comprehended *The Trust's* pursuit for the book and why the deadly tactics.

"Wait, we just destroyed the sphere so there should be no need now," Bennett suggested.

"There is one other," Viktor hesitantly said wondering if it was still a secret.

"What… where?" Bennett asked.

"Deep beneath the Temple I believe."

"Where did these spheres come from in the first place?" Bennett asked.

"That I am not certain about and really a question for the Monk himself, only he knows the truth of origins."

"Ok, so if we destroy the codebook, does it eliminate the threat?" Bennett asked.

"No it doesn't, there are still the Oracles."

"Oracles? What are they?" Bennett asked but had a feeling he knew the answer coming.

"Not what, Who. Men and women chosen by the blue crystal, something in their DNA that responds to the crystal radiation giving them life when all else die. Those spared end up bearing thirteen symbols across their chest as a mark of survival."

"Jeremiah was an Oracle then, he had symbols on his chest, right?" Bennett suggested.

Viktor replied, "Yes it also means he was exposed to the blue death onboard that vessel in Bermuda but worse the fusion markings indicate the blue crystal may have been used in some kind of highly destructive weapon. Divers never found any other significant pieces of the ship, so it seems like it was totally destroyed on impact? No torpedo had that capability, a directed energy pulse weapon did."

"Well that certainly explains why *The Trust* were abducting and exposing local villagers to the crystal at their Namibia Facility, they were searching for Oracles to reveal the remaining codes. Nicholette and I were part of one of their exposures before we escaped, we just didn't know at the time the device was protecting us," Bennett confirmed.

Viktor nodded in acknowledgment.

"So they have three codes counting the A bomb?" Bennett asked.

"No I believe they have four but two are causing them problems. During my time imprisoned I was consistently tortured to reveal what I remembered from the codebook, but it also meant them keeping me informed because in their opinion I would die at Kehlstein."

Bennett looked at his father for a moment before saying, "Well, they now have another, the fourth oracle, a Namibian villager named Matheus. Unfortunately, we led Logan Bannister to him and got captured ourselves."

"Logan Bannister, now there is one man I'd like to slowly inflict as much pain as possible. Have you had dealings with him?"

"Yes, but nothing I can't handle. OK we destroy the code book, but how do we stop the genocide?" Bennett asked.

"That can only be done by killing the Six and the other key members of *The Trust*, not an easy feat and then there is one more problem, Jeremiah. We don't know if he is alive, but it is clear, *The Trust* don't have him otherwise there would be no need for the codebook," Viktor suggested.

"So what, Jeremiah just vanished?"

"Yes it seemed that way," replied Viktor.

Bennett still curious asked, "Who exactly is *The Trust* and why am I getting visions of terminating the Six when I don't even know who they are except Herman Schwartz back at Kehlstein."

"Yes that was good work, Schwartz was a key engineer in the design of their final solution, a continuance of Adolf Hitler's plan to conquer the world. Now, the Fourth Reich builds strength from behind the power of *The Trust*, their vision to gain worldwide autonomy through fear, hastened by the discovery of the sphere's technologies. Tell me about your visions."

"They started a few days ago in Africa, after a somewhat unexplained arrival."

"Unexplained, what do you mean?" Viktor asked.

"One minute we were in Germany talking to Doctor Kraus and then the next in Botswana, with no idea how we got there!"

"Sigmund Kraus? He is still alive?" Viktor asked.

"No, he died from the Blue Death, found him dead after arriving in Botswana, the last thing we both remembered was talking to him just outside Berlin then attacked by an unknown force before waking up in Botswana," Bennett explained hoping a comprehensible explanation was coming.

"Sounds like the Eleventh Code to me, teleportation."

"Oh and this tattoo mysteriously appeared on us both," Bennett said as he turned his head to expose the back of his neck. The small tattoo became visible, a triangle with a circle inside. Viktor stared at it as silence strangled him and his face transformed into an expression of disbelief.

"I have never seen this in real life, only heard of it. You and Nicholette carry the mark of the Higher Order a society of beings the Monk claims once presided over Earth. He commonly preached a misinterpretation of epic proportion that people placed too much belief in the Holy Bible. Now we have nations at war and all because of some two thousand year old misconstruction of the truth. Now, tell me more about your visions?"

"I'm surrounded by a raging inferno with the ferocity of fire in my face while women and children all around are burning and screaming for mercy. The pungent smell of frying flesh fills the air as the earth below me starts to tremble and collapse. I look off in the distance and above the fire, I see the horizon rising rapidly as a three hundred foot tsunami of molten rock races toward me annihilating all life in its path. As it grows closer my skin blisters and ruptures just as the agony really hits me. Then out of the flames crawls the burning carcass of a man screaming in pain and calling to me. He outstretches one hand and tries to speak through his charred lips. I bend down and that's when I realise in horror, I'm staring into my own cauterized face and as his muttered words come out, the molten earth swallows us."

Bennett had given his recount while staring at the floor space at his feet and looked up at his father now edged forward in his seat listening.

"What did he, I mean you say?" Viktor asked.

Bennett stared back before answering, "That I had failed."

Viktor said nothing, he knew what it meant but refrained from enlightening him.

"Back in the cell at Kehlstein you said your name was Heimdall, why?" Bennett asked.

"What, hmm don't recall saying that. If I did then I don't know why," Viktor lied as he turned to look out the aircraft's window into the night sky outside and all the while thinking it was too soon to reveal everything to his son.

The flight time now entered the thirtieth minute and the new orders had reached the cockpit.

CHAPTER 99

ENDURING FREEDOM

Washington DC

The War on Terror had commenced, the US President granting full retaliation on key terrorist facilities inside Afghanistan after the hijacked airliners had slammed into the Twin Towers and the Pentagon killing thousands. Aerial bombardments, day and night lit up the Afghan sky. The sound of rumbling detonations made the American's presence felt while in the north, the Taliban vacated their land to fight alongside their brothers in the south.

The bombs and cruise missiles continued their coordinated destruction of targets across Southern Afghanistan while the US Administration watched on with anticipation of a quick takedown of the terrorist network. One man sat with a different view, he knew the real reason and his anticipations were vastly superior, the extraction could now move forward without interference from the Taliban.

CHAPTER 100

ORDERS

Hungarian Airspace
September 15th

"Nobody move."

The sudden yelling caught Bennett and the others by surprise. The flight had been smooth and quiet until two soldiers barged into the lounge area with guns raised.

Bennett rushed to his feet as the painstaking brunt of a M16 rifle butt struck the back of his head and dropped him dazed back to his seat.

"There has been a change of plans, direct Orders from the United States President himself," the Operations Sergeant announced as the two soldiers maintained their vigilance.

"And one more thing, your Temple in Nepal has been totally destroyed by a cruise missile," he added.

"That is not possible, you are lying!" Viktor called to the Sergeant walking rearwards.

"Have a look for yourself then," he returned with a small laptop in his hand.

Viktor and Marcus both looked down at the screen in disbelief at the sight of the temple burning. Both were in shock, it was forbidden, his holiness was never to be acted upon by the fist of war.

Viktor turned towards his son, "I am sorry, we must hope Nicholette can find her own strength."

"There must be something we can do? What could *The Trust* possibly achieve by destroying the Temple?" Bennett asked out of earshot of the soldiers.

Marcus quickly answered, "I suspect *The Trust* knew about the Mayan Sphere and attacked to steal it, they care not for the Council's sacred rule or the consequences it will bring. That sphere was a gift to the Mayan civilisation about the same time as Anubis but when they started prophesying the end of time it was removed for fear they were planning to misuse its power."

Viktor suddenly announced over the top of Marcus, "I know how to save her."

"What?" Marcus responded.

"I know how to save Nicholette. The First Code neutralises the crystal."

"But even if we had the book and found the sphere, deciphering the code would take too long and she only has a day maybe two at the outside," Marcus said glancing at Bennett and observing the confusion in the man's eyes.

Viktor continued to explain, "The First Code is different to the others, it activates the sphere like the others however, instead of a light show, an antigen is released into the air that neutralises the radiation within a few hundred feet."

Bennett looked around the aircraft interior, a standard 737 passenger jet but split into sections, the forward command section, the medical section and a larger section for troops at the rear. They sat in the command section under guard. In all, he counted eight soldiers, the Sergeant and presumably two pilots, the usual requirement on long hauls. He and his father combined with Marcus and his men made up an attack team of five unarmed men, odds not good in the confinements of a passenger jet, he thought.

He turned towards the others and whispered, "Ok it's rather simple, we need to take this plane and fast."

The Sergeant returned a few moments later with a satellite phone in his hand, "Bennett you have a call."

Bennett took the phone and answered. The voice of Whittaker came through, "Jon I am sorry about this, I had no say or control in the decision, the President wants you taken prisoner and has it in his head you and Viktor are enemies of the US. I was ordered out of his office just five minutes ago. My friend you need to commandeer that aircraft before it reaches its destination in Bucharest. I can provide assistance after that but it's off the radar, I'm already committing treason making this phone call. Advise when ready."

He handed the phone back, waited until the Sergeant had walked away before making their plans in the least conspicuous way possible.

CHAPTER 101

TACTICS

Romanian Airspace
September 15th

The 737 continued its course east towards Bucharest, estimated time of arrival now forty-five minutes. Viktor stood to stretch his legs and moved slowly as expected of an old man so not to spook the guards.

"Can I just check the woman, she appears to be having breathing troubles?" he said tilting his head towards Nicholette.

"Yes be quick," the guard responded after a quick inspection her way and at the same time raising his rifle towards Viktor in a threatening gesture.

Viktor moved to her side and while his hand lightly caressed her forehead he took the opportunity to snap off a mental image of his peripherals, the soldiers seated in the rear section.

"She needs a respirator," he informed the soldier.

As the soldier took a sideways glance towards his offsider, Viktor leapt with the agility of a King Cobra attacking its prey, the soldier never stood a chance. His neck snapped before his body hit the floor. His son, like a younger clone neutralised the other soldier in what looked like a mirror reflection. They snatched their rifles and turned towards the rear compartment cutting the remaining soldiers down in seconds as they reached franticly for their weapons.

The Sergeant attempted a retaliatory strike but it was too late. Bennett had already calculated the Sergeant's position, a clean shot from his rifle found its mark cleanly on the man's forehead and he collapsed lifeless to the floor.

Bennett walked back towards the cockpit.

"Gentlemen I realise by now you have sent off the distress call and soon we'll have fighters on our ass. If you want to survive this then I suggest you open the door. The alternative is not what you want," Bennett announced into the cockpit intercom.

One minute passed and still no response.

Marcus spoke, "We have to act quick, those fighters would be airborne now and becoming stealth should be our number one priority."

Bennett didn't need any encouragement, he lifted his weapon firing at the wall. His success confirmed when the plane shuddered and lurched sideways into a steep descent. Three more rounds into the door lock and they busted into the cockpit. The two pilots leant lifeless against their flight controls pushing them forward while the autopilot battled to regain control.

Bennett took control of the plane before making the call to Whittaker's private untraceable line, "Dom, we have control, what can you do for us?"

"Ok firstly, we tracked the helicopters from the Temple to a location near Patna in India, they haven't moved from there and there's been no other traffic in or out, I've got one dedicated drone keeping watch. You need to change your transponder code, there are two F16s with orders to blow you out of the sky, I estimate you have six minutes before they're in range to launch their missiles. New transponder code is being faxed as we speak with diplomatic clearance into Karachi. All your flight plans are in and I will fax them through to you."

Bennett responded, "I need it changed to Sydney, Australia?"

"Why?"

"Dom you have to trust me on this one, there is much to tell you but not now," Bennett replied hoping his friend wasn't about to go all Washington righteous on him.

"Well, just keep yourselves alive, I want a full debriefing on your return. Be careful, The Trust has roots dug deep across the globe and now it looks like our own President has been compromised. Good luck, call me when you hit Australia, I am assuming you will be heading back to Patna."

Bennett acknowledged and disengaged the connection. A minute later the fax in the command room buzzed to life sending through flight plans and a new transponder code. Bennett immediately altered course for Australia with two refuelling stops at Dubai and Singapore.

Back behind in the dark, the two hungry F16s lost the scent and retreated from the hunt. While back inside the 737, Nicholette slipped further beyond rescue.

CHAPTER 102

DEMANDS

Berlin, New Hampshire, USA
September 15th

The remaining five sat in the conference room only partially mourning the death of Herman Schwartz, their once respected colleague at the table of Six. The fall of Kehlstein had been unexpected and unfortunate but now they had another problem.

"Gentlemen, we have a new enemy," the Chairman said looking around the table, "Logan Bannister wants to play with the big boys. It would appear he wants to barter with the Mayan Sphere."

"Does he really think he can win against us," the Third member declared from the far end of the conference table.

"Well apparently he does. His wants fifty billion US dollars and ownership rights to Australia and New Zealand once the plan reaches maturation. In return he will hand over the Mayan Sphere and I believe Bennett's codebook," the Chairman said.

The Second member piped in, "What the fuck! Does he have the codebook now too?"

"No, but he claims to know where it is. Gentlemen, it is the Sphere we need and right now Bannister has it. Our priority is retrieving it at any cost." He paused and as he scanned around at the four men he added, "Listen up, I have an ingenious plan."

CHAPTER 103

HISTORY

Indonesian Airspace
September 16th

Eight hours out from Sydney, Bennett and Marcus sat in silence watching the darkness outside the cockpit. Turnaround time on the ground at their destination would be quick while Bennett retrieved the codebook from the safe house.

"I still cannot believe the Temple is destroyed," Marcus muttered breaking the quietness.

"Who or what is the Council?" Bennett asked.

"About ten years ago, the Monk claiming to have great knowledge of a secret deadly organisation approached me wanting my help. He talked of a group of six mega wealthy corporate men with plans to implement a New World Order paradigm and raved on about Armageddon, the destruction of Earth from a cataclysmic chain reaction."

"Hang on, how does the Monk know this?" Bennett asked while scanning the flight instruments. The cockpit was an exhibition of tiny yellow and green lights set against the backdrop of pitch darkness. Back behind them, Viktor sat deep in thought of the Temple's destruction and his years inside Kehlstein.

"He can see the future we believe," Marcus replied.

"Do you believe that?" an apprehensive Bennett asked.

"Once I got to know him, I discovered he possesses many unexplained abilities. When he came to me, I was working for the Canadian Special Ops Command and I really had no intention of leaving. After an hour listening to what he represented, I was sold on his lifestyle and philosophies. Something inside me changed that day, it was like he entered my soul and opened a doorway to a new utopian world that I simply cannot explain. All I know is that each day I woke with a feeling of happiness and it was the Monk I felt flowing through my veins."

He continued to recount his past.

"He explained how he was on a recruiting pilgrimage around the world in search of warriors. Men and women he could count on to protect the beliefs of the Earth's Council and end *The Trust's* onslaught. He explained it as an assembly of leaders from all the World's religious denominations and their primary charter was preserving the longevity of planet Earth. The Temple had been their place of worship for over two thousand years. Inside its walls, it offered sanctity and the only haven on Earth where enemies were best friends."

He paused a moment.

"A rift in the ranks fifty-five or so years ago caused uncertainty. One German Catholic become atheist took it upon himself to dishonour the Monk's protection and set forth building his own empire of power and control. From that, a group of men splintered off from the Council and *The Trust* grew into what it is today, a stealth conglomerate of wealthy benefactors."

Bennett broke from listening to receive a course correction update from Air Traffic Control and made busy adjusting the coordinates. A few minutes later, he had lifted their altitude another two thousand feet and were heading further south towards the north west of Australia. He couldn't help wrestle with the uneasy feeling they were being funnelled into an ambush.

When realising his audience was ready again, Marcus continued.

"Anyway the next day, I was on a plane to Nepal and the Temple where I grew to understand their beliefs and the dismal extent of our planetary future. The strangest part of it all was I never had any doubt, I never questioned my own decision to go. It was like he manipulated my thinking."

Marcus continued, "The big problem wasn't who splintered off from the Council but who took up ranks with them. Long since the destruction of the Nazi empire of World War II, remnants of believers have been waiting patiently to strike and rebuild their empire. Some say Hitler's dream to conquer the world lives on in the hearts and souls of the Nazi youth of the 1940's. It is *The Trust* and their Fourth Reich plan we must stop. They want a New World Order but it is based on Nazi beliefs and their extermination plans far outdo those of the Jews during the war. This is why they seek the Thirteenth Code, they need that pulse weapon."

Marcus continued, "The Monk says the planet is doomed anyway whether *The Trust* builds their weapon or not. But not from climate change or global warming as our Governments fool us into believing. Our true destruction comes from the repercussions of life and the overabundance of human life that the planet cannot support. The Monk has sat watching this unfold for many years and it is this that worries him most. Once we run out, then what? ... Adapt or perish is what he says."

Bennett asked, "Does the Monk have a solution?"

"That was something he refused to talk about, saying it would be out of his control, others would decide. None of us ever knew what he meant and now maybe we never will," Marcus replied as he just sat staring out the windshield at the speckle of stars. They continued to fly east across time zones while outside, the sky remained black.

Viktor still had more to say, more to explain to his son.

"I recall in July of 1961, being summoned to the US President's office where he offered me a top secret assignment. I was to track down Jeremiah, who if still alive would have been in his thirties. He said nothing about the symbols or connection to the bomb just that I was to find him. I was only to answer to him directly, advise no one else and I had his reassurance the Agency would not impede my progress. So after that I spent months trying to find Jeremiah I found nothing, not a trace anywhere. I reported back but he didn't seem disappointed, it was like he knew. He instead gave me a new assignment, one focused on various conspiracies of world domination, alien invasion and Government cover-ups. That was what changed me, things I unfolded gave birth to waves of curiosity and quickly my world turned dark with deceit and fear."

"I spent most of my life after that trying to stay alive, hiding behind aliases, and all because I had stumbled onto something big, a cover-up so large it went all the way to the President's administration. It became obvious why he had assigned it silently to me, he suspected something occurring right under his own feet."

"Then a few months later, the President was assassinated and I was assigned to a remote CIA listening post in Iceland, complete removal from the trail I'd discovered. *The Trust* were behind the assassination I had no doubt but I couldn't prove a thing, they cover their tracks well and silence anyone likely to reveal them."

"My research had revealed the existence of *The Trust* as an imposing force behind many of the world's governments using the manipulative power of money to carve their empires. I found tentacles everywhere I looked, but I never discovered all those responsible only that there were six senior executives from its conception. Those original Six had sat and watched the atomic bomb test and on that day in 1945 they initiated their plan of a New World Order, to conquer the Earth. The sphere would make them the real destroyer of worlds, not Oppenheimer."

He paused momentarily while Bennett waited.

"I became part of *The Trust* but not how you imagine. I grew unsettled by the Agency's attempt at silencing me. Even after my posting to the fucking coldest place on the planet I still tried to unravel various clues I found along the way. They knew I was doing it and didn't take long before they restricted my access codes. A few months later, I resigned from the CIA. Two hours after handing in my papers, I received a visit at my home by two elderly gentlemen. They represented *The Trust* they said, and told me of their grand plan for a better future. Initially I allowed them to recruit me out of curiousity for the truth but then when they threatened to kill Rose if I left, that was when things changed. That's their tactic, find people close to you and threaten their lives for loyalty compliance. From then on, I became barbaric, doing what they were doing to me, threatening or killing innocent people in return for obedience. It was Doctor Kraus who made me see reality and finally escape."

Viktor witnessed the recognition in his son's eyes at the mention of Kraus and continued, "I fled once I thought Rose was dead from the injection so I headed straight for the Temple offering my knowledge to fight *The Trust*. It was my intelligence that directly resulted in the death of key position holders but none of the Six."

Bennett asked, "How did you end up a prisoner at Kehlstein?"

"They had been tracking me for months, using the DNA signature of the Eighth Code in my body, it gives off a powerful energy signature easily detected by the right equipment. At the time I was unaware of this technology and was ambushed one night in Paris. The sedative injection acted immediately and I never stood a chance. Then sometime later, I awoke in the dungeons of Kehlstein. Lucky for me, I had the Eighth Code, it kept me alive through the torture, often starvation, sleep deprivation, silence and mind numbing darkness of my cell. Above all, it kept me sane, no one could survive the mental degradation of loneliness in a single cell for twenty years."

Marcus spoke again, "We had been searching for you for years and it wasn't until Pierre managed to infiltrate Kehlstein that we discovered your location, it was the Monk who always claimed you were alive. He used to say he could feel your life sign was trapped, that was all he could sense."

All three men went silent for a moment watching the lights of mainland Australia flicker below as they flew closer to Sydney, now only 45 minutes to the south.

"What is *The Trust's* final solution?" Bennett asked his father.

"Yes the Final Solution. Their master plan to control the world, monopolise everything and never fear anyone. Adolf Hitler initiated the idea, he wanted to rid the Earth of what he thought was filth, the Jews. So his solution was the extermination of six million and would have been tenfold if the allied forces hadn't stopped it when they did. The Fourth Reich gains momentum, the once Nazi youth now becoming powerful and their totalitarian dictatorship is fast approaching. The Final Solution is what they plan to execute with Meredith in orbit, selected targets and the annihilation of billions of lives."

Marcus piped in, "They have control of Meredith through the financial seduction of the General in charge of her and to make it worse, on the day the Twin Towers were attacked, they launched an armed attack on Area 47 in Nevada."

"Meredith?" Bennett expressed a questioning look.

"Killer satellite, a little secret left over from the Reagan Star Wars Program," Marcus answered.

"Ok, why the attack on 47?" Bennett asked.

Viktor returned the answer, "I didn't know but I bet it was to steal Lucifer's Funnel."

Marcus nodded, "Yes you are right Viktor, they ripped the facility apart killed twenty men and all for one ancient Egyptian artefact."

"Ancient Egyptian artefact, is that what you were told? The artefact you refer to is a large red funnel shaped diamond found in the desert near Roswell in 1947, and Top Secret documents I've seen indicate it came from the crashed alien craft."

Bennett asked, "You saying the Roswell crash did happen?"

"I'm only reporting what I've read in CIA documents, files marked never to be released into the public arena. The funnel was discovered a short distance from the wreckage and resembled something machined beyond our industrial capabilities. The diamond material had never been discovered on Earth and scientists could not drill it, scratch it, melt it, in fact they were unable to do anything to it. What they did discover with it was the light amplification characteristics were phenomenal. It was discovered by accident in the lab one day resulting in the total destruction of one wall and the opposite laboratory. Sadly two unsuspecting scientists died."

"What happened?" Marcus asked.

Viktor continued, "One of the scientists working on the funnel decided to use a laser on it in an attempt to discover any weakness, instead he unleashed its true potential. The laser was fired into the widest end, what occurred next was both disastrous and exhilarating for the staff working that day. The beam of light from the laser exploded out the narrow end with such directed force it melted the opposite lab. When I say melted it, I mean complete disintegration, nothing left including the two scientists inside the room, their bodies were never recovered. It all just vaporized into dust."

"Why hasn't it been used before now?" Bennett asked.

"The project was shut down, considered unsafe but more because one of the scientists killed was the son of a local Congressman. I believe some testing was continued covertly but never amounted to much, lasers of the time were not sufficiently powerful for the funnel to be used in war and the funnel was considered vastly unstable for real-time warfare," Viktor added.

"Ok, why now then, what use does *The Trust* have for it?" Bennett asked.

Marcus replied on behalf of Viktor, "The Thirteenth Code is why. It provides instructions to transform the power from the blue crystal into a directed energy beam using Lucifer's Funnel to amplify the beam's destructive strength. When launched from an orbital platform like Meredith it will transfer its energy at the Earth's surface."

Viktor broke in, "This is correct. Jeremiah's Scriptures also speak of the same destruction from the Thirteenth Code."

"The thing I really don't understand is the origin of the Spheres, the technologies would indicate alien and not ancient," Bennett asked both Marcus and his father.

Marcus answered, "Yes that question has been raised many times over the years and never adequately answered I should add. I suspect it is of ancient alien origins but is something the general population would not accept or believe, another reason it remains secret just like Roswell's cover-up remains unchallenged."

Their descent into Sydney airspace had commenced, another thirty minutes and Bennett would be on his way to collecting the codebook.

Meanwhile 9,000 kilometres away, Logan Bannister prepared for his next mission, one that would guarantee his reward.

He wanted Jeremiah's Codes.

CHAPTER 104

JEREMIAH'S SCRIPTURES

Airspace, Australia
September 16th

Viktor looked down at his old leather notebook held firmly in his hand, it had been close to twenty years since he last saw it and had mostly forgotten its contents. Now as he flicked through the pages it was coming back to him.

As expected their ground time in Sydney had been without delay and they were back in the air heading towards India and short stop in Jakarta for fuel and weapons courtesy of Whittaker.

Bennett sat at the controls watching his father intently scan through the book and hold up the last two pages. Text some English, some Latin and another completely foreign were scrawled out before his eyes. To the untrained eye, it resembled some ancient calligraphy perhaps more adequately placed on a thousand year old shrine.

"Can you see the symbols?" Viktor asked.

"No just text and what looks like smudge marks," Bennett replied having tried a few times since the Sanctuary to find the codes on the pages.

"I discovered this little trick," Viktor said holding the pages closer to Bennett.

"If you focus on the centre of the pages and nothing else, you only see the text right?"

Bennett nodded.

"Now watch but you must stay focussed on the same spot."

Viktor slowly moved the pages towards him and then further away.

"Stop, I see them!" Bennett almost shouted.

Viktor smiled remembering his own excitement when he first caught a glimpse of the symbols. "It all depends on where your eyes best focus to separate the symbol from the scripture. Once it does then your eyes grow accustomed to the depth of field required to see all of them. It is rather ingenious and lucky I had copied Jeremiah's writings exactly."

Bennett took the book and flicked to the first page.

His attention was drawn to a scripture written in English near the bottom of the page, a phrase he desperately sought.

...the cure rests before your eyes, death no longer, use it wisely and never again suffer...

Like the other pages, a series of thirteen symbols were scattered throughout the words and Bennett lightly caressed the paper.

"Yes it's the First Code, the cure for Nicholette if we find the sphere," Viktor added.

"Can you decipher it all?" Bennett asked.

"Yes and that's another reason Herman Schwartz fought so hard to break me, he knew I didn't just have the code book but that I could decipher it. I believe the only other person capable of this is Jeremiah himself."

"See here, it tells of the Oracles," Viktor said.

About halfway down the page was a scripture that immediately made more sense to Bennett.

...the Oracles grow strong and with them comes knowledge, chosen by immunity ... they walk among us waiting the arrival of the once highest Order...

Bennett flicked over to the last page, the thirteenth.

...Doom am I, dealing death to the worlds, engaged in devouring mankind. Even without your slaying them not one of the warriors, ranged for battle against thee, shall survive...

All went deadly quiet in the cockpit, neither men spoke just looked forward as the jet cruised north west across the Australian outback desert region.

Viktor broke the silence.

"Schwartz kept me informed of your life, it was just another one of their psychological torture techniques I suppose. Keep me online with thoughts of you on the outside and knowing they could terminate you whenever they wanted was an effective strategy by their measures. He told me you flew phantoms in the navy but came to grief over Afghanistan from a heat seeker. Then abandonment behind enemy lines I believe. I was angered hearing that but there was nothing I could do. I must admit the day I heard you'd survived and made it back to the US was the greatest day of my life."

He stopped talking and turned away, tears were building.

"Schwartz was correct, I was shot down and left to die," Bennett responded.

"Why?" Viktor asked as he wiped the sorrow from his eyes.

"That has tormented me for the past fifteen years, never found the arsehole responsible for denying my rescue. The best I could find out was it came from the top, some fucking pen pushing bureaucrat sitting in Washington thought it wasn't in the best interest of the US to go running special ops to get me out."

"I am sorry to hear that Jon," was all Viktor said in reply. Some things were best left alone because he could sense the intense anger in his son's voice. No point fuelling the inferno, he thought.

Lucky for him, Marcus appeared back in the cockpit with an update on Nicholette's condition. She had been in a coma the entire time with her life signs slowly decaying each hour, blood pressure lowering, pulse erratic and her breathing becoming laboured.

Soon she would be dead.

CHAPTER 105

SACRIFICE

Muzaffarpur, Northern India
September 16th

The buzzing sound of the alarm clock had become irritating, a noise known for its daily disturbance and ritual of rising for another day of commands and sacrifices. His consciousness aroused and his mind engaged for what he knew would be a great day for *The Trust*, the codes would be theirs and nothing could prevent the master plan.

The short rotund man walked to the bathroom of his hotel room where he peered into the old cracked mirror above the same conditioned basin. Staring back at him was a man he no longer knew. His pale sickly looking skin was out of place in downtown Muzaffarpur and though it was early morning, the northern Indian town was already ablaze with a deadly humidity. The sweat dripping off his face was enough to signal another uncomfortable day.

Eating was his favourite past time and it showed in every movement of his body. A small pair of round John Lennon spectacles clung desperately to the end of his bulbous nose fighting against the slide of sweat.

Richard Koehler was one of five remaining board members, one of the new supreme leaders about to unleash a war no nation could win.

Through the single weathered window he could see across the landscape of a massive grassy park and though he disliked exercise he still loved to watch others punish themselves. A group of young local boys were playing cricket and clearly enjoying themselves from the shouting and laughter echoing back to his room. He laughed to himself, it was bucketing down rain but still these boys played as if some morning ritual prevented their betrayal.

Behind him, his cell phone chimed to life.

He picked it up knowing who the caller was, he was right on time for the eight o'clock call. With no need to exchange pleasantries he spoke clearly and precisely, "It is arranged as planned, you will have your vengeance tomorrow, 14:00 hours, Muzaffarpur Airport. You know what we expect."

Koehler turned back to face himself in the mirror, he wasn't comfortable being alone in the field but the other board members had insisted on it. At least he knew today's orders would solve one of their problems. Jon Bennett had become a serious issue for *The Trust* and he had to be disposed of.

He fell back onto his hotel bed, closed his eyes to take in a moment of calm not knowing what waited for him.

CHAPTER 106

MUZAFFARPUR

Muzaffarpur, India
September 16th

They touched down shortly after 2pm into another day of heavy rain, temperature reaching 35 degrees Celsius and humidity well above comfortable. They taxied to an isolated area off to one end of the airport where two unmarked black Humvees waited with an anxious looking Indian driver in each.

Behind them, a US Military marked medical vehicle waited, engine idling while two soldiers with guns stood beside it watching the jet, their orders to transport Nicholette to a nearby hospital while Bennett's mission unfolded.

He and Marcus moved quickly to organise their team of three men and the weapons into the vehicles, their destination a small house in Hajipur to the north of Patna. There they would prepare their attack to steal back the sphere. Satellite photos faxed by Whittaker showed the target address earmarked by the same helicopter that attacked the Temple.

The doctors accepting Nicholette had been briefed well, a favour for a local diplomat to save the life of his daughter, a woman suffering terminal cancer in a queue for a trial treatment.

Bennett reluctantly walked away leaving Nicholette motionless on the stretcher, it wasn't time for her to die and he fought the emotional sorrow intensifying inside him. Within another five minutes they were heading south towards Hajipur with Viktor, Marcus and Bennett all riding together in the same vehicle while the remaining Guardians followed in the second.

Viktor broke the silence, "Did any of you notice we have an admirer?"

Marcus had missed it but Bennett had already locked in on the white Mercedes van ten cars back in the heavy morning southbound traffic. It had exited the airport car park at the same time they departed and from there it remained the same distance behind no matter how congested the traffic became. Inside two men sat, both of Middle Eastern appearance.

"Anybody you know, Jon?" Viktor asked from the rear seat.

"At a guess, I would say the Islamic Liberation Front, a small extremist terrorist group with a particular dislike for me. They think I led a seal team to the slaughter of their families in Kuwait."

"Did you?" his father hesitantly asked.

"No."

Rasheed maintained his distance ten cars back behind the two Humvees, he knew Bennett would undoubtedly know he was being followed and there was no advantage in taking out the vehicles now. He knew with Bennett and Bannister soon to be in close confines it would be easier to kill them both once the opportunity presented itself.

Viktor saw the flash and blue exhaust trail from somewhere off to their left inside a factory yard. He knew what was about to happen.

Marcus and Bennett had been focused on their followers and witnessed firsthand the impact of the RPG into the rear Humvee. It lifted off the ground and exploded in a nebula of fire and black smoke. The carnage devoured four neighbouring cars and sent a shockwave through the busy street. People fled and cars smashed their way towards safety as Rasheed watched with a hint of a smile lining his face.

Bennett turned and yelled at the driver, "Get us out of here...NOW." He had chosen to ride next to the driver but now a small black handgun pointing straight at him from the driver's hips had his attention.

"You are my prisoner, you must cooperate with me while I take you to my Boss," the driver commanded in his best English. He had never been adequately briefed on his human cargo and was under the belief he was transporting international arms dealers.

Bennett's hand action was swift and stealth, while his other hand pushed the gun muzzle forward as it discharged a round into the dash. The driver's head snapped rearwards under Bennett's strike and his neck broke severing the spinal cord. Viktor and Marcus returned their attention towards the front as they heard the gunshot and witnessed the driver's head fall limp to one side. All three knew *The Trust* had found them.

Bennett pushed the dead driver out the door into the chaos outside and pulled himself across behind the wheel. Already the panicking daytime commuters had caused traffic bottlenecks in every direction stripping them of any immediate escape and then the impact from a heavily laden four tonne truck bulldozed them sideways into the cars in the opposite lane.

Wedged in place and imprisoned, they had become sitting ducks for their attackers.

CHAPTER 107

NO EXIT

Muzaffarpur
September 16th

The afternoon rain storm continued to pelt down hard onto the streets of Muzaffarpur as Bennett slammed the damaged Humvee into reverse and floored the accelerator. Outside three armed men closed in on their position forcing Bennett to push harder against the wall of vehicles front and rear. The tyres spun at a frantic speed yet they moved nowhere under the burden of the truck pressed tightly against their left side. It had slammed into them at speed pushing the vehicle sideways and preventing their escape.

Inside, Marcus bit down hard to stop himself from howling in agony. The impact had crumpled the rear door inwards onto him and shattered most of his ribs. Beside him, Viktor had escaped most of it and scrambled for their weapons in the rear cabin. The men stalking their position carried Heckler & Koch battle rifles and as they separated to surround the vehicle, Viktor felt the cold hard steel of an M16 under his hand.

He dragged one out and threw it across to Bennett who was still struggling to ram their way out as the front windshield exploded from a volley of automatic gunfire. He threw himself down across the front seat under the falling shards of glass, twisted over onto his back and fired the weapon aimlessly in the direction of their attacker.

The incoming hail of bullets soon ceased.

"Ok we're shooting our way out. You two ready?" Bennett yelled above the roar of the engine and people screaming in the street. He peered over at his father who had shouldered his M16 and was cradling Marcus's shaking body in his arms. Bennett hadn't realised the man had been injured and their eyes met.

"Leave me Bennett, you cannot let them get the codes," Marcus stuttered as blood gushed from his every word and flooded down across his chest.

The sound of men shouting close by and the sudden heavy sounds of boots on the bonnet ended their escape. Two men in black appeared looking down over the top of their rifle sights aimed a few threatening inches from his face.

"Drop the gun and don't move," the lead man yelled.

Bennett stared into the two barrels and let his M16 drop to the floor, no point aggravating the situation. The assailants were all concealed behind black balaclavas and though their identities were hidden, Bennett recognised one set of angry eyes glaring at him.

Somewhere behind him a single shot rang out and more glass exploded across the vehicle's interior. Two other similarly clad men had scaled the cars beside them and fired one precise round into Marcus's head splattering Viktor's face in blood.

The small pinching pain of a dart and darkness descended over both Bennett men.

They had been captured and so too had Jeremiah's Codes.

CHAPTER 108

PATNA

Patna, India
September 16th

A gargantuan among Patna's landscape, the once motor vehicle assembly plant rose high above its neighbours on the southern banks of the Ganga River. Now it had become desolate, unused in years, overgrown with dense vines and a haven for vermin. Scattered across the floor partly assembled vehicle carcasses gave the impression of a once highly industrial arena.

Bennett sat with his hands tied agonisingly tight behind his back, a dark hessian bag loosely over his head suffocating all light and he could hear muffled voices somewhere close by.

The approaching sound of heavy boots crunching on loose metal caught his attention and as they came closer and stopped his eyes were drowned in light. The bag had been jerked from his head exposing him suddenly to the building's interior. He had no idea of the time or how long he'd been unconscious since the ambush, the dart had contained a rapid acting sedative that left him feeling weak and dazed. A quick scan forward and back alarmed him, he was a lone prisoner with no sign of his father and at least three men poised with guns ready.

Outside he could see the sun had broken through and the rain had eased. A massive rusty steel door stood half open giving him a view out over a flat section of bitumen similar to a car park or loading area. Further across the expanse he could just make out the nose section of a Mi-24 Gunship helicopter. It was the location shown on the satellite images.

"Where is my father?" Bennett demanded.

"Your father is alive for now."

He turned his head to witness Logan Bannister stroll across the floor in his usual cocky manner, handgun hanging loosely at his side and eyeballing him. It was the same set of angry eyes from behind the balaclava he remembered.

"Bennett you are really starting to piss me off."

"Where is my father?" Bennett demanded again ignoring Bannister.

"Like I said, he is alive but that all depends on whether you cooperate. If you do then he lives, a fair deal I believe."

"Go fuck yourself Bannister, I want to see him?"

The mercenary closest to him moved in to strike at his face before Bannister raised his hand in a commanding motion to stop.

"There is no need for brutality here, Bennett will tell us everything we need to know, won't you Jon?" Bannister suggested as he moved close and tapped him in the head with the muzzle of his gun.

Bennett glared back at him, "I will spare the brutality on you if you show me my father now."

Bannister broke into deep laughter at the very sound of his prisoner's continued defiance. "Jon, you are so bold and I respect that."

He turned to his two men in the background and called, "Get the old man."

One spoke quietly into his radio never taking his eyes off Bennett strapped to the chair. A few minutes later Viktor Bennett shuffled slowly into view, hands bound and impatiently shoved along by another of Bannister's mercenaries. He had been badly beaten, blood streamed down across his clothes from a number of facial gashes. One leg dragged leaving a thin smear of blood on the dusty floor and the grimace of pain on his face illustrated the torment he had endured.

They made eye contact like any father and son would do and Bennett caught a glimpse of the very thing taken from him as a boy, fatherly love.

He sat feeling the tightness of the zip ties restraining his hands and the blood rush through his body as anger swarmed his every cell. In front of him was his long lost father held captive by an animal no mother would want.

Bannister grabbed hold of Viktor and nudged him closer towards Bennett. "As you would know, I have the Mayan Sphere and now I have the code book. I thought our plan was flawless until now."

"And what plan would that be, Bannister, I know it wouldn't be yours. You aren't that smart," Bennett retaliated.

"Jon you cannot tell them anything," Viktor urged as Bannister unleashed a silencing backhand across the old man's head throwing him off balance and sending him toppling to the hard factory floor.

Somewhere behind him another more familiar voice sounded.

"Well that would be most unfortunate for all of you."

The look on Bennett's face announced his shock and Bannister laughed at the sight.

CHAPTER 109

BETRAYAL

Patna, India
September 16th

Bennett's mind raged a war of disbelief as a heavy set bald man walked casually across the factory floor from somewhere behind him. Enshrouded within a persona of command and control his every step declared he was in charge, walking past Bennett and only once giving him a minuscule glance. Disbelief and astonishment had taken a firm grip of Bennett and life as he knew it had just spiralled into oblivion. What faith he had in humanity died along with the arrival of his best friend.

Dom Whittaker casually dressed in jeans and a khaki suede jacket paraded to within a few feet of Bannister and paused at the blood smeared sight of Viktor, a vision he didn't care too much about. In his hand he held tightly the Mayan sphere while the other rested casually in his jacket pocket.

He looked from one prisoner to the other and gloated to himself how effective his plan had been. The Bennett's had been merely pawns in a much larger stratagem, one that would reward *The Trust* trillions of dollars and in his eyes, Earth's ultimate society.

Bennett watched him, his eyes signalling disbelief, dishonour and above all, endless questions. He sat stunned and speechless as Whittaker took the few steps over to his father kneeling on the floor and slammed a loaded left hook into the old man's face while the sphere remained firm in the other.

Viktor's pride lifted himself to his shaking feet, blood flowing freely from his mouth and knowing the man had done damage from the burning torment spreading inside his cheek and jaw.

"That's for fucking us around for so long and forcing my hand to involve your son," Whittaker declared as he stepped back from the strike zone letting Viktor find his stable footing.

He handed the sphere to Bannister and reached inside his shirt pocket.

"Viktor, as you can see I have your codebook so really not much use in keeping you alive any longer," he added while flicking through the pages and grinning victoriously towards him.

Viktor's entire imprisonment at Kehlstein had been about *The Trust* finding ways to extract the codebook's location from him. They had attempted all methods of torture without success but it was the mind probes that gave the closest results. In his sleep when he was mentally defenceless *The Trust* used their advanced technologies to delve inside his mind for the answers they desperately sought. Though it didn't reveal the codebook's location, it did identify Rose holding some knowledge and from that, Whittaker's plan unfolded to lure Bennett into his web.

He flicked over a few more pages, stopping momentarily to tilt them sideways and upside down. Though it had been subject of hype for many years within *The Trust*, no one had seen it except Viktor and now as Whittaker viewed it for the first time it wasn't what he had expected.

"What's wrong Whittaker, having a few problems understanding what it says," Viktor mumbled through his bloodied mouth. The facial blow hadn't just shattered his cheek bone it had slashed through his tongue from the impact of his jaws colliding. He stepped forward to face off against Whittaker as one of mercenaries ripped him backwards by his bound hands.

"What the fuck is going on Dom?" Bennett called.

Whittaker dropped his attack on Viktor and spun to face Bennett.

"Oh Jon ... there are many things you don't know. I must admit though, you have served us well and now we have the codebook all thanks to your efforts and your Soviet spy girlfriend."

Whittaker saw the bewildered look in Bennett's eyes, "What you didn't think I knew about her Soviet background. Jon I planned all this and played you like a puppet my friend."

"Why, I don't understand?" Bennett responded in a stunned manner bordering on shock.

"Jeremiah's Codes my friend. Quite simply put we needed them and suspected you could access them. You just didn't know it at the time and needed some prompting. So I devised an elaborate plan to flush you out of Australia and lead us to them. Some of it did not go to plan like blowing up the Anubis Sphere at Kehlstein but the board members knew the risks when we started, it was Jeremiah's Codes at any cost they ordered," Whittaker boasted knowing he wasn't giving the complete story.

Bennett was gutted, speechless and thinking through the events of the past weeks all part of a sinister plan devised by Whittaker. He needed more explanation but wasn't going to get it just yet. Beside him, Bannister had become frustrated listening to Whittaker catch him up on the deceit and interrupted the conversation.

"Whittaker, get the codes and let's fuck off from this place," he snarled at Whittaker.

Whittaker ignored Bannister and opened the code book to the first page facing it towards Viktor.

"Well Viktor you tell me how to decipher it."

Viktor said nothing, his returning look towards Whittaker said it all. Viktor Bennett had safeguarded the secret of Jeremiah's Codes for sixty years and was not about to fail himself now. Whittaker knew he didn't break during the entire time at Kehlstein so why would he now and so he switched his attention towards the other Bennett.

"Jon, tell me, where are the codes on this page?" Whittaker asked as he pointed the open pages at Bennett sitting three feet away.

Bennett looked and could easily see all thirteen symbols strung across the two pages.

"I don't know, and like you I can't see them, I think you have to decipher the written scriptures to reveal the codes," Bennett lied.

"Bullshit Bennett," Bannister snapped back at him. He grabbed Viktor by his hair and pulled his head back into the muzzle of his handgun. "You tell us what it says or your father enters the afterlife," an agitated Bannister yelled.

Whittaker stepped in and placed his hand on Bannister's gun, "Calm down Bannister, no need to shoot the old man yet, Jon will tell us what we need to know."

Bannister lowered his weapon away from Viktor's head. "Ok genius let's do it your way but if we don't have the codes in twenty minutes then it's my way," he whispered.

Whittaker knew extracting information from Jon Bennett wasn't going to be an easy task, he knew his tolerance to pain, his commitment to silence and above all, his pride was unbreakable. They needed to try various angles on the man, making him angry would never succeed but making him emotional might.

"With each hour that passes, Nicholette creeps closer to death. Now if you want to save her then cut the bullshit and tell us what we need to know," Whittaker said as he moved closer holding out the open pages towards him.

"I believe you are looking at Nicholette's only chance for survival. Somewhere on this page is the First Code and the cure for the dreaded Blue Death. Just tell me how to decipher the writings and she survives. Without it Jon, she will be dead. Mate you don't want that to happen, now do you?"

Bennett ignored Whittaker's attempt at the sympathy tack, it was a strategy he'd used many times himself, make him emotionally vulnerable.

Whittaker kept trying, "I've looked after Rose all these years and this is how you repay me, I am disappointed Jon."

Viktor piped in, "Whittaker you took care of Rose because she had knowledge of the codes. That's all it's ever been about, the codes not Rose's health. Tell him nothing Jon."

Bannister took one impatient step forward, raised his Beretta and squeezed the trigger.

CHAPTER 110

STRATEGIES

Patna, India
September 16th

Blood and brain splattered across the floor as the bullet exploded out the rear of the old man's skull followed by the unnerving thud of his lifeless body. Bannister lowered his weapon and turned to smirk at Bennett who had erupted into satanic spasms tensing in the chair to break free.

"Bannister you are fucking dead you gutless prick, you hear me... fucking DEAD," Bennett roared like an injured beast.

Bennett had lost his composure at the sight of his father's head exploding from Bannister's single bullet. The zip ties had carved deep lacerations into his wrists from the fight to free himself and a stream of blood dripped under his chair.

"You fucking idiot Bannister, there was no need to kill the old man yet," Whittaker screamed as he pounced towards him. The once field operative was still lightning quick with his hands and had stripped him of his weapon within a split second before Bannister had a chance to pull the trigger a second time. The mercenaries either side, though loyal to their commander were both taken off guard by the agility and skill of Whittaker who now had Bannister's gun pointed firmly at his head.

Back behind them, Bennett suffered the violent onslaught of rifle butts slamming his head and shoulders and like a caged lion primed to escape he continued trying to force himself upright clawing his way towards Bannister. Each time he was knocked back down by the men guarding him and the rage inside ignited. The Eighth Code in response replicated itself to give him a surge of lethal power until Whittaker walked to within arm's length and pressed the muzzle of his gun into his forehead.

"Ok enough Jon, settle down. Tell me what I need to know and I'll give you five minutes alone with Bannister." He turned back towards Bannister and casually remarked, "I was being generous, he only needs thirty seconds to dispose of you, weapons and all."

For a short moment, Bennett actually considered the proposal, the chance for revenge was intensely burning inside his veins.

"Come on Dom, the mercenary has no skills, he is a coward and hides behind big guns, just a gutless piece of shit, no wonder the Seals never wanted him," Bennett spat throwing bait to anger the man, he knew an angry man always made mistakes.

"I need to know where the codes are on these pages and you will tell me Jon because if you don't, I'm afraid Logan here will pay Nicholette a visit. Do you want her death on your conscience too?" Whittaker asked in his calm and controlled manner. Bannister on the other hand was provoked and impatient, he was thinking more of the reward and leverage the codes would bring him.

"Move aside Whittaker, I'll make the spook talk, he won't tolerate what I have for him," Bannister interrupted.

Bannister pushed past Whittaker heading towards the restrained prisoner, while his two goons hustled in close beside in anticipation of a brutal reaction, their weapons shadowing the prisoner every step. He clipped Bennett aggravatingly across the head with his hand as he edged by him heading towards the rear of the building. Bennett flinched and his anger rose higher than he thought it could yet not enough to snap the ties.

"Why Dom? Why all the deceit? I just don't understand how you could possibly be involved," Bennett asked glaring at his long-time friend.

He ignored Bennett as Bannister returned carrying a small metal briefcase. He placed it on the floor at Bennett's feet and lifted the lid to expose the contents. Bennett knew exactly what it was and the pain it inflicted was beyond tolerance for most people.

"Bennett you know what this is don't you? ... In fact I bet you've used it many times yourself to extract information from your victims," Bannister asked before breaking into laughter and adding sarcastically, "and you call me a gutless piece of shit."

Bannister continued to snigger to himself as he started removing syringes filled with yellow fluid. Whittaker watched on from just behind, he wasn't going to stop the mercenary if it meant getting the answers they needed. He was there to get the codes through any means possible and if it meant torturing his friend then he was fine with that.

Whittaker asked one more time, "Jon there's no need for torture if you just tell us what we need to know."

Bennett stared back and uttered what he thought would be a waste of time, "What's happened to you Dom? All those years you and I working together against pieces of shit like Bannister here. Tell me how does one change so much?"

Whittaker looked down at him and the inducing drugs at his feet and knew he owed him an explanation.

"For so many years I've sat back and watched the conflicts between world governments escalate and wars break out, the people never get a say instead they or their loved ones get killed. So many different religions and cultures on this planet means there will always be conflict and war no matter what we do to prevent it. The Board Members are about changing that, they are about a new society where war doesn't exist, a New World Order creating a complete state of balance for our planet. One government worldwide is what they stand for but first there must be human sacrifice. A one government world does not come without sacrifice and resistance, those opposed must be eliminated for the betterment of all. That's where the sphere and Jeremiah's Codes come into it," he explained and it became clear to Bennett the man believed his own allocution.

Bennett listened while Bannister prepared the injections and then responded.

"Certainly explains how the Nazi's fit into it, the Fourth Reich and their world supremacy vision... Kehlstein showed me that... death of billions worldwide. I saw the targets, North Korea, China, Middle East, Indonesia, Pakistan, Afghanistan and hell even a large part of the States, United Kingdom and Australia. Dom, this is insane, you can't be seriously supporting this madness, it's just another dictatorship but on a global scale of lunacy. Don't you remember we fought tirelessly to dismantle regimes like this and now, you and your mates are becoming the most heinous of them all."

"Yes it is madness Jon. You know I thought about bringing you on-board with *The Trust*, but I knew your morals would never have allowed it. Instead I devised a plan to use you to help us so in a way you are with us," Whittaker added as he nodded towards Bannister giving him the go-ahead to commence the psychometric torture.

Bennett knew there was no point in resisting, he couldn't help look down at his dead father laying in an expanding puddle of dark red blood flowing outwards across the floor from the hole in his head.

Bennett felt the first injection enter his arm, an angry jab declaring what was to come. Then a warm tingling sensation drifted up and commenced seducing his mind as the second injection pierced the side of his neck with similar ferocity as the first. The third was more painful, the substance injected was thick and cold as it advanced slowly up his neck into his brain. Like molten wax spilling across bare skin he could feel it searing inside his veins and the blistering itch that followed was intolerable.

Bannister took a step back admiring the initial stages of his work and from there, he watched as Bennett's eyes glazed over and his mind succumbed to the invasion of drugs.

"Soon he will be ready," he told Whittaker.

A slurred voice from the chair sounded, "What plan ... you played me. Tell me, what plan?"

"It was quite ingenious Jon. Your father wasn't helping us, his imprisonment in Kehlstein didn't exactly go as we planned, he told us nothing except that the code book existed. He did tell us in his sleep that your dear old Aunt Rose knew its location too. But she was too far gone to give us anything. You know I kept her alive all that time, *The Trust* wanted her dead but I convinced them she held the key to the whole plan. I just had to get her to talk to you Jon so a little mental stimulation each night for about a month worked perfectly. Her dreams were polluted with satanic verse and deadly scenarios of Armageddon induced by *The Trust*. After four weeks she was on edge screaming out in her sleep, quite the part she played and at no time did she even know it."

Whittaker stopped briefly to think of Rose and the parts he intentionally left out. Bennett didn't need to know what he did to her after they'd visited her a month ago. He continued.

"So I set up a plan that would flush you out and get you on the scent. We enlisted an old friend of yours, the ILF to hunt you in Australia but make sure you escaped. You see I knew you'd come running to me then, some things about you are predictable. Once I had you, it was just a matter of making sure you headed in the right directions. We knew Nicholette Sponarava was closing in on us and would do just about anything to complete her mission. So we leaked her information suggesting you had knowledge of the codes location, that way it took some pressure of us and she'd unknowingly help us find the codes. The Council's priority was or is the elimination of *The Trust* but Jeremiah's Codes take priority over any other except confiscation of the sphere itself."

Bennett mumbled, "Afghanistan... why?"

"Yes Afghanistan, why did I send you there? Well quite simple really, I needed some bogus verification on terrorists with stolen nukes that would get approval from the President for a justified military strike on Afghanistan. Your friend Sergi Saranovik was working for me and accepted a substantial pay cheque to double cross you but of course he never got to cash it, rest his soul."

"No nukes?" Bennett murmured.

"You are quick Jon, correct there were no nukes," he laughed. "Deep within those mountains is the only other known blue crystal deposit in the world. There is enough to fuel our campaign ten times over. We suspect it came to Earth millions of years ago by a meteor with the main section hitting Afghanistan and a smaller splinter smashing into Namibia."

"Anyway, we had a problem extracting it, the Taliban sabotaged our everyday mining efforts. Bannister here couldn't stop them, as you know, fucking useless mercenary."

Bannister moved uneasy on his feet, he was both embarrassed and infuriated at his failure.

Whittaker continued, "We needed to remove the local Taliban tribesmen and fast. There were over five hundred spread out through the mountains that made eliminating them one by one near impossible not to mention time consuming. I thought if Washington feared nuclear material in the hands of terrorists then they would engage an immediate invasion and our problems with the Taliban would be over. Sadly it wasn't the case, the President didn't accept you as a reliable source and chose to ignore the threat."

Whittaker could see Bannister getting edgy to attach the electrodes, he was salivating to inflict pain. He enjoyed making Bannister wait, it gave him that superiority over the man and so he continued to provide Bennett with explanation.

"We needed the damn Taliban off our backs and the only way was by military force but justification did not exist. That's where we used Al-Qaeda and their hate for the West. Once the green light was given by the Six, the plan became reality and as you know, various airliners crashed into the Twin Towers. For the sake of three thousand people we got what we needed, a retaliatory strike on Afghanistan which flushed the Taliban out of the northern mountains to fight. The little mining operation of ours in the north became unnoticed and way down the priorities for the locals. Never thought for a minute, I'd be enlisting terrorists to aid us in our cause."

Bennett's head was starting to sway forward and back, his focus drifting and his speech making less cognitive sense. "Must not use thirteen," he slurred like a drunken man.

"Come on Jon, this whole hunt is about the thirteenth technology, our master plan depends on what it can do, so much power and so much control for us. Our air dispersal systems are still not sufficient to provide large scale elimination, it simply requires the machining of too much crystal dust. The orbital platform is our best option and with the intense power generated by Lucifer's Funnel, I dare say no one can stand in our way."

He paused briefly and walked towards Bennett, grabbed him by the shirt collar and screamed into his face, "Tell me how to read the codes."

Bennett remained silent like the well trained agent he was, he would not succumb to pressure under any circumstances. Now was no exception, he could feel his own mind fighting to regain control, presumably the Eighth Code adapting to the chemical cocktail surging through his bloodstream.

"Ok Bennett it's time for you to start talking, I've had enough of your silent bullshit. Move aside Whittaker I need to attach the electrodes and show you how real torture is done," Bannister announced as he edged his way to grab Bennett's shirt. With two hands, he yanked Bennett's shirt open to expose his bare chest.

Both men stumbled a few steps backwards in amazement at what they saw.

CHAPTER 111

THIRTEEN

Patna
September 16th

With his shirt ripped open, Bennett sat back in a state of mental disruption, mind muddled by the drugs yet he knew why they had stood back. He had seen the symbols appearing on his chest over the past days and did his best to keep them hidden. It was something Bannister never expected but Whittaker on the other hand had the inkling from his sources in the field. *The Trust* had been so focussed on finding the codebook that here was the carrier of the Thirteenth Code right under their noses the entire time.

"I'll be damned... it's true," was all Whittaker could say.

He had received obscure reports from his source inside the Council about claims of Jon Bennett holding the balance of power. But it wasn't until field operatives discovered a blind African man proclaiming one man held the secret scripture to Armageddon. At the time they laughed it off on the ramblings of some superstitious witch doctor who was suffering the psychotic effects of chewing too much Khat plant.

Whittaker walked closer to Bennett and leant in for a more rewarding inspection. He reached out and delicately ran his fingers over the strange looking symbols that in the fading light of the factory had a luminous glow similar to that of the blue crystals in the dark.

Whittaker turned towards Bannister, "You know what this represents?"

"Yeah another set of codes."

Whittaker broke into a deep belly laugh, "Not just another set, it's the Thirteenth Code and it changes everything."

"What do you mean?" Bannister asked.

"Deciphering that damn codebook is no longer important and..." he paused thinking about what it was he was about to say.

Bannister had caught on quick and finished for him, "and we don't need Bennett any longer."

Whittaker suddenly finding himself with a conscience looked away from Bennett thinking how for so long he hoped this day never arrived. Twenty years of friendship was always going to be a hurdle no matter what happened.   The board members didn't care when he raised it, Bennett was always just collateral damage in their eyes.

On the other hand, Bannister hated the man and so needing no further motivation he walked towards the defenceless Bennett, an excited finger on the trigger. At one foot away he aimed his handgun directly at his head while a few steps back behind him, Whittaker said nothing. It was easier for him to turn away and let Bannister do the dirty work.

CHAPTER 112

KOEHLER

Patna
September 16th

Koehler hated the overcrowded streets of India with its heat and obnoxious odours wafting through the air. The thought of Schwartz's fate at Kehlstein continually played on his mind and whether he'd be the next victim to perish at the hands of Jon Bennett. Right now, he felt only marginally reassured as he sat with Rasheed and three brothers of the ILF a block from the old vehicle assembly plant. He had opposed Whittaker's idea to bring Bennett into the game and now, the man was killing them off one by one.

Koehler commanded the Africa/Middle East Sector and for twenty years he manipulated governments, the military and the local industry leaders to secure non-negotiable control for *The Trust*. He always knew his job was the easiest, US dollars bought anything in the corrupt African governments and his private army was cheap and impressionable. The Middle East was not so simple with so much conflict in religious belief and hatred towards the West. He found it almost impossible to gain their trust and money offered no persuasion. Consequently, that region became his first target for Meredith.

Each board member had a specific region of Earth to control and prepare. Like the others, Koehler chose his geographical targets, large areas of population considered most threatening to birthing the New World Order. It was *The Trust's* mission to expel problems before they surfaced and so Koehler had picked targets inside Iran, Iraq, Somalia, Libya, Syria, Algeria, Sudan and Angola. He knew taking control of the oil rich provinces gave them political dominance in any society still dependant on the use of fossil fuels.

Koehler had been particular in the design of his sector's implementation phase. Air dispersal of blue crystal dust would dispose of most in the larger populated areas while local hired guns would deplete the remainder. His colleagues on the other hand, had different challenges in selecting their ground targets. With highly populated cities, greater military sites and economical strengths meant a gargantuan volley of pulse strikes into the Earth's surface were required. In total, over a thousand deployments of Meredith's energy pulse weapon would initiate a terrifying series of deep land tsunamis across four continents decimating the surface and everything on it.

Rasheed didn't like Koehler because to him he was just a little weasel condemning life without his hands ever bloodied. He didn't care much for their new world dream or the bloodbath dictatorship it would incite because in his belief no one was more powerful than Allah.

Half an hour earlier they had witnessed the explosive ambush and watched as Bennett and his father were dragged from their wrecked vehicle by Bannister's men. From there they covertly pursued them south through the streets of Patna to the factory and waited. Rasheed knew timing was everything, he wanted Bennett but the deal was to kill Bannister and take the sphere. It meant being patient, something he wasn't comfortable with.

CHAPTER 113

EXIT STRATEGIES

Patna
September 16th

The sound of boots pounding the floor combined with gunfire was all Bennett heard as something heavy slammed against him.

A few seconds earlier, Whittaker had suddenly remembered the symbols fade when the subject dies. It had occurred once during the Namibian tests when a survivor attacked a guard and was shot. He died within minutes and the symbols immediately vanished from his skin. It was a costly mistake for *The Trust* at the time not knowing if it had been the Thirteenth Code.

Whittaker had acted quickly and charged Bannister shouldering his handgun off target. In the same movement he kicked out at Bennett landing his size twelve boot squarely in his chest that sent him toppling over.

Bennett opened his drug blurred eyes to witness Whittaker wrestling Bannister's gun and somewhere the rattling sounds of automatic gunfire were growing closer. He fought against the restraints like a drowning man clawing for his last breath.

Rasheed's men had stormed the factory and without warning obliterated two of Bannister's mercenaries while outside, Koehler sat in the car waiting the all clear.

The building's interior erupted into war with rounds ricocheting across the closed confines and deflected off the surrounding machinery. Bannister broke from the struggle and raced for cover while Whittaker grabbed Bennett's arm and lugged him, chair and all, away from the incoming barrage of bullets. The floor either side of their position was littered with old disused assembly line structures and steel benches once used to sort thousands of vehicle parts that now sat dormant covered in years of dust. The onslaught of Rasheed's small but elite outfit pushed Bannister and his men to take cover where they returned fire the best they could.

Whittaker kept low, pulling Bennett into the protection of a large conveyor belt once used to push car parts along to their final design. Bullets chinked as they deflected and ricocheted off the rusted steel frames narrowly missing them both. Either side, Bannister's men returned their own ferocious ensemble of rapid gunfire as Whittaker pressed his gun harder against Bennett's head.

He knew Bennett's abilities were subdued and he sliced the zip ties releasing him from the confines of the chair. The drugs flowing through Bennett's body had dulled his reflexes and minimised his ability to think quickly or strike with his usual cobra like velocity. As if his hands were out of sync with his mind and the encroaching double vision clouded his coordination, he offered no resistance to Whittaker yanking his arms behind his back and binding them agonisingly tight.

Bannister had dived for cover behind another conveyor machine where he scanned the incoming formation of combatants all dressed in green army fatigues and black head banners. He counted at least three on the far side of the building carrying attack rifles and from the way they moved in covering formations he was sure they had military training. At that distance they appeared intimidating but it was the single dark figure walking boldly along behind that he feared the most.

He took aim and steadied himself against the steel struts of the conveyor. There he squeezed the trigger and let loose with three short bursts. The first found its mark into the chest of the lead man ending his advance dead in his tracks. The other two missed the intended targets. Another hailstorm of rounds blasted Bannister's position all deflecting high off the machinery he crouched behind. His few remaining men had taken cover further over and waited for the opportunity to counter attack.

Back behind them, Whittaker still with Bennett under guard looked up towards the roof rafters where two of his commando team were expertly concealed. A nod of his head was all it took.

Within seconds, two of Bannister's mercenaries were cleanly executed in the back of their heads. The soldiers used silenced weapons and not even Bannister knew his men had just died. He hadn't spotted his new enemy above him, the assassins with orders to kill everyone in the factory because unlike Whittaker, Bannister had come there that day without an exit strategy.

More silenced shots reached their targets and Bannister lost the remainder of his team.

Rasheed crouched low cloaking his position behind an old vehicle chassis, he was well trained and battle hardened but now he felt forced to reassess his surroundings. Something he thought didn't add up, the enemy had gone too silent for his liking. No movement or noise was unusual and so he stood to entice an answer. Nothing happened, no sudden shower of bullets or movement. With his gun raised to eye height, he stepped from behind the engineless car frame and called to his men to provide cover.

Only a short distance separated him from the conveyor hiding the dead men and so he advanced slowly across the floor stopping every few feet to resurvey the area from behind his rifle sights. Still nothing, no movement or sounds from among the mass of machinery further over. His men slowly moved with him, maintaining cover over their leader as they stepped almost in unison. A few cautious steps and Rasheed reached the first of two large conveyor units crossing his path. He paused, raised his gun high and hoisted himself up onto the long jaded platform that once held the underbellies of vehicles progressing along the assembly line. He peered down at the dead bodies of Bannister's men sprawled in a sea of their blood. He knew then they had a new enemy.

Rasheed turned and yelled to his men as the first bullet brushed his shoulder catapulting him off the conveyor onto the floor next to the dead men. At the same time, Bannister launched himself from behind the second conveyor unleashing more rounds towards Rasheed, all missing him. Rasheed's men had reacted swiftly to intercept Bannister's assault on their leader and attacked with their own volley of automatic fire while Rasheed did the same from the floor. He had rolled to his back, lifted his AK47 and released the magazine's contents at Bannister's position shredding the metal sheets but not the target.

A quick change of magazines gave Rasheed another thirty rounds however, as he did something high above him caught his eye. Perched high in the rafters a dark long object was suspended from the roofing. It wasn't till it moved towards him that he realised what was in his sights. The soldier clad in dark fatigues blended with the roof and the matrix of rafters surrounding him giving the impression of some huge cocooned insect. Then Rasheed caught sight of the second soldier a few feet further over with his rifle aimed at him.

"SNIPERS… SNIPERS… in the roof."

Rasheed screamed to his men in his native tongue and pulled tight on his trigger. With the snipers exposed, it only took a few seconds before they both hung lifeless from their harnesses.

Under the rampage of gunfire, Bannister crawled behind a pile of scrap metal and waited clasping his gun for the opportunity to escape. The hard steel of a gun muzzle pressed firmly into his head changed that.

"Move and I kill you."

Bannister considered for a brief second to fight until his quick sideways glance warned him otherwise. Out the corner of his eye he caught a glimpse of a Middle Eastern man and knew it was Rasheed

Mahdavi, the same single dark figure he'd seen entering the building ten minutes earlier. He had heard the stories of his merciless killing of Iraqi troops during the Iran Iraq war and he was well known for his superior hand to hand combat.

Rasheed pressed his gun deeper into Bannister's head, it was clear he wasn't about to start playing any games with him. He wanted to find Bennett and deal punishment but first he needed the sphere and then kill Bannister.

"Tell me … where is the sphere?" Rasheed demanded as his team appeared alongside.

"I don't have it, but Whittaker does, he is somewhere here in the building and he has Jon Bennett," Bannister replied hoping Rasheed would take the bait.

CHAPTER 114

TRAITOR

Patna
September 16th

Outside the car factory, the rain had completely cleared and the sun was blasting its warmth down onto the steaming roadway. The surrounding streets were void of movement typical for that part of Patna except for two men scurrying along, one carrying the burden of zip ties behind his back and stumbling every step of the way. From high above, sniper crosshairs followed their every step while keeping watch for the enemy in pursuit.

Bennett had been forced to keep a hurried pace with Whittaker who continually pushed and shoved at him to move faster. With his leg restraints severed and his hands still bound, Bennett found it difficult to resist the coercion of a gun in his back. He glanced up at the rooftops and though blurry, he caught sight of three dark silhouetted snipers.

In the chaos of Rasheed's attack, Whittaker had taken the opportunity to flee the building, prodding Bennett along at gun point towards his hire car parked in the next street. Everything had gone to plan, the snipers in the rafters gave them an escape, he had the codebook and sphere and best of all, he had the Thirteenth Code inscribed across Bennett's chest. From there it was north to Muzaffarpur for a quick exit out of India and onto the next phase of his plan.

"Never pictured you as a traitor, Dom," Bennett remarked finding his usual speech was returning.

"Traitor, what the fuck Jon, you have no idea. You think trying to save mankind is being a traitor? The human population is doomed unless we do something, just too many fucking people and not enough resources. At least *The Trust* has the balls to do something about it whether you support their methods or not. What are our Governments doing? Yeah jack shit nothing except make it worse."

"Do you really think exterminating billions of innocent people is the best way?"

"Has to be done Jon. Just shut up and keeping walking."

"You fucking lunatic, there will be no planet left to save when you use that pulse weapon," Bennett snapped back.

Whittaker replied while at the same time clouting Bennett across the head with his gun, "No one believes the old Monk, his prophecies for this world are beyond ridiculous, now shut up."

Bennett fell silent as they approached Whittaker's car, a late model silver Bentley Arnage looking out of place among the industrial dumpsters and aging buildings all around.

"You don't know his plans, do you?" Whittaker laughed as the three shooters from the roof joined them.

"We have a problem Boss. Our boys on the inside are dead and those gunship choppers are winding up," the lead sniper quietly informed Whittaker.

"Ok we can't assume Rasheed or Bannister are dead and it means they will be coming for Bennett and the sphere," Whittaker announced before adding, "Rasheed is most dangerous and the moment you drop your guard your dead."

The soldiers loaded their weapons into the car all with Whittaker's last comment on their minds.

CHAPTER 115

GUNSHIP

Northern Patna
September 16th

Like the raindrops of an approaching rainstorm a few single rounds struck the brick wall next to them before a torrential deluge of bullets followed with some piercing the car's boot. Whittaker pushed Bennett into the rear seat where he was firmly sandwiched by two soldiers. Another couple of seconds and their car was churning up dust and mud as it fishtailed under the grunt of the powerful Bentley engine silencing the chinking of rounds hitting the rear chassis.

Whittaker kept a close watch on their tail as the car accelerated through the lonely industrial area of western Patna. Even though it was late Sunday afternoon and the surrounding factories were closed, the roaring engine and screeching tyres were sure to draw unwanted attention as they entered the neighbouring housing colonies.

The massive frame of a Soviet made helicopter gunship passed at speed overhead rocking their car and the surrounding buildings in its wake. It rose up and turned back downwards like a dragon preparing to heave a belly of fire into their path. It stopped and floated only feet above the houses either side where the howling turbulence of downwash rattled roof tiles and shattered windows.

Under each winglet pod hung a threatening arsenal of slender air to ground missiles and from the nose dangled a Gatling gun waiting anxiously to obliterate them. The pilot from behind his blackened helmet had the car centred in his crosshairs and waited Bannister's command. Tucked in behind but slightly higher, Bannister sat anxiously waiting the show and not taking his eyes off the car racing towards them.

Less than twenty minutes earlier he had Rasheed's gun in his back until Richard Koehler walked across the factory floor and offered him a lifeline.

"Hold on!" the driver yelled as he slammed down hard on the brakes and yanked the gearshift to reverse. Whittaker and the others braced themselves as the car skidded and slid to a halt while the back wheels spun up gaining traction in reverse.

Bannister watched as the Bentley vanished under a blanket of swirling blue tyre smoke and gave the command. A rocket launched from under their left winglet with a deathly hiss leaving only a thin smoke trail and careered overhead of the fleeing vehicle. It found its intended target, an old dilapidated building where it struck without mercy. Brick, timber and fire exploded skyward before crashing back down blocking the narrow road and the car's escape.

"FUCK… GO… GET US OUT OF HERE," Whittaker screamed as the gunship launched its second missile.

Bennett was flung sideways as the missile lifted the back wheels and hurled it sideways against the concrete wall of a nearby apartment block. The gunship descended skimming the rooftops as Whittaker snatched a rifle and fired at the cockpit.

The first of three rounds pierced the windshield and sliced through the pilot's shoulder followed by the other two deflecting off the frame. In grimacing pain, the pilot pulled his gunship high into the sky with Bannister screaming in protest.

Like a rabbit fleeing a bird of prey the Bentley scraped along the wall as it accelerated away smashing and deflecting off parked cars. Back behind them the pilot wrestled against the searing agony in his shoulder to fly his machine with Bannister frothing at the mouth in anger. He lowered the nose and rattled the Gatling across the escaping car's path. Up ahead the car's escape ended at a Mosque, there was no way out and he only needed one missile to trap them.

Whittaker had seen the dead end and lifted himself out the window and fired back at the gunship except this time his accuracy was thrown out by the severity of the car's manoeuvring. The pilot kept in pursuit nursing his blood soaked shoulder and pulled tight on his trigger finger.

It was the third missile he'd fired, though this one struck the roadway under the car's tail catapulting it upwards in flames and crashing back down onto its roof. Whittaker and the others had been tossed loose inside and all three soldiers were dead from single gunshot wounds to their heads.

Whittaker on the other hand was alive and staring into the muzzle of a Beretta 9mm still smoking from the three lightning quick taps. He had dropped his gun during the rollover in preservation of not losing the sphere.

"Are you going to kill me too Jon," Whittaker asked while at the same time considering his options for attack.

"Give me the sphere and codebook and we can negotiate your death," Bennett responded. He had slit the ties using a small razor blade concealed within the back of his trousers. As the car flipped and the soldiers lost their seating he grabbed the closest of their side arms. From there it was a matter of rolling with the car and firing the shots.

Further back along the street, Rasheed's soldiers were preparing to rope themselves down from inside the belly of the gunship as the car came to rest on its roof in the middle of the road. With twenty feet either side to the houses, the vehicle had become an easy target.

Bennett pushed himself from the wreckage onto his back and fired a volley of shots towards the gunship moments before another barrage hit the left turbine, someone else had joined the shoot. The pilot yanked hard on the controls and fled.

Whittaker was trapped in the vehicle with his leg caught under the collapsed dash and still clutched tightly at the sphere in both hands. He had been quick to retrieve it back at the factory when the shooting started.

"Jon don't you ever dream of a free life, away from the persecution of always looking over your shoulder. I can give you that and more money than you ever imagined. Think of our friendship, what you and I have been through together," Whittaker pleaded.

Bennett bent down and pushed the gun into his head, "I should kill you right here, you traitor and friends we are not. Now give me the sphere and codebook."

Whittaker held stubborn.

One shot sounded and Whittaker bellowed in agony. The bullet tore through his leg and exploded out the other side into the seat. He grabbed his leg dropping the sphere and Bennett repeated, "Give me the sphere and codebook or the next round will be in your knee."

"Come on Jon, we can both be winners from all this. Just think rationally for a minute mate. It means you finally get what you want, sanctuary from that life you so desperately run from."

Bennett swung hard with the butt of his handgun claiming Whittaker's head as the car wreck came under attack. The whining roar of the gunship rising above the Mosque and the Gatling spraying its venom sent Bennett dashing for cover amongst an old disused fruit stall tucked tightly in between two houses. There he crouched low keeping close watch on the wreck, Whittaker was unconscious and the Gatling rampage had ceased.

Screams and singular gunshots from inside the house opposite pulled his attention from Whittaker as the first of three men dressed in dark green and head banners exited the front door. Rasheed's men had rappelled to the roof and shot the residents as they descended towards the street where they moved quickly and in formation towards the overturned car. Each carried an aggressive style shortened attack rifle continually directed towards the car until they too came under siege from shooters further along the street. All three dropped and crawled as more shots chased their tails through the mud and road sludge lining the roadside.

Bennett too felt the deluge of rounds as they deflected off the building behind him and he sprinted low for cover. He had no idea who was shooting however, he couldn't risk losing the sphere and codebook so after a few minutes flat on his back, he leapt out onto the street towards the wreck.

The whistling scream of an inbound missile threw him sideways into the roadside sludge while he covered his head from the blast and fire. The impact had been precise and the thunder confirmed it with the detonation of the car's fuel tank.

Bennett raised his face from the slime still partially deafened by the cracking impulse of the explosion and wiped his eyes to witness his hell. The Bentley had become a burning twisted heap of metal and the sphere was lost, devoured by the intense heat. Whittaker was dead he smiled, but at the same time he felt sadness. A once good friend was gone yet worse, it meant Nicholette would die without the First Code and the sphere.

Across the street, the firing had started again jolting him to his open unprotected position just as one of the men in green appeared scowling from behind his rifle sights.

"Get up Bennett, hands where I can see them," he called in a heavy Middle Eastern accent.

Bennett pushed himself to his feet and flinched as two shots brushed close by his head. One speared the man's chest while the second blew his head open. Somewhere to his right, a rocket grenade riding a plume of ashen exhaust screeched the length of the street rising and accelerating as it passed.

The gunship's underbelly blew apart as a set of powerful hands grabbed Bennett from behind.

He fought to regain his footing however, his captor was too strong and he was dragged fast into one of the many houses lining the street. Up above he witnessed the passing of the gunship as it toppled over belching black smoke and disappearing down behind the roof tops.

CHAPTER 116

STRANGER

Northern Patna
September 16th

Bennett turned to peer into the cobalt blue eyes of an old man, something he wasn't expecting from the overpowering hand strength strangling his shoulders. His sun darkened face was a roadmap of aged lines with eyes uniquely contrasted by the surrounding bloodshot whites. Half his face was obscured behind a mass of grey almost white beard that flowed down in three platted tails across his chest. His clothes were that of any local Indian, long robed shirt and white pants somewhat dirty but coexisting with the other community men. He was unusual looking, almost alien and clearly not of Indian homage.

"Jonas Bennett you must not be captured, the Monk needs you to have strength," the old man muttered.

He spoke English with an unusual accent, something Bennett couldn't quite place but it was strangely familiar.

"Come on we must hurry, a car is waiting for you," he demanded.

A sudden flash and they dropped to the floor as CS gas smoked the house and automatic gunfire perforated the walls. Outside in the street, the two shooters wearing gas masks walked cautiously towards the front door. While back inside, Bennett and the old man crawled fighting for breath towards the rear door doing their best to stay conscious. They could feel the rancid taste as the toxic fumes scalded their nose and throat and the disorientation took hold. Somewhere in the white smoky haze dark figures moved quickly towards them and hoisted them to their feet.

Bennett was dragged half running until the sun struck his paining eyes and he squinted to see the narrow confines of an alleyway. He gulped for fresh air to flush the gas from his lungs and broke into a fit of convulsive coughing.

"We must keep moving, you will be ok," a deep English voice sounded as more gunfire rattled from behind them in the house. Bennett looked back and though his vision was a little blurred he could make out the shape of a gunman crouched at the doorway firing into the building covering their escape.

"I'm ok, I'm ok," Bennett announced as he pulled free and shuffled up to the same pace of his saviour. "Who are you?" he asked looking into the weathered face of a man in his forties, strongly built and wearing battle dress in the shades of brown and grey.

"We are Guardians here to protect you, there is a car waiting for us in the street."

Up ahead the old man too had recovered and was making fast towards a backstreet similar to the one they'd just escaped from. At the end of the alley, an aged olive green Mercedes sat with its engine idling. Local folk had gathered on the pavements watching, drawn by the shooting and explosions but as Bennett and the Guardians appeared they scampered back into the shadows.

Surprised at the vehicle's mighty grunt, Bennett hung on as the driver like in a fierce contest of dodgem racing smashed his way through narrow corridors and backstreets scraping buildings and ramming other cars. The car's droning horn had become his friend as he held it on giving the locals warning of their perilous approach.

They continued at high speed for the next five minutes until they hit the massive expanse of the Mahatma Gandhi Setu bridge over the Ganga River. It stretched north for miles and as the sun kissed the western horizon they darted amongst the build-up of traffic maintaining their hefty speed. No one spoke, the driver wasn't taking risks with slowing down and so the Mercedes rocked and slid as it swerved other cars. They kept a vigilant watch behind until taking the first exit towards Hajipur on the northern side of the river.

The road turned to loose gravel, mud and potholes yet the driver kept up his urgency while some distance away the second gunship commenced spinning up its turbines.

Bennett watched and held tight as the car pulled hard right into a short driveway before skidding abruptly to a stop outside a small brick farmhouse.

"We wait here," the driver said as he exited the vehicle followed quickly by the other Guardians. The old man wasn't so eager and remained seated in the front waiting for privacy. He turned to look penetratingly into Bennett's eyes and asked as he extended his hand, "Please I need to see your prophecies."

Bennett sat a little shocked, he had no prophecies or any understanding of what the old man was referring to. He had developed some unexplainable subliminal trust for the man and he extended his own hand in response. Their hands fused together and the old man smiled, his vision had been reached, and finally he had some glimpse of the future. He released his grip, he knew Bennett carried the thirteenth markings under his shirt and he'd confirmed the Monk's belief after months of travelling and covertly observing. He had sat back watching from the shadows just a pair of bloodshot eyes in the dark analysing Bennett's every move.

"So the great Monk is correct, you are the Thirteenth Oracle," he said after a brief moment of thought.

"What prophecies do you see?" Bennett asked.

"If you cannot see them then you are not ready to administer such responsibility. What is important right now is your safety until you can learn to conceal your markings."

"Conceal? How do you mean?"

"When your mind is developed, you will acquire the ability to hide your markings to the world. They will vanish from your skin only to return when you permit it."

"It feels more like a curse to me," Bennett complained.

"You Jon Bennett hold the power of existence, the Ace card if you like. The Thirteenth Code is not everything you are led to believe, there is so much more it can provide but it is the prophecies that will guide you," the old man added as his attention was drawn to a sudden commotion outside the car.

They both exited the Mercedes as the same Guardians appeared carrying rocket grenades. Inside the farmhouse, Bennett could see movement of at least eight more men all strapping rifles and ammunition across their shoulders. In the sky to the south he saw why.

The first series of missiles hit the house ripping it open killing three Guardians in the strike. The others scampered for cover while in the air above them the gunship gained altitude before rolling over preparing for another attack.

Bennett had found cover behind an abandoned tractor overgrown in long grass and there he watched as the next round of missiles decimated the remaining house structure. The surviving Guardians returned fire however, the Gatling was slowly picking them off one by one.

The same Guardian who saved him in Patna appeared with blood streaming down his face.

"We must go," he yelled as he dived in behind the same cover.

"Where?" Bennett responded.

"Muzaffarpur, there we can get you out of India."

"Wait there is something Bennett must know," the old man called as the Guardian pulled Bennett to his feet.

CHAPTER 117

DASH FOR LIFE

Hajipur
September 16th

Bennett bent down to hear the old man above the clatter of machine and Gatling guns behind them. The dusk lighting was still good and the burning farmhouse provided an orange and gold flickering ambience that reflected an unusual glow from his skin.

"*The Trust* has Sponarava at Sadar Hospital in central Muzaffarpur," the old man said.

The gunship had launched more missiles this time lifting their Mercedes ten feet in the air where it ignited into a ball of bright orange fire resembling a fireworks display executed by Satan himself.

"We have another car hidden at the next farmhouse, about five hundred yards," the Guardian shouted as the blast wave steamrolled them into a stumbling run.

"Name is Simon, Simon Johns, ex British MI6," the Guardian announced out of the blue as they pounded the roadway distancing themselves from the helicopter.

"British Secret Intelligence Service?" Bennett laughed in response as Johns fell to the ground.

The sniper bullet came in high hitting Johns cleanly in the right ear and jettisoned out the other side of his head taking with it half his brain. Bennett dropped for cover next to the dead body as the dirt next to him sprayed up as another high speed round zeroed in and missed him by just inches.

Bennett pulled himself forward and pushed his legs through the sand and dirt crawling for the cover of a large Baobab tree that towered over the road. It was massive, almost the width of a car and beside it a small wooden hut was dwarfed in its presence. With just over twenty feet to crawl he launched himself and sprinted slipping every few strides in the loose surface. One sniper round clipped his leg and he toppled forward. The next round slammed into the tree at his head height and he yanked himself to the safe side away from the sniper's incoming barrage.

He leant back against the tree to catch his breath and ripped a strip of material from his shirt. His gunshot wound had opened the gates to a torrent of blood and it was leaving a distinctive trail across the ground.

He wrapped it tight restricting the flow, the bullet had passed clean through the outer edge of his right thigh and he knew the bleeding would stop. He also suspected the Eighth Code would expedite the healing.

The sniper had ceased the attack and even as Bennett lifted himself and darted the few steps to the neighbouring hut there was no reaction. There he fell to the earthen floor amongst the putrid odour of animal waste and scampering rats. The day's light was vanishing and soon he would be an easy target under a night vision device, he needed the dead Guardian's gun if he considered himself a chance at all. A faded crunch of a boot on gravel pushed him back down low behind the hut's wall where he focussed on listening.

Somewhere close by he had company.

CHAPTER 118

MISTAKE

Hajipur
September 16th

Dressed in all black and trying to blend with his surroundings, the sniper crept lightly towards the tree following Bennett's blood trail. He paused, lowered himself into a crouching walk around the massive tree trunk until he caught a glimpse of a single bloodied boot. He stood for a better shot and took two more silent steps forward. Finger on the trigger he pounced to find two empty boots.

A few minutes earlier, Bennett had spotted him skulking through a clump of trees on the far side of the road. He stripped himself of his shoes, planted them to entice the sniper and waited. Once the gunman stepped from the line of sight behind the tree, Bennett sprinted bare foot towards the dead man's gun.

As the scuffling sound of someone running finally caught the sniper's attention, he spun and hurled himself to the ground behind the telescopic sights of his Remington. Bennett swooped low into a body slide across the loose dust while at the same time reaching and grasping the dead soldier's gun.

The sniper felt the fleshy thump and searing sting as two bullets tore through his shoulder and pelvis just as he zeroed Bennett into his crosshairs. The round through his pelvis had shattered the bone into razors slicing through his femoral artery and opening a tap towards his death.

He fired one round and fumbled to reload the next when the pressure of a gun muzzle in his head subdued his motivation and he dropped his gun.

"Yeah wise move, now who the fuck are you?" Bennett demanded noticing the sea of dark blood expanding under him.

He kicked him over to his back to stare into the face of a Guardian, one of the three who dragged him and the old man from the battle in Patna.

"What the fuck is going on? You're a Guardian. I don't understand, why kill us?"

The dying man muttered, "So many things you don't know," before his body started convulsing in shock from the blood loss.

"What? Tell me," Bennett demanded as the man's eyes rolled back and his head slumped to the side signalling his death.

Bennett raised himself to stand and looked around expecting company. Darkness of night had closed in and the sounds of the gunship and gunfire to the south had gone silent. He pilfered the remaining spare ammunition from the dead men and limped north keeping to the concealment of a dense tree line until a farmhouse in darkness came into view.

As he edged his way closer, he recognised the distinct shape of a car hidden beneath a dark coloured tarp. It was the vehicle Johns was referring to he suspected and yanked hard on the tarp.

Even under the cover of darkness it was an impressive sight that took him by surprise. He stood staring at the sleek design of a black V12 Jaguar built sometime in the late 80's and in immaculate condition, a machine built for absolute speed.

He climbed into the driver's seat to find the key in the ignition and various weapons strewn across the rear seat. Perfect, he thought, as he turned the key and the engine roared to life with the pulsating thump of the massive V12. It screamed road supremacy as he pushed his foot against the pedal and accelerated away into the night along deserted narrow dirt roads carving through the farming fields in and around Hajipur. He reached the main northern highway doing ninety miles per hour weaving past the traffic heading towards Muzaffarpur.

The car sat smoothly at speed and Bennett didn't relent keeping his foot down hard against the pedal only easing up momentarily for the tighter corners or to dart around the semi-trailers using the coolness of night to cart their produce. He didn't expect the road in front of him to erupt into a tornado of fire and fruit as one of the trucks detonated under the impact of what he thought was a missile.

He pulled hard left to evade the raining debris and pushed full throttle pressing the Jaguar into a violent fishtailing shudder as if suffering some mechanical epileptic fit. It gained speed quickly under the influence of the immense horsepower and within seconds he had it back under control. A few feet overhead a gunship tore past dousing the car in a hurricane of downwash.

He slammed down hard on the brakes and spun the wheel towards another narrow road shielded by thick overhanging Baobab trees either side resembling a tunnel.

Like a mouse hiding from a cat he slowed to a cautious crawl feeling the gunship's thunder from above the tree canopy stalking his movements. In the near distance just outside the cover of the trees he could see a cluster of large sheds and silos silhouetted against the already dark surroundings.

He floored the Jaguar towards the largest of the three sheds just as the helicopter's Gatling blasted holes across the bonnet. At forty miles per hour Bennett smashed his way through the twenty foot high shed doors screeching to a halt deep inside the building.

The pilot floated his gunship forward edging the nose through the decimated doorway and using the spotlight he focussed on the Jaguar.

The radio crackled, "Update, where are you? Have you got Bennett yet?"

From around the edge of the doorway Bennett stepped centre stage into the spotlight tucked tightly in behind the targeting scope of a Stinger missile. For the pilot responding to the radio call, it was all too late.

The missile released and obliterated the cockpit cremating the pilot within a split second. The explosive force pushed the helicopter sideways and drove it nose first into the ground snapping the five rotors into twenty foot spears slicing through the shed like tissue paper. The fuel tank erupted peeling back the gunship's metal skin as if opening a tin can and as the ammunition ignited in another bright flash of orange, the fire leapt to engulf the sheds.

Bennett had not waited around to watch the gunship's death, he was already back in the Jaguar accelerating along a back road towards the highway and then north to Muzaffarpur.

After thirty minutes of uninterrupted high speed, he was walking through the front gates of Sadar Hospital in search of anything looking like an isolation unit. He walked past nurses and doctors but no one questioned him or disrupted his advance. It wasn't a large medical facility by any comparison and within another few moments he reached a hallway posted with restricted signs every few metres and the overpowering bitter odour of cleaning fluid.

Another few steps and he turned a corner where a smooth polished steel door caught his attention. It was more the sign he was interested in, small yet distinguishable.

Contamination Unit
No Unauthorised Entry
Strict Bio-Security in Effect

He pulled his handgun from his waist and pushed down on the handle. The door sprung ajar an inch with an electronic clunk and he stepped through.

CHAPTER 119

LESSER EVILS

Sadar Hospital, Muzaffarpur
September 16th

Nicholette's pale blue body stretched out motionless on a hard steel hospital bed, her beauty still the centre piece even with death making its presence felt. The coma was keeping her alive for now but with every passing hour, the blue death in her veins spread and killed more tissue cells. Her long dark brown hair dangled loosely from the table while her half naked body showed signs of coldness and severe blood loss. Tubes and electrodes hung from her nose, mouth and ears signifying her more as an evil experiment than a patient.

Bennett stood staring not concerned that either side two armed men were removing his weapons. His eyes had tunnelled in on Nicholette's ghostly image while in denial his mind growled at her impending death. Behind the bed a little pale man dressed neatly in a black suit stood watching him and waited patiently to draw his attention.

Bennett expected an ambush the moment he set foot inside the room but for some unforeseen reason he had continued despite being completely out of character for him. Once through, the heavy steel door swung shut behind him followed by a loud hiss as air expelled to seal the room airtight again. For the first time in many years, Bennett had made a mistake allowing emotions to disrupt his usual psych.

The entire room clinical and cold had the pungent scent of disinfectant resembling more a morgue than a hospital ward. He hadn't been prepared for her deteriorated appearance or the agitation he felt in his heart as he gazed upon her with what he realised was love.

"Mr Bennett allow me to introduce myself, I am Richard Koehler, my colleagues and I have a proposition that may interest you," Koehler said as he looked down at Nicholette, "one that will save this beauty's life."

He continued, "We both want the same thing, you need and we want the Mayan Sphere."

Bennett spoke for the first time taking a sideways glance to judge his enemy's strength, "the Mayan Sphere was destroyed along with Dom Whittaker back in Patna."

"Arh Mr Bennett you are wrong, Whittaker is alive and still in possession of the Sphere, he was dragged from the car before the missile hit."

"How do you know this and what about Bannister, is he alive too?" Bennett asked.

"No Bannister was killed in the helicopter crash. Whittaker on the other hand was pulled from the car wreck by, we assume his terrorist friends, here see for yourself," Koehler said as he extended a PDA towards him.

Bennett took the small device and watched satellite imagery show the gunfight in the backstreets of Patna as it occurred less than three hours earlier. He saw the upturned Bentley in the street, himself running for cover while three men advanced on hands and knees from behind the car. It was then he witnessed as Koehler had said, one of them drag Whittaker's body from it and return for the sphere.

"So what are you proposing?" Bennett asked handing the device back.

"I propose we work together to find Whittaker and the sphere and in return your girlfriend here will receive an injection of our newly enhanced Eighth Code. It will not cure her but it will provide her more time while the sphere is located. Once we have the sphere, then she will have her cure, as you would know, the First Code can save her," Koehler said trying to look genuine and convincing.

"What if I refuse?" Bennett replied knowing it wasn't an option anyhow, it was a catch 22 but Nicholette's life depended on it.

"Well you both die and Whittaker wins," Koehler announced.

"Can't say I like any of those options... how do I know you won't just kill her anyway or whether your Eighth Code will prolong her life?"

"Our new version works just like yours but with some improvements and whether we kill her, well that's a risk you just have to take," Koehler said.

Bennett thought for a minute before answering, "Ok, but first I want her injected now and then we can discuss plans to find the sphere."

Koehler's phone rang and he walked from earshot. A short moment later he returned and said, "Whittaker just flew out of Muzaffarpur with the sphere."

"Do you know where he's heading?" Bennett asked.

"No, his flight plan is under diplomatic restraint, covert, but we are tracking its movements."

"I want her injected now and I'll find Whittaker and get you the sphere, but I want confirmation of the injection. I want to see it for myself."

"We need to fly her to our Kyrgyzstan facility to administer the injection where she will be provided the best care while you do your part. Do we have a deal?" Koehler asked.

"Yes we do, there are things I need, weapons, explosives and clearances," Bennett said.

"Whatever you need, but I warn you Mr Bennett, any hint of you double crossing us and your girl here dies," Koehler declared.

Bennett was directed outside with the two guards to where another group waited. Nicholette was transferred to a waiting ambulance while he was shadowed by the guards into a nearby troop carrier followed by a short journey to the airport. He noticed they all spoke German and weren't mercenaries like the usual guns hired by *The Trust*. Each sat with an air of militant self-discipline saying very little and appearing serious. These men he could see were professional.

They arrived and boarded an awaiting Bombardier Aerospace business jet, Koehler's personal air transporter. There Nicholette was placed in the rear section of the cabin and Bennett was restrained further forward because Koehler was taking no chances.

Koehler's cell phone rang once more, this time he waited till he'd walked well away before answering it. He knew the incoming caller ID, and was pleased at the name displayed on the screen, it meant his insurance plan would be activated.

CHAPTER 120

KYRGYZSTAN

Orto-Tokoy, Kyrgyzstan
September 16th

A thousand miles later and they landed at an off the chart airfield just northeast of Orto Tokoy in Kyrgyzstan. On public view it resembled an old rundown hydropower plant feeding from the Orto Tokoy reservoir set tightly between two steep mountain ranges making it ideally concealed. Underneath the mass of grey derelict buildings, another maze of tunnels and chambers similar to Kehlstein penetrated deep into the Earth.

After a rugged landing caused by the gale-force down winds off the mountains, Bennett was led away by four of the guards into a nearby building that appeared as though it would collapse at any minute. A solid electronic steel door slid slowly across revealing a modern lift large enough to drive a truck into. He and the guards entered the lift where they descended what he thought was at least a thousand feet passing through a dozen levels along the way.

It stopped and the lift doors rolled open onto a large sterile room, an area roughly the size of a basketball court with computers and other electronic devices scattered throughout. On the far side another smaller lift had opened and Nicholette's body was wheeled out on a stretcher by a man in a long white lab coat.

Just off to her side, Koehler stood waiting.

"Mr Bennett, this is where we prove our side of the deal," he announced as he lifted a small silver briefcase onto the table next to him. He opened it showing three syringes of a purple fluid, each marked with a series of numbers.

"We've worked hard at improving the Eighth Code's design, it's a more self-learning and robust version now," he proudly explained.

He nodded to the man in the lab coat who took no time to administer the first two syringes into the rear of Nicholette's neck. It was a dangerous procedure and only needed the needle to move slightly off centre and the patient would be paralysed or worse suffer a catastrophic brain seizure.

"It has to be injected into the spinal cord so it feeds directly to the brain's nervous system, she will spasm for an hour or so while her body adjusts to the microscopic stimulators but then after that she will improve and gain consciousness within a day or so," Koehler added seeing the concern on Bennett's face.

Koehler nodded again and she was administered the third serum before a small vial of blood was extracted from her arm. The lab technician looked at it closely and smeared a small drop onto a microscope slide. Just above them, a large flat screen came to life with an image of Nicholette's blood in its true basic existence of cellular life with one distinct difference. Moving among the resident cells were tiny cylindrical objects metallic in appearance except moving with a purpose, not floating. Each foreign object raced from cell to cell programming the new DNA message, her body already starting the transformation from human to something yet to be classified.

Bennett watched her natural bodily defence system, her white blood cells attacking the invaders, surrounding them and then swiftly retreating. He witnessed for the first time the blue death in action feeding on the live cells, small blue spiked objects of varying sizes attaching to her healthy cells. With each attachment the cell would immediately dissolve. As the minutes passed, more cylindrical objects replicated before his eyes and attacked the blue death, closing in but only neutralising it for a few days perhaps weeks at the best.

Slowly Nicholette's body began to shake and spasm in a clenching display of agony as the injections took hold.

"It is fascinating isn't it? The way the body recognises they are friend not foe, and how quickly they take control at the molecular level. Advancement in nanotechnology of this magnitude will mean an illness free world, cancers no longer existing, mental and physical disabilities extinct. The perfect race of people designed and bred by *The Trust*. You see Jon, our vision for Earth is a pure society, a place where people live in peace, free from fear and above all, life spans five times that of now. This is what we have always wanted, the ability to live longer. Our enhanced version extends a human's life another 400 years. Can you see the benefits and demand?" Koehler explained growing anxious at his own recurring thoughts of wealth and control.

"Yes but who gives you this power to decide what is best for the Earth and how many have to die before you can fully implement your plan?" Bennett threw back at him. He added, "And you say no more fear but isn't that your final solution, a plan to annihilate most of the population and then force the remainder to bow to *The Trust's* reign of terror?"

"Jon... Jon... Jon, No you have it all wrong. Without *The Trust* there is no future for this planet, it cannot possibly continue to sustain life at the current population expansion rate, half the world is at war, over a quarter is starving and already the majority of economic markets are failing. This planet needs one Government to take control and steer it to safety and a long healthy future. That Government is what we propose, all others must go and the political bullshit that now wrongly shapes our existence. Without it, this planet is doomed," Koehler said in defence of their fifty year old plan.

He continued talking without a break, "For years the Monk and his World Council have promised a solution to the overcrowding, depleting resources and degradation of human values. He kept saying it would one day reset itself, waiting on the resurgence of their higher order. It is all lies. They live by prophecies of the reappearance of our maker and in complete desperation of an Earthly event that will never happen. Climate change, global warming all these things they claim is just the start but if we wait, it becomes too late."

Bennett listened, he could see there was more to come.

"The great Führer had a vision. He wanted the perfect race and the ultimate society but it came with a cost, the initial extermination of six million Jews. We are simply carrying on with his ultimate dream," he added.

"Your plans are pure genocide massacre and madness, not to mention the cataclysmic destruction the orbital pulse weapon will cause the planet," Bennett argued.

"Jon, I fail to understand this way of thinking, so little is known about the technologies of the Thirteenth Code but yet the Monk and his disciples seem to argue its devastating side effects. Our own research contradicts what they say but enough said about that for now. I want to fully confirm our side of the deal, but first we need a specimen of your blood," he said changing the subject quickly.

"Why my blood?"

"Quite simple really, I want to prove to you that what you have is what Nicholette has in her blood, that way you know we are good for our part of the deal and free up your mind to deliver on your part," Koehler answered.

Bennett extended his arm as the lab assistant took a small blood swab. Just like Nicholette's sample it was placed under the microscope and displayed on the screen. He looked up in amazement and almost disbelief, his blood was largely overpopulated with the same synthetic organisms as Nicholette, except tenfold in numbers. They moved throughout his blood work with a purpose like dogs mustering sheep.

Koehler didn't wait for comments and moved on with his instructions, "Whittaker's last tracked path had him heading for Tehran, there we expect him to gather forces and go underground. We cannot afford for that to happen. It is your job now to find him and bring us the sphere and codebook. A private jet is waiting up top to take you and a small team of my men to Tehran, there you will meet up with more men I have on the ground. Whittaker is smart as you know and will anticipate our move, he may not expect you to be part of it."

"I prefer to work with my own team and people I trust so your team is not needed," Bennett defiantly announced as he looked at the entourage of guards standing watching him, fingers on triggers.

"Yes I did anticipate you saying that so I arranged an old friend to accompany you," he said as Scott Douglas walked into the room. Bennett turned to see his old Australian intelligence officer mate turned drug lord standing smiling at him, an expression of *I'll do anything for money* on his face.

"Scott here will be your team with four more joining you in Tehran, he has been fully briefed on the situation," Koehler added.

Bennett returned a confused expression, but he knew Douglas and at that moment he was a better choice than any of Koehler's men. They spoke briefly a few words of greeting before Koehler's guards directed them back into the lift and towards the surface. Up top, the night sky was littered with cloud and a cold wind blew fiercely down through the Orto Tokoy valley from the west.

They walked out from the lift towards two business jets parked on the tarmac, one Bennett had flown in on while the other, an old model Westwind was whining up its two engines in readiness for departure. They were directed towards that plane and pushed up the stairs. As he found the first step, Koehler grabbed his arm and wedged a brown envelope into his hands, "Here you might find this interesting reading, and just remember Nicholette's life is riding on your success."

Bennett climbed the stairs and found a seat next to Douglas where he wasted no time asking questions while the jet found its way into the sky and the two hour journey west towards Tehran.

"How the fuck did you get involved in this?" he asked Douglas.

"Mate a few days after you left Khan Abad I got a visit from Koehler and that same Bannister fella we met in the mountains. He offered me a deal I couldn't refuse, and at the same time boost my opium trade to a wider sector of the market. It seems those poor villagers died from something called Blue Death. Koehler and his mates were doing some weird experiment shit, exposing them to some blue crystal in the ground around my poppy fields," he explained.

"Why you now, what have you been told?" Bennett asked.

"I don't really know much, the deal was to keep my mouth shut and in return they paid me ten million US dollars, gave me importation protection and hey, they even wiped my arrest warrant in Australia. Couldn't really say no to all that but it did mean helping them take care of problems from time to time. That's why now, this is one of their problems," he answered knowing he'd given a slightly different version of the problem than what his friend was thinking.

They spoke for another hour, neither knowing what lay ahead, only that Whittaker had landed two hours earlier onboard the same 737 Bennett had hijacked out of Germany. Douglas had fallen asleep leaving Bennett to open the envelope given to him by Koehler.

CHAPTER 121

MORE SECRETS

Airspace over Kyrgyzstan
September 16th

Inside the envelope, Bennett found an eight page bound document, with official letterhead of the US Secretary of Defence and watermarked Top Secret in red across all sheets. At the top of the first page appeared the words *CIA Operation Sabre 1986 – Experimental Genetic adaptations of a CIA Field Operative.*

For the next half hour he consumed pages of scientific jargon about CIA experiments transforming men into field operatives through their genetics solely from the exposure to the appropriate environmental triggers. It detailed using local operatives to help guide the experimental targets on the ground in Afghanistan, Iran and Pakistan. Targets were kept unaware of the experiment usually placed in the alien environment by accident or made to think it occurred that way.

In an effort to reduce training costs, the CIA considered it more effective to start with men and women guaranteed to not fail the rigorous training, people selected based on their DNA. Operation Sabre they hoped would prove genetics impacted on whether a person's body could quickly acquire the skills required for clandestine operations leading to the early identification of suitable personnel.

He read on until he reached the first experimental target's name, that's when it hit him like a twelve foot wave back at Gracetown beach. On that page one name rose up at him.

Jonas Viktor Bennett born 15/05/1960

He was thrown back fifteen years remembering the horrors he chose to forget, the constant nightmares and reflection of the deadly survival all at the hands of the US Navy but now the CIA as well. He realised with disgust he had been deliberately shot down over war torn Afghanistan in 1986 to fulfil some experiment for the Agency, some experiment based on his father's abilities as an operative. He was furious, that period of time shaped his life, destroyed part of him, deeply wounded his mind and set him up for a lonely retirement.

He read on while his mind twisted in fury at the thought of being used as a lab rat, and on top of discovering Whittaker's plan to use him to expose Jeremiah's Codes. There was no one left to trust in his life, even Nicholette was not who she said she was.

The other three targets he didn't know but were all killed during the experiment, written off as killed in action just like he was, the easiest way for the US Government to cover it all up and offload liability. The official document in his hands showed him as the only successful test case recruited into the CIA on his immediate return to the US. The next two pages showed his results from both physical and mental examinations, an assessment of his field combat skills, weaponry skills and use of explosives. It went on to illustrate him as a unique soldier of espionage, someone perfect for clandestine operations.

He reached the final page when the jet suddenly hit turbulence somewhere over western Turkmenistan, dropping two hundred feet and scattering everything around the cabin including Douglas who had been sleeping unharnessed.

The turbulence accelerated to a more violent shake as the jet entered the down draft of a storm cell with gale force winds pushing the small eight-seater in every direction. The cabin lights had extinguished and the pilot fought to maintain control, he had foolishly ignored the radar storm warning in favour of the quickest route into Tehran. Now he was attempting to fly through the left ventricle of the storm and was paying the price.

Bennett clambered his way into the cockpit to see the pilot sweating in fear and strangling the controls. Outside, the sky lit up purple, blue and green as lightning streaked across their path followed closely by thunder snapping at its tail. Each time the thunder pounded so too did the jet's fuselage with violent vibrations that felt as though the rivets holding the wings together would release at any minute.

Bennett threw himself into the empty co-pilot's seat and scanned the instruments while the pilot showed no objections, he was happy for the support and dying alone had never been in his bucket list.

Douglas appeared in the cockpit, "What the fuck is happening? Crashing wasn't in the travel brochure Jon."

Bennett had always liked Douglas's sense of humour in times of near death and this was no exception, he chuckled to himself.

"It's ok mate, travel insurance will pay for your funeral, now probably best to go buckle up, it's going to get rough," he called back to Douglas over the sound of thunder and metal stress as the plane flew at

450 miles per hour 30,000 feet above the dark desolate landscapes of Turkmenistan.

Douglas fought the plane roll to find his seat while mumbling, "Fucking great, insurance wasn't included, and how the fuck can it get any worse than this." At that moment he found out, wind shear struck the nose driving the plane into a steep dive and hurled his body head first into the rear cabin wall knocking him unconscious.

Up front, Bennett had taken over the controls relieving the pilot of a likely stress induced heart attack. The man was well over weight and struggling to find his breath amongst the pressure of the moment. The radar screen flashed red, orange and blue of the storm engulfing the small jet and their only chance now was to fly on straight through. Bennett knew flying in storms was never a good idea where the wind forces alone could rip the wings clean off like turkey wings at Thanksgiving.

Emergency lighting in the cabin caused a soft amber glow enough for him to see rearwards and there was no sign of Douglas. He called back, "Scott you ok?"

No answer...

After calling out two more times with no response, he reluctantly handed the controls back to the still anxious pilot and moved rearwards trying to remain upright against the plane's gyration.

He found Douglas unconscious and bleeding from a large gash to his head, flat in a prone position at the rear of the plane. He lifted the man's enormous weight and dragged him to the closest seat all the time fighting the storm's vibrations. As the jet rolled abruptly sideways from another windshear impact, his own feet fell from under him.

Another few minutes of wrestling with the g-forces and he managed to lift Douglas's limp body into the seat where he buckled him in tight. The man's head hung forward dripping blood into his lap but his medical care would have to wait.

Lightning every five seconds lit the cabin up like dancing strobe lights and he clawed his way back towards the cockpit using the few seats to pull himself along. The jet lurched violently left rolling over and throwing him hard against the aircraft's sidewall. The impact knocked him flat to the floor and there he laid a brief moment while the jet found some horizontal stability again. In the dim light, he caught sight of the document he'd been reading as the storm hit, it had fallen onto the floor and separated at the last page.

The lightning continued to light up the cabin interior giving an eerie ambience but what he saw simply added to the horror of the night and his unknown life. He looked in disbelief, it was not possible. He made one quick lunge and grabbed the single piece of paper pushing it under his shirt while wrestling his way forward to the cockpit and strapped himself in.

Almost twenty minutes after entering the storm they were finding the western edge and breaking out with their lives and amazingly, the jet in one piece. Tehran was only forty five minutes west and they would commence their descent soon.

Somewhere behind them, a British made surface-to-air missile had just launched from the back of a truck and was racing towards them.

CHAPTER 122

RAPIER

Airspace over Eastern Iran
September 17th

At just after midnight local time and at a speed tipping the edge of Mach two, the Rapier missile careered into its target.

The pilot's neck snapped on impact, his head and body driven forward by the blast only feet behind the cockpit. Fire rushed the cabin moments before the sudden depressurisation inhaled it back out the ruptured fuselage into the night air.

Beside the dead pilot, Bennett's body slouched against the controls, the blast's shock wave had been more forgiving and only knocked him unconscious.

Back behind them, the cabin was torn open to the pitch black of night after the missile missed the left engine. In the last second searching for its mark, the Rapier had turned tightly and smacked square into the cabin just behind the cockpit. Now the jet slipped sideways and downwards towards the mountainous terrain north of Nosar, eighty six kilometres from Tehran, increasing speed as it fell into a spiralling death roll. Control was lost and the descent rate quickened by the second as it passed through 25,000 feet.

Warning bells pitched a frantic chime mostly drowned out by the angry roar of air rushing through the cabin from the five foot gaping wound in the jet's skin. A panel of lights near the centre of the console lit up like a Christmas tree flashing orange and red while two screeching sirens bellowed. One signalled the rapid depressurisation happening inside the aircraft and the other more specifically meant the autopilot had disengaged after the abrupt slap on the control stick from the pilot's dead body.

Bennett didn't stir, he remained motionless as the jet's frame started to buckle and scream in a metallic creaking pitch. Further back, Douglas sat holding intensely onto life, he had jerked back to consciousness just as the missile struck. Like some terrifying nightmare, he awoke to see a fireball rush the cabin interior and then drown out as a raging vacuum jettisoned it back out.

He grabbed the small yellow emergency oxygen mask flapping above his head while the jet descended into a left rolling slide towards the ground. The deafening rush of air and the snap change in cabin pressure was like someone had just clobbered him over the head with a club. Disorientation had set in and his ears felt ready to explode.

"Fuckin great and I signed up for this shit?" he thought as he unbuckled himself and clutched at the seat fighting against the clawing winds of depressurisation.

The jet careered through turbulence and Douglas was flung sideways losing the oxygen mask and his footing. He crashed hard to the floor and slammed against the sidewall knocking all breath from his lungs. The air sucking towards the hole and the plane tilting dragged him forward across the floor but as he stumbled to his feet, the effects of the reduced oxygen dealt him a harder blow. His legs collapsed and his vision began to fade and blur as the starvation of oxygen eroded his awareness. Falling where he did was his saviour.

At his fingertips he felt the cold cylindrical steel of an inflight emergency oxygen bottle and he rushed the mask over his head. A few deep breaths and life raced back through his body that reignited his forward staggering plight towards the cockpit. Though less than thirty seconds had passed, he thought it had been minutes and the mountainous terrain of eastern Iran would be looming.

He was a big strong man yet it took all his strength to fight off the tentacles of the outside air snatching at him as he pushed past the blast hole.

The pilot he could see was dead by the precarious positioning of his head and the constant gush of blood from a gaping neck wound. The blast had shredded the bulkhead behind the pilot's seat resulting in a mass of tiny jagged metallic strips slicing through his seat and body.

Just off to his right, Bennett was slumped forward in the co-pilot seat, unconscious with only abrasions across his face. His breathing was laboured and Douglas slapped the oxygen mask on him. All around him warning sirens sounded over the rushing air while lights flashed orange and red across the instrument panel. He surveyed the cockpit in despair, he had no experience as a pilot and had no idea where to start.

He did what he thought best and yanked back hard on the controls using his strength and weight to raise the nose. The dead pilot's overweight body made it difficult to get full leverage and as he glanced around the instruments, one in particular was spinning down at a fast rate passing through 15,000 feet losing two thousand feet every minute.

He yelled and slapped Bennett's face trying desperately to wake the only person on board who could save them.

CHAPTER 123

CONTRACTS

Cherat, Iran
September 17th

Three Iranian men stood watching their prize sink rapidly towards the distant dark horizon, a hint of orange and red flames trailing off behind it. They had waited patiently in the dark with their one British made Rapier missile loaded in its launcher atop an old Iranian army truck. Their orders had been laid out precisely, wait until the phone call before launching. The missile's guidance system had been pre-programmed with the target's transponder codes but they knew nothing more of the reasons behind their mission. Preparations had been last minute when word came of Bennett's flight to Tehran on board a jet owned by *The Trust*.

As a small aircraft was heard roaring distantly above them across the sky, the cell phone had rung. The order to launch had been received and the missile responded up into the star filled sky with a plume of red fire spewing from its tail. They waited and watched towards the west for the next five minutes until the Rapier did its job.

They packed up feeling confident no one could possibly survive the approaching crash and made the confirming phone call.

"It is done as you ordered, a direct hit."

When the phone clicked dead, the Monk turned to his chief Council members at the conference table and they all applauded because a serious threat had just been eliminated. Whittaker and the codebook were next.

CHAPTER 124

DAMAVAND PEAK

Airspace over Eastern Iran
September 17th

On board the spiralling Westwind, lights flashed in unison across the instrument panel and audible warnings continued to screech. Douglas had dragged the dead pilot from his seat and slid into his place when Bennett failed to respond. Now as the jet continued to lose altitude he had no forewarning of another problem waiting in the dark.

Damavand Mountain the highest mountain in the Middle East peaking at 18,000 feet sat in their direct flight path and soon they would slam into it at over 300 knots.

Douglas pulled back the controls until the jet commenced a violent shake and a new warning chimed above the others. Bennett's arms twitched and his head shook blurting a murmuring sound from under the mask. His eyes opened and he pulled the mask away to holler, "Need speed, we're stalling."

Bennett had woken to hear the stall warning and knew the wings were about to lose their flight capability. The airflow across them had dropped to a critical low speed after Douglas had pulled the nose high in his panic to avoid an impact with the ground.

"Nice of you to join me buddy, kinda in a jam here," Douglas squeezed out. For the last couple of minutes he'd wrestled against the aircraft's rock and roll grasping fiercely at the controls until it felt like his arms would rupture from the tension.

Bennett grabbed a firm hold of the throttle and rammed full power from the engines while driving the control stick forward dropping the nose with a jolt. Douglas knew his place and released his aching arms to witness Bennett react without the slightest hint of fear or stress. The shaking stopped almost immediately and the stall warning silenced along with the autopilot and depressurisation sirens leaving only the sound of rushing air inside the cabin.

"We aren't clear yet!" Bennett called as he scanned the panel and searched the cockpit for the right navigational map.

He knew what terrain spread out below them but worse he knew Damavand Mountain waited somewhere ahead of them in the dark. He rechecked the instruments and rolled the jet hard left raising the nose as they climbed through 15,000 feet. Their original flight path had them passing a few miles south of the mountain peak into Tehran however how far they had drifted north he didn't know. The lack of city lights in the distance had him concerned and he realised then they were behind and below the mountain's highest point.

"We've got a problem," he declared.

"Huh," Douglas responded as the ground proximity warning fired up.

All he heard next was Bennett screaming, "FUCK, HOLD ON."

His warning came too late as the rugged mountainside appeared in the aircraft's lights, two thin beams streaming out from each wing tip towards what lay ahead. Rocks, boulders and then a sheer cliff face flashed into view pushing Bennett into an emergency frenzy as he yanked hard back on the control and rolled further left.

Airspeed had dropped back to below 350 knots as he pushed the jet into a steeper climb and commanded full power from the already straining engines. Douglas had lost his joking persona as his face transformed to a sickly grey watching Bennett for the first time displaying a sense of uncertainty.

The nose had lifted high and Bennett could feel the vibrations of the jet struggling against the sudden change in direction made worse by the constant impact of the cyclonic mountain down drafts driving against the fuselage.

Douglas held silent clutching his seat in a death grip while the harness dug deeper across his chest with every shudder until one brutal whiplashing jerk forced two words from deep inside him, "HOLY FUCK!"

For a second he thought it was their demise not knowing the right wingtip fuel pod had clipped the cliff face and exploded like a grenade tearing off a small section of the wing. Bennett could feel from the sudden stiffness in the controls that not only had the wing been damaged but the aileron was jamming making the directional control that much more difficult. He looked out the side window at the wing and in the dark he could see something flapping in the wind. The rubber de-icing boot had peeled away from the leading edge and clung desperately to the wing in the gale-force air flow where it thrashed wildly.

The sudden loss of fuel weight to that side catapulted the plane into an aggressive left roll forcing Bennett to release the control as it snapped over at wrist breaking speed.

While Bennett fought to pull the jet back to horizontal flight, Douglas could do nothing except hold on like riding a raft down the flood induced river rapids of the mighty Tsangpo River in Tibet.

"We got a big problem. The right fuel tank is gone and the aileron is jammed," Bennett called.

"Have we got enough fuel to get to Tehran?" Douglas responded hoping for the answer he wanted.

"Fuel is not the problem, the right wing has sustained too much damage to keep us in the air," Bennett yelled as he wrestled against the yawing and rolling.

Bennett knew the terrain below was riddled with ridgelines all the way into the city and confronting them was most likely a suicidal manoeuvre in the dark. He watched as the altimeter wound down losing height quickly and though he had the right engine at full power to compensate for the loss in uplift he strained to coordinate the needed combination of rudder and aileron.

He looked across at Douglas looking somewhat pale and caught his eyes.

"We're losing height too fast. Get ready, I'm crash landing this battered beast."

Douglas nodded in a hesitant unsure way and called back, "What's our chances?"

"There's a valley with a road about thirty miles to the south. Unfortunately at our current rate of descent we won't make it and ditching somewhere much less comfortable is our only option."

The onset of turbulent updrafts funnelling up from the rocky ravines grappling and buffering the airframe convinced him the ground had just become dangerously close.

The gusting winds worsened closer to the ravines and steep ridges throwing the aircraft up, down, sideways and occasionally pushing a half flip. It felt like a cattle train carriage rattling and it took all Bennett's concentration to command as the remaining headlight showcased the edge of a wide ravine.

"Hold on, it's going to be rough."

No sooner had he spoke when the ground filled the windscreen.

CHAPTER 125

MATES

40km east of Tehran, Iran
September 17th

Douglas raised his hands to cover his face as the ground rushed up smashing the windscreen. The jet's underbelly had struck a tall monolith of solid granite gutting it like a fish and spearing it forward into the rapidly falling slope of a steep wide ravine. There it ploughed uncontrollably driven by momentum and gravity.

The ravine was unforgiving and scattered with boulders amidst rocky outcrops that made it more a demolition run than a controlled crash landing. For close to thirty seconds they both held onto anything they could while the jet was battered brutally from side to side before splitting in two with the nose section continuing to tumble downhill.

The rear section and wings splintered left and ignited the moment they smashed against the ravine's rugged sidewalls. It launched a fireball a hundred feet into the night sky casting a beacon for miles around.

Further down the ravine the cockpit and partial cabin slowed to rest inside an old rain gorged gully. There they sat momentarily as Bennett unbuckled himself while at the same time looking towards his friend bleeding profusely and coughing blood. In the impact, the force had shot the nose wheel strut up into the cockpit and through the right side of Douglas's chest, slicing through a lung and part of his abdomen. Shock was rapidly setting in with his body starting to tremble.

Bennett slid from his seat just as he heard Douglas groan a few wretched words and force his quivering hand towards him.

"Mate I'm sorry."

"Hey hang in there, I'm getting you out," Bennett reacted, however quickly lost his enthusiasm once he caught full sight of Douglas's injuries. A three foot metal strut protruding through his torso and into the seat meant he wasn't going anywhere.

"No Jon I am sorry. You don't deserve it. Leave me," Douglas mumbled as blood started to stream from his mouth and down his neck.

The blazing fireball further up the slope behind them was showering them in a dim flickering light that displayed the dying man in an eerie ambience. Bennett could see defeat in his eyes and as his breathing became increasingly shallow and laboured, his pulse grew weaker and his speech acutely slurred. So there in the dim fire light, Bennett held his friend and listened to his struggling speech one last time.

"I am sorry mate… my mission… kill you if his man failed… return the sphere to Koehler."

Douglas paused to catch what breath he could and then added.

"That's not all mate… they paid me… so you think there were nukes in northern Afghanistan. Too much cash to refuse… you know me, it's all about the money," he said as he laughed and coughed at the same time with more blood spurting from his mouth.

Bennett was confused and side-tracked by Douglas's sinful confession.

"Who paid you and why?" he asked.

Douglas was becoming weaker by the second, his eyes fluttered and his voice was riddled with gasping breaths signalling the end was near.

"Bannister… set it up for *The Trust*… he contacted me before you came… all I had to do was spread the radiation story in the mountains… take you up there… they would do the rest."

He struggled hard to get the words out, it was his Sacrament of Penance. With all his remaining strength, and as his last request for forgiveness, he reached into his jacket's left pocket to reveal a small flat screen monitor. He pushed it towards Bennett and in his final frail speech said, "This tracks the Sphere… Koehler gave it to me… Whittaker has no idea about it." He pushed it harder into Bennett's hand as he convulsed one last time as death smothered him.

With his friend dead, Bennett crawled from the wreckage, through the twisted jagged metal that was once the front of the cabin and pulled himself to his feet. He looked up the slope towards the bright orange flare of dancing flames. Though it created a beautiful contrast to the dark Iranian night, he knew it was like rotting meat to flies and soon the locals would be swarming. That meant the Iran Revolutionary Guards would be on their way.

He didn't care too much about Douglas working against him, he had never trusted the man anyway and money would always win with him even if it meant killing his own mother. What did disturb him was who shot them down. The thought bounced back and forth through his head as he continued to survey the dark mountainside and twiddle with the device in his hand.

He had no exact idea of his location, Damavand Peak was behind him to the north and somewhere to the south was the highway he'd seen on the map. The night sky was ablaze with stars and a half moon that shed some light over him and his sloping surroundings. Each side of the ravine a sheer rock face rose high above his position.

But before he started his southerly trek he looked down at the device in his hand. It was no bigger than a cell phone and resembled a thin flat screen monitor. He pressed a button along the top edge and the screen illuminated into a map of Iran with a green dot flashing in the center. Zooming in on the image showed the sphere's position at an airstrip on the eastern side of Tehran.

The device he realised was a tracker using GPS to not only show the location of the sphere but also his position on the ground. He zoomed in closer on the satellite imagery to reveal a small village just over the next ridgeline to the west and possibly a vehicle he could steal. During the crash, shards of windshield had deeply lacerated his arms that now throbbed with every slight movement made worse as he started to climb his way out of the ravine.

Thirty miles to the west, a single helicopter appeared low in the sky loaded with highly trained soldiers to commence the search for survivors. The man sitting next to the pilot did not belong with the others but it was his dollars driving the charge.

CHAPTER 126

NEW AGE SPIES

Berlin, New Hampshire, USA
September 17th

Two men of German descent sat scrutinising a wall of monitors inside a dimly lit room hidden from the world. It was one of three discrete operations rooms of yet another high security facility owned by *The Trust*. They knew their orders and both had studied the briefing papers countless times in the past month, now they just had to keep Jon Bennett under constant surveillance. The only problem for them was they had lost him in Kyrgyzstan and a sense of panic was building in the room.

Each day and night was the same as they scrutinised satellite and surveillance camera feeds from around the world, all in the search for Bennett. They had quickly learnt in the first week of duty the slippery nature of their target and wasn't until they developed a computer program to isolate his heat signature that everything became easier. It was the Eighth Code racing through his body that radiated a unique energy signature but for the operators it still needed endless hours of low terrain scanning to pick it up. When it did lock on, alarms sounded and it was game on.

Set amongst a conglomerate of business houses in the fast growing town of Berlin of northern New Hampshire, the Heydrich Institute had gained notoriety for its life saving achievements in the medical world. What people didn't know was how it formed the public front for the North American arm of *The Trust*.

The phone rang followed by an arrogant sounding male on the line.

"I need eyes in the sky over Iran, coordinates coming through now. Bennett was in a jet that just crashed at this location. Report back if there are any survivors." The phone went dead.

Twenty seconds later, their fax machine buzzed to life spitting out a single sheet of white paper with a set of numbers in bold type across the top.

35°56'32.55"N, 52° 6'46.59"E

The men and women leading their working lives in and out of this monitoring room had access to every piece of advanced spy technology the world could offer and right now they were dialling up a Soviet owned satellite just passing over Kazakhstan. Seven minutes passed before the coordinates came into view on the wall screens and the men were somewhat relieved.

The screen displayed one large fire on the edge of Damavand Mountain and using infrared they were able to distinguish the outline of the wings and tail section. A little further away they spotted the nose section and a less intensified object slowly moving south.

One of the men tapped a short command into his keyboard and executed the heat signature software.

"There… it's Bennett," he said pointing at the screen and zooming in the full extent to show a lone person walking along the crest of a ridge towards a clump of village lights. The digital output was displayed in a small window in the right-hand corner and it met the correct radiant intensity for Bennett's Eighth Code.

The other control man activated the second monitor and zoomed back out to show a wider field back towards Tehran.

"Looks like he has company coming his way too," he added.

Further to the west, a helicopter was flying a direct route from Tehran towards the crash site. The first control man picked up the phone and dialled the usual number.

"Sir, Bennett survived, he's walking south and there's an inbound chopper on direct route to the site, what do you want us to do?"

"Keep tracking its progress, I want to know the instant it deviates from its current path towards Bennett." Nothing else was said and the phone disconnected.

Somewhere over the south Indian Ocean, a small cylindrical satellite abruptly altered its western path to head north towards Iran. As its spiderlike legs commenced unfolding in all directions, two large doors peeled away at the front to reveal her canon extending. With her laser systems arming, Meredith obeyed every keyboard command she received and accelerated towards Tehran. George Anders had complete control of his girl and now he had his second mission after downing Bennett's jet at Kehlstein.

CHAPTER 127

EYES IN THE DARK

Damavand Mountain, Iran
September 17th

Bennett kept walking in the direction of the small village stumbling every few feet on loose rocks and stones. The mountain air had suddenly become bitterly cold from the increasing wind gusts racing down the mountain side and he strained to breathe as each gust chilled his lungs. He estimated the village was only a few kilometres beyond the next ridgeline but getting there was his next predicament. It was steep and under the dim lighting of the stars he could see there was nothing allowing him the footholds needed to climb. As he stopped and searched for an easier path, a new distant sound caught his attention. The wind howling and echoing through the ravine had made it near impossible to hear anything but now something was pitching in and out over the top of it.

He dropped into a crawling manoeuvre across the loose sand to behind a nearby rock formation where he waited and listened to the sound intensify into the thumping slap of helicopter rotors thrashing the air. It was approaching with speed and hugging close to the ground while a bright beam of light extending from the nose scavenged the ravine floor in front.

The dark silhouette of a Bell 205 helicopter roared past only a few dozen feet above him and showing no signs of slowing down as it started veering left up towards the next ravine.

The thunderous clap of the rotors shook the ground as it clawed its way into the gale force wind leaving a suffocating whirlwind of dust churning around him. He remained hidden while it settled but it wasn't long before he realised the helicopter wasn't his only problem.

The ravine in which he found himself was lined both sides by ridgelines of at least forty feet high and the floor was scattered with deep gullies and more rock formations. In a military sense he had stumbled into an ideal ambush site and the enemy could be concealed anywhere.

Suddenly the rocks behind him exploded in a shower of granite shards as a volley of gunfire arced above his head. The shots came in quick and accurate forcing him to scurry low to the ground with more pursuing his every stride spitting up sand under his boots. He zigzagged the best he could to avoid the onslaught until one loose stone threw his footing and he stumbled forward onto his hands and knees.

The shooting stopped.

Further off in the dark, three highly trained riflemen had stopped their advance because they knew their rabbit was cornered and ready for the slaughter.

Bennett spread himself flat on the ground reducing his enemy's target as something next to him in the sand moved.

CHAPTER 128

RASHEED

Tehran Airspace
September 17th

The room was small, heavily scented with aviation oils and mostly in darkness except for the light penetrating through the one single doorway behind him. As his eyes adjusted to the dark environment, Bennett discovered his helpless situation. The chair under him was heavy and both his hands and feet were bound to it with zip ties that tore unforgivingly into his previous binding wounds. Outside the room he could hear a helicopter winding down its rotors and the sounds of vehicles arriving.

His head pounded with a throbbing pain and he had no idea how long he'd been unconscious. He recalled stumbling to the ground at the hands of an unknown shooter and the sand erupting around him to reveal a dark human shape. From that point everything went dark as a single dart shot into his chest releasing a fast acting paralytic agent.

The soldier had laid waiting camouflaged under the sand for Bennett to enter his zone. His colleagues had done their part, mustering Bennett into his path and it had become an unavoidable trap. The soldiers had watched him traverse down the mountainside and before that had tracked his movements using the radiation signature pulsating through his blood. Their orders had been to take him alive.

Bennett twisted his head in a strained effort to catch sight of the approaching sound of boots scuttling across the concrete floor. Behind him the silhouette of a large man appeared through the doorway and then another man though smaller. Bennett turned back and sat confident just staring forward into an empty brick wall.

A man's ragged voice broke through the silence, "You coward dog, you ran from me in Australia. But now you are finally here to pay in blood for your sins against my family."

Rasheed stepped forward lifted his rifle butt and drove it fiercely into Bennett's back punishing his right shoulder blade and near shattering it. The sudden unexpected rush of pain arched him backwards in the chair and at the same time he bellowed out an excruciating howl that resonated across the hangar floor.

Like he'd done many times, he called on his mental training to block out the pain and focus on his next move. He asked in his usual defiant way, "Hey asshole, who are you and what do you want with me?"

This time the other man stepped to within view and landed a solid fist into his jaw, a punch worthy of any heavy weight boxer. Bennett had seen it coming and tilted his head to deflect most of the impact and the accompanying pain.

Rasheed spoke again, "I'm surprised you don't recognise my voice. My name is Rasheed Omar Allah, and you are the infidel dog who will die today but not before you beg for my forgiveness."

"Why?" Bennett asked thinking the voice had some familiarity.

"Like your coward brothers, you come, you destroy, you kill but you have no understanding of why, but still you think it's your business to control my people by brandishing your guns and bombs. And now you ask why. You are an ignorant Infidel. Death will soon come but first I will punish you for my brother's death. You Jonas Viktor Bennett killed my brother Ahmad and his family when you attacked his house in Kuwait on August 1st 1997 and now you must pay for your sin in blood."

Rasheed had not moved from behind him while he spoke and the light from outside camouflaged his appearance with a silhouetted darkness.

"You are misinformed, I wasn't in Kuwait when the attack happened, you are threatening the wrong man and you have pursued the wrong person all this time," Bennett boldly announced back at him.

Rasheed stepped forward again this time swinging his rifle butt across the side of his prisoner's head. The strike split Bennett's ear open like overripe fruit and his blood started streaming down his neck. The Iranian's pent up anger was showing, he had planned this day for three years and now his control was failing him.

"Well Bennett you have to excuse me for not believing you, when even your government sacked you for that very sinful act, and what is worse, you committed it against the family of your once friend."

Bennett knew not much could be said to negate his false actions so widely publicised as true, front page of most newspapers worldwide meant the Senate Inquiry was never going to be impartial and all forged from a political set up unbeknown to the same audience.

He turned his head in another attempt to catch sight of his tormentor and asked, "Once family I don't understand?"

In the darkness, Rasheed walked to a position in front of his prisoner exposing himself for the first time. He raised his hand towards the ceiling where he found the single hanging light bulb. The room erupted in candescent light momentarily blinding Bennett and making him squeeze his eyes shut before the adjustment could begin.

As his eyes found visual stability, Bennett witnessed his captor looking down at him and with the full exposure of light finding his face, he gasped in disbelief at who he was beholding. He could feel Rasheed's dark Middle Eastern eyes flooded with hate penetrating deep into his soul and shredding him apart from the inside. Rasheed's brother had been close to him and losing him tore a hole right through his heart, a mental wound that had never healed.

Bennett took a quick glance around the room and then back at Rasheed while he fought desperately to make sense of the situation. He felt confused why this man of all people would believe the lies of the Kuwait attack.

Rasheed stepped forward and spat in Bennett's face leaving the hostile discharge trickle down his cheek violating his dignity and adding further confusion.

"You coward dog, you didn't just kill my brother, you killed his wife and his seven children, my nephews and nieces. Your intelligence was wrong, yet you still continued to kill everyone in his building. Five floors of families died that day, people I grew up with. They were not your enemies, they were not at war with your country but your soldiers still murdered them with their guns and explosives."

"Soheil, I cannot believe it is you, we are old friends. You once saved my life and I returned the favour more times over, have you forgotten our trust. Surely you remember that. You must believe me, I wasn't in Kuwait when that atrocity occurred. I would never do that, I am the same Jon Bennett you taught and took me in as your brother."

Like an electric shock zapping his body, he came to the realisation that the ILF was led by Soheil and it was his old friend attempting to assassinate him these last few years.

Bennett looked into the fierce eyes of a man he once trusted with his life, a man he knew as Soheil Mahdavi, an intelligence officer with the Iranian Government and the man who saved his life after being shot down in 1986 over Afghanistan. This could not be right, he thought, this man was his friend, Soheil taught him how to survive, how to fight, how to be the best operative. It was this man who shaped his entire life, who taught him to become the CIA's most lethal human weapon and the reason why he was recruited in the first place. Soheil and his men in 1986 rescued him from certain death at the hands of the Soviets or if not them, then certainly the Mujahedeen Rebels would have killed him.

"My real name is Soheil Mahdavi as you know it but I, like you, have many aliases, Rasheed Omar Allah is one of them. I do not believe you, I have seen classified reports from your Government of your involvement. So do not try your pathetic lies on me, you dishonour my intelligence with everything you say."

Rasheed stepped forward and in one mighty action of his rifle butt slammed it hard into Bennett's face. He felt the grinding gravel sensation as a tooth shattered and fell from his blood filled mouth. He spat narrowly missing Rasheed's boot while he tried vehemently to free himself conjuring up all the available strength he could.

He looked up at his captor, the man he realised looked much older and weathered, his face an expression of revenge and he could feel the heat of hatred radiating from the man's eyes melting his flesh. Their eyes locked, both defiant and non-surrendering, this time Bennett returned his own stare fuelled by the agony of the facial assault.

Rasheed had worked himself up, his composure was lost to the anger deep inside as he released two well placed left and right blows to Bennett's exposed face who without his defences was an easy target for attack. Then another two followed by another, all finding his face and hammering his nose and cheek bones. Bennett could do nothing except receive the undue punishment and wait for the next round. He could feel the warm metallic taste of blood as it trickled into his mouth and overflowed down his chin soaking his shirt.

The lashing continued for what he thought was hours though only a few minutes in reality had passed while his face became a mosaic of blood and abrasions and his mind lingered towards unconsciousness.

Abruptly the attack ceased and his head slumped forward limp from exhaustion. Rasheed had stopped his bombardment and walked from the room leaving Bennett to regather strength and his mental bearings. A few minutes passed before he returned carrying a small black metal briefcase and placed it meticulously onto the floor next to the chair. Inside Bennett knew what to expect, an arsenal of pain inflicting instruments and neurotoxins capable of slaying even the strongest of minds. Two dull clicks and the case sprung open to expose what Bennett had imagined.

He chuckled to himself thinking how ironic it was, that Rasheed once taught him the gruesome art of effective torture and the methodologies to quickly extract information from the most stubborn operatives in the field.

He also knew that whether Rasheed intended to rip fingernails out, cut off his fingers one by one or apply electrocution, it wasn't about extracting information, the moment was about inflicting maximum pain.

The heavy scraping sound of boots from the direction of the doorway caught Rasheed's attention and he turned to greet the leader of his hired soldiers.

"Rasheed, I have a message for you."

Rasheed spoke briefly in quiet with the man. What he heard pleased him and aroused his motivation for torture.

It was time...

CHAPTER 129

ILLUSION

Sepehr Airport, Tehran
September 17th

Rasheed crouched and rummaged through the contents of the briefcase with ruthless determination in search of one specific item, the very thing that would cause Bennett most discomfort. The selection before him as he looked down was plentiful and under normal torture conditions would be sufficient but not this time. What he needed was a last minute inclusion in his repertoire of pain devices courtesy of *The Trust's* bio weapons department.

With a small black device looking similar to a tiny television remote tucked inside his hand, he stood once again to face Bennett. In his other hand, he delicately caressed what would become Bennett's worst nightmare.

"It appears we have some time before your friend Whittaker arrives, he too has unfinished business with you. What I find humorous in all this is that he was the one who led us to you, starting with your location in Australia. You Americans cannot be trusted when friends turn on each other and this is exactly what you did to me," Rasheed declared as he nodded his head towards the soldier standing behind Bennett.

Just as Rasheed started laughing, Bennett's world plunged into darkness followed by a hint of claustrophobia as a pair of strong hands snapped his head rearwards. Time was not being wasted, the man behind had slipped a black bag over Bennett's head and as he pulled it tight across Bennett's mouth and nose, the air started extinguishing from his lungs and his struggle for life ensued.

As his lungs screamed for sustenance and asphyxia took a dangerous hold, the grip of death around his throat grew stronger as each second passed and all the while, he could hear muffled laughing behind and in front.

Every muscle and tendon in his body was at war and fighting to keep their host alive giving the distinct impression of someone having a seizure. Panic had consumed him and the air deprivation was winning the mind battle to survive. Bennett continued to fight but the weight compressing his mouth and nose was too great to break free. The burning in his lungs was all he could feel as the final remnants of the oxygen gave life to his blood. Above the muffled laughter and his own fighting grunts, he could hear himself gasping for breath under the bag whilst the sound of laboured breathing close to his ear signalled his murderer's presence.

As a final fighting gesture before death, Bennett's arms and legs released one last retaliatory uprising before the Kevlar bindings defeated him. With his energy depleted and his motivation to survive forfeited, he slumped back into the chair waiting the end.

Muffled voices filled his ears as the laughing dissipated and dizziness swept through his head. He knew at that moment, death was approaching.

As he sat waiting finality and everything drifted weightlessly inside his head, a single voice grew louder and more audible. He had no strength or vision yet for a minuscule moment in time he thought God was consoling him as he approached the gates of Heaven.

The soft soothing voice broke into something else.

"My two nieces died like this, suffocating under the rubble made by your rockets. I hope you are enjoying the same feeling they endured just before they died," Rasheed whispered so close Bennett felt his spittle and expiration on his ear.

The bag loosened and an immediate deluge of oxygen flooded Bennett's lungs as his gasps for air broke into convulsions desperately attempting to reach his fill as fast as possible. The bag still hanging loose across his face made it tough to inhale deeply and so he gulped what he could with a frenzied ambition to survive.

The electrifying zap of a cold syringe needle penetrating deep into his neck meant a new terror was entering his body but he was too oxygen deprived to care. It was not until the cold burning sensation flooding its way down from his head to his toes that jolted him to an alert state. As the neurotoxin tore through his body, his nerve fibres had no choice but to surrender control to the invaders. *The Trust* had specifically designed the toxin to build an alternate neuron network so an artificial interface could provide the control they needed over his brain.

From one end of the device, Rasheed extracted a long thin stiff metallic rod no thicker than a needle and moved in behind Bennett. There he placed his free hand on Bennett's head and with the other rammed the rod into the soft fleshy section below the base of his skull. Even in his numbed state, Bennett felt the stinging ping as the rod entered and breached his spinal cord transmitting an immediate pulse of muscular tensing agony down both arms. It only lasted a brief moment yet with each slight movement of his neck, he felt a violent burst of pain like fingernails scraping across a blackboard.

A few seconds and it started.

A cold itching tingle spread down through his body, a feeling that intensified with every second. He wanted to scratch violently and rip at his skin to cease the frustration but underneath it all, a nerve-wrenching terror was building. Something evil had been released and now it crawled just under his skin trying to break free with each movement.

The mental horror of clawed flesh eating beetles ripping and gnawing their way through his skin overwhelmed his consciousness and sent him into the oblivion as a wave of carnivorous invaders tracked up his neck into his face and head. Their barbed legs slashed his skin like razor blades while a row of oversized incisors masticated his flesh. Bennett tried to shake them off but he was powerless and defenceless to their feeding frenzy.

"I did not kill your family, I am your friend. Please stop this madness, I beg you," Bennett screamed seeking refuge while his pain tolerance showed signs of failure. His mind in turmoil, the excruciating pain had become too much to handle, and his mental stability was swiftly fading. The small carnivorous creatures like piranha devoured his flesh, ripping through raw nerve endings and like the worst toothache each bite sent an earthquake of agony vibrating through his body.

Rasheed was pleased with his new toy.

"You see Bennett, this fancy new device takes torture to a whole new level. It transmits a signal to that rod embedded inside your spinal cord and well let's just say becomes your worst nightmare," Rasheed explained but made no mention it induces the victim to visualise and feel almost any terror imaginable and the mind's natural phobia becomes an effective starting point.

The rod acts as the neurotransmitter sending signals to the brain while the toxins neutralize the real time physical awareness. For Bennett, his view of reality had changed to a horrifying virtual world built solely on his own worst subliminal fears from his childhood.

All his life, he had suffered a terrifying phobia of beetles but more specifically, he was terrified of the flesh-eating kind. As a young boy living in a rough North Queensland country town meant he had to grow up fast. Avoiding the constant bullying campaign by the senior school boys was near impossible and practical jokes were their daily ritual. However, one day near his seventh birthday that all changed.

He would never forget camping one night with Jim Roberts in the Mount Cook Forrest just south of their homes in Cooktown. That night, a group of the town's troublesome boys ambushed them while they slept. They staked him down and cocooned him inside his sleeping bag where he couldn't move. They filled it with beetles and other crawling insects and left him there overnight. Roberts got off lightly, he was dragged away, stripped naked and strung up in a tree hanging by his feet.

Next morning, Aunt Rose raced to their rescue only to find a traumatised six year old boy screaming and crying in a psychotic state. She pulled him from the bag to discover his small body completely red raw from the bites and scratches he had endured. In eight hours of terror, his subconscious was branded with the hottest of irons, one that would never heal.

Strangely about two weeks later, the same three boys vanished while fishing five miles up the Endeavour River. Their dinghy was located drifting with no signs of them anywhere. After a lengthy search, Police eventually filed the case as a suspected crocodile attack something not uncommon for the area. As Bennett grew older he often wondered whether his father and Rose ever had anything to do with their disappearance as it was never mentioned in their house.

"Kill me", Bennett screamed a muffled cry from under the bag, "FUCKING KILL ME."

He could not think anything other than the hundreds of clawed creatures gnawing their way under his skin and eating him alive. Their jagged teeth ripping through his flesh and tearing nerve endings was too much to bear and he laboured on the edge of blacking out.

Rasheed knew turning the dial on the device higher would escalate Bennett's subconscious state of fear but right now he wanted more conventional revenge and so flicked the switch to off.

The crawling bugs dissolved to a memory, his flesh intact and not desecrated like his mind had deceived him. Unlike awakening from a nightmare, his sense of relief quickly dispersed when suddenly, the black bag lifted and a flash of searing white light pulverised his retinas back to the reality of the room.

Rasheed stood before him with his wild animal eyes stalking his prey and preparing for the kill. He lifted his hand high above his head and in a powerful backhand action struck Bennett hard across his face, breaking his nose on impact and sprouting a new fountain of blood from an already mangled face. He had endured bashings in the past, however, it was always the facial attacks that stung the most but more from humiliation. Three more times, Rasheed sought his revenge with strikes to the face and each time it punished more than the last and each time more blood flowed.

"You will cower before me and beg for mercy, something my brother's family did not receive in their final hours of slaughter," he demanded as he unleashed one more uprising backhand across Bennett's face.

Bennett remained strapped tightly to the chair and with no signs of it releasing he was forced to take every inch of punishment. His head hung forward from the exhaustion and his hair dripped sweat mixing with blood as it spilled to the floor. He sat motionless, breathing heavy to maximise air and regain composure.

A strong calloused hand grabbed his throat and pushed his head backwards to expose his bloodied and broken face. Rasheed firmed up his hold and pulled himself in close to speak. "You are a filthy swine, confess your sin and let my brother hear you from his grave."

They locked eyes, Bennett defiant to the end and only a few inches apart. He could smell the Iranian's foul stale breath and felt his spittle charge from his mouth as he yelled into his face. The grip tightened while Rasheed clenched his teeth harder to help drive greater force into the murder of his old friend.

An authoritarian voice barked from the doorway.

"Rasheed, that's enough, let him go."

He glanced up towards Dom Whittaker striding across the room and giving Bennett his waited opportunity. At the very moment he felt the grip loosen around his throat, he launched a violent head butt squarely into Rasheed's face, splitting open the man's chin. Out of reaction, Rasheed's offsider drove his rifle butt deep into the fleshy muscle between Bennett's neck and shoulder.

As Rasheed regained his stature and shook off the retaliatory attack, he drew his handgun and lunged at Bennett. Pressure on the trigger and pushing the muzzle deep into his mouth determined to end it there and then after humiliation had become the overriding factor.

His finger twitched while Bennett's throat suffocated the muzzle. At point blank range, it was a certain kill shot, his head would explode out the rear with everything inside and from there, no return.

Bennett just stared back at him, waiting.

CHAPTER 130

THE CODEBOOK

Sepehr Airport, Tehran
September 17th

Rasheed regained his composure quickly and stepped back hesitantly while lowering his weapon at the same time. He wiped his chin with his sleeve and looked down at the blood before laughing. "You attack me like a rabid dog but you still think you are above the law. You have become an ignorant fool but soon your punishment will be dealt."

At the height of his vehement rage Rasheed had shown his control and professionalism to desist. He knew Whittaker would have shot him in the head before he had the chance to pull the trigger anyhow so finding restraint was his priority. As he turned and caught sight of Whittaker's gun pointing at his face he confirmed his belief.

"Thankyou Rasheed, you have done well. Soon he will be all yours as promised but first I have unfinished business with Bennett," Whittaker declared pushing past him to stand over their prisoner.

His first impression of his old friend was of someone who had just endured thirteen rounds with a world heavyweight champion, his face a sea of blood and deep gashes. His eyes looked beat and his body slumped like an old man. Whittaker laughed at the sight and walked closer, "Jon you are looking a little worse for wear my friend."

He moved to within Bennett's blood polluted sight to expose Viktor's codebook in his hand.

"I see you have reunited with your old buddy Rasheed or Soheil as you once knew him. I hope you got to reminisce," he laughed at his own attempt at humour.

Bennett just returned a cold glare through half-closed and swollen eyes failing to verbally respond mostly because he couldn't. Unbeknown to Whittaker revenge was still at play. Rasheed was making sure of it by gradually turning the dial on the device. The effect on Bennett was immediate as the tip of a razor sharp knife pierced the skin of his scrotum. He cringed and fought to escape, trying desperately to release the pain through screaming outbursts. Arching his back, howling towards the ceiling, the knife continued to split the skin and lever one testicle out from under the flesh. He could feel the nerves and fleshy tendrils stretching and snapping one by one with the pain shooting up into his abdomen inducing a fountain of vomit. Tears rolled down his face leaving track marks through the dried blood giving off similarities to a walking dead Halloween mask.

The Director of National Intelligence showed no compassion, he wanted something from Bennett and knowing Rasheed was rotating the dial could work to his advantage.

He stepped in close towards him, "You have to understand something Jon. I never wanted it to come to this, but you left me no choice. Before I leave Rasheed to finish his business with you I need one last thing from you."

He reached down and pulled open Bennett's shirt. The Thirteenth Code touched the light for the second time since the car factory in Patna. He opened the codebook to the last page and held it alongside Bennett's chest. He stood scrutinising the book yet still his recognition was blank, the page was crowded with variations of English, Latin and some foreign hieroglyphics that uttered complete mystery. Nothing on the page looked anything like the blue tattooed symbols across Bennett's chest.

"Why can't I see them Jon?"

Bennett rolled his head and looked up at him through blurred vision and pain instigated delirium and said nothing.

"I certainly hope your father did not die in vain, now tell me how I see the God damn codes?" Whittaker demanded furiously.

Bennett tried to answer but the agony was intensifying with Rasheed turning the dial and it wasn't until he started to lose consciousness that Whittaker seized the device out of Rasheed's clutches.

In the process of Whittaker snatching the device, the codebook had slipped from his hand and as it hit the floor Rasheed swiftly pounced to scoop it up. He had heard the stories about it but never understood its importance or what it had to do with Bennett.

He looked down and like Whittaker, he could only see unfamiliar text. He flicked through the pages while Whittaker grew impatient at an arm's length away.

"Why all the hype Whittaker, what's so important about a book full of gibberish?" Rasheed asked holding it up at him.

At a few paces away, Whittaker suddenly could see things from a different perspective.

"Well I'll be damned," was all he could say.

On the page where text filled the lines, images had vaguely materialised. On loose inspection they resembled an array of lines intersecting other lines, circles, triangles and squares reminding him of Ancient Alchemy he'd seen in text books at university. Though all had been hand drawn, they were strikingly similar to those on Bennett's exposed chest.

Whittaker stood mesmerised by the tattoo, like a teenage boy catching his first arousing sight of a naked woman. He broke from the trance and reclaimed the book from Rasheed and flicked through the other pages. On each a different set of thirteen symbols rose up from behind the text and he thought how strangely it gave the impression of some 3D children's book.

As he glanced back towards Bennett, something else caught his eye.

CHAPTER 131

BENNETT'S NEMESIS

Sepehr Airport, Tehran
September 17th

Just under the top of Bennett's trousers, a sheet of white paper protruded. Whittaker had seen it and walked over, reached down and snatched it up.

"What is it?" Rasheed asked.

Whittaker unfolded a crumpled piece of A4 and knew immediately what it was. He turned to Rasheed and inviting their prisoner to hear said, "It's something Jon has been searching for, something plaguing him for a very long time, his obsession for personal justice against those who abandoned him in Afghanistan. It is his answer!"

Bennett was still suffering from the hallucinogenic after effects of the device and feeling the residual burn of the imaginary knife. Through his clouded vision, he had seen Whittaker snatch the paper. The single torn sheet was the final page of the official document he'd found earlier on the floor of the crashing jet.

"So Bennett doesn't know!" Rasheed commented with a slight hint of smugness.

"That it was me, no," Whittaker returned looking directly into Bennett's eyes waiting for the response.

Like an avalanche of snow breaking loose above his head and nowhere to run, Bennett gasped with disbelief at the announcement. A new emotional roller coaster snagged him followed by the sudden onset of a deep hate and a revengeful desire to make Whittaker pay. Right then he had never wanted to kill a man more than Dom Whittaker.

"Yes Rasheed, I have never told him, it wasn't worth the problems it would have caused the Agency," Whittaker added.

Quickly Bennett's mind cleared of the agony and he knew without the restraints, he could snap Whittaker's neck with one swift move. Instead he struggled to release himself, his fury returning and beckoning the Eighth Code to give him additional strength while he glared murderously at Whittaker. He wasn't sure whether it was the breach of trust or the mental scar that Afghanistan had caused him but right now Whittaker was in his sights.

"You are dead, hear me, DEAD," he screamed like a man who'd just witnessed the rape of his wife and daughter.

Rasheed laughed, he was enjoying watching his enemy suffer in a different way and he joined in, "You see Bennett, it wasn't all just your good friend here, I launched the missile that brought your Phantom down."

Muscles and tendons flexed from the strain to break free while the zip ties gouged deeper into his skin spraying more blood as Bennett fought with the most violent ferocity imaginable. He had instantaneously transformed into a raging inferno of hate and revenge and nothing else mattered now except breaking free to kill Whittaker. The chair rocked but its weight held it firmly upright.

"Jon, calm down, it was never meant to kill you. The plan was always for Rasheed to shoot you down, rescue you, mentor you, expose you to the appropriate environment and manipulate the development of your field skills. Operation Sabre made you the best field operative the CIA has ever had, better than your father," Whittaker proudly informed his former friend.

Whittaker continued talking.

"I know what you want Jon, I know what eats you. It was me. Yes, I gave the order. We fed false information and satellite images to your carrier fleet so in their opinion, you were killed and your jet, destroyed. We sabotaged your radio so you really had no chance. Our plan was never for you to be rescued, a successful operative should know how to survive and find his own way out. It was our belief that you possessed the right DNA to quickly adapt and acquire the skills needed to survive. Rasheed was our controller in the field and he had his orders."

Bennett slouched back in the chair, it was no use fighting any longer and all his energy had been depleted in absorbing yet another twist of his life. He finally spoke, "So all my life has been some experiment for you and the Agency? Was being my friend an act too?"

"No Jon, that part was real life, nothing about our friendship was ever planned, it just happened and for what it's worth, you were the best friend a man could ever have."

"So what now? You have the Thirteenth Code and all the other codes in my father's book," Bennett snarled at him.

"Well I guess I do owe you some explanation before Rasheed kills you, I can see he grows impatient by the second."

Rasheed was pacing the room working himself up for the final slaughter.

"We expect that once the Thirteenth Code is entered into the Sphere, a set of detailed instructions will be released showing us how to build the laser cannon harnessing the full destructive power of the crystal radiation. It should show us how to insert Lucifer's Funnel into Meredith's cannon and then concentrate that power one million times giving birth to our very own nation destroyer. This weapon when fired from orbit will have the destructive force to annihilate a small country like, say, Belgium. Think of it as a subterranean regenerator, it disintegrates everything back into the ground giving life back to the planet."

"Lucifer's Funnel is pure evil. Why do you think it has reference to Satan?" Bennett fired back at him.

"Yes we know what it is, we have known since it was located near Roswell and that so called downed weather balloon," he sarcastically replied with a smirk on his face knowing the truth behind the Roswell incident.

"As for Satan, well that would also infer there is a God and clearly your security classification was never sufficiently elevated to know the adverse truth behind the religious origins of humanity," he added in a more serious tone.

Bennett returned a cold disinterested stare and Whittaker continued.

"In 1914, a German Archaeologist was exploring an old catacomb under the Ancient city of Saqqara in Egypt where he stumbled across a stone wall covered in alien like symbols and Ancient Latin scriptures. The symbols were the same as those on the sphere and after the text was finally translated it made distinct references to Lucifer's Funnel," Whittaker explained.

Bennett sat listening prolonging his death and calculating his chances of escape.

Whittaker went on, "One main scripture stood out, *Beware the bearer of the Thirteenth Code for he will rule the world with the power of Lucifer's Funnel.*"

Bennett looked down at his exposed chest and the blue markings.

"Yes and that would be YOU Jon," Whittaker responded the moment he saw his prisoner scrutinising himself, "and those symbols across your chest hold the key to utopia on Earth."

"Yes but at what cost?" Bennett snarled back at him.

"Our way maybe radical but it gives Earth a fighting chance and a healthy future for thousands of years to come."

"I don't understand, you are working against *The Trust* still you claim their vision," Bennett questioned.

"I am not opposed to their vision. It is just that some of the men behind it cause me great concern. I don't think the world is ready for the Fourth Reich and another Adolf Hitler just yet. We need a more stable government platform, one worldwide institution we can trust if we are to survive their proposed holocaust," he answered.

"How do you even know the Thirteenth Code will give you the weapon they claim?" Bennett asked.

"The Roswell crash gave us our first clue. The same markings and symbols etched into the twisted metal and down one side of the funnel. At the time it meant nothing until the Saqqara wall markings were translated. From that day on, a team of linguists at Area 47 worked around the clock unravelling something truly amazing. The craft prior to the crash had been armed with a similar weapon however it broke apart on impact. The funnel had been hurled half a mile away and from the translation, it had formed the integral component of the weapon."

Bennett interjected, "It will destroy all life on Earth including you and *The Trust*. There will be no utopia just a desolate wasteland for thousands of years."

"You are very wrong, we have already completed a series of tests and based on what we know so far, the pulse travels outward not downward. What the Monk claims is bullshit, a cataclysmic chain reaction will not occur. Our last successful test flattened an entire apartment block and that only used a micron speck of crystal and no funnel," Whittaker proudly announced.

"Whittaker, you are a weak coward and soon to become part of the most horrific act of mass genocide in the history of Earth. I bet Silvia is just so proud of you mate? Oh and what would your son think of you now if he was still alive. Gee dad you're the best, you just exterminated six billion people, way to go dad!"

Like hot metal rods submerging into freezing water, the hiss of fury could almost be seen steaming from Whittaker's ears. He had been attacked personally, his old friend knew just how to twist the knife and introduce the right topic, his dead son.

He glared into Bennett's eyes and with one well aimed right fist landed it squarely into his face. It stung like the other eight or ten times he'd been punched in the head that night except this one had an extra rampaging bite and split an inch long gash across his cheek.

"Come on Whittaker, you're getting soft in your old age, you used to have a good right hook on you. It's sad how old washed up fellas become, not much use for anyone really," Bennett verbally retaliated while he could feel the increased warm flow of blood trickle down over his jaw.

"Listen here you fucker, you'd be long dead if it wasn't for me. Washington wanted you eliminated however, it was me who buried the contract on your head," Whittaker snapped back.

"Dom, you are just a bureaucrat, a diplomatic pencil pusher all tucked up in your nice suit and tie, a yes no man to the President. A puppet is all you are, nothing more and you couldn't call the shots if Silvia's life depended on it. As for your dead son, well maybe he'd be alive today if you'd taken the time to be a father to him not some jackass blackmailing his way to the Whitehouse," he said dangling succulent bait at Whittaker.

Like a pack of ravenous sharks scenting blood in the water, he turned his fury on Bennett. "I should kill you myself, you sorry arsehole. I have fucked your life so much, it actually should be me who kills you. Fuck mate, I even had you sacked from the Agency, quite ironic really don't you think, I recruit you and I sack you," he said as he started laughing in a vindictive way.

He was angry, his emotional rage did what it always did, took over his thinking and Bennett knew how to work the man's weakness. He continued with his raging verbal retaliation towards Bennett. "You know I find it hilarious now that your sacking was caused by the Thirteenth Code. You claim I can't call the shots, well then how did the Senate Inquiry not know you were recovering stolen nukes in the Soviet Union when the Kuwait attack occurred. Yes that's right Jon, I destroyed those records and substituted some nice new condemning field reports and secured the right men to support my fabricated evidence. I call all the shots and have always called the shots, just like the Kuwait attack. We needed a site to test our prototype crystal laser on board Meredith in orbit. It was as good as any and it had a great cover story, the ILF were enemies of the US anyway."

Just like clockwork, Bennett thought, he knew Whittaker of all people would know the truth of his sacking, it was just a matter of pushing the right buttons. It was all unfolding as he'd pre-empted.

All the while Rasheed was standing behind waiting and only half listening to all the verbal bantering between the two men.

Whittaker had grown restless of the argument and said, "I will call one last shot for you Jon. Rasheed, he is all yours, make him suffer like no one has ever suffered before and then kill him."

On that command, the ILF leader lifted his handgun and pressed it into Bennett's right kneecap. He hesitated a moment and pulled the trigger...

CHAPTER 132

FRIENDS

Sepehr Airport, Tehran
September 17th

Whittaker, in a confused state collapsed to the floor with one hand cupping his bleeding chest wound while the other drew his handgun back towards Rasheed. In the last second and as he prepared to shoot Bennett in the knee, Rasheed had turned his gun towards Whittaker and squeezed the trigger twice. The two bullets tore their way through Whittaker's flesh and bone before exploding out the other side into the wall.

Whittaker had been shot in the chest from the rear, the gaping hole under his hand evident the bullets had exploded on exit taking a fist size chunk of flesh with it. Rasheed had missed a direct heart shot but instead the projectiles had desecrated his right lung. In the time it took to hit the floor he had returned four shots, two finding Rasheed's off sider in the head and the other two at Rasheed.

In the final few seconds as he pressed his gun into Bennett's knee, Rasheed had comprehended what Whittaker said and the realisation of the truth cracked him hard. In Bennett's eyes he caught sight of the man he once trusted and a man who was not his enemy. He raised his handgun towards the real enemy walking out the door and fired two quick rounds into his back. A coward act for a coward, he thought, as he watched Whittaker collapse to the floor. It was not until a volley of shots rebounded back at him that he realised he'd missed the man's heart and for his mistake, two bullets lodged deep inside his abdomen. The unexpected impact toppled Rasheed forward clutching his stomach and plunging him onto Bennett as Whittaker dragged himself out through the doorway leaving only a thick trail of blood to show his path. An immediate encore of small firearms rattle from just outside the door signalled Rasheed's soldiers entering the fight.

Rasheed emptied his clip into the doorway in search of Whittaker's damaged body but all he found was empty concrete flooring. The man was gone.

"Cut me loose," Bennett said in an almost frantic way as he scanned the doorway.

While his hands shook from the shivering nervous hysteria of his belly wounds, Rasheed pulled a knife from his belt and slashed the bindings from Bennett's hands and feet. He had just enough energy to answer Bennett's request before slumping onto the floor where he started gulping uncontrollably like a drowning goldfish. Death was swiftly approaching.

Bennett reached behind his head and curled his fingers around the long metal spike. He knew the risk but still he gave one mighty rearward yank and without any effort it exited cleanly. Bindings and rod removed he was now free to move.

As he flung himself from the chair, Rasheed reached up and grabbed his arm with such force it dragged him down to the floor. His dying declaration came as Bennett looked into the man's fading eyes and listened intently.

"I am sorry my friend, I was fooled by trickery and deceit … should have trusted you to know you would not betray a friend. Allah awaits me, please find forgiveness..." Rasheed murmured as his eyes went lifeless staring at him. His body went limp and his hand fell away from Bennett's arm. Soheil Mahdavi or Rasheed as he was more commonly known was dead.

Bennett lifted himself to his feet, grabbed Rasheed's handgun and collected what ammunition he could from the dead man's pockets. As he riffled through the pockets of both dead men, he stumbled onto the small tracking device Scott Douglas had given him to locate the Sphere. In the excitement to torture Bennett, Rasheed had neglected to inform Whittaker of the tracker.

Outside, the clatter of automatic rifles and occasional rocket propelled grenades exploding was amplified by the hangar's tall tin structure. With a gun in hand and a second under his belt, Bennett edged his way out into the unknown war. Staying low he ran to the cover of a small training aeroplane where he surveyed the battle field.

Under the reflections of the building's lighting, he was surprised to see the Bell helicopter sitting motionless on the tarmac. He was sure a grenade would have slammed into it by now. Off to his right, three of Rasheed's men were returning fire at whoever was attacking them. Further over past them behind another small Cessna aeroplane, he caught a quick glimpse of Whittaker stumbling through a side door. The unrelenting gush of blood had drowned his shirt and he was growing weaker by the minute. In his hand, he clutched tightly onto a grey satchel roughly the size of the sphere.

Bennett sprinted low and out of sight across the hangar floor towards Whittaker's escape route. There was no point drawing the attention of the gun battle towards him, he thought, as he ducked in behind the Cessna to prepare for the assault on the doorway only a few strides away. A loud explosion buffered the wall beside him followed by random bursts of automatic gunfire that pressed him tight to the floor.

He waited until the shooting eased before launching towards the door where he slipped through unnoticed to outside the hangar.

On the ground under the exterior lighting, he could make out the downed body of one of Rasheed's men. A deepening stream of dark blood flowed from his head and by the jagged piece of shrapnel wedged in his face, it was clear he was dead.

Bennett advanced from behind the sights of his handgun keeping a close eye on his darkened surroundings, he knew Whittaker's lethal capabilities and though he was injured he would fight like a wounded hyena backed into a corner.

Adjusting his eyes from bright light to almost no light impeded his retaliatory response to a new barrage of automatic gunfire coming from somewhere out in the darkness. The shots tore holes through the wall behind him narrowly missing his head as he fell to his hands and knees into the protection of an oversized steel rubbish dumpster a few feet over. It provided him the cover he needed though the gunfire quickly stopped the moment he fell from sight.

Somewhere further over the deep rumble of a truck engine could be heard but the rasping breathing of someone close by grabbed his attention.

Slumped against the end of the dumpster, Whittaker had the look of a defeated man with blood drained skin and glazed eyes. His clothing was drenched in blood that glistened under the partial lighting and had already streamed a few feet across the ground.

He rested with nothing, the sphere and codebook were both gone. He looked up into the muzzle of Bennett's gun.

"Arh Jon, you are too late, he has the sphere and Viktor's book," he announced in laboured breath.

"What... Who?"

"Bannister," Whittaker replied.

Bennett stared at Whittaker, wanting to slam the trigger rearward and kill the man yet there was a small piece of him that refused his cold-blooded murder.

"What do you mean? Bannister is dead."

"Well it must have been his ghost that knocked me to the ground and took the sphere from my very hands. No Jon I am sorry but he is very much alive. So if you want that sphere you better get going. There is a transporter plane at the eastern end of the runway, that's where he's heading," Whittaker said knowing he was dying and no further use in hiding information from Bennett.

Bennett kept his guard up scanning the area and watching Whittaker. He could see the red tail lights of a vehicle fading as it drove at speed towards another well-lit hangar a few kilometres over. Bannister, he thought, and turned his attention back down at the Director of National Intelligence.

"Why Dom, what happened to you? Why *The Trust*?"

"Silvia, mate. That's what happened."

With his gun still aimed squarely at Whittaker's head and only an arms distance away, Bennett offloaded a quizzical look that needed no accompanying words.

Whittaker responded in between the straining gulps for air and the increasing shivers from blood loss.

"They killed Josh, made it look like a drug overdose. The ultimatum was simple, I cooperate or they kill Silvia." He paused trying to expel his words.

"That's why I worked so hard at patching up our marriage, keep her close and keep a watchful eye over her. I thought if I could gain some advantage over *The Trust* with the sphere then it would keep her alive."

Bennett listened but after the recent events and discoveries, he was not too compassionate towards Whittaker's predicament.

"What about Sabre?" Bennett asked.

Whittaker took a moment to suck in more air and fight back the pain.

"Yes that was me and others, no one expected you to survive so when you showed up a year later, new orders came out to silence you. I was so impressed with what you'd done, I acted against the order. I only got away with it because I knew people in Washington and had dirt on a number of Congressmen."

"Who gave the order?" Bennett asked as he stood up to peer over the dumpster at the sounds of shouting from around the corner of the hangar.

"Here… it's the last signature," Whittaker replied pulling the piece of paper from his pocket, the same piece he'd taken from Bennett earlier. Bennett snatched it just as more gunfire struck the dumpster forcing him back down. To their right was an open grassed field stretching out a few hundred yards with small aeroplanes parked in two rows. Back the other way was the door and then further around to the front was the tarmac. Somewhere on the other side was presumably Bannister's men shooting at them.

Whittaker reached inside his jacket pocket as Bennett snapped to alert, "Hey not so fast, your hand, let me see it," he said pushing his gun firmly into Whittaker's head.

"Steady on, it's no weapon but something you need," Whittaker said as he slowly removed his hand and extended it towards Bennett.

"I know I have done some bad things Jon and I never expect you to forgive me but I am begging you to protect Silvia. She knows nothing of this and she does not deserve to die. Here take this," Whittaker said as he pushed a small PDA device towards Bennett.

"What's this?"

"It contains names of the board members and other influential men inside *The Trust*," Whittaker replied before adding, "be careful you don't understand how high up this all goes."

Bennett took it as Whittaker slumped sideways onto the ground and started convulsing. He had lost a massive volume of blood and he was nearly dead.

"Glasnost… encryption," he muttered from face down on the ground.

"What?" Bennett called as he dropped to within a closer hearing distance.

"Glasnost…"

The firing ramped up harder and crucified the steel bin forcing Bennett to cower as Whittaker slumped unconscious. He knew the gunmen were just keeping them contained for some unknown reason so the moment it paused, he stood and fired at anything moving. Ten rounds and two aggressors dropped dead to the ground. They had been advancing quickly and were easy targets at close range. A third shouldering a rocket grenade appeared.

The bright flash of exhaust was spectacular in the night but also frightening as the rocket launched towards him and Whittaker.

CHAPTER 133

STOWAWAY

Sepehr Airport, Tehran
September 17th

Logan Bannister glanced back over his shoulder at the hangar as he sped towards the waiting transport plane. Beside him on the front seat was Whittaker's satchel with the Mayan Sphere inside and in his left shirt pocket, he had the codebook well secured. Only a few minutes earlier he'd made a phone call to Koehler while his men had Bennett and Whittaker pinned down outside the hangar. He knew what was coming and didn't want to miss the light show.

Back outside the hangar, Bennett laid stunned on the grassy field from the full brunt of the explosive shock wave slamming across his back like an airborne sledgehammer. Catching sight of the rocket grenade had been enough warning for him to turn and sprint however, avoiding the surging fury of air pressure that followed was impossible. The dumpster was hurled ten feet into the air as if made of coolite before crumpling against the hangar wall beside it. There it erupted into a mini inferno of voracious flames climbing the wall and spewing out burning rubbish.

The gunfire had stopped and Bennett clambered to his feet still guarded behind his gun sights as he caught a glimpse of a vehicle racing away at speed in the direction of the eastern runway. Coward, he thought, and walked back towards the burning dumpster. Except for the crackling of fire, there were no other sounds, no gunfire or men shouting in the distance, and as he moved closer, no Whittaker on the ground only the spill of his blood. Like a small stream building in torrential rain, a flow of blood appeared from under the twisted bin and ran red across the ground to his feet.

For a brief moment, Bennett stood fixated on the twisted metal and Whittaker somewhere crushed beneath it. Poor bastard, he thought, as he turned towards the direction of the escaping vehicles. As he did, a bright blue flash high above him pierced the night sky and shot downwards.

He'd seen this before at Kehlstein and shielded his eyes while he started to run. The energy pulse struck the building with such driving force the entire eastern side collapsed inwards on impact followed by an astronomical detonation as aviation fuels joined the eruption.

For the second time in the space of a few minutes he was slammed face first to the ground as the earth under him heaved upwards and ruptured open either side. Back over his shoulder, the hangar was engulfed in flames and collapsed inwards causing more explosions as aircraft fuel tanks ignited under the climbing nebula of black smoke and ash.

He clawed his way and stumbled over moving rock feeling each stride slipping through the breaking surface. The pulse had driven its full destructive force through the floor of the hangar and into the subterranean rock where it surged outwards and upwards. A second pulse drove downwards with greater explosive impact than the first annihilating the remaining building and whacking him forward off his already stumbling feet.

A white blinding light came next.

He had kept up a fast pace running and though every few strides his legs buckled under him from the shaking ground he still reached a safe distance from the impact zone. The sudden bright spot light in his eyes took him by surprise and the two Iranian police officers shouting to drop his gun and get on the ground removed the confusion he may have had.

Bennett lowered himself to his knees and tossed his gun before extending his open hands in a gesture of surrender while the officers moved cautiously towards him with their handguns drawn. Bennett said nothing and he could see the distraction in their eyes as they both looked past him at the inferno. They had arrived in response to reports of gunfire at the airport just as the first pulse struck the hangar and startled their advance. Then as Bennett appeared running and stumbling towards them they both froze and spun their vehicle's spot light onto him.

Bennett saw the glint of handcuffs and felt the first officer grab his arm as the other stood back with his gun directed towards him. Explosions were still sounding in the background as drums of aviation fuel ignited like grenades in a small skirmish, each breaking the officer's concentration until one final crowd stopper erupted. The underground fuel tanks had ruptured under the seismic movement from the second pulse and all four detonated as one.

He used the distraction to disarm the officer and turn the gun on his partner. One shot landed dead center in the second officer's chest knocking him loose on his feet while the second tapped into his forehead. It happened so fast the first officer only felt Bennett's hand strike his neck and his body go limp as Bennett stole his sidearm. The bullet entering his head at point blank ended any likely retaliation.

So in the reflection of the blazing hangar Bennett stood looking down at the two dead police officers feeling guilt and strangely a sickening feeling in his belly. They had been innocent in this war against *The Trust*.

He regathered his thoughts and claimed their vehicle, a relatively new Mercedes before accelerating out onto the runway heading east with the headlights off. He didn't slow down to ponder Whittaker's fate, *The Trust* had just cremated his crushed body with Meredith's pulse cannon.

Within a few hundred yards of the eastern hangar he could see it was a hive of activity with men running and forklifts slithering. Like the hangar just destroyed, it was a single building large enough to house a family of Boeings and in the darkness of early morning it couldn't be missed. Lit up like a beacon to every moth on the planet he sighted the lone aircraft out front on the apron, a C-130 Hercules military transporter.

Sirens in the distance signalled the approach of the Tehran Fire Department and Bennett knew the place would soon be swarming with law enforcement like flies over rotten meat. Once word got out that two of their own had been killed then every cop in the city would come hunting for revenge.

Bennett pushed down hard on the accelerator and jammed it in place using a long police baton he found rolling around on the floor. He then hurled himself from the speeding vehicle into a rolling manoeuvre across the side dusty ditch where he came to rest on his back.

As he jumped back to his feet in the concealment of the ditch he watched as the Mercedes held its course towards the hangar and a business jet parked inside. The transporter had already started whining up its four huge turbine propellers with an amplifying growl as they sliced and shook the still air.

As he expected, the car ignited on impact with the jet starting a frenzy of commotion in and around the hangar. Men ran from everywhere attempting to extinguish the fire while another group ran towards the Hercules with guns out and ready. Among them, Bannister barked orders to get airborne immediately and stopped to peer out into the darkness surrounding the hangar, he sensed it was the work of Bennett.

He turned back towards his men and ordered a protective guard around the plane not knowing it was a waste of time.

In the time it had taken for the car to crash, Bennett had made his way up the rear gang plank and concealed himself underneath a new armoured assault vehicle bearing Iranian military markings. There he hoped to remain undetected for the duration of the flight not actually knowing their destination but presumed it would be back to Kyrgyzstan and Koehler.

CHAPTER 134

SNARE

Airspace over Turkmenistan
September 17th

Inside the tin shell of the transporter, Bennett could hear men talking and laughing up front above the monotonous hum of the engines. Occasionally a few would wander back into the cargo bay and carry out inspections by pulling on chains and shaking various timber crates. It had been a while since he had slept and already the night was edging towards day so he climbed quietly into the vehicle above him. At least five men sat up front and amongst them with his feet up and looking every bit cocky was Logan Bannister sucking on a cigar unaware his enemy was so close.

The weather conditions over Orto-Tokoy had turned evil, winds of cyclonic strength slammed against the mountains sending a continuous backwash of windshear across the valley and pounding the narrow airstrip. The Hercules felt every gusting tentacle as it made its final approach coming in high to maintain speed and control. The pilot had made countless landings onto this airstrip but never as frightening as this one and his paling face showed the fear.

Clutching the flight controls unforgivingly, he edged the huge bird downwards and prayed he timed it right. One wrongly directed wind gust could slam her nose first into the ground or slide sideways into one of the mountainous walls of rock either side.

The Hercules's wheels bit the asphalt surface bouncing five times while the wind grasped a tighter hold in a last ditch effort to claim a victim. Even as it started slowing, the wind still terrorised its wings trying to flip the aircraft that forced the pilot to maintain his firm hold all the way to outside the facility's hangar area. There it stopped and the unloading commenced with the assault vehicle driven off last into the rear of the closest of three hangars.

Fortunately for Bennett the windscreen and windows were heavily tinted black making it difficult for anyone to see in as he drove past Bannister's men. Next to him on the front passenger seat was the dead body of the man sent to drive it off the plane. Now he just had to get out without being noticed, he thought.

He parked not far from the main building and hurled himself from the vehicle disappearing silently in behind a stack of empty timber crates. There he waited and kept watch across the compound, an area roughly the size of a basketball court. The sudden glow of a bright light caught his attention as a large elevator door rolled open and Bannister and three others walked in.

The sun still hadn't broken above the eastern mountains leaving much of the compound in semi darkness and his position well hidden from the remaining men on the surface. A forklift carrying a large steel crate appeared and as it turned towards the elevator he broke from his position to follow it keeping low out of the driver's sight. As the elevator doors rolled open the forklift bumped forward with Bennett hanging close to its rear.

The doors closed and the elevator started a slow descent.

While the driver waited and belted out heavy metal on his headphones, Bennett maintained his position tucked in behind where he activated the tracking device just as a siren overhead started howling. The dead man in the assault vehicle on the surface had been located.

He hurled himself up onto the forklift to face a startled driver now removing his headset and clutching at his sidearm. Bennett lunged snatching the gun and fired two rounds upwards into the man's head through his chin. In the short struggle the lift had stopped and he could feel it surging towards the surface.

Less than a minute later, the lift doors slid open to an awaiting group of armed men all ready to decimate the room with bullets. The forklift sat engine idling with the dead driver slumped over the steering wheel and black exhaust fumes filling the compartment. The men cautiously edged their way forward into the lift, their guns at the ready in anticipation of Bennett jumping at them through the increasing smoke screen. None expected the forklift's fuel tank to erupt in a hellish bombardment of fire knocking them over with ease like bowling pins.

Three levels further below, Bennett forced his way onto Level Four.

The burning rag in the fuel tank had acted as a fuse while it gave him time to climb down the elevator shaft after escaping through the emergency hatch. The sphere's tracker had led him to level four where he levered open the doors and climbed through into a narrow corridor well lit under florescent lights and no one to greet him.

The tracker flashed the sphere's location somewhere a short distance to his left down another narrow corridor except all was too quiet, he thought. His instincts were eating at him and his heart rate pounded against his chest. So he proceeded with calculated steps, a handgun in each hand, one Glock and one Beretta courtesy of the dead police. Every few seconds he checked the tracking monitor, the sphere was behind a closed door at the end of the corridor.

He stopped and listened, still nothing.

He pushed the handle down and stepped into the room with both guns up ready for whatever waited.

Like the corridor, it was well lit and empty. On first inspection, it appeared as a medical room, clinical in colour with examination tables along one wall while a series of fridges with blood bags lined the other. Across from him were two closed doors giving no clues where they led.

He rechecked the monitor and it bleeped the sphere's location inside the room and then he saw it.

At his feet was a small metal object the size of a coin and immediately a rush of anxiety washed over him. Koehler had fooled him and it could only signal an ambush. The tracker had been removed from the sphere and used as bait to lure him into the snare.

"Hello Jon," sounded a voice from close behind him.

He spun around, both guns outstretched and prepped to unleash the fatal shot except he froze in disbelief.

CHAPTER 135

CYBORG

Orto-Tokoy, Kyrgyzstan
September 17th

The room was morbidly quiet except for the woman's voice.

"I have missed you Jon," Nicholette said as she, like Bennett, aimed her dual handguns at his head.

That moment catching sight of her steam rolled his emotions with a sense of desire yet confusion still played havoc on his mind. Nicholette Sponarava had made a remarkable return to the living when less than twenty four hours earlier, she had the faded appearance of a ghost with death looming.

"You look shocked Jon, did you not expect this?" she asked not lowering her weapons. As if a mirror image, he kept his guns aimed on her and finger prepped to tap off enough rounds to ensure an escape.

"I don't understand, what has happened to you? What about your loyal obedience to the Monk or are you one of these idiots now," he responded without fear of her guns and sighting Koehler and Bannister enter the room through the doorway behind her.

"Yes Jon, I agree you look shocked. Did you really think I would take a risk bringing the Russian goddess of death back to life when I know her mission isn't exactly in our favour. She has assassinated too many of my colleagues yet her skill set is too valuable to kill her off," Koehler said with a somewhat aggravating smirk.

"What have you done to her, what was in that injection?" Bennett demanded switching one gun to Koehler's head and the other still firmly locked onto Nicholette. Bannister walked slowly away from Koehler and Bennett tried hard to cover both with only one gun. His peripheral vision was all he could use on Nicholette and he knew he had no chance without taking the first shot.

"The Eighth Code as promised Jon except with one other small improvement I neglected to inform you about. This version manipulates the mind to see things our way. So think of her more as our loyal soldier, she can put those killing skills of hers to good use for us now," Koehler explained changing back to his usual arrogant German way.

Nicholette stood poised with weapons ready, she had become a cyborg with steely expressionless eyes and focussed on the man she once secretly admired in a more than professional way. He penetrated back into her eyes trying to find something, a small mental trigger to activate her subconscious but there was nothing.

He wasn't real sure if she would shoot, she was famous in the espionage world for not bluffing and taking life without hesitation or guilt yet right now Bennett had a feeling she needed commands to act. Acting on that perception, he transferred his firepower to cover Koehler and Bannister.

Bannister started laughing.

"Come on Bennett, put your weapons down, you are outnumbered, not even you can out gun yourself here," Bannister said moving in closer towards Bennett and adding, "One command is all it takes before Nicholette destroys you."

Bennett knew when to concede and lowered his guns to the floor. It was then he noticed Koehler holding the grey satchel in one hand and the codebook in the other.

"Koehler, you can't kill me anyway, I'm too valuable to you," Bennett declared.

"And why is that so?" Koehler asked putting his hand up to stop Bannister's advance.

Bennett opened his shirt to expose the Thirteenth Code to a disinterested Koehler.

"Yes yes the Thirteenth Code is plastered all over you. Yes I know but you see Jon, I can read the Codebook and so don't really give a shit about your fancy tattoo.

Bannister's raucous laughter irritated Bennett.

"Yeah Bennett I told him about your artwork so I guess this means we can kill you after all," Bannister added while amusing himself tapping his gun muzzle into Bennett's battle worn face.

Off to their side, Nicholette lowered her eyes focussing on Bennett's exposed chest. Koehler walked over to Bennett where he removed the Mayan Sphere from the satchel.

"This is what you failed to retrieve for me?" he said as he pushed the sphere out towards Bennett and added, "We had a deal but Logan succeeded where you did not."

He stopped talking, looked at the robot beauty and said, "So I guess that means your girl is now really his. What do you think about that?"

Bannister disengaged from Bennett's side and walked the few paces across to his new maiden.

"Thankyou Mr Koehler, I will make good use of her and a few privileges on the side too I'm sure," he said as he ran his hand through her dark chocolate hair.

Without hesitation Bennett responded in anger, "You lay one finger on her and your death will be slow but it will be the pain that eventually kills you."

She lifted her eyes and a glint of light caught Bennett's stare. A small tear had formed in the corner of her eyes and glistened in the room lighting. Their eyes locked while Bannister tried his hardest to aggravate him by stroking her hair and shoulders.

Koehler had grown impatient of the bantering and gave the command on exiting the room, "Nicholette... kill Bennett."

She smiled her best seductive way and quickly tapped off two rounds without hesitation.

CHAPTER 136

EMOTIONS

Orto-Tokoy, Kyrgyzstan
September 17th

At such close range, the two bullets from Nicholette's gun easily found Bannister square in the chest and drove him rearwards onto his back. The momentum of him falling carried his unconscious body across the tiles slamming him into the wall. In the preceding second, there had been no time to lift his own weapon in defence and Bennett knew it the moment she broke her eye contact with him. Assassins don't take their eyes off the target unless they're not the real target.

A barrage of gunfire flooded the room from the doorway while Nicholette returned her own equally frightening display of firepower. Bennett dropped to his knees, retrieved his weapons and joined in the gunfight as they both heard the clang of a metal object clatter across the hard tiles.

A heavy blanket of grey smoke engulfed them and an overzealous gunman wearing a respirator mask fell to his death as he pushed through the doorway. The gas canister was fast drowning the room in tear gas and already it was starting to burn their eyes and force an agitated response.

Bannister showed signs of slight movement followed by deep coughing. His bulletproof vest had denied penetration of both bullets and now he struggled to catch his breath as the gas intensified. The same was happening for the other two making it near impossible to aim and shoot just as the door burst open and automatic gunfire sprayed across the room. Though the toxic gas was like needles in her eyes, Nicholette still returned sufficient accuracy to force the shooters back out of the room and find cover from the barrage of her trigger fury.

"Come on," Bennett yelled as he pushed open one of the doors behind them. Firing a few more rounds across the room into the mass of smoke which gave them a little more time to escape and she sprinted through the doorway on his heels.

Nicholette suddenly stopped.

Like a small child suddenly finding a forgotten twenty-dollar note in their pocket, she pulled out a small metal ball from inside her jacket. A small dull grey sphere the size of a golf ball appeared in her hand. It was one of three she'd taken from the armoury a few hours earlier and now she was arming it as bullets hit the walls and ceiling. Bennett did his best to keep the men back with an aggressive routine of suppressive fire.

"Whatever it is you're doing, can we get it done fast, I'm almost out here," he screamed as he looked down at his remaining ammunition.

Nicholette held the ball in her hands and rotated the top half one complete revolution. It started beeping slowly at first and then quicker as a single green light illuminated. She looked back at Bennett and an explanation was not needed, it was obvious to him what she had. She turned and with her best underarm rolled the grenade towards the smoke.

"Run we only have a few seconds!" she yelled and leapt into full sprint.

A tsunami of life sucking fire and shrapnel surged through the corridor consuming everyone in its path as the grenade detonated. The device designed and built at the Kehlstein facility had a destructive force tenfold that of any modern day hand thrown explosive device and had desecrated five human lives in a flash.

A shockwave of intense heat followed forcing Bennett to use his weight to bump Nicholette sideways into an emergency stairwell. There the crushing impact threw their bodies together as one rolling onto the stair landing. As the emergency door self-closed, tentacles of ravenous fire clawed their way inside scolding clothes and stroking her head leaving the rancid taste of smouldering hair in the air.

For a brief satisfying moment, they paused in the anticipated comfort of each other's arms, her body hard against his and deep inside their souls, the warmth of passion raged to life. Even with the odour of burnt hair, her womanly scent overpowered Bennett like it had done the first time they met and he felt an urge to kiss her soft lips.

Suddenly she spoke and broke the embrace, "What about the Sphere? We need to get it back from Koehler."

"No time for that now, we have to make our way to the surface, Bannister will send more men," he replied as he placed his arm around her waist and lifted her delicately to her feet. Something beautiful had just transpired between them, a feeling of adoration and a need for each other.

A small green light above the door gave them a slither of light in the darkness of the stairwell that painted her face in a soft seductive glow. Somewhere off in the distance men were shouting and edging their way through the debris of the collapsed ceilings and walls, getting closer with every second that passed.

The noises severed their hold and Bennett took the lead up the stairs hesitating briefly on the third step, "Thanks for back there, you saved our lives."

Without delay, she launched the three steps into his arms and their lips pressed together. In that point in time, they felt the love and passion for each other made more prominent by their lips dancing in a field of ecstasy. He wanted more and she responded pulling him closer into their hungry embrace while his fingers softly caressed her face and neck. Both felt the arousal deep within their bodies as they fell deeper into the abyss of euphoria.

They both tried to break free but like magnets, the force was powerful until the sound of men behind the door threw them apart.

"Fuck... Come on, time to move," he whispered and led the way up the stairwell.

The facility, like Kehlstein, was nuclear strike proof and hundreds of feet below the Kyrgyzstan surface meant the emergency stairs were slow going and physically demanding.

"What happened to you here?" he whispered above his laboured breathing.

"Not real sure, I remember being sick but then something else took control of my body. Something very powerful I couldn't resist until you showed up. The symbols on your chest started flashbacks of us together but I think it was the emotions that gave me back control."

Bennett brought her up to speed with the recent events until the sudden echoes of heavy boots pounding the stairs silenced the briefing and they quickened their pace.

"Ok we've only got two handguns and little ammo. How many more of those fancy grenades you got?" he struggled to ask while gasping air and flooding in sweat.

"Two and a stick of C4 ready to go," she replied also in a heavy breath.

"Ok good, we take out this stairwell at the surface. I blew up the main lift on my arrival. That should give us a sufficient head start," he advised.

"There is still the emergency lift on the other side of the facility that we need to destroy," she added.

They reached the top landing within a few minutes and sat catching their breath listening for an ambush waiting outside the surface door. All was quiet except for the sounds of the men pounding the stairs in pursuit a dozen or so flights below.

Bennett pushed the door slightly ajar to give a sneak view of the interior of an aeroplane hangar. The early morning had lightened enough to glimpse a business jet parked at the far end and an awaiting welcoming party. He and the soldier sitting atop a green army jeep met eyes just as he swung his mounted Gatling canon towards the door.

Next to him, three more men stood with assault rifles looking tense and ready to engage a fight.

The Gatling gun spun to life spewing a rampage of ballistic punch directly at the solid steel door sending Bennett scampering back deep inside. He and Nicholette pushed their way down the stairwell where the enemy both sides had them pinned.

CHAPTER 137

THE THIRTEENTH CODE

Orto-Tokoy, Kyrgyzstan
September 17th

Koehler like a child with a new toy rushed the two levels to the viewing room where the empty pedestal waited. Similar in design to Kehlstein, the Kyrgyzstan facility had a specific high security theatre built for observing the sphere's projections and a smooth aerated ceramic dish to hold it. He hurried the positioning amidst drowning in his own deluge of excitement. He and his colleagues had scoured the Earth in search of Jeremiah's Codes and more importantly the Thirteenth Code for longer than he could remember but now he held them in his hand. He never expected the emotions he was experiencing as the sphere commenced floating and slowly spinning on the tiny columns of air streaming up through the pedestal.

Beads of sweat had formed across his pale blotchy forehead and as he looked down at the last two pages, small droplets rolled off his nose and fell to the paper. There they diffused outwards through the sixty year old scriptures and symbols leaving part of the Thirteenth Code streaked and blurred.

Like his shirt on fire he dabbed the book dry in a rage of panic at the thought of losing the one thing that meant extorting the leadership from *The Trust* and the supremacy he had dangerously desired for so long.

He reached forward, his fingers shaking with anticipation and tapped the first of the thirteen symbols, a circle dissected by a cross and a triangle. He continued cautiously taking his time to certify each symbol matched precisely the one on the page pausing every few seconds to wipe his face with his sleeve to dry the deluge of sweat.

He had never physically entered codes into the sphere and the moment was fast becoming the greatest day of his life.

Twelve symbols entered yet nothing was happening, he thought, and now it was time for the last, an unusual square rising up through a double barred cross. He rechecked the codebook and located the same symbol on the sphere before applying the finger pressure needed for activation.

One by one, the symbols illuminated pulling Koehler closer, mesmerised by the growing shimmering beauty and the hypnotic trance that grew more powerful with every passing second.

A brilliant flash of white bleached light burst outwards from behind each symbol swallowing the room and deflecting off the walls and floor. Koehler was blinded for that brief few seconds as he pulled away covering his eyes and in sudden doubt of what was happening. With his eyeballs feeling scolded, he forced them open to witness a display of grandeur across the tall cone shaped ceiling.

Above him in columns and rows were hundreds perhaps thousands of mathematical equations and technical schematics centred around a clearly distinct image of Lucifer's Funnel. He stood gazing like at a star filled sky suppressed by a feeling of astonishment at the complexity and sophistication of truly advanced science. It was a priceless piece of artwork no one could afford.

A tear rolled off his cheek and hit the floor as he lifted his cell phone and dialled a preprogramed number. It had just become the greatest day of his life and he had to announce his long waited demands to the Chairman.

The phone call was heavily encrypted and soon chimed inside a luxurious office deep inside Washington DC. The Chairman was a powerful man, highly respected in society and the political arena yet at the same time he was feared by all those around him. It was his tenacity for detail that earned him the position at the helm and subservient to the two elderly Gentlemen.

Born in a small town just outside Berlin during World War II, the Chairman was the only child of an influential German Gestapo Officer, a Nazi with direct ties and friendships to the Fuehrer himself. Fearing execution for humanity crimes at the end of the war, his father fled Germany to raise him under an inconspicuous identity. Now the Chairman headed a dozen major corporations worth trillions and held an influential political seat. It was all part of their grand plan.

"Yes Richard, what news do you have for me?" the Chairman asked as the phone connection went live.

"I am looking at the Thirteenth Code, spread across the ceiling as we speak," he replied boldly.

Silence fell across the line for the next few seconds while the Chairman pondered the truth.

"How did this happen? Why was I not informed before now?" he eventually demanded in a raised angry tone.

"That does not matter now, I have it, not you and it is time we talked business," Koehler responded.

"Is that so… then what is it you want Koehler?" the Chairman asked.

"I want complete control of the Southern Sector, unquestionable leadership of all settlements in the Southern Hemisphere and also... I want..."

Koehler stopped mid-sentence looking at the sphere that had now changed colour to a bright fluorescent green.

"Koehler, you still there?" the Chairman asked.

Koehler gave no answer, only a gurgling sound as the line went dead.

CHAPTER 138

DEMOLITION

Orto-Tokoy, Kyrgyzstan
September 17th

Outside the emergency stairwell, the Gatling gun stopped its vociferous barrage and cycled down to a whistling squeal. Behind the bullet scathed steel door, Bennett and Nicholette huddled together covering themselves against the splintering walls as hundreds of rounds pierced through searching for their flesh. Further down below them, the sound of boots pounding the stairs grew closer ahead of the heavy breathing of about five men.

"A few minutes are all we have," Bennett whispered watching Nicholette scrounging inside her jacket pocket.

"This won't be effective unless it's timed just right. Detonation takes seven seconds," she declared as she revealed one of the small grenades.

"Ok hold for five seconds and then let it go," he added hoping his elementary understanding of gravity was accurate for the detonation to occur somewhere close to the men a few levels below.

Stella twisted the top half to initiate the countdown sequence. The green light activated and Bennett signalled the five seconds.

"Three... Two... One... GO"

The ball rolled from her hand and free fell into the darkness below.

The deafening roar of the blast came quicker than they expected as it detonated unleashing a blazing holocaust and accompanying death. They pressed themselves to the back wall of the upper landing away from the scorching heat and flames while down below men howled like injured dogs. The pursuit team were mostly incinerated on impact yet a couple weren't so lucky and instead, lay dying in their own molten flesh.

"Poor bastards," Bennett said as he helped Nicholette to her feet.

Cracks started appearing under their boots as the stairwell collapsed from the impact. Within just a few seconds, the entire landing on which they stood jerked downwards as it broke away from the sidewalls only to hinge on the steel reinforcement bars that creaked and groaned under the bending stress.

"What now?" Nicholette shouted as she clung tightly to the top stair rail.

"Out there, take our chances with the Gatling. We use your last grenade as a diversion to get out the door."

The landing shook and fell as the primary support pillar collapsed. The rumble of concrete falling and crumbling became deafening and fire turned to black suffocating smoke belching up at them.

She pushed the door open just enough for Bennett to reach through. As expected, the Gatling wound up smashing rounds at the door as he tossed the grenade.

The seven seconds passed and the blast rattled the door.

CHAPTER 139

FLANK ATTACK

Orto-Tokoy, Kyrgyzstan
September 17th

Bennett shouldered the door open with his body weight and lunged through into the open space of a large aircraft hangar. He caught a sideways glimpse of fire and smoke to his left yet no immediate gunfire was there to cut him down. To his right was a business jet at the far end, though reaching it was a long unprotected sprint of at least fifty yards.

"Come on lets go," he screamed as he felt Nicholette anxiously shove past him.

She had stepped through on his heels with her guns raised towards the smouldering jeep and Gatling gun. She slowed, did a quick scan for signs of threat but still she witnessed nothing except flames and three men sprawled in their own blood, missing various limbs torn hellishly from their bodies during the detonation.

A spurt of gunfire sprayed across their path narrowly missing both and forcing them flat to the floor where they crawled on hands and knees to find the only cover nearby, a small crate of canned food.

Outside the hangar, the same Hercules he arrived on sat lifeless on the tarmac but it was the business jet, Bennett had his eyes on. On the side of the Gulfstream luxury aircraft was the name Richard Koehler inscribed in large fancy gold letters and what fitting way to escape, he thought, but on Koehler's own private jet.

"I make three gunmen to the right of the fire near the Herc," Nicholette whispered as she snuck another peek and added, "Looks like movement coming our way, trying to outflank us."

They leant back, both with a single gun in hand and with only enough ammunition for a very short gunfight. Behind them a group of three men advanced towards their position, two moving out wide to flank attack them while the one behind kept his sights aimed towards the crate. Bennett leant in close to Nicholette and whispered his plan.

Less than thirty seconds later, they rolled out from behind the crate aiming wide of their position. It didn't take much time for them both to aim and shoot their targets. Four single shots rang out as both men collapsed to the ground, life extinguished from the first bullet.

No sooner had the remaining gunman seen his colleagues fall simultaneously to the ground had he felt the first of four rounds slice through his chest. Like Nicholette, Bennett had seen the third man as he shot his target and instantly rolled to tap two rounds at the man's chest. Nicholette had done the same manoeuvre like a mirror image of his. The result meant the third gunman fell dead to the ground with four bloodied holes in his chest.

As per his plan, Bennett pounced to his feet and sprinted towards Koehler's jet.

Meanwhile on the backside of the main building out of their sight, the emergency elevator doors opened and one lone man walked out, long barrelled rifle in hand.

CHAPTER 140

SHOOTER

Orto-Tokoy, Kyrgyzstan
September 17th

Bennett reached the Gulfstream and lowered the front stairs while Nicholette provided them cover from behind the crate. She had just a few remaining rounds and she knew accuracy was crucial.

Nothing moved and with the morning light responding from the sun's rays making their appearance over the mountain, she felt uneasy. Her instincts clawed at her as she surveyed the hangar and the adjoining tarmac. Back further over and out of full sight was the main building, yet like standing naked in a curtainless room she felt vulnerable.

Behind her, the jet's twin engines whistled as the compressors wound up and the fuel ignited into a humming roar. If more men were to come then now was the time, she thought, as she took one last full scan of the area before turning towards the jet and running the dozen or more strides.

At the opposite end of the hangar, a controlled finger prepped the trigger and the scope zoomed in on the fleeing woman centring her in the crosshairs.

It took Nicholette no time to reach the stairs, part of her falsified American life was true, she was a national standard track sprinter and fast running did come easy. She took her first step onto the staircase at full stride just as the single high-speed metal projectile tunnelled and spiralled its way through her abdomen and finally wedged itself into the third step of the stairs.

Her body collapsed forward striking the stairs with a thud that sent an alarming vibration through the aircraft that Bennett felt as he prepared to roll the jet forward.

He looked out the cockpit window rearward towards the staircase.

"Noooo!" he screamed and leapt from the seat not seeing the shooter walking towards the jet, gun up and aimed.

CHAPTER 141

TRAIL

Orto-Tokoy, Kyrgyzstan
September 17th

Bennett hurled himself down the stairs towards Nicholette dragging her bloodied body up each step. While one hand reached out desperately fighting to grab the railing, the other covered half the hole in her stomach. The bullet had exploded on exit ripping with it part of her abdomen. Dark crimson blood oozed through her fingers and streamed down into an expanding puddle on the step below.

Jumping the last three steps, Bennett reached down and lifted her blood soaked body up into his arms just as the heavy rattling sound of high revolution gunfire ripped and shredded the jet's tail section. He turned to face their enemy boldly walking towards them labouring with the heavy Gatling gun from the jeep and as spent shells spewed out the side, he continued to unleash metal hell on the aircraft. The longer he attempted his impersonation of the Terminator the weighty gun wore him down and the fatigue showed on his face.

The engine closest to them ignited and burst into flames. Bennett knew the fuel line was next and after that, the tanks would take out half the hangar. The Gatling clanked as it emptied its last round followed quickly by the metal thud as it dropped to the hangar floor and the familiar gunman stepped clear with his handgun up covering Bennett.

Logan Bannister had his sights firmly centred on Bennett's head while strapped across his back was the sniper rifle he'd used to shoot Nicholette. He advanced as if playing a tormenting game, not shooting at Bennett when he could have easily with the Gatling. Bennett fired a fast combination of rounds towards him and though they narrowly missed, it forced Bannister to take cover behind the crate of cans.

Once the firing had stopped, Bannister raised himself and fired half a dozen rounds towards Bennett just as the fuel line ignited.

The tanks exploding lifted him off the ground and drilled him rearwards across the hangar floor sliding on his ass. Another few steps closer and he would have worn the full wave of its fury but instead it only licked his face as it passed over. He laid winded from the hammering strike and the warm feeling of blood filling his pants accompanied by a growing agony down his right leg. He lifted himself up and with one strong grip ripped the piece of metal shrapnel from his leg while watching the burning carcass of the once luxurious aircraft.

His face already showed gruesome markings of previous battles but now it was worse, scalded raw in patches from the brushing flames. As the hangar creaked and collapsed in places, Bannister shielded his eyes from the blazing inferno in search of Bennett's dead body. Leading towards the rear of the hangar was a trail of blood ending at a closed door.

Bannister opened the door and edged his way through into the darkness of a dense shaded forest.

CHAPTER 142

LOVE

Orto-Tokoy, Kyrgyzstan
September 17th

The forest floor was cold and dark while hanging above, a dense canopy of branches and leaves closed over to largely deny the sun's existence. It grew thick scraping against the facility's eastern hangars and buildings that was now proving ideal for Bennett and his escape from Bannister. He carried his wounded accomplice deep into the darkness of the trees where behind a clump of thick shrubs he concealed their presence. He lowered her down across his lap and for the first time witnessed the gravity of her injuries.

Motionless in his arms, Nicholette's breathing had flattened and her eyes wilted under the strain of her suffering. Her lower body was a mass of blood and yet more oozed from the wound in her belly.

He gazed down into her dying eyes and they returned a penetrating stare except something was different. He could feel it, an emotion he had long pursued.

Her body shook violently as more blood spilled to the forest floor and her body temperature dropped dangerously. Her face had drained of all colour but her eyes were still seductively beautiful even on the ledge above death. She grabbed his hands with all her remaining strength and her pale lips edged open.

Her voice croaky from the pain and weakness came out soft and he had to lower his head to hear her words.

"I'm sorry," she murmured as another violent convulsion yanked her body towards finality.

"Don't talk, save your energy," was all he could say back, his emotions were spiralling out of control as he held her close and stared into her eyes like lovers separating for the first time.

"I always dreamt I'd meet you again after the Soviet Union," she struggled to say and at the same time lifted one hand towards his face. He took her hand in his and kissed it softly while feeling the hypnotic pull of her eyes as they penetrated his. With all her strength, she raised her head up off his leg and he spontaneously reacted, the urge had been too powerful to resist.

Her soft lips met his and they kissed for what seemed like an eternity to him. He caressed her face with his hands and looked deeply into her eyes just as a ray of sunlight pierced the overhead tree canopy. As the sun wrapped its warmth around them and her eyes sparkled of green emerald, he became entranced in her full beauty.

She reached up with both her hands and clasped his tightly. She took a deep breath and said, "I will miss you Jon Bennett," before exhaling for the last time.

Her hands went limp and fell from his grip while her eyes fixated past his, staring out into nowhere. Her life had finally passed and now she lay lifeless across his lap.

As a tear fell down across his cheek and dripped onto hers, the deadened sound of a bullet slicing through wet leaves threw him face down in the dirt. During the past few minutes, he failed to notice the forest floor illuminating under the streaming morning sunlight and his position had become visible to the approaching assassin.

He snapped a peek above the leaves to spot the dark shape of Logan Bannister perched some distance away behind the barrel of his rifle. Bennett went stealth amongst the trees leaving Nicholette's body hidden under the bushes.

"Bennett I know you're out here, come out and fight me like a man," Bannister called out.

Like a Velociraptor stalking its next meal, Bennett slid and sprinted low through the bushes leaving only a trail of silence. Bannister squinted through his riflescope yet he saw nothing and he became edgy at the sudden quietness.

"Bennett you can't hide from me," he called out again hoping Bennett would give off some clue. It came almost immediately.

"Why would I need to hide from a piece of shit like you," Bennett quietly announced as he pressed his gun into the back of Bannister's head.

Bannister laughed and flung himself left as Bennett squeezed the trigger.

Click…

The gun jammed.

Bannister spun knowing the sound and launched his own retaliation from the hip as he yanked his handgun from belt to eye height. The whole manoeuvre took only a split second and Bennett ran as the bullets chased him through the thick shrubs deflecting off tree trunks.

"I said it before Bennett, you can't hide from me," Bannister called out just as he caught sight of him vanishing through the same rear hangar door.

Under the flaming light, Bannister gave the impression of the half-incinerated cyborg as he walked slowly back into the hangar with guns ready and his face blistering from the burns.

While Bennett watched from behind timber crates at the other end of the hangar, Bannister reached into his pocket and removed a small silver device. He looked down at it and then up in the direction of Bennett's position before engaging automatic mode towards the crates. The timber shredded like paper as rounds smashed and ricocheted off it.

Bennett knew now he was being tracked and remained hidden from sight but with no weapon, he had just become an easy target.

CHAPTER 143

SAFEGUARD

Orto-Tokoy, Kyrgyzstan
September 17th

Blood trickled slowly at first as Koehler convulsed violently in his own foul vomit. His eyes had exploded from his face, he had gorged his own tongue and now his internal organs were dissolving to a thick black sludge of blood and flesh. His skin had started to split and peel from his body as the Blue Death continued its attack.

His agony during death had been beyond comprehension and for the last five minutes, he had a front row seat at experiencing just what he had ordered others to suffer.

Inside the viewing room, the sphere still radiated a vibrant green haze of death, a safeguard implanted by the Monk a few years earlier when he learnt of the mole amongst his Guardians. The original Mayan Sphere had been substituted with a lethal twin replica only requiring the Thirteenth Code to activate its deadly payload. Designed to appear authentic, the ceiling projection lured the victim in for an effective close range kill and the Blue Death radiation was released.

The sphere started flashing a sequential order of light intervals each growing faster and disappearing one by one.

CHAPTER 144

REVENGE

Orto-Tokoy, Kyrgyzstan
September 17th

The bullet storm clattered as Bennett covered his face from the shards of timber splintering in all directions. Somewhere on the other side, Bannister limped towards him leaving a trail of blood across the hangar floor while the scraping of his boot signalled he was wounded.

As Bannister paused to reload, Bennett rolled to his feet and launched himself into full stride towards the assault vehicle parked around the corner of the next building.

A wild spray of rounds from Bannister's gun clipped his left leg just below the knee and he stumbled bouncing awkwardly across the hard asphalt tarmac. He tried to raise himself but his leg failed him on first attempt and Bannister lunged at him.

Bennett rolled to his back to stare up into the dark smoking muzzle of Bannister's gun.

"Well Bennett, this is it, say your prayers," Bannister announced peering over the top of his sights. Below him, Bennett pushed back feeling a low thundering rumble from somewhere deep below followed by a slight ground tremor. It was his chance and he quickly swung his good leg out and up into the man's crutch while at the same time Bannister jerked wildly at the trigger. Three shots expelled, all missing.

The ground under them erupted upward and opened up. As if struck by an earthquake, crevices appeared in the asphalt and stretched across the compound collapsing building structures as they travelled.

As the earth swallowed the hangar behind them, Bannister stumbled forward onto Bennett. The sphere just like the previous one had detonated a thousand feet below them with the force of a low yield nuclear warhead and the resultant shock wave was pushing a cataclysmic domino effect towards the surface. Soon the entire above ground complex would plunge into the earth like the victim of a massive sink hole. All over the compound, gas lines were rupturing and fires were igniting into small infernos that quickly spread to the adjoining buildings before they too were engulfed by the underground.

Bannister had dropped his gun and Bennett seized the opportunity. He slammed one head strike after another with his fists feeling the soft squelch as the man's nose broke.

From then on, they were locked in a fierce hand-to-hand struggle while Bannister tried arduously to reach for his gun a few feet over on the asphalt. His fingers brushed the metal barrel as Bennett hammered his knee into his unprotected face. Bannister responded with blood gushing from his nose and lifted himself up into Bennett's chest driving with his legs as he did. The clash threw them both toppling over into a shallow crevice where they wrestled against each other's pride and fight.

The ground either side continued to buckle and shake yet they exchanged punch for punch with the occasional kick and head butt. Bennett was by far the better skilled fighter but Bannister was heavier and stronger and once he was in close confines the fight became stacked in Bannister's favour. Bennett had to fight like a slippery eel not allowing him to take hold until a flash of shiny steel caught his attention.

Bannister had pulled a long hunters blade from his boot and like an Olympic fencer was lunging forward thrusting the knife towards him. Ducking and weaving awkwardly on his wounded leg was all Bennett could do to prevent impalement.

Half the hangar floor had sunken and the runway was cracking like thin ice on a frozen lake. Further north along the collapsing tarmac was his means of escape and soon that aircraft too would drop from sight.

"You know Bennett, I really don't know which would be more satisfying, killing you or when I killed your father," Bannister said as he waved the knife at him preparing to strike.

As Bannister made a lunge towards him, Bennett side stepped grabbing his arm and with lightning quick hands slammed the syringe needle hard into it pushing the plunger all the way. The effect was almost immediate.

Bannister's legs buckled and he fell forwards before clambering back to his feet in desperation of survival. He staggered while his muscles lost their sense of reality and his mind started going numb from the toxin pumping through his body. He tried to talk but an unrecognisable blur was all Bennett could hear as he watched his father's killer fall to his knees and the knife slip from his open hand.

When Rasheed died back in Tehran, Bennett had pocketed the mind controlling device and a syringe filled with the prep drug. Now he was using it in the best way possible, to take revenge on a man worthy of it. Bannister had become imprisoned inside a human shell devoid of all control and there was nothing he could do to change it except watch Bennett disappear behind him.

Showing no signs of compassion, Bennett drove the thin metal spike into the back of Bannister's neck through to the spinal cord. He turned the device on, twisted the dial to its maximum setting and stood back to watch retribution come to life. For the next minute, Bannister fried in his own horrific nightmare and entered a frantic psychosis, he tried to run until Bennett speared the hunter's knife cleanly through his left knee almost severing it from the leg.

Bennett watched and from only a few feet away he witnessed how vengeance was now at its sweetest however, with the ground growing more unstable by the second and sections of the runway dropping, he had to move fast.

A familiar vibrant blue flash caught the corner of his eye while he watched Bannister kneeling and bawling in terror, tears flowing fast down his face and screaming for redemption.

The energy pulse struck the Hercules with the ferocious pace of a meteor strike. As the fuel tanks erupted, pieces of wings and fuselage rocketed off in all directions narrowly missing them both.

He rushed to pick up Bannister's handgun while the ground heaved violently swallowing more of the buildings. Another flash of blue light smacked the ground, this time the main elevator building.

Bennett knew what he needed however before he did, he turned and without guilt or thought he tapped off three precise shots.

Bannister slid lifeless to the ground and his terror abruptly ended with the three bullets ripping his head apart.

Bennett hurried back into the forest where somewhere up the mountainside a pulse struck with a high pitch roar. The quiet stillness of the trees became a distant uneven rumble as rocks and boulders stampeded from somewhere above. Another pulse strike, this time close to where he moved and the forest burst into flames. Just as the small forest animals ran for their lives, so too did he stumbling every few strides on his injured leg.

He reached the spot among the bushes where he had left Nicholette's body just as the fire lashed at his back and the smoke strangled his breath.

Nicholette was gone, only a pool of blood remained.

CHAPTER 145

CRASH

Orto-Tokoy, Kyrgyzstan
September 17th

Two more pulse strikes collided deep into the mountain tossing chunks of earth into the air and raining down onto the forest below. An avalanche of volcanic proportion was building as the mountainside loosened and shifted on itself.

Fire closed around him and then from behind the inferno came the first car-sized boulder smashing through the trees followed by others. He turned and ran, stumbling at first and confused.

Nicholette was gone, but how? She was dead, she had died in his arms. How she could just disappear played on his mind.

The narrow runway faded into the northern distance as Bennett hobbled towards a small black jet parked to one side. Behind him, the runway kept collapsing into the sunken facility below and cracks were stretching their way north.

Time was running out and he knew it.

The noise of rocks colliding grew louder as the avalanche built speed smashing into the forest and breaching the perimeter. Climbing the stairs of the Cessna Citation business jet he could see a number of larger boulders had rolled out littering the runway.

Within a few minutes, he had seated himself in the cockpit and fired the two engines ready to taxi. He had enough fuel he hoped to reach northern India so he released the brake and the jet jolted forward into a steady roll.

The sun had risen higher in the sky and the weather looked healthy for flying just as the windshield lit up vibrant blue as another energy pulse smashed to Earth. This time it struck the ground next to his jet driving up a wave of earth and asphalt across his path. The shock wave smashed into the aircraft's nose, spinning the jet sideways and almost flipping it over. Desperately out of time, Bennett shoved the throttle full forward whining up the jet turbines for maximum power responding smoother than he expected. The jet was old and from the initial appearance, he had been dubious whether it would make flight.

With a straight stretch of bitumen running parallel to the river and mountain ridges, he pushed the jet's speed towards take off. In the distance, he could see more mountains rising steeply off the end of the runway and the immediate need to pull altitude once airborne. Back behind him another huge explosion rocked the main building with flames and smoke erupting upwards like a small volcano. The underground fuel storage tanks had just ruptured from the shifting earth and ignited giving birth to a new fireball. A massive black mushroom cloud rose swiftly while under it, thousands of rocks swarmed the complex as half the mountain rolled across it.

He turned back towards the runway as the jet's speed passed through fifty knots and another energy pulse smashed into the runway narrowly missing his right wingtip. The jet shook and rattled as the speed increased with each vibration, feeling like the rivets holding the fuselage together were popping yet he pushed it onwards.

At eighty knots, a flash of blue light swarmed the cockpit as a pulse tore up the runway thirty yards in front leaving a grave for the jet and him.

"FUCK!" he screamed clutching the controls tighter.

Keeping full power, he lowered more flap and yanked back on the controls. The plane started to lift with the nose wheel rising first while the rear wheels gripped the bitumen all the way to the trench. Bennett looked out the windshield at a crater the size of a bus and could only silently pray.

He felt the sudden dip and shake as the jet floated over the small canyon before another lighter thump as the rear tyres skidded on the other side. His speed had been enough for the wings to offer the lift needed to fly and now his task was missing the mountain ridge directly in front. One plane crash into a mountain was enough for him, he nervously chuckled to himself.

Missing the ridge proved easier than he had calculated with no weight on board and holding full power for longer. Down below, the facility had mostly collapsed into the ground with the remaining ground structures littered with fire and rocks. The mountain still crumbled onto the site burying it deep and overflowing into the river. Random explosions still engulfed parts of it and a mass of black smoke funnelled south driven by a strong northerly wind. His fuel status was good and he set course for Islamabad in Pakistan, a distance he estimated should only take ninety minutes flying time.

He climbed to 30,000 feet and settled into an efficient cruising speed somewhere crossing over the southern Kyrgyzstan border into Tajikistan. Eventually he knew the airspace restrictions would become an issue for his flight path and without a registered flight plan, he would certainly attract unwanted attention. For now, he relaxed back and gazed at the clear blue sky extending into the distance while the clouds rolled out 10,000 feet below him.

Ten minutes into Tajikistan airspace he screamed, "Shit will they ever give up."

Without hesitation, he throttled up to maximum and banked hard left pulling more G's than he thought the plane could survive. An energy pulse had rushed vertically across his flight path and if not for his quick fighter pilot reactions, he would have flown directly into it.

He pushed the banking manoeuvre into a steep dive towards the surface of Karakul Lake reaching the maximum airspeed the wings could withstand. Two more near misses flashed by making the jet shudder and shake while he kept pushing it downward and altering direction to prevent Meredith locking on. Another five minutes and he was skimming the surface of the lake heading south towards the rugged Pamirs Mountains. At a few hundred feet above the ground, he considered himself safe from his predator in orbit, the jet's body hidden amongst the many ground signatures making it impossible to locate.

To the east a violent storm cell was tracking his way and the increasing turbulence ripped and tore at the aircraft making the low level flight almost impossible. He pushed on through fading visibility and an urgency to gain altitude until a brutal down draft sent his jet spinning and slamming into a valley of ice, rock and snow.

CHAPTER 146

NO SURVIVORS

Virginia, USA
September 17th

The young officer sat forward of his supervisor in the control room and they were both satisfied with the satellite image displaying on the wall monitor. Meredith had failed where Mother Nature had not, they snickered. What they looked at was a plume of thick black smoke trailing back from a badly twisted metal carcass of an old Cessna Citation Jet.

"Sir, no survivors, the escaping jet was completely destroyed on impact with the ground," the supervisor reported into the phone.

The Chairman listened to the report and hung up. He sat alone in his Washington office and a smile broadened across his face confident Jon Bennett was finally dead.

CHAPTER 147

GHOST

Virginia, USA
October 10th

George Anders did what he did every time he entered the Virginia facility, processed himself through the usual security scanners before accessing the primary control room. Once inside, he prepared his usual double strength espresso and checked his emails. Things had settled down since Bennett crashed somewhere in the Pamirs Mountains a few weeks earlier and *The Trust* no longer considered him a threat.

He took his usual seat at the laptop and punched in the various lengthy security codes connecting him to Meredith inside her space dock floating in orbit. Another series of key strokes and he set into motion the daily ritual of diagnostics across her systems while he prepared the first of a dozen software upgrades. The extra work required for the upgrade meant he wasn't going home for days.

The control room was quiet except for the occasional blip of a computer as each diagnostic test completed its cycle and moved onto the next. He was competent at what he did and preferred to work alone so when he heard an unusual noise behind him, he immediately swung around to investigate.

His mouth dropped in both shock and horror.

A grey haired man stood only a few feet behind him and in his extended hand, a Glock was confidently aimed at his head.

"Who the fuck are you and how'd you get in here," Anders nervously asked thinking of how he was going to get to his own gun on the far side of the room.

"Just handover the laptop and I won't shoot you," the man demanded.

"Now if I was to do that I'd be dead anyhow, so you see, your threat doesn't really hold much weight," Anders announced as he started to push himself up from the chair thinking he had a chance against an old man.

Two silenced shots muffled the room's stillness and Anders slumped back down while his head rolled to the side with two small bleeding bullet wounds. His employment within *The Trust* had been short lived.

"Well I just saved them the hassle," the old man said to himself as he carefully picked up the laptop. He wasn't there to dance in negotiations, he was there to take control of Meredith.

He slipped out the same way he snuck in, an underground tunnel unknown to most. The building where they based their Meredith operations was an ex-CIA safe house not far from the CIA Headquarters in Virginia. It and the surrounding twenty hectares of forestry had been sold off a few years earlier as part of the Agency's budgetary cutbacks and though it remained a top secret location, it was for a different clandestine organisation. He knew its layout well and its greatest vulnerabilities were the mass of underground tunnels leading in all directions.

He hurried from the tunnel to his car concealed on the western side of the forest and disappeared into the night like a ghost.

CHAPTER 148

NIKITA

Washington DC
October 10th

Bennett under the pseudonym of Paul Benson drove unnoticed down Pennsylvania Avenue to his hotel amongst the tourist precinct of Washington DC. There he walked casually to his room and removed the face mouldings and old man's wig. In the eyes of *The Trust* he was dead and so a ghost he had become.

He had almost perished in the inhospitable mountains of Tajikistan but not from the plane crash. He knew that if he was to escape *The Trust* he had to die or at least convince them he was dead. In the last few minutes of the turbulent flight, stress fractures had appeared across the wings and rivets were popping like champagne corks at a wedding forcing him to crash land. Selecting the least dangerous path, he lowered the underbelly down onto a wide valley of what he hoped was deep snow. It hit without mercy biting down hard into the icy snow at just over 160 knots and tobogganed out of control until a soft patch caught the nose. From there it ploughed deep into the snowfield like a diving submarine and quickly came to rest almost totally submerged.

Bennett had been strapped in tight and had to dig his way out through the freezing snow, all the time thinking it had been somewhat more smooth riding than the crash into the barren hard terrain of Iran the day before.

With the use of Nicholette's C4 explosives, the wreckage became a flaming orange beacon against the stark white background and with the cover of the overhead storm clouds he walked away undetected by satellite.

A day later, suffering from extreme hypothermia he staggered into a small mountain village. Tajikistan had always been a haven for ex-Soviet spies and securing an exit back to the United States went off without a hitch.

Now inside his hotel room, he relaxed back with bourbon in hand and opened the laptop. From his jacket inside pocket, he pulled out Whittaker's PDA and fired it up. Whittaker had been pedantic about keeping records mostly so he could blackmail his way into higher places or in this case, keep him and Silvia alive.

It had taken Bennett days of searching to find the files and it wasn't until he remembered Whittaker mumbling something about Glasnost that triggered the clues. Embedded inside an image of the beautiful Saint Basils Cathedral in Moscow was an encrypted text file. It wasn't the beauty of the church that Bennett most recalled, it was Nikita Topoluk, a local barmaid living on the outskirts of Glasnost that Whittaker fell in love with. He had fed her promises of marriage and a wonderful life in the United States but that all ended the day she was brutally murdered in her apartment, an event Whittaker had always argued stank of KGB. The truth Bennett later discovered was Nikita Topoluk was an agent working for the Chinese sent to steal Soviet secrets.

Bennett opened the encrypted file using the only password he thought appropriate, *Nikita*. It unfolded into a text document of mammoth proportion outlining a historical account of Whittaker's involvement with *The Trust* and how he set up infiltration networks within the US Government and various other governments around the world. Sections of it had clearly been deleted causing him confusion but it was the names of the Six and significant installations around the world that he was more interested in.

His thoughts drifted back to Nicholette. It had been her mission to exterminate the Six and the PDA was the perfect assassin's aphrodisiac for just that. He had spent days reading and rereading the document to build an understanding of what they were and to devise his final mission.

The Trust, he discovered, was an amalgamation of predominantly German mega corporate businessmen forged from the failure of World War II. It spanned the five continents and controlled every major financial institution around the globe. The list of men and women involved was devastating and then there were the twelve hundred benefactors, mega wealthy families wanting a chop at an extended life in paradise all at a non-negotiable cost of fifty million US dollars each.

The PDA told him their New World Society was destined for governance under the Fourth Reich and was only until the discovery of the Sphere of Anubis that their plan was born. In 1945, six men of influence sat in an old house somewhere in New Mexico watching the first ever detonation of the atomic bomb and it was there they confirmed the sphere held the key to their plan's success. From that small secluded house they set forth into the world to build their empires and prepare for the uprising.

Already Richard Koehler and Herman Schwartz were dead leaving only four members of the Six remaining. Killing three of them meant nothing to him however, the Chairman was worth the wait and needed just the right approach.

Bennett tapped a few keys and executed the overriding command for Meredith to leave her home for the last time. Whittaker had played the large part in securing General George Anders and in doing so acquired the operating instructions for their killer satellite. He entered the first of her target's coordinates and sat back to wait while indulging in another celebratory bourbon.

Sometime later that night, the entrance to the Afghanistan mine erupted in fire and rock, men scrambled as a chain reaction unleashed deep inside the blue crystal mine just north of Khan Abad. Within no time, the reaction went nuclear, the result of a thousand tonnes of crystal fusing under the energy pulse impact. The world's media would confirm nuclear weapons in northern Afghanistan as the largest ever recorded mushroom cloud rose towards the heavens. From that, the US invasion was publicly justified except the lack of nuclear radiation would go unpublished until a few years later.

In various other newspapers around the world, articles appeared of chemical warehouse fires, unexplained seismic activity in the mountains of Utah and a recidivist arsonist on the loose destroying large office blocks in a small town called Berlin in the New Hampshire. In tune with their heritage, *The Trust* had chosen the American made Berlin as their predominant town to orchestrate much of their chaos plan.

Meanwhile in a Western Australian newspaper, a story appeared on the front page of unexplained lights in the western sky. Witnesses in the small coastal town of Port Hedland reported sighting a huge meteor with trailing fire race across the sky and crash somewhere over the coastal horizon. Experts announced it as space junk suffering the ravages of the Earth's gravitational pull and all were happy. At that point in time, only one man knew the truth.

Bennett sat watching as Meredith had her life incinerated until the re-entry inferno disintegrated the camera and the live video feed went dead.

He smiled as he removed the laptop's hard drive and hammered it into oblivion, he had more unfinished business to take care of but that would have to wait until the next day.

CHAPTER 149

STRONMEYER

South Pacific Ocean
October 11th

On the eastern coast of a small remote tropical island north east of Tahiti, a luxurious beach shack smouldered in a pile of blackened timber debris. Once worth millions with breath taking views of the South Pacific Ocean, it was obliterated in a matter of seconds. On the ground only a few feet from the front door, the charred body of the owner was decomposing under the hot and humid Pacific sun when only the night before he had rejoiced in the tranquillity of his utopia.

Professor Klieg Stronmeyer had played his part well, convincing the world and in particular the wealthy of the Earth's impending death. While *The Trust* incited fear through Stronmeyer's sermons, the mega rich came screaming for sanctuary and with them the extra billions *The Trust* needed. Stronmeyer did not care, he was awarded his share of the millions and his little chunk of paradise in a small cluster of remote Pacific islands.

The night before had been no different to any other, devoid of cloud and a gentle sea breeze lapped at his face while he sipped his vintage malt whisky. He stood and gazed upwards, mesmerised by the countless thousands of sparkles flickering and reflecting off the dark ocean below.

A bright flash of blue light grabbed his peripherals and he turned sharply as Meredith's energy pulse struck his home. For a hairline in time, nothing transpired as his whiskey glass smashed onto the timber deck. Like a great white shark attacking a seal, the radiating wall of fire and force rushed out incinerating his body as he stood.

The fire would rage for days taking in half the island's jungle yet no one would see it or arrive to investigate.

CHAPTER 150

FINAL DECEIT

Dallas Conference Centre
October 14th

Senator Denzil Brown dressed in his finest black suit stood from his table of dignitaries and pranced towards the podium absorbing the congratulatory atmosphere along the way. Men and women stood to applaud his presence while those closest extended eager handshakes. One man in particular, a freelance journalist for a small time political magazine stepped anxiously from the media booth and shook his hand vigorously with a firm grip.

He grinned and quickly said, "Senator, you deserve this moment."

Brown's protection team of suited goons pounced on the reporter propelling him backwards into the media stalls among his colleagues voraciously shooting countless snapshots. Brown glanced back at the reporter, a little confused by the outburst from a media person, and though his hand tingled slightly, he thought nothing more of it and continued with his moment of glory.

He reached the podium and turned to face 350 of his constituents standing and cheering. He was the key speaker on this auspicious day, an event to declare his long overdue run for the United States Presidency.

He cleared his throat to open his address while the audience seated. But before he did, he took one more perturbing look towards the reporter, a blonde haired man in his forties wearing jeans and t-shirt. He was standing only a short distance away and watching but something wasn't right, there was something disturbing about his eyes when they shook hands. The reporter was smiling, he thought, but then he realised it wasn't a smile, the man was smirking and laughing towards him. Like an out of control freight train, it hit him, the reporter was Jon Bennett.

Two days earlier, three of his colleagues were each found murdered in their homes from a single bullet wound to their heads fired from presumably a sniper. Police were left clueless on the motivation behind the shootings however, Brown suspected different. On his own orders, his personal security was tripled at his home and he took no chances by cutting his public engagements in half to be safe.

"Bennett…" Brown announced except no one heard his muffled words.

His body started to tremble unnoticeably at first as he grasped each side of the podium to hold himself upright. The toxin had entered his brain and taken immediate control. He attempted to yell but he was frozen in time. He tried to point towards Bennett yet his body refused and as he watched, Bennett smirked back at him, he knew it was over.

His body engulfed by a violent spasm collapsed heavily to the floor knocking the podium over as he fell. Blood gushed from his mouth as he bit through his tongue while the ferocious agony of the Blue Death strangled his muscles. As he struggled to inhale air and women screamed in the background he could see the blurred vision of his nemesis walking away.

He watched as he heard the muffled desperate voices of his bodyguards trying to save him, screaming for the paramedics and pushing his loyal servants back. In the background, Bennett casually strolled out of the room taking one last look as he did. No one noticed in the chaos of the moment and like blood in the water for sharks, the photographers swarmed in a feeding frenzy to get that bestselling photo. Bennett enjoyed what he was witnessing, a sight he impatiently waited for fifteen years.

Brown convulsing out of control could no longer think like the animal he was, fear had taken its rightful place and the anguish of approaching death became undeniable. His heart exploding in his chest signalled the end for the Senator.

Outside Bennett walked away from the Dallas Conference Centre with some satisfaction he'd just executed the Chairman, the head of *The Trust's* board of management. The pin he used during the hand shake was covered with blue crystal dust, fitting he thought for the man behind it all.

The Chairman had been Senator Brown, the man with a vision for Utopia but what he had kept secret was his sinister methodology to radically cull the world's population. He wanted reform but it would never happen through policy changes and so his master plan started with Meredith and what the Thirteenth Code could deliver.

The Senator had been born Dietrich Himmler, son to a prominent German banker with strong familial ties to the once Nazi party of World War II. He and his family immigrated to Boston when he was a young boy and within a year his name was changed to avoid the humiliation of being German at a time when World War II had just ended. He worked hard, earned his first million by age twenty five as a stock trader and eventually moved into politics when he was in his mid-thirties. He quickly gained momentum with his radical beliefs towards world domination and aligning with the rebirth of the Nazi party's Fourth Reich. He formed significant ties to other influential German capitalists and wasn't long before he found himself at the helm of *The Trust*, unbeknown to all those around him in politics.

Bennett walked to his car parked a few blocks away and took his seat behind the wheel. There he pulled from his pocket the crumpled back page of the Sabre document and looked down at it. Three names appeared.

Dominique Whittaker

Robert Johnson

Denzil Brown

Johnson, Bennett knew, had died in a horrific light plane crash in the Utah Mountains a few years earlier and at the time received media hype and speculation of foul play. Nothing was ever proven and the plane had disintegrated on impact leaving physical evidence out of the question.

It was the third name on the list that ignited Bennett's rage. It was Brown who had refused his rescue from Afghanistan. Whittaker's PDA disclosed it was Brown who sanctioned the attack on the ILF building in Iran using Meredith's laser. Coincidently, it was the same man who humiliated him in front of his peers at the Senate Inquiry and dishonourably discharged him from the Agency for that same cowardly act.

In the end, Bennett had good reason to hate the man and apply his own summary justice. It was always these men who walked free, never accountable and always hiding behind the cliché of plausible deniability. Not this time, Bennett laughed, as he heard the far off siren of an ambulance racing towards the conference centre.

Whittaker's PDA had revealed many things about *The Trust* and the deadly influence of Denzil Brown. What disturbed him though were three memos from Brown to Whittaker. Each made reference to someone higher than Brown however, all were nameless. Bennett had sat through two sleepless days exploring the PDA opening every file and every email but he found nothing to identify this person. Not even Whittaker had named the person or perhaps he didn't know. But one thing for sure, Bennett knew there was still one more person of authority out there turning the wheels.

Like he'd witnessed on the screen in Kehlstein, the PDA listed hundreds of targets for annihilation. The primary targets in China, India and the United States were programmed first for deployment based on the greatest concentration of human population. In total, it detailed over three hundred sites worldwide earmarked for a cataclysmic holocaust beyond anything imaginable.

One report by a leading German impact physicist hypothesized the destructive force of Lucifer's Funnel combined with the compressed blue crystal would punch a land tsunami over a kilometre deep with a radius of a few hundred more. It would completely annihilate everything and everyone on the surface similar to that of a massive meteor strike. But their insanity did not stop there. Whittaker's encrypted file exposed mountains of information about their proposed plans to exterminate millions by the dispersal of a blue crystal aerosol.

Absolute lunacy, Bennett had thought at first, however as he read more, he started building an amended appreciation of the master plan. Bennett had long thought society was on a collision course with reality, that one day vital resources would run dry and the masses would perish at the hands of the world's greedy.

He sat a moment longer in his car reflecting on the past few months wondering if it was actually over. He'd lost many friends in the time, learnt many secrets of his past and most of all, he still had the passion to love someone. So many years as a hardened spy taught him never attach himself, never place someone close at risk and yet Nicholette died because of him. The thought slapped him back to reality and the heartache he chose to bury deep inside burst to the surface like an air bubble rising up through water.

He started the engine and drove off with his destination decided.

CHAPTER 151

BEGINNINGS

Broken Head, Australia
Two weeks later...

The sun edged its way over the watery horizon sending a beautiful morning shimmer across the headland and surf break. For the first time Bennett returned to Australia under his real name and settled on the east coast of Australia. As a two metre swell pushed hard onto the coastline off a wild storm at sea, he found himself drifting amongst an inquisitive bunch of dolphins frolicking nearby. Jumping and darting among the waves they sent a message of freedom and coexistence out to all around them. Bennett loved the peace they transferred, it was the best mental therapy session life could offer.

Two weeks had passed since Senator Brown died on the podium and police were still struggling to find a suspect or even a true cause of death. Doctors confessed they were baffled writing it off as a rare kind of severe radiation poisoning. Somehow, the Senator had come into contact with a radioactive substance but what and where they did not know.

An hour of solid surfing had been enough and so he returned to shore, not really knowing what to do that day. As he walked from the water, an old man passed him by and acknowledged his presence before stopping to ask about the surf. He walked with a heavy stoop and his skin looked too pale for the beach and sun. He gave the impression he was old but still he moved without effort like a young man.

"Do you find your peace?" the man asked.

"What do you mean?" Bennett returned still half walking towards the sand dunes.

"The waves and ocean, does it relax you? Does it make you find calm with yourself I mean."

"Ah yes it does, there is no better way."

"That is good, I am pleased," the man replied and walked off.

Bennett stood watching him for a few minutes as he grew smaller into the distance along the beach. Something was different about the man he thought, the aura around him was almost breathtaking. Somehow he knew him but couldn't place how or where from. It was like déjà vu, a familiar feeling he'd known the man a long time and with him a sudden sense of safety washed over his body.

He shook it off and turned to leave just as a fellow surfer walked past and commented, "Man, cool tattoo. Where you get it done, it's a wicked colour hey!"

He looked down at his own bare chest, the Thirteenth Code was the brightest he'd ever seen it. Alarm bells sounded inside his head, something about the old man had caused the tattoo to appear but now he'd vanished from the beach. Bennett raced towards his home, a small timber plank beach cottage set well back from the beach amongst thick forest, ideal for any obsessive surfer.

He stopped abruptly, someone was standing on his front porch.

He walked cautiously towards his house along the bush track carved out by the years of surfers seeking their daily fix. Already he felt at home in the surfing wilderness of Broken Head, a tranquil secluded community south of the famous Byron Bay. But now he was not so sure as his fingers wrapped around a loaded handgun expertly concealed under a log.

The person didn't look threatening, a woman in perhaps her sixties he first thought. She was standing with her back to him as he approached.

"Who are you and what do you want?" he said aiming the gun at the rear of her head.

"Jonas, there is no need for guns, put it away," she replied without looking behind.

She turned to face him, "Now come here and give your Aunt Rose a hug."

He froze in mid back step, his weapon tilted downwards. She was a picture of health in contrast to what he remembered a few months earlier.

"Rose, I don't understand, you look so... I mean I saw you at St Marika's and you looked deathly and frankly you scared me."

"Yes we have much to discuss, but first I want you to meet someone very special," she said as she pointed out over his shoulder towards the same beach track. Walking towards them was the old man from the beach.

"Jon I want you to meet the Monk, ruler of the Himalayan highlands but more importantly the spiritual leader of Earth's Supreme Council."

He hadn't really noticed in the glare on the beach that the man was very unusual looking. His skin was almost transparent, so milky white and his eyes were narrow slits but much larger than the average human. He stood there a brief second thinking the man looked like some alien not of this Earth.

The man extended his hand and Bennett accepted a warm but gentle handshake more reflective of an old fragile man. The moment they touched an electrifying chill ran through his body like he'd just grabbed a low current power cable. For a brief moment he couldn't let go, their bodies synching with each other, so it seemed.

"Jonas Bennett you are a brave warrior. We thank you for what you have done, for without you, *The Trust* would have won and desecrated the Earth with the pulse weapon. Your father was a brave man too, he sacrificed his life for the Council and the longevity of Earth. So many good people have died but not without sacrifice."

Bennett turned towards Rose, "We have much to talk about, let's go inside," he added as he pointed towards the front door.

Once inside he opened by throwing a line of questions towards her, "Ok I know how my father became involved in all this but you Rose, I do not."

"Jonas I was not always just your dear old aunt. Your father enticed me into the ways of *The Trust* and their vision for a New World while you were still young. When we learnt of their real plans to exterminate billions of lives it was time to exit."

Bennett just nodded in understanding.

"I became romantically involved with one of the Six you assassinated just recently," she added and Bennett wasn't sure whether it was aimed at making him feel guilty or she was just simply stating the fact.

"But I don't understand, you are so well now," he asked.

"Dom helped me," she briefly said before adding, "he injected me with a new strain of the Eighth Code shortly after you and Nicholette visited me. It acted quick, I think about two days and I walked out of there, AWOL I might add."

"Whittaker did that for you, why?"

"Dom may have done some bad things in his days but he always loved me and never wanted me to suffer. He took a huge risk to administer me that serum but it came with a price. I vowed to protect Silvia and so now she is safe, she didn't take the death of Dom too well but she is living a comfortable life out of sight of *The Trust*," Rose said.

"What, *The Trust* is still active, I thought I ended all that."

"*The Trust* infiltrated every government on the planet, there are sleeper cells spread across each continent just waiting the commands to activate," the Monk interjected.

"Commands? Who from?" Bennett asked.

"We are not sure but we believe the Six took their orders from powers above them and this is why I am here," the Monk stated.

Bennett looked puzzled.

Rose stepped into the conversation, "Jonas we need your help to identify who they are. The Council needs you but more importantly I know Viktor would want you to do this."

Bennett remained silent thinking of his dead father and the events of the last few months.

"There is much you do not know but in time you will see things from a different perspective, a new enlightened insight into life on earth," the Monk said as he turned and walked out the door. Bennett wanted to follow but his legs failed to respond, something powerful had a hold of him and he couldn't fight it. Rose remained inside not surprised by the Monk's sudden departure, the rest was up to her.

"He is right, there are many things you do not know and you must be on your guard at all times. The Eighth code is not what it seems but I am forbidden to speak of it."

"Forbidden, why?"

"You, me and a dozen or more others are infected with it," she said abruptly stopping realising she'd said too much.

"Infected? What do you mean infected?" Bennett asked.

"Jonas I've said more than I am allowed, the transformation has already commenced and you, I or anyone cannot stop it now. Please I am not permitted to tell you anything, the Monk has eyes and ears everywhere."

"Okay, then who are these Elders I hear about?"

"Jonas, do you believe in God?"

"I think it's about faith, and if it gives people hope and happiness then yes I do," Bennett answered.

Rose asked another question, "Do you believe the events of the Holy Bible about Jesus delivering God's message and his abilities to heal people? I ask that because I would like to know if you think Jesus was human."

Bennett wasn't certain where she was going with the conversation yet he answered it anyway. "I think that if the story of Jesus is true then he was a man with a gift, extraordinary powers perhaps given to him by God."

"Yes extraordinary powers he did have but not granted to him by the God you learn about in Sunday School," she said.

Bennett raised an eyebrow clearly unaccepting of his aunt's view.

"You must understand something, for many years the people of this planet have only been told what was considered best for them. If they knew the undocumented history of Earth, then I am afraid we might have wide spread panic."

"Rose are you inferring that God was alien, some extra-terrestrial being from another world?"

"It is what the Monk advocates and he claims his prophecies declare the return of the Elders from that world, the true makers of humanity. For some unexplained reason I believe him. You bear one of Jeremiah's Codes, haven't you seen their coming in your dreams?" she asked.

Bennett replied, "Visions, only destruction and death, nothing about aliens or what the Monk claims, tell me where Jeremiah really fits into all this?"

"Not sure, some speculate the mythical Atlantis. He was located in the waters off Bermuda with no explanation for his being there. The Monk has never made any comment about him, though many have asked the question."

"Hmmm pretty wild accusation, not sure I would believe that one," Bennett returned.

"Did you know it was Jeremiah who dragged you from the gunfight in Patna?"

Bennett looked shocked and thought back to the old man he'd left at the house under attack from the gunship.

"Jeremiah had followed you keeping watch because all along he knew you carried the thirteenth code," Rose added.

Bennett had a sudden realisation thinking about Jeremiah.

"The codebook has been destroyed but Jeremiah alive poses a threat doesn't he?"

"Yes I am afraid so, Jeremiah does need to be eliminated," Rose replied.

A few hours had passed and a dark wild storm was building in the west, the thunder was already rumbling in the distance. Bennett and Rose had much more to discuss and they settled in for a busy afternoon while outside the storm grew more dangerous by the hour.

CHAPTER 152

OLD MEN

Undisclosed location,
Antarctica Continent

The two elderly gentlemen sat in the heated comfort of an all-terrain vehicle while outside the bitter subzero blizzard winds smashed against the windows and made visibility impossible. Somewhere in front of them was the excavation site deep in the side of a towering mountain of ice and rock.

They were excited and sat impatiently waiting for the news from their workmen. For the past decade they had sought its location, a craft believed of extra-terrestrial origins just like Roswell and now the time to prove their suspicions was on them.

Both men were over the century in age and if not for the Eighth Code flowing freely through their veins then they'd be either dead or incapacitated in a nursing home. They had led controversial lives, contributing to significant changes in world history, some good but also unspeakable genocide acts and world war.

The radio crackled to life and the Englishman lifted the handset.

"Is it there?"

"Yes Sir, just as you said. It has suffered damage but the weapon is in one piece."

"Excellent, I want it out asap and shipped to the island."

The men had new plans. Construction of a new covert facility inside a remote South Pacific island off the coast of Chile was well underway. The Monk would never stop them this time.

The German spoke in his usual strong Deutsch accent never once inclined to master the English language and so the Englishman always struggled a little to understand him.

"You have done well, at last we have the Thirteenth Code weapon," he said breaking into half a smile, something he was never known for.

The Englishman simply replied, "Yes Adolf you are correct, it is a great day for the *The Trust*."

CHAPTER 153

HOPE

One month later

The phone next to his bed buzzed, it was 1am.

Static and silence at first but then a distant female voice broke through.

"Jon please help me, I can't get out?"

Then men shouting in the background, a heavy thud and the phone line went dead.

Bennett tried calling the number displayed on his cell phone but there was nothing, no service whatsoever. The woman was gone.

How was it possible, he thought? How could Nicholette still be alive?

He sat thinking his next move, was it real or some new elaborate ambush in play.

. . . .

Paul Gilmour